The House at Lobster Cove

A NOVEL BY
JANE GOODRICH

BENNA BOOKS
an imprint of Applewood Books
Carlisle, Massachusetts

For my best ones.
—Jane Goodrich

The author wishes to thank the Phillips Library for their permission to cite, quote, and publish from the MH 70 Francis W. Crowninshield Papers, Phillips Library, Peabody Essex Museum, Salem, Massachusetts.

Cover and title page illustration by architect Robert Swain Peabody circa 1885, courtesy of Boston Architectural College.

Library of Congress Control Number: 2016959103

978-1-944038-02-1

Published by Benna Books
an imprint of Applewood Books
Carlisle, Massachusetts 01741

Benna Books is a boutique press for artists and writers.

To request a free copy of our current catalog
featuring our best-selling books, write to:
Applewood Books
P.O. Box 27
Carlisle, MA 01741
Or visit us on the web at: www.awb.com

10 9 8 7 6 5 4

MANUFACTURED IN THE UNITED STATES OF AMERICA

The House at Lobster Cove

*"Died. George Nixon Black, 86, Boston capitalist & philanthropist,
onetime largest individual taxpayer in the city, in Boston.
Servants Gombi & Robrish were willed $73,000."*

TIME MAGAZINE "MILESTONES," November 12, 1928

*"Every spirit builds itself a house,
and beyond its house a world, and beyond its world a heaven.
Know then, that the world exists for you....
Build therefore your own world."*

RALPH WALDO EMERSON

Boxer
1927

The dog simply slipped off the cliff. Or leapt, or flew, no onlook-er could later say just what had happened. There was only the sound of the young St. Bernard running down the path, the skittering of its claws on the rocks, and the dog was midair, ears flying, a gloriously happy look on its face, its front paws punching forward in its peculiar way, which earned it the name Boxer. Then the dog disappeared into the sea below.

Bathers on Singing Beach found the body washed up a few days later, and the stable boys brought it home in the back of the dray. Down in the garden where he had instructed that a hole be dug to bury Boxer he found the men leaning on shovels, wiping sweat from their faces. The dog was a stinking heap covered by a frayed horse blanket, its white paw thrust out from beneath it, stiff and splayed open.

He remembered another dog he had years before, as a boy. A mon-grel dog, small and short-haired, which followed him home from the wharves one day and ended up staying. His father had not wanted the "little cur" in the house, but he took to loving the dog because it lis-tened to his boyish troubles with interest and sympathy in its dark choc-olate-colored eyes. When this dog died, the Irish girl took it away before he could see it again, and he did not know where it had gone until, by accident, playing in the back of the house he saw the dog's small white paw protruding from the pile where the servants put the garbage and the night soil.

Now, as an old man, he often dreamed about both dogs. He would always see the white paw, never knowing which dog it belonged to, and then he would wake suddenly, dizzy and sweating.

On nights like these he would rise and sit on the edge of his bed. He always wished he could call for Francesco, but he never did. The best thing would be to have Francesco read to him, as he often did in the daytime now, but he would never allow himself the foolishness of calling a grown man to his room to comfort him at night. To wake Francesco with such a request was something he could never do.

So he would dry his face with a towel and imagine Francesco's voice, its soothing baritone timbre. He had hired him for his voice, but since that day the valet had proved to be wonderful in every way, and he had grown to depend on him for many things.

He remembered the first time he heard the voice at the villa in Taormina where Francesco had been employed. The splendid house, with glorious gardens, had been taken for the season by an old friend of his mother; a woman also from Boston, then in advanced age but remarkable salubrity. She had a quick eye and was famous for her ability year after year to secure the houses with the finest views for the lowest prices. The excellence of her table was also legendary and worth the long cataloging of the hostess's health which accompanied each meal. Often he would escape the company of the elder women by retiring to the stone piazza to smoke.

The view from this vast coast appealed to him, the thin line of light resting on the far horizon, the familiar black shape of the Isola Bella. Even in those days the dark bowl of the sky with its millions of stars was starting to lighten as electric lights grew more and more popular in the town. On that night the voices of the kitchen boys in the laundry yard below drifted upward to his solitary figure. Before he even finished cutting the end of his cigar, he had already picked out the sound of the remarkable one.

The voice was sonorous and knowing, and, despite the fact that its owner was obviously quite young, it had the quality of an elegy. It had burrowed into dark places and returned unscathed. Deep in its cadences were bravery, expectance, and a mote of the libertine because the voice belonged to one who had known pleasure and joy. It was enchanting for the eavesdropper to close his eyes, inhale the smoke, and listen to the spectrum. The voice could be wall, or bridge, or roof, or bed. It was capable of every possible form of consolation. He strained to hear each word of the foreign dialogue to catch the tones of the one voice, he knew then, he wanted to hear forever. His Italian was quite imperfect, but he knew the boys were sometimes talking about him.

"Signor Nixon," they said several times in their conversation. *"Signor Nixon è Americano."*

The evening wore on much longer than he expected, even after the supper party had broken up. He remained in the narrow street beyond the back entrance of the villa, sitting on a wall, consuming cigars and watching the small door. When it finally opened and a young man, as attractive as his voice suggested, emerged, Nixon approached him.

Affecting the bravado and nonchalance of his race, the young Francesco was at first impassive, but as he began to understand about America, the house there by the sea, and the salary, Nixon saw his brown eyes widen.

Francesco was the only thing he was ever actually able to claim he had stolen.

Of course, his name was not just Nixon. There was more to it than that. His Christian name was George, after his father, and his surname was Black. In fact, he shared the entire three-word name with his father, but it never quite fit the same on either man. He loved the name Nixon, but it seemed to him bookended by two words he disliked, so over time, for him, these disliked words fell away, unused.

Nixon liked best the sound of the name. It was masculine, strong, and grounded, all qualities he was unsure he possessed. It also had a secretive feeling, perhaps enhanced by the hiss of the spoken "x," and something in it reminded him of a thing desirable and forbidden. He even liked the act of writing the name. He had the choice of stopping at the delicious "x" and crossing it then, or postponing the crossing and completing the whole word before going back and putting the finishing slash in place. His father would cross his "x" when it presented itself, halting mid-word, and then continuing on. Nixon always made himself wait.

"Nixon!"

The air was so cold the voice sounded false and metallic, but he knew whom it belonged to. Its owner struggled through the deep snow not yet cleared from the paths in the Boston Common to the spot where he and Boxer stood. The man was thrust forward, working his arms and legs briskly, with great clouds of breath surrounding his red cheeks and mustaches. But Bob Peabody was all energy always, bearlike, enthusiastic, forever in the moment, like a great heaving engine.

"Nixon, man, you look like the king of the Eskimos."

Nixon quickly considered this. When he first decided on walking out, the Russian sable–trimmed coat seemed the thing. Indeed, Francesco had laid it out for him, and Nixon liked its thick collar and beautiful rust color. He looked well in it, he knew. Even the lady artist who painted ivories had asked him to pose in it when she made his likeness. The temperature sat far below zero and the sun on this February day was a weak disc in the eastern sky. All around the Common, coal fires from thousands of rooms sent up perfectly straight plumes of smoke from chimneys. Boxer wore a coat, arguably as elaborate and silky as his own, and he could see how standing in the snow they made a humorous pair.

"But it is you who resemble the walrus with your pair of frozen tusks," Nixon laughingly replied.

"'Tis true," Bob said, but he was already bending over, both arms around Boxer, ruffling the dog in a half-hugging, half-wrestling way, paying no attention to the long white hairs gathering on his coat sleeves.

"So who are you then, big boy?" Bob asked. "Is this Hub or Boxer? I can't tell them apart anymore. You're magnificent, anyway."

Boxer, however, remembered exactly who Bob was and to show his recognition promptly smeared the side of the man's cold cheek with his long tongue, which appeared suddenly, a startling pink, extravagant in this drab landscape of midwinter. Bob deposited a small handful of snow on the dog's head and continued ruffling the great mane of fur around his neck.

"Does he carry a keg in there for you, Nix?"

"He's Boxer, Bob, and no, but there's brandy across the way at number 57, and smokes, if you'd care to walk back with us." Nixon gestured with his head toward his townhouse on Beacon Street.

"Ahhh, if only I could," Bob replied. "I'm off to a meeting I'm afraid, and one I'm not anxious to attend. Walking in this snow is a good excuse for lateness."

He laughed again and dropped another snowball on Boxer's head before he turned to go.

"Annie told me just yesterday how she'd love to see you for supper. Why don't you come by on Wednesday night?"

"If I'm not frozen in," Nixon assented, nodding.

"Yes, what I would really like is to be playing billiards on your porch." Bob patted Nixon on the shoulder. "Wednesday, then."

Bob touched the dog's head once more before he resumed his push through the heavy snow, thrusting his hands deep into his pockets, one of which, Nixon knew, also held the sketchbook.

Man and dog began their own trek back to the house at Beacon Street. The snow excited Boxer and he wanted to romp, so Nixon let him leap ahead, his large body and luxurious tail cutting a path through the drifts Nixon was glad to follow.

Something compelled him to fix his eyes again on the receding figure of Bob Peabody, trudging in the direction of Tremont Street.

My porch, Nixon said to himself with a little laugh, shaking his head.

Even at this distance he could still see in the bearing of the departing man's shoulders, the boyhood friend of forty years before. As his own booted feet crunched in and out of Boxer's path in the snow, he could clearly recall the summer picnic at the Crowninshields in Nahant, just before the Civil War. He himself had been a guest, but Bob was one of thirty cousins—for the half of Boston Bob was acquainted with was the half he wasn't already related to.

Sprawled out on the warm grass, Nixon had seen the sketchbook emerge from Bob's pocket for the first time. By the end of the long afternoon it was filled with page after page of girl cousins with parasols and croquet mallets, infants on their mothers' knees, and carriage horses dozing in the shade—all captured between the small book's covers, which he closed with a quick snap and secreted away in his vest.

All the young men admired Peabody, and not just for his ability to render. He was a fine athlete, entirely likable, and he caught the girls' smiles as often as not, but it was something deeper. Whatever he saw he could grasp, whatever he planned he could achieve, and his thoughts were always ahead of whatever else he was doing. While Nixon and the other fellows had little idea of what they would be doing the following Saturday evening, Peabody knew what he was going to do next year and the year after that. Harvard, the École des Beaux-Arts, and on to become the finest architect in America.

There was never any doubt in his direction or in his success in following it. Many years later, after Peabody's practice had begun, the two men traveled in Europe together. Nixon watched again, fascinated, as entire buildings were absorbed by Peabody's gaze and reemerged recognizably and charmingly from the tip of his rapidly moving pen. In a few deft movements, which seemed to flash from the iris of his eye, down his arm, and through his fingers, the Doge's Palace in Venice or some decrepit farmhouse in France would appear boldly in the sketchbook on his knee.

His eyes went far beyond the facade of a structure. Like an anatomist, he cut buildings open in his mind and examined them. Chimneys and dormers were flayed and penned in all directions on the pages. Floor plans emerged behind rows of windows, maps of hallways from renderings of pediments.

Nor were buildings his entire oeuvre. Far from it. Trees and vistas presented themselves up and down margins. Children and dogs leapt across the sketchbook's gutter, and boats...there were always boats of every variety, from full sail to dry dock, appearing like small inky fancies between the practical problems of construction.

So when Nixon as a middle-aged man desired his own seaside retreat, the sketchbook came out again. Stroke by stroke on those pocket-sized pages the marvelous house was built, and because the friendship between the two men had been one of many decades, the foundation was one of familiarity and love. Drawn into the rows of sea-facing windows were the births of each of Bob's children. The romantic tower remembered Marianne, Nixon's beautiful doomed sister. The fantastic, impossible archway was mindful of sunset evenings spent in the reflection of the exuberant Piazza San Marco, and the porch where eventually the billiards were to be played felt like the far-off day of the picnic at Nahant.

Indeed, on the winter night when Bob unfurled the linen roll of finished elevations, Nixon went dizzy with recognition at the sight of it, so intimate and accurate was the portrait.

Kragsyde. The still, perfect point of peace in Nixon's privileged yet necessarily clandestine life. Kragsyde, the house at Lobster Cove. The dual act of artistic genius and affection that flowed from Peabody's pen and became the masterpiece of his entire career.

Nixon noticed his feet were getting cold. In the palm of his hand he felt a puff of warm breath and Boxer's tongue. They had made their way to the curb of Beacon Street, and Boxer had his head cocked, his brown eyes imploring him for direction. Nixon smiled. Taken suddenly from his business of plowing trails to the task of trying to decipher his master's intent, Boxer's nose was heaped with a perfect pyramid of snow. His ears pricked and the snow scattered away as they both became aware of a repetitive banging. Nixon looked in the direction of the sound, just across the street at number 56 where, on the step next to his own, he saw Bigelow's man with a shovel chopping at the accumulated ice.

Or was that someone knocking at the door?

Yes, it must be, and his feet really were cold.

"*Signor* Nixon?" the lovely baritone bringing him back into his Beacon Street bedroom, back again on the edge of the bed, barefooted, shivering a bit, with a towel on his head. "*Signor* Nixon, I have your tea."

"Yes, Francesco, come in," he said, pulling his red carpet slippers toward himself and creeping his feet into them.

The forty-year-old Italian appeared at the bedroom door with a teacup and saucer in his hand. It was Nixon's favorite salmon-colored cup with the paper-thin porcelain edge. Tiny wisps of steam curled above it. Francesco placed the tea in the accustomed spot on the desktop and gently removed the towel from Nixon's head and draped it around his neck.

"Did you sleep poorly, sir?" he asked.

"I was too hot, or too cold. I can't remember."

"Shall I see Will and have him check the boiler?"

"No, no, it won't make a difference; it is just me."

Francesco was circling the room; opening the interior shutters to let the daylight in. It was a sunny day, and Nixon could hear auto traffic on the street. He squinted at the slits of sun coming from the outside. He reached for his pince-nez eyeglasses on the table and clamped them on the bridge of his nose. He rose from bed, with surprising mobility in his back today, but unsteady because his feet were chilled. He moved toward his desktop and the tea and took a sip from the cup. Francesco passed him his dressing gown.

Nixon was in the habit of writing a few one-word notations in a diary each day to help him remember his dreams. With outstretched fingers he pulled the slim volume from a shelf on the desk. Standard Diary 1927. In the top drawer he rummaged for his pen, unscrewed the cap, and shook the ink into the reservoir. Still standing, he flattened out the pages of the small book with his left hand and held it steady while he located the date, April 24. Carefully he wrote "Boxer" in the space provided, coming all the way to the upturned tail of the letter "r" before returning and crossing the "x." Both their names had five letters, both centered with an "x." He had never thought of this before. He sat down again, heavily, on his bed.

"Francesco."

The valet did not answer immediately but looked at him directly, turning from where he had been in the closet. "Yes?"

"I've outlived them all," Nixon said, and shivered.

"Yes, sir, you have." And then, "It won't be long now."

Nixon did not move, but his eyes widened, and a warm rush ran up his spine. Had he heard what he thought he heard? Would Francesco say such a terrible thing? Would he ever dare? But Francesco was leaning in the closet, quietly removing the clothes he'd chosen for him today, laying them out piece by piece in the shape of a dressed man on the bedclothes. What an awful thing to say, but how wonderful, too. It wouldn't be long now. He looked again at the valet's face. Francesco was carefully placing clothing down, smoothing collars, brushing away a speck of lint. He did not look like he had said anything. His face was handsome, his mouth inscrutable.

Perhaps, thought Nixon, touching his hand to his forehead, it was not Francesco speaking at all. Perhaps it was God. Their voices were the same.

Quick Water
1852

Not many days after the melting snowfalls became stretches of cold rain and a faint green quickened in the boggy roadside places, talk of the log drive began.

All through the frozen Maine winter, men in logging camps deep in the woods had awoken each morning to the sound of the camp cook pounding an iron rod against an old saw blade suspended from a concussy pine. "Turn out! Turn out! Daylight in the swamp!" he shouted. There followed a general fumbling for clothing stashed beneath bunks and a round of coughing and spitting as men stumbled over the hard rutted ground outside the bunkhouses. The kitchen cat ran furtively across the boughs piled on the split-shingled roof of the cookhouse. The bullwhackers and teamsters were already up, their harnessed beasts bumping and shouldering one another and breathing their muzzles into icy beards in the waning darkness. Behind them, a row of groggy men stood leaning into a dug trench, suspenders dangling, wisps of piss steam rising before them.

Soon the whole company would be seated, filling their bellies with salt pork, biscuits, gingerbread, and strong tea. They ate in silence to preserve their energy for the day. For the next ten hours, as soon as the sleds carried them down the haul road to their cut, they would be felling and bucking timber, the backbreaking and monotonous winter work of the Great North Woods. Their days were unvaried, punctuated only by long

Sundays used for shaving or mending, and the occasional death of one of their number. There were a dozen ways to die, the most common being struck by a "widowmaker," a branch that remained hung up overhead after a tree had been felled and then came crashing down.

Depending on the outfit, horses or oxen would twitch the twenty-foot logs out of the woods after the men had cut and bucked them. They would be sledded back down the haul road, piled in great stacks on the ice of the river, and when the riverbed was full, laid up and down the banks. Here they would remain until the ice-out.

Downriver, in Ellsworth, no one knew exactly when the log drive would begin, except by word of mouth, but to the lumberjacks the day announced itself suddenly. The weather would change imperceptibly, but the huge piles of logs on the river would groan and tremble, and old-timers swore they could smell the night when the ice would fail and the whole mass would begin to move. The air had a scent, they claimed, and sure enough, by morning the logs would heave and shudder and the earth around the camp would tremor as though by an earthquake; a sudden roar and the logs were on the haul.

The men were prepared, of course. As soon as the logs came loose and the haul began, a whole new set of rules and jobs came into play. To those who worked solely in the woods as lumberjacks, ice-out signaled the end of their long spate of work, and they could leave with their pay. Others traded their hobnailed boots for a different pair with greased leather waterproofing and cork soles sporting sharpened spikes, and began to work the drive. These were the rivermen, and every boy in eastern Maine dreamed of being one.

There came a day at the end of April in 1852 with weather as fine as summer. The log drive had been running for a week, and George Nixon Black Sr. decided to see for himself the progress of the timber down the river. He drove out to a spot near where the west and east branch of the Union River joined. Along with him came nine-year-old Nixon, his son, and his nephew Henry who was just a few years younger. The boys had seen log drives before but from areas close to town, where logs were calmly floating near the mills. The work of a river driver was always dangerous, but at the mills the action was more subdued. The thought of seeing the rivermen driving the logs in quick water had the boys dizzy with excitement.

The threesome left Main Street in a small wagon with a picnic packed for the day. Ruby, a mare owned by Henry's father, Alex, was in the harness. There was a cleared field along the edge of the river where George planned to observe the drive, and when he arrived he maneuvered the stiff-sprung wagon close to the water. George was no longer a young man, but his arms were strong and he handled horses well. Just shy of the age of forty, he was a little thick in the middle and a little thin on the scalp, and his shoulders were rounded by years of decisions and desk work, but his face was not without an attractive quality. He had dark thick eyebrows and unusually strong blue eyes, a feature he'd passed on to his son and his two daughters. His eyes possessed a great clarity, as did his entire countenance, and one felt upon seeing him that he was a man of good judgment. If his face had a flaw, it lay in the shape of his mouth. He had a habit, in concentration or during effort, of pressing his lips tightly together, which gave the effect of melancholy as well as determination. The truth was, he was capable of both.

"You boys keep your hats on," he commanded. "You'll have sun-burned ears by noontime if you don't." He then pointed to a bucket wedged in the back of the wagon. "Nixon, bring that down to the river and fill it up for Ruby, and mind the mud."

Nixon did as he was told. Sliding out of his seat, he could hardly take his eyes off the sight before him. The bend in the river looked not like water but like bark, like the skin of something living, some reptile, writhing and grey, and he could hear the roar of the white water beneath. Jammed between logs were the white teeth of ice shards, jagged treacherous bergs.

Henry was soon beside him whooping with delight. Henry's mother had been light-haired, and his small blond head bobbed up and down as he capered on the bank, waving his hat at the men out on the river who were crawling on the logs.

Henry was too young, but Nixon calculated quickly how close these men were to disaster, as they waded up to their waists in icy black water or stepped deftly from one log to another, lifting and prying the slippery timber. Often a log snapped back and only by the quick aversion of his body did the riverman avoid being dumped into the rapids. A leg could be crushed like lightning,, and if a man fell under the churning logs, he'd have little chance in finding an opening at the surface, let alone one where his head would not be knocked off. If a man had to wade to do his work, he did so keeping an eye out for his safety as he steered logs with his hooked pole. Then he chose a passing log, sprang aboard, stuck his cant dog into it, and rode it away, skillfully stepping from one moving log to another to make his progress.

"Who are those men on the other side, Uncle George?" Henry shouted. He had not stopped jumping up and down since he'd climbed off the wagon.

"Those men are tending out, Henry," George replied. "They need to keep the logs out of the still spots and push them back into the quick water."

"What if they stay in the still spots?" he asked.

"They could pile up and cause a jam. One jam and logs can get so hung up they can't get them untangled."

"Then what do they do?"

"They call in the jam cracker," George said laughing.

"Is that true?" Nixon interjected. "Is there really such a job as jam cracker?"

"Not officially," answered his father, "but there is always one boss who is a cracker at breaking jams. He comes in and surveys the situation, looking for the key log, the one log they can move and bring the whole jam down. It's dangerous work."

"Why do they go so fast, Uncle George?" Henry wanted to know.

"The water is good this year, just the right depth. When the water is low, the logs get stuck on everything. When the water is too high it can toss logs into the air and up on the banks. Then the rear crew has to go with the teamsters and fish out every stranded timber. It loses money. If they tear up a farmer's field, we have to pay for the damages. Good rivermen keep the logs in the river, and moving down it. This part of the river is a hundred-foot drop from here to your grandfather's first mill in Ellsworth. A nice easy slope."

"What about this field?" said Henry. "Could logs fly up here, right now?"

"They could," said George, "if the men didn't pay attention, but we've got good crews here. They'll keep them moving with water like this, and sluice them right under the bridges, neat. Logs have been landing safely in the catch booms downstream all week, and our sawmills are going day and night. It's going to be a money year."

By and by the three sat in the back of the wagon and unwrapped their picnic, still watching the rivermen work. A log drive was something to see. There were dozens of men, most with short tattered pants, cut to keep them off their feet and ankles. There were many Frenchmen, always joking and sometimes singing, and their dress was dapper, often accented by a colored sash or an unusual hat. Many of the men smoked pipes as they drove, and it seemed to Nixon amazing that they could keep a pipe so well balanced at the same time they wrestled huge logs through ice. There were some Penobscot Indians too, quiet and taciturn, among the garrulous Frenchmen. They handled especially well the few double-ended bateaux skirting the edges of the drive. Nixon had heard stories of Indians shooting dangerous rapids in these boats for fun. From the look of their faces they seemed incapable of doing anything just for fun, but he never doubted they could shoot any rapid they pleased.

"Look!" shouted Henry as he jumped up in the wagon, scattering the picnic food balanced on his lap. He was pointing to the slow water on the inside of the river bend at some distance from where they sat. There in that quiet water floated a raft on which stood a team of harnessed horses, their driver beside them.

"Look, Ruby, look!" he shouted again. "River horses!" Ruby turned her head when she heard her name, blinked once, and resumed dozing in the sun.

George chuckled, shaking his head. "They're moving a team. Makes easier work on a raft than through the woods."

As the sun moved to its afternoon place, Henry, who had tired himself out, fell asleep on a pile of canvas in the back of the wagon. Nixon and his father continued watching the drive.

"There is a lot of money gliding by out there," George said to his son, smiling and tousling the hair on Nixon's head. "This is just the long lumber. They have not even begun to float the small logs for the shingles or shooks. It's going to be a good year."

Nixon watched the men and the thousand logs as they surged along. Only now, in the back of the wagon, with his father leaned against the bed edge and his cousin sleeping in the canvas, did he realize: Everything in the river belonged to his family. Every riverman within sight worked for his father or grandfather. Nearly every forest, every log, every horse, every sawmill downstream, and even the schooners the finished lumber was loaded into belonged to his family. The thought made his eyes heavy, and he wanted a place on the folded canvas with Henry. He was sleepy too.

The little town of Ellsworth was as rough-cut as the timber floating through it. On a map it appeared as an irregular cross plunked down at the place where the Union River began to taste the sea. Like the timber, most people who found themselves at this crossroads were on their way to somewhere else.

Several commercial businesses and a few hotels vied for the attention of any traveler passing through the few streets, either to Bangor or Boston, Bar Harbor or farther Down East. This same traveler could find, during the day, most any necessity he required at a dry goods store or druggist or blacksmith. At night too he could procure most of the goods desired in those hours, from a hotel room on Main Street to the usual vices down on the riverfront in the area known locally as Rum Row. If it was culture or amusement he was seeking, however, he found it in short supply.

For Ellsworth was then, and always continued to be, a distinctly commercial town. Like most communities, the land and natural resources established the conditions for its development. Early settlers saw a place where they could turn a profit and then never sought anything else. Diversion and scholarship came to town of course, in the form of various lectures, concerts, or other festivities, but these things seemed always to be on wheels or under sail and disappeared in a few days. They did not root well in a soil fertilized for industry and trade.

Even the finest mansion in town reflected this taste. It was Woodlawn, the home of Nixon's grandfather, John Black, one of the richest men in Maine. This fine brick residence was set high up on a rise above the river, providing a view of its entire prospect and a direct sight line to his wharves and the many ships there. The entire face of the lovely structure was lined with a bank of gleaming triple-hung windows, offering John Black the view he most relished, across his carpeted double parlor, down his sloping lawns, right to the bottom line.

"Children!" said George as he walked into the doorway of his home at the end of the workday. "Let's walk to the river and have a look. There are more ships in today than I've ever seen before."

Little did George realize, however, he'd walked into a surgical the-ater. At a table in the parlor, his wife and two daughters were focused on a limp object. Nixon was sprawled at their feet, digging around in a small tin box. Mary, his wife, held a needle and thread in her fingers and stared intently at the tabletop, her light-brown hair snugged tightly at the nape of her neck with one strand escaping near her forehead. Like George, she was no longer young, her quick girlishness mellowed now into something warmer, larger, and slower, which was to him equally appealing. She took no outward notice of his arrival, and tucked her hair back over her ear.

Marianne, the elder and more lovely of the daughters, watched with her chin resting in her palms. Her hair was like her mother's but more golden. Almost thirteen, she'd just begun to pin it up like the older girls. Her large eyes were all he could see of himself in her, the same almost exotic blue of his own. Her skin was exquisite, milk and roses, and she seemed suffused with health and beauty. Indeed, there was something regal in her entire appearance, and in personality too she was quiet and queenly. She seemed a happy girl but always cool, with her emotions well contained.

Agnes, the little one, was cut from an entirely different bolt of cloth. Feisty and vocal, she gripped the table with furious little fists, straining to peer over its edge. Standing on tiptoe to watch, and still wearing short dresses, she was four years old. Her hair was dark and wavy, tending already to frizz. She was a physical child, running and stumbling and often indifferently bruising herself on immobile objects. George noticed her mind ran as fast as she did. She missed very little of the goings-on, and George often caught her looking at him with eyes that seemed far older than four. He was inclined to think when both sisters were grown he would have on his hands beauty and haughtiness, and brains and temper.

"Jenny Lind is having eye surgery!" Nixon cried, leaping from the floor as his father entered the room, scattering buttons from the tin box across the carpet.

"Is she?" George answered slowly, realizing the limp object on the table was Agnes' rag doll, who in no way resembled the popular Swedish singing sensation. "How has she been blinded?"

Agnes began to snivel. "I looked everywhere for her eye, Papa. I don't know how it got lost."

"Nor do I," Marianne cut in, "when you drag her around by the hair all day."

George caught the laughing eyes of his silent wife.

Agnes began to wail. "It's not true. I look after Jenny. She comes everywhere with me!"

"Exactly," said Nixon. "Besides she's not blinded, she's one-eyed, so she can still see. I've picked out an eye for her from the button box. I found a good brown one to put next to her blue one. Then she'll look like the dog over at Cooper's." He laughed and winked.

Agnes wailed even louder. "Noooooooooooooo!"

George scooped her up and rested her on his hip. "You sound like Jenny Lind yourself, child. Why don't we let old Jenny lie blind for awhile and we'll go see the ships. Your boat is down there too, Agnes."

"My boat is there?" she asked excitedly, ceasing to cry.

"Yes, little girl, it's down there with more than fifty others."

"Fifty ships in?" Mary asked as she straightened.

"Nearly sixty," he replied.

"I'll tell Ann to keep the supper a little longer," said Mary. "Sixty ships is something to see."

"What about Jenny Lind?" Agnes sniffled, reaching out toward the table where the one-eyed doll lay near the sewing basket.

"Don't worry about her," George said as he reached with his free arm for a strip of cloth from the basket and pulled it over the doll's eye. "She's sleeping."

It would take only minutes for the family to walk down Main Street to the corner below, where the bridge crossed the river. Stepping out onto the porch of their house with its four columns, they could see the entire distance. Sizable elms lined this portion of the street, and above their own white house was a nearly identical structure belonging to George's younger brother, Alexander Black. On summer nights with the windows open, Nixon and his cousin Henry could converse from their bedrooms across the hedge growing along the lot line. Henry's mother died in that house, Nixon knew, just after Henry was born, and the thought of this event always made him shiver a bit when he looked in the windows, but he'd been too young himself to remember when it happened. Henry had a new mother now, named Susan, and two sisters.

Below their house were the broad verandas of the American House, Ellsworth's finest hotel. Nixon loved living next to the hotel. Interesting people came and went, bringing all kinds of carriages and horses. Often in the evenings, men would retire to the hotel veranda to smoke and talk. Nixon and Henry hid in the hedges to eavesdrop. The porch smokers told jokes and gossiped, and were often drunk, so the boys heard wonderful things. By the time the same gossip floated up through the floor registers to his bedroom from Ann or Ephraim working downstairs, or his own mother talking softly in the parlor with his aunt Susan, chances were Nixon had heard it already.

It had not rained for a week, so street dust was swirling in the late spring breeze as they stepped to the plank sidewalks just beyond the American House. Here the big trees ended and the commercial section of the town began. Low-roofed wooden storefronts, built cheek-by-jowl, progressed down the sloping hill to the water. They passed Colvin and Peck's apothecary, where medicines were compounded and leeches could be seen wriggling in a glass jar behind the counter.

Marianne paused by the window of Luke's Millinery. Since wearing her hair pinned up she had taken a lively interest in bonnets and ribbons. Nixon regarded Dr. Osgood's door with disgust as they passed, remembering the tooth he'd left in the old butcher's pliers when he was eight. The dentist did a brisk business this time of year, when the lumberjacks came out of the woods with toothaches they'd nursed all winter.

At the corner just before the bridge was another hotel, the Ellsworth House, and just opposite was his father's store. It had a black sign with gold lettering: G. N. Black and Co. A few more paces and they reached the bridge, the perfect viewing platform for the lively center of Ellsworth.

Activity spread in all directions. From upstream, the din of sawmills, now operating twenty-four hours a day, could be heard. The logs from the drive were sorted in the big catch booms according to marks made in the winter woods by lumberjacks with their axes. Each ax mark was like a cattle brand and identified the owner of the log. Once counted and sorted they were ganged together and floated to the mills. There were many types of mills: single and gang sawmills, box mills, shingle mills, and clapboard mills, all turning out the wooden products used in everyday life, from the construction of buildings to the wooden boxes and barrels used to package everything.

Below the bridge the view was amazing. The water was obscured by the decks of ships. A sea rat could have climbed and jumped his way from the nearest ship to the farthest without getting his feet wet, simply by crossing from deck to deck. Hundreds of masts poked into the air. Eighteen wharves and half a dozen shipyards lay in this distance, and each one had sailing coasters lying three or four abreast taking on lumber or unloading cargo just brought in.

Any product not made in Ellsworth arrived by boat, and the wharves were crawling with men carting loads of salt, coal, and grain, loaded in wicker baskets or hoists and hand-carried or dumped into waiting wagons. A quick sweep-out, and these loads were immediately replaced with departing lumber. When the holds were stuffed as full as possible with newly cut wood, more was stacked on every clear space on the open decks and hung out over the rails in piles as high as possible, still allowing the sails enough space to be handled.

Shipbuilding too was ongoing in the midst of this movement of cargo. At Seth Tisdale's yard, downriver near Indian Point and beside the bridge at Sam Dutton's, the frames of ships under construction stood. To Nixon, they looked like fallen animals, stripped to the bone on some field of battle, as they loomed, in mist or obscured by the smoke rising from the fires that heated the pots of tar used to caulk them. Always the smell of these small fires burning, and of cut wood, tar, pitch, rope, horses, smoke, and water.

These smells, and the sounds of shouting men, huffing horses, groaning yards and hoists, and the clatter of tools and saws and wagons, was constant to Ellsworth throughout the spring and summer. Only on Sundays did the noise cease. The wharves were a reminder that this was the industrial heart of Hancock County, and as long as this heart beat, the residents were content.

"Where's my boat, Papa?" Agnes was clutching the bridge rail trying to make herself taller. Her bonnet had fallen from her head and was dangling by its strings. Mary replaced it as George lifted Agnes again in his arms and balanced her on his hip. He pointed down the river.

"With the blue flags, dear, down at grandfather's wharf. Isn't she a beautiful ship? Eighty tons, sweetheart, and just as fast a runner as you are," George said with a smile.

Agnes beamed and sought out the ship named after her, now being stacked with long lumber on its main deck. The ship had been built when Agnes was just two years old.

"I've never seen anything like it," Mary said. "Why is it so busy?"

"The season and the prices, I'd guess," George replied. "The harbormaster must be near crazy berthing this lot." He let Agnes slide down the front of his coat and placed her two feet on the bottom bridge rail where he balanced her with his hand.

"Where is the *Rambler*?" asked Marianne, her hand shielding her eyes from the late afternoon light.

"Down in Nahum Hall's yard, Marianne. Do you see the ribs of her hull sticking up there?" He pointed to a half-constructed ship. Its hull, being formed, was propped in place with spindly cribbing.

"I like the name *Rambler*, Marianne." George said. "I'm glad you've named her. I'm no hand at naming ships. She'll be one of the biggest we've built when Nahum finishes her."

"They have such beautiful names." It was Nixon speaking this time. His son was a sturdy boy, dark-haired, with the family blue eyes, and something of the rosy skin of his sister Marianne. He was going to be a tall man, George thought, taller than either himself or his own father. Nixon was a kind, soft-spoken boy with a quiet humor and great fondness for the family horses. George, who shared this passion, looked upon his son's equine enthusiasm with approval and noted with enjoyment the hours Nixon spent brushing and currying the animals, and talking to them in loving tones. Nor was the boy afraid of work, as he eagerly helped Ephraim clean stalls and polish harnesses. George had taught Nixon to ride, and the two sometimes took the horses up for a run on the land around Woodlawn. For a dreamy and tender boy, Nixon also possessed a streak of toughness, which George realized with some surprise. The boy was a brave rider. Nixon, despite his youth, was also a good judge of what was desirable and bad in a horse. George took pride in his son's astuteness, but there was something in it that rattled him too. Like George, Nixon was a good judge of the soundness of an animal, but he was also able to see something in them George could not. George might see a horse was fine and healthy, but Nixon could also see it was lovely to look at, a characteristic George would only notice at second glance, or perhaps not at all.

"Yes, Nixon, the ships have wonderful names. If you knew what they meant you'd never have to study Greek or Roman history in school," said George. His eyes scanned the names of the ships within his sight. There was the *Zeus*, the *Hermione*, the *Ianthe*, the *Montezuma*, and the *Nauseag*.

"I don't think I want to study Greek," Nixon said, "I don't want to know the names, only hear them. I don't think I could remember them all."

"You'd remember them well enough if they were racehorses," said Marianne.

"How many boards are out there?" Agnes asked suddenly, tired of hearing conversation with words she could not understand.

"Boards?" George asked, stymied by the sudden turn in the topic. "Why, thousands; more than the hairs on your head."

Agnes giggled. "Are they all for building houses?"

"Most will be used for that."

"Do they all belong to us?"

George laughed heartily. "No, dear, not all of them." Which was the truth, but barely.

"It looks like a forest out there," Nixon said, leaning with his head in his hand on the bridge. "All those masts were trees. Cut down once, and now standing back up."

George looked down at his son. The boy was placid with his chin slightly raised, his eyes slightly closed, and his pale face turned into the wind off the river. George felt he was witnessing a remarkable serenity, almost a state of grace.

"We'd better go home to supper now," said George. "We don't want to be down here after dark."

Few people would seek out the riverfront of Ellsworth as a place to pass the night hours. After dark Water Street went from a place of work to a place of trouble. The street itself was filled with muddy ruts turned up by the heavily loaded wagons passing through it each day. Sometimes these holes were filled with brush to afford the teams some traction. Manure and garbage formed a daily top layer so anyone who dared step off the wooden sidewalks chanced wading ankle deep in a rank soup.

Opposite the wharves was a string of buildings, mostly chandlers and sailmakers, as well as small saloons selling food and drink. The only illumination on the street escaped through the mud-splashed windows of these establishments or emanated from the flickering coals of the ever-burning tar pots. Large rats alighted from the vessels and, emboldened by this cover of darkness, could be heard rustling in piles of debris wedged between buildings. Men too skulked in doorways, with eyes that shone, their booted feet scuffing the planks of the sidewalks, and their fists riding in their pockets.

Rum was the main attraction of this area after dark, but not every man was looking to challenge his liver. Women were rare in this district; Ellsworth's population was too small and insular to support a bawdy house of its own, but there were always a few young brothers ready to broker an encounter with one of the slow-witted sisters in their households to fetch some extra money. Shortly after any nightfall these young salesmen could be seen, leading cautious sailors up some side street to a modest home, where babies could be heard crying and where thin dogs pulled and whimpered on their short ropes in the darkness.

After ice-out the waterfront became most volatile. With sailors in to pick up lumber, and woods workers down after deliveries, the little town throbbed with strangers. Never quite welcome by the section of the populace that profited from them, this annual influx of tough, seasoned, and often worldly men brushed up uncomfortably against the local roughnecks. It was a situation in which men indifferent to a fight clashed with men sparring for one, and rare was the night when fists did not fly. Fists flew over cards, fists flew over bets and women and heritage and perceived slights. Generally fists flew simply for the diversion of fighting. Men grappling with one another regularly rolled out into the street pursued by a tavern owner with a cudgel. Usually one combatant ended up in the cold water of the river, sobered up and swimming away.

A year earlier, Nixon and Henry witnessed such a brawl. It was early evening on a pay-night, a time known for rowdiness with toughs full of bluster and money hitting the taverns. Nixon once heard his father describe pay-night as "hell let out for noon" and there was truth in this humor. It was precisely why the boys were out. Hungry for glimpses into a male world not encountered in their own homes, they devised any pretext to spy on the activities common in Rum Row.

Prominently located was the Eagle, a two-story wood frame structure which had never seen paint. Streaked grey and brown, it had a precarious exterior staircase leading to rooms somewhere in its upper regions. Snow and ice were a six-month feature of the local climate, but the roof once built over this staircase for protection from these elements had long perished and lay in a heap in the cramped space between the Eagle and its neighboring building. Passing the Eagle in the winter, Nixon often noticed the waterfall of ice flowing down these stairs.

Nixon liked the Eagle. It had no sign identifying it. It was distinguished from the other taverns by a carved wooden eagle above its doorway. This eagle had suffered as much abuse as the stairway. The bird was missing one fierce-looking claw, and the bottom of its gaping beak was broken, placing its face in a continuous state of alarm. Unlike the building, the eagle was painted, but one of its angry eyes had lost its color so it no longer looked like it was defending its aerie, but winking. Whenever Nixon passed this place in a carriage, his father would always say, "If that eagle could talk."

As the boys neared the Eagle, the door burst open and three men came tumbling out. The oldest was bald and wore black armlets. He was grasping one side of a struggling bearded man who appeared very drunk. A heavier man also had hold of the struggler and was pushing him along with his knees and thighs. In unison the two men dumped the bearded man face down in the mud.

"You keep your trouble out of here!" the bald man shouted, his red face contorted with anger.

The bearded man was a riverman. Nixon saw at once he still wore his spiked boots with his pant legs tucked into them. He moaned a little, rolled over in the street, and spat before leaping quite adroitly to his feet. He had dark hair with curls that ran down the back of his neck just a bit farther than was fashionable. Probably he'd not been near a barber for some time. He was quite tall, taller than the men who'd pushed him into the dirt, but slimmer and more wiry. He wiped his face on his sleeve and spat again.

Henry and Nixon had seen men thrown out of the saloons before, but what happened next caused them both to step back and duck behind a pile of crates in surprise and caution.

The voices of a dozen men roared from the doorway of the Eagle, and a small group emerged, pushing before them a barrel-chested fellow with a bulbous nose and huge arms and hands. They lurched him forward, slapping his back, prodding him with some force.

"Don't take that smart talk, Eli," one of them said.

Eli threw his arms back thrusting away the hands of the crowd behind him. He wore a dirty shirt unbuttoned at the neck with a cluster of wiry hairs spilling out of it. His hands were enormous and awful, like slabs of meat. Nixon thought at first they were deformed in some way, but they were just covered with scabs. He did not seem as drunk as the riverman, and once off the sidewalk he peered around looking for his quarry, crouching slightly as though he were short-sighted.

The riverman looked feverish as well as drunk. His skin had a greenish cast, but he stood tall and regarded Eli with a strange look of disinterest, his arms hanging limply on either side of his gnarled-looking upper body. Nixon noticed though that the fingers on his right hand twitched.

The crowd surrounded the two men like hungry dogs circling a carcass. Some hurled insults and appeared agitated, others stood quietly with their arms crossed, still holding their glasses or smoking. To a man, they were a rough crew, with dirty clothing and skin and disheveled hair, their eyes glittering. They seemed to be mostly men who worked on the wharves and lived locally. There were no other rivermen. Deprived of his clientele, the bald man came out of the Eagle to lean in its doorway, wiping his hands on a rag that looked more soiled than his hands.

A fat onlooker with greasy side-whiskers shouted out, "Kill that sum bitch, Eli!" and, as if startled by this, Eli jumped and hurled himself at the riverman, throwing punches with his scabby fists at the side of his opponent's bearded face.

The crowd whooped in delight, and one strange man leapt into the air slapping his knee and laughing the laugh of an idiot. "Haw-haw-haw, hee-haw," he brayed, sounding to Nixon's ears like a complaining mule. This man was skinny with a sunken chest and humped shoulders. He could have been any age from a hard-used forty to eighty, it was impossible to tell. He was toothless, or nearly so, and his lower face was sunken to the remaining bone.

After these first hard punches, the riverman fell back on one of his knees, but quickly recovered and retaliated with punches of his own. Nixon could see the spiked boots he wore put his footing at a disadvantage. His strong, muscular body moved quickly, but his mind seemed elsewhere. Perhaps the riverman was just drunk, but Nixon concluded he was not yet fighting with everything he had.

Eli was, though, and when a punch he delivered spun the riverman back on one heel and turned him around, Eli spied his chance and threw his burly body into his staggering opponent, grabbing the back of his scalp with one hand and pounding his kidneys with the other. Eli threw the riverman into a pile of lumber on the far side of the street. The riverman groaned and fell to his hands and knees, a long slimy string of blood hanging from his mouth.

"He's going to beat that riverman, Nix," said Henry, standing behind his cousin. "Look at his bloody hands. I bet he pounds someone every night."

The riverman rose slowly, and once standing, ran his tongue around the inside of his lips, fishing for a dislodged tooth, which he spat on the ground at his feet. Eli staggered back, his own face cut and bleeding, and dropped both his arms down hard, snapping his wrists and hands as though to shake them dry. "Goddamn rummy," Eli muttered. "He won't look so pretty now."

"Haw-haw-haw-hee-haw." The skinny man laughed, clutching his ribs in great enjoyment. The hooting ring of men jostled and chuckled in approval. In the excitement of the fray, the boys had edged out from behind the crates and now stood at the elbow of the toothless muleman. At this proximity Nixon could smell the sour odor that clung to him, and saw the yellow in his eyes and skin.

In the lull, the fighters still leveled their eyes at one another, circling cautiously in the gravel. The riverman's face was pounded, bleeding so the neck of his shirt was stained with a red bib. He still seemed unsteady, and blinked repeatedly as though to clear the vision in his eyes. Eli's left eye was swelling and he was more winded, the heaving of his chest audible in the silence.

Very slowly the riverman smiled, allowing his pulpy lip to thaw from its malignant curl to a full grin, which revealed the tooth he just lost not to be the only one missing. He jutted his chin toward Eli. "Is that the best you can do?"

Eli roared and ran directly at the source of the insult, grabbing the riverman's shirtfront and flailing him with his huge fist. Spit, sweat, and blood flew in a spray around his head like some unholy halo, and the riverman was forced on his knees again. Eli slid back. "You stupid bastard!" he screamed, the strings of tendons in his neck straining and red with rage.

The riverman, still on his haunches, held up both hands in defeat, a small river of blood running from his face and ears. Eli stepped back with his head raised and his hands flat on his hips, as the riverman placed his own hand on the ground for support and slowly rose, still holding his other hand aloft in a gesture of truce as he stood, half-bent in the center of the circle of men, who were now closing in on both fighters.

"Haw-haw-haw-hee-haw! Haw-haw-haw-hee-haw! Haw-haw-haw-hee-haw!" The skinny man was beside himself with delight and leaned forward to Eli, who had turned to laugh with him.

"Eli!" The name was suddenly shouted toward the victor, who turned rapidly to answer it.

Suddenly upright, the riverman stepped once toward Eli, and with a great lunge kicked his foot high toward the shorter man's face. The heavy hobnailed boot made contact with Eli's jaw and lifted his entire body from the ground at the impact. The circle of men behind him broke, as they gasped and stepped out of the way, while the boot with the sharpened spikes broke Eli's jaw and raked the skin of his face, opening rows of deep furrows. Eli fell hard to his knees, his elbow bent over his eyes.

"Haw-haw-haw-hee-haw!" the mule-man brayed, and suddenly he turned to the boys. His toothless gums leered like a gash across his own face. He grabbed Henry under the armpits and hoisted him into the air. Nixon was amazed at the swiftness and strength of the sallow man and tried to grab Henry's foot, but Henry was held suspended, out of Nixon's reach, wide-eyed, with his surprised mouth frozen into a mute oval.

Eli was slumped in the muddy street, clutching his grotesque face, blood running in small streams between his fingers and down his arms. A single onlooker leaned over him. The riverman had staggered into the alley of the Eagle, and Nixon could see him there, bent and clutching his belly. The rest of the men, bored with the fight, were going back inside the Eagle or drifting away.

The mule-man stepped toward Eli and prodded him with his foot. He still held Henry suspended in the air above Eli's terrible face. Nixon saw his cousin's shoes jiggling above Eli's bloody head, and his struggling arms slashing at the mule-man. "Haw-haw-haw-hee-haw! It's the lumberjack's smallpox, boy! The lumberjack's smallpox! Now he'll be marked for life! Never turn your back on a riverman!"

Nixon jumped again toward Henry, but just as soon as he'd grabbed ahold of him, the mule-man dumped the boy in the dirt. Henry screamed when he hit the ground, then got up and began to run down the street.

"Henry!" Nixon cried, but his cousin was ahead of him, racing home. "Haw-haw-haw-hee-haw!" Nixon heard the sickening laugh behind him and thought he smelled the sour man at his own back. Heading for a shortcut he thought the mule-man would be unable to follow, Nixon shot toward the alley next to the Eagle that led to a grassy hill where he could make his way though dooryards to safety.

Running as fast as he could, he gripped the corner of the sagging building and tore around it. Suddenly he felt his own feet sliding out beneath him, and he could not reason why. The thought of the icy stairway flashed through his brain, for it felt like he was on ice, but it was April. Slipping, he felt himself falling on his hands and knees. When he landed and lifted his scraped hands to examine them he realized the sickening cause.

The riverman had vomited in this alley, and Nixon had fallen into the pool of it. Nixon's stomach churned as he rose to keep running. His knees were soaked. The smell! He looked at his hands again, and, not wanting to wipe them on his pants, wiped them on the wall of the Eagle, then scrambled up the grassy hill, clawing his way between the buildings with a thickening in his throat and eyes stinging with tears.

In the center of the table was a silver bowl filled with strawberries. Someone had arranged them prettily, entwining some of their leaves among them.

Nixon smelled the berries before he saw them, their odor so strong and familiar, as he poked his head into the dining room where his party was to be. Finally it was July, and today was his tenth birthday! Two digits at last, and there was to be a celebration here at grandfather's home, Woodlawn.

A "strawberry party," Marianne called it, which sounded rather girlish to Nixon, but he did like strawberries. Better than the strawberries, his mother told him there was also to be ice cream, a treat made at special times. Nixon loved ice cream and the funny way it was made, in a large bucket that had to be cranked and cranked.

Nixon poked about his grandfather's dining room. Here lived the rewards of riches. He ran his fingers along the table where the strawberries were. A white tablecloth hung nearly to the floor. Silver and cut glass gleamed, dishes painted with exotic scenes and Chinamen awaited delicious foods. Near the fireplace, where one could still smell the sweet scent of winter wood fires, brass shovels and tongs leaned against the wall. Heavy candlesticks appeared on many surfaces. Opulent curtains swept the floor. Nixon walked with his face close to the tall sideboard. Two knife boxes stood like soldiers, one at either end, with many silver handles lined up within. The area between the two was empty. Somebody would probably bring flowers.

Nixon climbed under the sideboard. In past years he'd done this with ease, but now his shoulders were too wide for him to fit on his side, so he lay flat on his belly and scanned the room from floor level. Under the sideboard one could smell the rich oils rubbed into its rare wood and see the animal-paw brass feet of the dining table across the room. In his own house down-street, one could always hear the sounds of Ellsworth, but here at Woodlawn one existed in silence, in an enveloping and pervasive calm. The sun's glare struck the trees outside, and in some distant part of the house voices erupted in laughter. Here, he felt he was at the bottom of a sea. In the light of the windows above him he could see slow-drifting particles of dust, like tiny fish swimming in the air.

Two shoes and the hem of a skirt entered the room. It was Franny, he noted with relief. She was on a visit to Ellsworth and he recognized her taffy-colored dress as the same one she had worn at supper at his house the previous night. She crossed the room and stood directly by the sideboard, where he heard the small thud of something heavy being placed on it. He saw a blossom fall to the carpet. She was bringing the flowers.

"You're spying, Nixon," her warm, low voice said.

"Yes," Nixon said, wondering how she always spotted him. "I usually am." He liked Franny. She was the only one he would dare say such a thing to. She was older than his parents, and her husband had died not long ago, but she was secretly funny. She had dark hair with tiny threads of grey in it, like pinstripes, and dark, happy eyes.

"Oh, I am aware of this," she replied flatly, but Nixon knew she was smiling. Different from other adults, she always knew what to say and what he was really thinking. Most adults who'd not seen him recently would comment on what a good-looking boy he was, remark on how much he'd grown since their last viewing, and then ask about his schooling.

Last night, upon her arrival at his home, Franny merely greeted him when she came in the door. Later when Nixon took her to the stable to see the new bay horse, she asked him if Miss Hight, his teacher, was the old pinch-face she looked to be. Nixon laughed heartily. No other adult said such things.

Franny poked him with the toe of her shoe. "Why don't you go into the parlor?" she asked.

"There are just girls in there."

"Your grandfather Black is there."

"He's blind." Nixon was beginning to hurt from lying still under the sideboard.

"I know that dear, but he likes to see you."

Nixon laughed loudly. "But he can't see me."

Franny poked him again with her foot, this time a bit harder. "Come out from under there, you fool; you know what I mean."

"Well, he doesn't know who I am."

"He has almost thirty grandchildren, Nixon. Just tell him who you are."

"Henry couldn't come to my party," he said suddenly.

The entire time they had been talking, the hem of Franny's skirt was moving slightly. Nixon thought she was arranging the flowers. Women always fussed with flowers. When he mentioned Henry her skirts stopped moving.

"Father sent me across to their house this morning, but Uncle Alex wouldn't let Henry come."

"Did Henry say why?" Franny asked.

Nixon hesitated, although he did not know quite why. Perhaps he should not have spoken of Henry at all. "Uncle Alex said it was indecent. Henry thinks his father might be warm at him."

"Why, dear, what did Henry do?"

"We don't know, neither of us knows what indecent means. Henry thinks it has something to do with getting his father's book wet yesterday by bringing a glass of water into the parlor."

Franny was quiet for a long moment. "Oh, I don't believe Henry has done anything to make his father angry, Nixon. He's a good boy."

"Anyway," Nixon said as he quickly rolled out from under the sideboard and caused Franny to jump back, "now I am the only boy at my party." He remained lying on the floor and smiled at her above him, clutching the fallen blossom he'd rescued from the carpet.

Franny regarded him with eyes brimful with fondness, followed by a smirk and raised eyebrows. "This is the last birthday you'll be able to fit under there."

Nixon stepped into one of the large parlors with Franny steering him, her hands on the top of his shoulders. "Here is the fugitive," she announced as she propelled him into the grand rooms. The large space had two fireplaces, one at each end, made of a swirly marble, which his grandfather once told him came all the way from Philadelphia. A line of windows ran along one wall and these windows were constructed of three sashes rather than the usual two so they could be opened to form doorways onto the porch outside with the long view down to the river.

At the far end, Marianne and Mother were sitting on sofas by one fireplace. Agnes, as inclined to the floor as Nixon was, could be seen sitting cross-legged beneath the curious table that sat against the wall with a mirror beneath it. She was dangling Jenny Lind and gazing at her reflection.

Grandfather was, as always, facing one of the tall windows with the river view.

"Nixon," he said, turning toward the sound of Franny's voice. "The man of the hour. Ten years old. Come here next to me."

The old man's hands fumbled across Nixon's shoulders, questing, and finally gripping them tightly. The gesture reminded Nixon of the day when he and Henry found an injured bird in the back field, and the nervous, unsure feeling of the creature's claws as it gripped his hand while he held it.

Even with sightless eyes, his grandfather bore a curious and friendly look. Nixon understood the old man was powerful and wealthy, admired and deferred to by others. He'd come to America from England when he was not much older than Nixon himself, and had cannily positioned himself into becoming the manager of the Bingham lands, the million or more acres that lay in the vast watersheds of the Kennebec and Penobscot Rivers. He was not very tall and shaped like a barrel with a thick chest, which made his slightly bandy legs seem shorter than they actually were. Full of vitality and quick-witted, his ambitions had not allowed him to be content with the management of someone else's acreage. He'd become a huge landowner himself and one of the biggest timber operators, with markets up and down the Eastern Seaboard serviced with his own lumber from his own mills, shipped in his own vessels.

"You are so tall, Nixon," his grandfather said, still running his hands along his grandson's shoulders. "Bigger each time you visit me."

Nixon supposed his grandfather always enjoyed good fortune because he had demanded it. There was something awesome in his self-assurance. Nixon could not imagine John Black plagued by doubt or hesitation. Yet, the clutching hands and the few remaining wiry hairs that sprung from the places above his ears seemed so vulnerable. In age, he had found his first real adversary, and age was going to win.

So too were the damaged eyes windows of mortality. Nixon could never keep himself from looking at them, and their presence disturbed him deeply in a way he did not understand. But the staring was irresistible, and he only took care that others did not notice him doing it. One of the old man's eyes was an awful yellow orb, lolling in its socket. The other, which apparently retained some recognition of light and shadow, turned grotesquely to whatever angle it required to register any sight.

Grandfather Black's eyesight had been failing for some time now, long before the death of his wife, Mary, last year. Nixon's grandmother had been a bland and motherly woman, given to flushing and bustling about. She was always soothing and quelling, and moved constantly in a nervous wake of appeasement. It fell to her to mediate between grandfather and the housemaids. In the early years of his dimming eyesight, Grandfather would insist the tall windows with the river view were not being cleaned properly and repeatedly instructed the maids to remove the streaks he saw there while searching for his docking ships. When the "dirty" windows became a family joke even Grandfather himself understood, Grandmother Mary went on and on, making sure the housemaids neither cleaned the windows often enough to make them sullen, nor infrequently enough to displease the man who could no longer see out of them.

"Look, Nixon," his grandfather said, pointing to the wall between two of the tall windows, "Franny says the *Fame* is in. Do you see her? Is she all unloaded?"

"I think so, sir," Nixon answered, peering at the ship docked far below. He didn't know one from another at this distance.

"Did you enjoy your studies this year, boy? Miss Hight is one of the good ones, I understand."

"Yes," Nixon said. No, Nixon thought. He and Franny glanced at one another.

"Papa!" Agnes suddenly cried as she jumped out from under the table in the opposite parlor.

George had stepped hurriedly into the room, pulling off his hat and smoothing his hands down his waistcoat. "Has the birthday started without me? I'm sorry, I was delayed at the store."

"The *Fame's* in, George," Grandfather Black said. "Is she unloaded?"

"Nearly," George replied, shaking his head and laughing.

"Well, then that's it," Grandfather said clapping his hands together and then rubbing them briskly. "Now it's time for strawberries."

After the strawberries and ice cream, Nixon lay on the branch of a tree that overlooked the brick front of Woodlawn. Sleepy from the food and the hour, he stretched along the length of the stout bough with his feet wedged against the trunk. His chin on his forearms, he watched his family. His mother and Franny sat on the porch intent in some feminine conversation. Agnes was crouched down on her haunches peering into a flowered bush, while Grandfather poked its leaves with his stick.

From his elevated perch Nixon could see Marianne walking slowly toward his tree. She wore a dress with tiny flowers sewn on the surface of the fabric. Threaded through her elbows and garlanded in a swoop at the small of her back was a periwinkle-colored shawl that Nixon guessed Marianne knew set off her eyes beautifully. He was aware suddenly that something was moving very fast and realized it was his heart. Pale and lovely, Marianne was magnificent. She was fingering something small she held in the palm of her hand, and Nixon watched with pride as his elder sister passed beneath his branch and toward the driveway beyond. He waited until he could see the slightly curled blond hairs at the nape of her neck before calling to her.

"Marianne," he said softy, "what do you have in your hand?"

"Oh, Nix," she replied, looking up at him as he hung overhead. "They are little seeds, from the columbine. Grandfather says if I scatter them around they will grow and come up next year in lots of colors. He told me a rhyme: "Columbine, you're a dusty fellow, your feet are tipped in gold.""

"Let me see," Nixon said, sliding off the branch and climbing down, lowering himself slowly at first, then with a long drop to the ground. The two crouched under the tree as Nixon examined the dark, round seeds. Nixon offered his sister his pocket handkerchief and tied it to store the seeds. They sat together on the grass, Nixon cross-legged and Marianne with her knees propped up before her. She'd wrapped the periwinkle shawl over them and was tugging the corners around her ankles, aimlessly tying and untying it.

"Let's go see the horses in the barn," Nixon suggested.

"No," Marianne answered. "There are horseflies up there. You know how they bite me."

"I wish Henry were here," Nixon said. "It would be more fun."

"His father won't let him come here now," Marianne said. "You know that."

"No, I don't," Nixon admitted. "Why won't Uncle Alex let him come?"

"Nixon," Marianne dragged out his name, and rolled her eyes, "you are a dope. Grandfather Black means to marry Franny."

Nixon felt a funny throbbing in his throat. "But he's so old—and ugly."

"I know, and the uncles are angry at him, and at father for siding with him."

"But why?"

"They think she wants his money," Marianne said.

Nixon considered this. "Aren't we all rich?" he asked his sister.

"I guess so," Marianne replied. "All I know is everyone is fighting. Mother is very upset." The two sat in silence for some moments.

"Do you think she wants his money?" Nixon finally asked.

Marianne slowly twisted her scarf ends around the tips of her fingers. "No, not really."

Nixon sighed and lay back on his elbows with his legs stretched straight before him. "I think he just likes her, as we all do, and her husband is dead, and Grandmother is dead."

"Mother says Grandmother hasn't been dead for a year, and since Franny is Grandmother's niece, people will say bad things," Marianne replied.

"Well," Nixon said, followed by a long sigh, "I'd marry her."

The day had been thundery, and for a time in the forenoon it rained with great force. Nixon was confined to the porch during these hours, desultorily making battlefields of the old green-and-red-striped canvas cushions from the chairs there. In these musty fields and caves, he commanded charges and retreats with his lead soldiers, but he grew hungry and hot and tired of them, leaving them in wrecked formations on the wooden floor.

After his noontime meal he'd gone back to play again, but while lying on the floor setting the little hussars in place, he fell asleep. He dreamed he was hiding in the ferns at the swimming place on the river where all the boys were warned not to go and went anyway. Secreted in the green and verdant hideaway, he was watching the older boys swim. He peered at them from behind the fronds which smelled like cut hay, and in the dream he had yellow eyes like a tiger.

He woke, disgusted, on the porch floor, with his shirt twisted uncomfortably under his side and his cheek buried in a drool-soaked wet spot on a moldy-smelling cushion. The sun had returned, and even though the rain had passed, water still sputtered in a muddy patch of earth near the corner where it leaked unsteadily from a canted eaves trough above the porch.

Marianne was sick. She had been sick for a month. "Scarlatina," his mother said, which sounded like something beautiful, or maybe like something beautiful and slightly dangerous, like the swimming place in his dreams. Apparently, it was one and not the other, as he was kept away from Marianne's bedroom on the warning he could catch from her the painfully sore throat and headaches she suffered.

Colleen, the laundry woman, told him scarlatina was a fever that made your tongue turn bright red. She also said you could get so hot your brain would boil and you could die. A few days after hearing this he stood at the door to his sister's bedroom, with the toes of his shoes just on the edge of the threshold. His sister was sitting upright in her bed, embroidering a sampler.

"Marianne?" he asked quietly. "Is your tongue bright red?" She stuck it out at him and he saw indeed it was, and also had a strange white patch in the center.

"Is it still red?" she asked him back.

"Yes."

"Is the white spot still there?"

He nodded. He chewed on his lip and swayed unsteadily in the doorway.

"Is your brain hot?" he asked.

"No," she answered. "Go away."

That conversation was more than two weeks ago and she was still in bed. He wondered, sweeping his soldiers into their wooden box, when she would get up. Her brain had not boiled yet, but he began to think something was badly wrong. Dr. Mason had come a number of times. Nixon didn't like Dr. Mason. He reminded him of one of those green insects you could find sometimes in the leaves of small trees. A mantis. Yes. Dr. Mason Mantis with his skinny legs that folded and unfolded as he crawled out of his carriage, and his popped-out eyes, and his clutching hands. Whenever he came around something was made worse, especially if you were a child.

A few days ago as Nixon skulked in the hallway, he saw through the crack of the door Dr. Mason laying his ear on Marianne's chest. His black greasy hair just beneath her chin; how awful for her! Later, Nixon overheard him speaking with his parents about "damage to her heart."

Her heart! That was even more important than her brain, wasn't it? He'd begun to doubt the story of the boiling brain. After all, Colleen was a laundry woman, and everyone knew her husband was often found sleeping in the street after drinking too much.

It must be her heart. It had to be something. Usually on Thursday afternoons he and Marianne attended dancing lessons at Mrs. Whidden's. Mrs. Whidden would tie a beaded sash around her waist and play the piano while the students practiced the gavotte, the quadrille, and the redowa. With Marianne's illness he'd been forced to attend alone and always ended up in the marching cotillion with the cross-eyed Bullard girl. Mother had given Marianne the sewing sampler to pass the time. Mother's own voice was anxious and high-pitched ever since Marianne had taken ill, and Father sat in his chair in the evenings, rubbing his hands together, over and over. That was never a good sign.

Nixon crossed the porch and pushed the cushions back into their places in the outdoor chairs. He listened inside the house. It was quiet.

The water splashed off the roof, and there were the faraway sounds of the town, but the house itself was silent. His mother must be lying down. There was no telling where Agnes was, but she would keep his secret in any case. He was going up to Marianne's room. Everyone else had been there and no one had gotten sick.

Nixon made his way across the carpeted parlor and slid his box of lead soldiers onto a shelf in the bookcase. Then he slunk into the front hallway. He rubbed his hand across the wooden bump crowning the newel post and lay his foot quietly on the first step. The fifth step up squeaked on the right side, so he put his weight on the left. The ribbon of carpet hid the rest of the sound of his ascent.

Marianne's door was ajar. He placed his finger on an upper panel, pushed it slowly, and stepped into the room where he'd been forbidden to go. Marianne lay on her side, facing away from him. Her window was cracked an inch and he could again hear the sound of the roof water, which was softer upstairs. From here it sounded almost like a fountain. He'd never seen a fountain, except in a picture in a book, but imagined it would sound like this. Marianne the princess in her castle and her fountain in the courtyard.

Here, though, was no princess. Marianne lay with her arm exposed on the counterpane, its entire length covered with densely packed red spots like the skin of some animal. Only her palm was still white. Topsy, her doll, whom Nixon thought was put away because it was too babyish, lay twisted between her pillows. Her bed was narrow, but her head still looked small in the width of it. Her hair was always the color of bronze and even in sickness it seemed to shine in the dim light. He always noticed how the gold highlights sparkled in near darkness and then went dull in the sun. Today her long hair lay in two braids tied with pale blue ribbons.

Nixon wanted to touch her head, to put both his hands around it. He wanted to hold its warm roundness, his fingers stretched as around a ball, and he reached out, but then thought better of it and pulled his arms back to his chest.

Instead, he crossed around the bed to the side where she was facing the open window. Her cheeks and forehead were covered with the red rash too. The ties near the neck of her nightdress were undone and lay plastered against her sweating neck. He reached out and touched the spots on her arm. They felt like sandpaper.

He sat down in the chair beside the night table, and the cushion made a too-loud squashing sound. Marianne slowly opened her eyes and focused them. Always a startling blue, today they seemed to glisten. Their surface seemed coated with oil, and they both beckoned and re-pelled. Different from before the scarlatina. Nixon saw that behind them was someone trapped, as though under a pane of glass. There was, inside his sister, a terror of some kind, pressing on all corners of her spirit, feeling around frantically to find a way out. Yet she laid perfectly still.

He stood up, frightened, and went back around the other side of the bed where he did not need to look at her. He hesitated a moment, won-dering if he would be discovered, decided he did not care if he was, and lifted the covers of her bed. He slid down under them next to his sister and put his arm around her small waist, pulling his own body up close.

"Is your tongue still red?" he asked.

"I don't know," she answered.

They lay together until it seemed she was asleep again. Nixon could not keep his hands from her small, vulnerable head. Lifting himself care-fully, so as not to wake her, he leaned with his weight on one elbow. Reaching out with his clumsy fingers, he drew their tips down the parting in her hair, from the crown of her head to the nape. He did this again and again, staring at the little trail of skin visible between the taut hairs. She was going to die. He shivered violently and felt a sob burst in his throat. He swallowed back hard. He did not want her to die. As he did this he felt her tiny shoulders cave in on themselves a bit. She reached to the back of her head to cover with her speckled hand his own hand, frozen in her hair. Her palm felt as though it would burn him.

"Marianne," he asked, "are you going to die?"

"Not today," she replied.

Later, deep in the night, he awoke in his own bed. A bright light had crossed his closed eyes and illuminated the room. Before climbing out from under the sheet and walking to his window, it happened again. The leaves of the big tree, the grass, the clapboard of the house were all visible in the quick white light. He watched in awe as the lightning flitted before and behind the clouds. The powerful force of the light moved from one part of the sky to another and several times blinded him as though it were the sun. The magic part was the silence. That such bolts could cross the heavens with perfect stealth, unknown to anyone who was not standing by their window, watching, was more than he could imagine.

Marianne had not died that day. Nothing had happened. It was the day Nixon began to wait for it to happen.

Odd Job
1852-1854

◎〜◉ John Black stepped out of his double parlor on November 21, 1852, with a new wife and only one son who remained on speaking terms with him.

That son stood in the driveway shaking hands with the Reverend Tenny as he climbed into the carriage for his ride back to the parsonage after the small wedding. Lazy flakes of snow had been weaving a long slow path from the sky to the ground all day, their first appearance this season.

"I thank you, sir," George said. "It meant much to Franny it was you who officiated, and we all appreciate your coming here to the house to accommodate Father's blindness."

"Not at all, George," the Reverend Tenny replied. "It gives me great pleasure to unite the two. May they offer one another many years of comfort and happiness with God's blessing."

"We hope it so," George assented and shut the carriage door with a tight click. He stood on the whitened gravel with one arm lifted in a gesture of farewell watching the carriage descend the gentle slope, trailing narrow lines from the wheels in the thin snow dust. Father was animated and joyful during the short ceremony and the meal after, and Franny had seemed cheerful and calm, but George was exhausted.

In the forenoon before the marriage, George saddled his mare Flicker and rode slowly to Woodlawn. Earlier there'd been a weak sun, but it was scrubbed slowly away by the snow. Approaching the property through the fields and thin woods behind it, the great roof of the house began to be visible to the lone rider, and while counting the six tall chimneys, George experienced the sudden proximity of his childhood. He remembered when they were constructed, surrounded by the mason's staging and gazed on with pride by his father. The bricks for them and much of the house itself came as ballast in the ships, a savings his father took a delight in. He valued those sorts of things.

George had to admit his own natural inclination toward containing costs, as his father had bequeathed to him a large portion of his own restless ambition. Father and son had worked agreeably side by side for many years. George enjoyed the land management and timber business from the start, possessing a natural ability to assess and speculate in real estate and a love of the complexities of manufacturing lumber. He even enjoyed the tedium of the bookkeeping, as his soul was soothed by order and in many ways he desired a monotonous and predictable life. With his father's worsening eyesight and age, the older man began to rely on George for more and more, a responsibility George shouldered lightly. Now there lay before him a chasm between the way things once were and the way they were soon to be, which George could not imagine being able to cross. George did not know whether his father was unaware of the ways in which their world was about to change, or if he simply did not care.

During the previous summer, his father had called George to Woodlawn and told him of his plans to marry Franny. She was Frances Hodges Wood, the widow of one of the old man's business associates and the niece of his recently deceased wife. His father had not expected George would make any objection and would not have been deterred from his plan even if he had. In thinking of the prospect, George really could find nothing wrong with it, and his imagination could not lead him to be outraged like his brothers.

The trees through which he and Flicker passed were leafless and solemn, dreaming perhaps of summer. The snow enclosed them in a thick silence. He imagined he could hear it falling, covering the dead leaves and withered ferns. But all he could hear was Flicker's soft breathing, regular and comforting. He began to think he was probably not nervous at all.

Ahead in a clearing stood the family tomb. His father had it constructed some years before, and several of their blood were buried here. It was a large earthen mound, overgrown with grass and little purple violets in the warmer months. Today it was covered only in the gentle snow, and as George and Flicker circled it, he noticed it was imprinted with hundreds of small tracks in elegant laced circles. From horseback it appeared the surface was penned with a light wispy handwriting, but George realized the tiny tracks were the footprints of a family of red squirrels who were probably bringing their winter stores in with the tomb's occupants. The thought pleased him. His mother was buried here, and the burrowing would probably please her too, as she loved all small creatures.

Of course, his mother had been jealous of Franny. His father always had an eye for Franny, and everyone knew it. It was never an eye of lust, but more an eye of approval. Franny had a quick mind and sought to be valuable through her talents and her differences. Never afraid to speak her thoughts, and armed with a dry wit, she would spar with a man as quickly as agree with him, and thus earned the disdain of women, like his mother, who'd always triumphed by being submissive. It was Franny who first made his father aware the "dirty" windows were his problem, not the fault of the housemaids, and she did it by teasing him about it. No one else would have dared it, but he was the sort of man who delighted in the frankness, and Franny knew this.

George loved his mother and knew his father had been devoted to her as well. She was a tender woman, full of quiet feeling and genuine desire to make others feel loved. Gentle and caring of her children and grandchildren, she was best with the ones who needed loving steering. George was born quite able to steer himself so he never availed himself of the part of mothering his mother was most adept at. He recognized it but never required it, and his own independent streak could easily understand what his father found so desirable in Franny. While his mother would be the woman to turn to for sympathy, Franny would be the one to turn to for advice.

George also realized his own understanding would count for nothing at the present moment. His brothers were furious about the marriage and would soon be even more enraged when they learned that their father had chosen to pass the management of the millions of Bingham acres on to him. No matter that his brothers were all apathetic businessmen, and that the responsibility was vast; they would only perceive the act as a slight, and he would soon be drawn into the position of the villain. George did not know how he was going to weather it.

After stabling Flicker at Woodlawn, George approached the back door of the house. There was a lamp burning in the window of the stairway. *Happiness is not always a part of the things which have to be done,* he thought, and as his eyes traveled down from the high window he noticed a figure in the kitchen yard. A woman in a dark blue dress with her hands clasped together at her waist, standing in the snow. It was Franny.

He walked up to her and stood close enough that he could see the icy flakes in her dark hair. She was not a beautiful woman, but she was handsome, with appealing eyes which spoke plainly of everything they ever witnessed.

"I saw you at the tomb," she said, reaching out her hand to grasp his own. "I'll never replace her."

"No," George replied. He focused his eyes on her small gloved hand threaded in his and felt suddenly he wanted to cover it with both his hands, to protect it from some danger. "Can you stand the blame?" he blurted out.

Franny lowered her head and briefly touched the bridge of her nose with the two forefingers of her unclasped hand. "As long as I am blameless," she replied, raising her eyes to his. As always, Franny's virtue wore the costume of audacity. He admired her courage.

"We'd better go inside and have a wedding," he said, smiling, still holding her hand, as they stepped toward the kitchen door.

George paused and looked out again at the first snow of winter. When the day was done, the anger would belong to his brothers and the blame to the bride, but the pain would belong to him.

It was to be a first-rate snow fort. The roaring storms of January left an expanse of glistening wind-packed snow behind Nixon's house in the broad field beyond their stable. To Nixon it was a blank canvas begging to be built into a city for play. Now the sunnier days of February had come at last, and he headed out with his shovel and sled, with the idea of making a tunnel through one of the hard-packed drifts.

Though there were no structures in the field it could never be described as empty. The space, used communally, had been home to seasons of leaf houses, kite flying, firefly hunts, and games of rag tag. In the summer the tall grass there was intersected by the beaten-down paths of walkers who cut through it to and from the town's dirt streets, and there was seldom a time when the waving flag of a dog's tail did not appear among a group of children. Nixon had crisscrossed it all his life.

"'Lo!" a distant voice shouted.

Nixon looked up from where he was cutting snow blocks for his tunnel entrance but could only make out the shape of another boy against the strong sun.

"Can I dig with you?" the small voice asked as it drew nearer, and Nixon's heart jumped. It was Henry!

Since grandfather and Franny had married he and Henry had seen little of one another. They tried, but the short days of winter and the fact they attended different teachers made it difficult. Everything had changed. Their mothers no longer gossiped in each other's parlors and their fathers crossed the streets to avoid one another. If Henry and Nixon met, it was usually on the arm of a parent tugging them in opposite directions.

Nixon felt embarrassed and angry when other boys laughed about the fight in his family. Neither of his parents took any notice of this, but Nixon's face burned with shame when other boys sniggered. Nixon noticed other people acted as if their family deserved it. This he puzzled over. What had been their crime?

Losing Henry was the worst thing. He was sure Henry felt the same, but it was impossible to act as before. Something irreparable had thrust itself between them, heavy and permanent.

The day after the wedding, Nixon was told by his father it would be best not go to Henry's house anymore. Nixon flung himself on his bed in anger, and looking out his window he saw Henry's head resting on the windowsill inside his own room. Henry waved one hand sadly, and Nixon knew he too was confined at home. The boys tried to speak through open windows in whispers, but the weather made that impossible. They attempted secret hand signals but did not have enough movements to convey all they wanted to say. Eventually, the day came when one or the other forgot to look out his window, and not long after Christmas Nixon tried to stop looking entirely. Once in a while he would look across to Henry's lit window for the strange pleasure of making himself feel worse.

It was the window that troubled Nixon most. It was an unblinking rectangle, like an accusing eye reminding him each time he saw it that things were no longer right. Filled with a longing he did not fully understand, he only knew there was something he wanted dearly that he could not have. On nights when his loneliness for Henry was at its worst, Nixon found he could be soothed by taking his feather pillow from beneath his head and holding it in his arms. Even better was lying flat on his stomach and putting the pillow on his back, where the weight of it felt comforting and helped him grow tired and sleep.

Now Henry was here! With his sled and shovel!

"How are you out?" Nixon asked. "Does your father know?"

"I don't know," Henry said. "I just told them I was going to play in the snow, and I came over."

"But what will we tell them? They'll see us and get angry."

"No, they won't, Nix. Old people never come out in the snow. They don't even like to go out on their doorsteps. We all look alike bundled in our coats. They'll have the housemaids holler us in."

Nixon pushed his slipping cap back away from his eyes and surveyed the deep drifts. "You're right, they'll never wade out here."

"Just in case, let's not shovel a path, and let's build the biggest fort we ever made," Henry said, his smile wide and glowing.

For weeks whenever they could, the boys constructed. Often they worked independently, and coming out to the site found with delight something new the other had made. They decided at the onset to build the walls of their fort high, so they could scurry unobserved from the windows of the houses along Main Street.

Henry's father, Alex, who was a great one for books, had a library, and

Henry found within it a book on the churches and castles of Europe. In the evenings he copied drawings from its pages, and the boys tried to build some of the designs in the snowbanks. Nixon was fascinated with the drawings, learning the names of the buildings' parts. It was all wonderful. Flying buttresses, battlements, basilicas.

The happiest days were when they worked together. The February weather was fine and their fort grew quite large. Their plan of high walls resulted in a warren of trench-like pathways crowned with crenelated battlements, as seen in the castle book, replicated with blocks of snow. They built rooms for stores and a keep to jail captured prisoners. On discovering one corner was an area favored by local stray cats to pee in, that became the latrine, and the boys took a great thrill peeing in it too. Their favorite part of the fort, however, was a room they called the snow cave. A huge pile of gathered snow stacked up against a hardened drift packed by the winds and reinforced by some icy layers was carved out into a little room, completely enclosed. There was only one crawl-through entrance and the boys spent hours inside. They could lie flat on its floor and talk, shoulder to shoulder, entirely unknown and unseen. One day they tried to build a fire inside, but found they were immediately smoked out the door, where they lay in an outside snowbank coughing and laughing. Each night they carefully sealed and disguised the entrance, so it had to be dug out to be used again.

The day came when the boys went to the fort to find they were not alone. Other boys were working in the snow. Charlie Perry and Tom Stimpson were digging their own fort. Nixon and Henry felt their hearts quicken with excitement. None of the boys had exchanged anything other than a wave, but all knew what was to happen. At last their fort was to be tested in a war!

New preparations had to be made. The buried barrel, which was the well, had to be covered so it could not be poisoned by the enemy. Their fort was on the higher ground, but it could still be undermined by possible chargers with shovels, so a stack of laths was brought in from behind the sawmill and an afternoon was spent whittling the ends into sharpened spikes. They had read about *chevaux-de-frise,* and these wooden spikes sticking out of the snow would deter any plans to storm and undermine their walls. Mitten-clad hands formed hundreds of snowballs. They fashioned three types: powder balls to hurl at faces to blind and wet them, ice balls for extra sting, and a coveted store of carefully crafted snowballs, each with a stone hidden in the center.

Nixon saved the blue cloth from feed bags Ephraim used in the stables, and he cut and assembled a dozen pointed flags from this and more scavenged lath. They jabbed these flags into the corners and high places of their structure, christened it the Black Fort, and patiently added to their piles of balls, awaiting the day of the battle.

When the first barrage of snowballs flew by his head, Nixon was entirely unprepared. He'd trudged out earlier to the fort, certain he was alone. There was a warm, unsteady wind and clouds streaking overhead shredded by its blowing.

He immediately noticed their flags had been yanked out of the snow, and one was even snapped in half and tossed into one of their trenches. This was a bold and aggressive challenge, as usually boys did not defile each other's forts outside of an actual battle.

Nixon knew that neither Tom nor Charlie had books of castles at home to look at, but their fort was hastily built and with none of the enthusiasm he and Henry took in making theirs. The fun was in the planning and building. In truth, neither he nor Henry built their fort with any idea of having a real snowball battle, although it was certainly welcome. Tom and Charlie only built a fort after seeing theirs and only in hopes of a battle. His mother had often reminded Nixon that not all boys had the advantages he did, but Nixon understood what the broken flag meant. This winter Tom and Charlie would knock down the flags; next summer they would join the older boys at the swimming place where they would jostle and fight and eventually blacken eyes and come home with their own eyes blackened; a few years more and they would buddy up with the young men who joined the Cast Iron Band gang that prowled the streets and did illegal things. Nixon knew his own path and personality would never take him there.

His thoughts wandered thus as he circled the fort, replacing the flags, pushing them deep into the snowbanks. Then a large snowball grazed his head.

"Wake up!" Tom shouted and howled with laughter.

Nixon crouched down, recoiling from the chunk of snow lodged in his coat collar and now biting his neck with cold. He slid along the snow trench on his backside to the piles of snowballs he and Henry had stacked. The top layer were frozen together, but with one kick of his boot they loosened and he hurled his own salvo at the taunters.

For several minutes it was back and forth, with all the boys getting in some good hits, but it was two against one, and Nixon was getting tired and sweaty. Where was Henry? Was he even nearby?

One of the flying balls hit Nixon squarely in the right ear and it stung mightily. He was breathing hard now, and beginning to fear he could not keep up. The knees of his pants were soaked through, and his nose was running, requiring he keep wiping it on his sleeve. Charlie threw a snowball and it knocked Nixon's hat from his head.

"Hey, moneybags!" Charlie yelled. "Your granddaddy will buy you another."

A fury rose up inside Nixon. He was sick of the boys laughing at his family. He was sick of having everyone know what he wasn't even sure he knew. He was angry about the broken flag and that he would be expected for some reason to forgive it. He was really angry the battle was taking place without Henry. It should be two against two; Tom and Charlie knew that. Henry would be sadly disappointed. Nixon fired snowball after snowball in a rage, hurling them across the distance between the forts.

With a sharp nose for panic, Tom and Charlie sensed Nixon was faltering, and the two charged up the edge of their fort. They'd run out of snowballs anyway, not having made many beforehand, and decided to make a run for Nixon's fort. Nixon saw the boys charging toward him and quickly assessed the chance they might jump on him and attempt to give him a beating. He was mad enough not to care and puffed up his chest and shoulders. Tom and Charlie plucked two of the lath spikes dotting the snowbanks and ran toward Nixon, flailing them like bats. They knocked down another flag and started digging at the wall of snow that formed the outer edge of Nixon's fort. They were trying to destroy it! Nixon kept hitting them with as many snowballs as he could heave in their direction.

Suddenly a shape appeared behind Nixon's right shoulder. Nixon recognized Henry at once, but it was Henry moving in slow motion. No matter how many times Nixon later tried to recall what happened, he was never able to speed up the movement.

Henry, coming from someplace in the direction of their homes, leapt upon the rear bank of the snow fort, beside Nixon. For the briefest moment Henry was suspended in air above the snowy trench like some sort of avenging angel, a look of calm joy on his boyish face. His spiky blond hair surrounded his head like the rays of the sun. His right hand held something dark and dangling, and Nixon forever believed he saw a wave of dark water swirling in a wake, midair, from within it. For it was water, a simple bucketful, and Henry brought it triumphantly down on the dumbfounded heads of Tom and Charlie, who were staring up at him aghast under their slipping woolen hats, mouths open, noses running with snot and snow.

"Sniper!" Henry yelled, as he slopped the gallon of slushy water in a great spray across the enemy heads and slid down the bank to land flat-footed in the trench, where he spilled the last pint of water across his own feet.

"Ooops," he said, noting his wet boot tops, but only Nixon heard this, as Tom and Charlie were already gone, howling across the field toward their homes.

They had little time to savor their victory. For a few minutes the boys huddled in the walls of the fort, laughing at Henry's successful surprise attack. They discussed ways in which Henry could explain his soaked pants and shoes to his parents. Chattering happily, each exchanged his version of the snowball fight, but soon both boys fell silent. Suddenly and awfully, their fort was already in the past. They had won the battle, but Henry was as wet as the boys he'd vanquished and had no choice but to go home too.

Sometimes, childhood slides away unnoticed, its last day as elusive to memory as its first. Other times its end can be marked with perfect accuracy, slipping from one's grasp after a word or gesture, sometimes momentous but usually ordinary. At these times the memory of that end is then carried like a stone in one's pocket, heavily or lightly, depending on the weight, but never again without daily notice, because it is the first of many such stones.

As an adult Nixon marked the end of his childhood by the moment of his parting with Henry at the snow fort, for the boys never played side by side again. His wet cousin, back turned, plodding toward home, dragging the empty wooden bucket that a half-hour before had changed their world, Henry may as well have been the picture of his own boyishness turning its back and leaving him forever. When Henry got to his dooryard, he turned and faced Nixon, and held his hand aloft, silently.

"'Bye, Henry!" Nixon shouted, spatters of rain hitting his cheeks. The ragged clouds that arrived that day now began to release a cold two-day rain, which accomplished what Tom and Charlie could not. By the end of the week the Black Fort had melted away.

Building the snow fort had stirred Nixon's interest in making things. During the long wet spring of 1853, Nixon tried his hand at constructing little models carved and shaped from wood. The castles he and Henry tried to imitate in blocks of snow were a bit more easily attained with blocks of wood, and Nixon's clumsy hands attempted many such miniatures. By the arrival of summer, his skills were such that his carvings were readily identifiable and his fingers rarely bandaged after a slip of his penknife.

In making his wooden models Nixon quickly exhausted the wood he found in the stable at home, so he often made forays to the sawmill to find usable scraps. There, rolling in a pile of sawdust one day was a small, strange dog. It was a dirty white mongrel but carried in his veins the blood of some terrier type. The dog approached Nixon slowly, creeping along on its belly, with the upright stub of its tail wagging. Two intelligent, dark-brown eyes regarded first the boy, and then the gunny sack the boy was placing wood scraps in. Nixon decided the little dog had seen the inside of a gunny sack before, and slid it aside as he reached his hand toward the dog's face.

"Who are you, then?" Nixon asked the small beast, which cocked its head at the sound of the voice and answered with a soft whine.

The dog looked as though it had survived many wars. Its right ear was an upright triangle that rotated and pricked at every sound. What remained of its left ear was a ragged edge, the rest probably torn away in some adversary's teeth. One front leg had been broken and healed in a crooked shape so the toes tipped inward, and both back legs seemed to have suffered a similar fate.

Its face was comic. The wiry hairs around its muzzle were quite long, like the bristles on a chimney cleaner's brush and just as black. In fact this black mottled color extended from its snout all across its muzzle and past the eyes as if the face had survived some explosion.

The dog allowed Nixon to stroke its head and moved closer, creeping on its belly.

"You are a funny little thing," Nixon said. "Do you belong to one of the ships?" Assuming this to be the case, Nixon patted the dog, hoisted his gunny sack, and started to return home. He was a quarter-mile along before he heard the determined huffing of the dog behind him and turned to see a stiff-legged little fur ball with an erect tail following him ten feet behind. Long accustomed to his injuries, the dog could move quite quickly on its twisted legs, but the sight was one that made Nixon laugh out loud.

Despite returning the dog to the wharf, and trying to outrun it back to the sawmill, Nixon found the dog following him for the rest of the day. Back home with his wood, Nixon saw the dog run past him and out into the field. He watched the funny little one-eared head hopping like a rabbit through the deep grass.

The following morning, the little dog sat waiting at the edge of the property. As Nixon approached, the dog crouched down on its belly again, whined, and suddenly leapt up and bounced on its four stiff springs into the field. Nixon followed, wondering as his own legs moved beneath him why he was doing so. The dog came to a sudden stop in a spot where the grass was trodden down. Nixon knew the pup had passed the night curled in this spot, and then realized with a strange apprehension the sleeping place chosen by the little dog was the same area where the snow cave had been last winter.

Nixon threw himself in the grass beside the panting dog. He felt dizzy with something, perhaps the dazzling sun, perhaps joy. Reaching out, he placed his hands around the misshapen creature's body for the first time. The dog was surprisingly sturdy despite its tiny size, with fur that was softer than it appeared. Nixon parted the fur and examined the dog's skin. Tiny fleas ran from the intrusion. He ran his fingers along the ragged ear. It felt tough as a hank of rope. Nixon stroked the dog's neck and discovered at its base a gnarly lump. He knew this lump was more dangerous to the longevity of the dog than any other wounds, but the pup seemed sound and its eyes were bright.

He could not keep this dog. His father would never allow it. The dog had fleas. It had a lump on its neck. It probably belonged to one of the ships. It regarded him with unblinking eyes from the circle where the snow cave had been.

Still, Nixon lifted the small dog with a hand under its chest and carried it across the field. Some determinations cannot be fought against. Nixon knew he had been chosen.

"Oh no, you don't," Ann said, as she saw Nixon carting the dog into the backyard where she stood shaking out a rag.

"He's followed me for two days," said Nixon.

"I don't care if he followed you all the way to Saint Peter's gates," Ann said. "He's not comin' in the house until I hear different."

Nixon screwed up his face. Ann was always talking about saints, usually while scolding him.

"He's a good dog," Nixon said, "and smart too," as though this would convince a scowling Irish housemaid with her fists on both hips.

"Well, he looks plenty hard-used to me," Ann said. "You keep him outside or ask your mother."

Nixon sighed and sat heavily on the porch with the dog in his lap. He knew there was no point in asking his mother as she would only tell him to ask his father. Still, there might be some use in trying to get her on his side before his father arrived home.

His mother and Marianne were in the front room sewing. Since her daughter's illness, Mary Black was stalked by the fear of the girl's death. She'd lost another daughter, Caroline, in infancy eight years before and retained the clear memory of leaning over her child's small, shrouded corpse, in this very parlor, and cutting a lock of her blonde baby hair for a memento.

She recalled the rain of that long-ago September evening dashing across the windowpanes like handfuls of small pebbles, and how she had held the tiny curl in her palm and felt a strange cold fire behind her eyes. She had thought of her surviving children, Marianne and Nixon, sleeping upstairs, and the awful premonition ran through her with a certainty she had never forgotten. "The unbearable can happen," she had thought, "and then it can happen again."

Now the premonition lurked around Marianne, unseen by everyone but her mother. Mary knew it was unreasonable. Dr. Mason had given several reasons to hope the girl's heart was not damaged irreparably by the scarlatina, but Mary could not deny the voice she heard. There were times when her anxiety grew so fierce it was all she could do to keep from clasping Marianne in her arms, to hold her fast, to keep her from slipping away.

She enjoyed sewing with her daughter, or engaging in any repetitive household task. There was the pleasure of teaching her, but commonplace work also seemed to prohibit any drama or misfortune. Enveloped in the mundane, she felt safe.

Today, they were binding a trim to the sleeves and hem of a dress. Marianne's pale fingers were mastering the exacting task of pinching the fold of the red velveteen tightly and feeding it accurately onto the surface of the dress fabric while tacking it securely with a needle and thread. Agnes was also present, but having spent the morning running her dolls around the baseboards of the room while on her hands and knees, she had tired herself out and was snoring in a large chair.

"Take tiny stitches, dear," Mary reminded. "Don't hurry and let them get too large. They need to be nearly invisible for the trim to be pretty."

When a loud whoop sounded outside the front window both women turned to see the head of a small animal bouncing within its frame. Was it a dog? Surely it was Nixon whose inexpertly disguised squeak was chirping, "Hello! Hello!" each time the animal's head was hoisted into view.

Marianne put down her sewing, and she and her mother crossed the room. Outside, Nixon stood on a wooden crate holding the ugliest dog they had ever seen. It was one-eared with a face that appeared to be covered in soot.

"Nixon! Quiet down!" Mary said, raising the window sash to its halfway position. "Where did that come from?"

"He's been following me," Nixon replied. "Isn't he the strangest little dog?"

"He looks like he's had his nose where it didn't belong," Marianne said. "Where did he come from?"

"He followed me from the wharf."

"Oh, then he's off one of the ships." Mary said. "You'd better take him back."

"I already tried, and he won't stay. I think someone left him, or he ran away. He slept in the field last night," Nixon explained. "Do you think we could keep him?"

Before Mary could object, a squeal of delight erupted from beside her. Agnes had awakened and stood by the window shouting. "A doggie! A doggie!" before bolting away to join Nixon and the mongrel.

"You two stay outside with that dog," Mary ordered, "and wait until your father gets home."

Waiting on the porch was interminable for Nixon and Agnes as they strained their eyes looking for the figure of their father returning from his store. When George finally did arrive he found both his children dandling a frightful-looking beast. Nixon explained how the dog came to be there, and George had to smile when he considered the creature's spunk and survival.

"He does look as though he's been run the wrong way through a dirty pipe," George commented dryly. He eyed the homely little mite, whose twisted feet were padding with excitement in time with the stub of a tail which was beating out its own tattoo on the porch floorboards. He noticed a red strip of ribbon tied on the creature's tail.

"Look how well he wears a bow, Papa," Agnes pointed out proudly, gesturing to the bouncing, beribboned tail.

George rolled the dog on his back and searched its underside. "Let's see what else this little cur is wearing." Taking note of the scattering insects, he raised his eyebrows. "Nixon, this dog is covered with fleas."

"Please, Papa, can't we fix him and keep him?" Agnes asked.

"I will think about it," said George. "Put him back in the field where he belongs, and come and wash yourselves for supper."

As George mounted the steps and entered the cool darkness of the stair hall, he saw his wife and daughter bending in the parlor as though searching the floor for a lost coin. Mary stood up as he entered and leaned on the back of the wing chair in a corner.

"Are we to have a dog now, George?" Mary asked, looking weary and impatient.

"A dog who lives in the stable perhaps." George replied. "What are you two hunting?"

"We've lost the last strip of trim for Marianne's dress and are frantic trying to find it. The dress will be spoiled without it." Marianne looked up at him, flushed and desperate.

George flattened his lips into their customary line and touched the unfinished dress heaped on the parlor table. "This red trim?" he asked. Mary nodded.

"I'll go fetch Nixon and Agnes for supper," he said, "and we'll all look for it together."

Outside, the children were still playing with the dog. George squatted down and untied the red velveteen ribbon from the tail of the creature. He pointed with one finger toward the field in silence, but Nixon understood the command.

"Ag," he said, dangling the ribbon from his fingers, "take this inside to your sister."

My cup runneth over, Nixon thought as he lay in bed that autumn. He knew his psalms from church sermons, of course, but did not really understand them. They could be memorized more easily than most things, without really trying, as one learned a song. Perhaps this was why the words "psalm" and "song" sounded so alike. But what cup? And what was running over?

On this autumn night, snug beneath his counterpane, Nixon believed he had solved the puzzle of cups running over. Owing to two wonderful, unexpected events he felt his own heart filled with more happiness than he imagined possible. Feeling this, he remembered the lines from the psalm.

Not only had his father allowed him to keep the stray dog, but another miracle had happened. A week after the dog was accepted, Nixon spotted his father riding Flicker up the street with two new horses tied behind her. One for himself and one for Marianne!

Nixon had been promised his own horse when he reached the age of twelve, but he'd just turned eleven and had not even dared to anticipate this possibility until another year. The horses had arrived bearing names, and his, a sorrel mare named Lucy, was like a dream come true.

The dog was not given a name. As a condition of keeping it, Nixon was to bathe it at once. The pup's soft regular whines turned to howls when stuffed into a tub and soaped with pine tar. As Nixon lifted the twisted little body in and out of the water, chasing fleas from the furry belly and running a worried hand across the lump on the dog's neck, he tried out several names. None seemed to describe accurately the sincerity and grit he found in the animal's brown eyes.

"You already know your own name, don't you?" Nixon asked the dripping dog. "And you are not going to tell me." Nixon knew he could never intrude on the dog's own secret. The battered dog had lived a whole life of which Nixon knew nothing. Adventures, battles, narrow escapes, faraway travels—who knew what variety of experiences lay inside the tiny furry head? The mongrel would be allowed to keep its name to itself and would not have to endure the indignity of another.

After a lifetime of dipping, scrubbing, and picking, Nixon decided the dog would pass any inspection his father decided to render. Amazingly, George only gestured toward the stable and told Nixon the dog must live there. When Nixon placed it on the hay pile, the dog whined in protest until Nixon realized it wanted to be covered with hay. When the evening ended, Nixon closed the stable door quietly, a pair of chocolate eyes watching him from between hay straws. He prayed the dog would be there in the morning.

Nixon had not needed to worry. The following morning the pup was sitting on the floor of the stable with its tongue lolling. It padded its forefeet excitedly, stood on its hind legs momentarily, and circled an object on the floor. Nixon saw the focus of the dog's delight. Before him lay a large grey rat. Its feet were stuck in the air like four pink gloves and its long worm-like tail lay in a straight line like an exclamation point.

"Ratter," George said, raising one eyebrow and flattening his lips when the rodent was shown to him. "Good. The pup will earn his keep."

The dog and Lucy got on well, but caring for them kept Nixon's hands full. Now that he was riding out nearly every day, Nixon was covering more miles. Looking backward astride Lucy, Nixon noticed the little dog struggling along on bent legs, trying to keep up with the horse's easy gait. So Nixon fashioned a sling for it to ride in. Tied from a triangle of old sailcloth, it made a pocket for the dog to sit in, suspended from the saddle pommel. The solution was a good one, as the three could then go together on all their ventures. Every day the dog's eager head and dark eyes could be seen poking out from the sling bouncing against Nixon's knee, while Lucy's patient hooves pressed onward.

Thus the late summer and autumn passed in unhurried happiness. By the night when Nixon lay beneath his covers pondering psalms, a great hole in his heart had been filled. He felt warmly toward everyone and inclined more than ever to being good.

But what exactly was good? Encouraged for as long as he could remember to be good, he found as he got older the notion of goodness more difficult to decipher. Certainly goodness was not something easily grasped. While it often appeared plainly, it came dressed in disguise as well. To obey goodness was obviously not humanly possible, thus the sermons and psalms. The temptation was to not worry about it and just go on as always, but others seemed to mind. This led to the problem of complying with others' definitions of goodness. For Father, it seemed to revolve around diligence, for Mother around something like kindness, but Nixon knew Miss Hight, his teacher, only required silence and a clean shirt.

Adults were surely not good. The men who beat each other on Water Street seemed a fair example of badness, but why was it, then, that the men who watched the fights seemed worse?

What too of his own family? Was Franny really bad? Why did the uncles hate her so? Was she really looking for Grandfather's money? If one could suspect Franny of desiring his money, it was only one further step to suspecting the uncles wanted his money too. Uncle Alex and Uncle Will would no longer speak to Grandfather. Nixon knew if he behaved this way to his own father he would be punished. No one insisted the uncles be good.

Lying in bed, looking out the window at the moon, hours could be spent in such wondering. When he was younger it was easier. The day was either sunny or rainy; if it was a good day there were no lessons and if it were a bad day there was a visit to the dentist. Now he realized he was going to have to pay attention to motive. This, apparently, was something adults had to do. The realization made his heart feel heavy and sad.

Nixon believed his own father was good. He was stern and did not put up with "tomfoolery," but he was kindly. Was there a reason he gave in so easily, letting him keep the dog? What was the reason for the early gift of Lucy? Was it because Marianne was going to die? Or was it because Nixon no longer had Henry to play with? Did his father even notice about Henry? If so, it was nice of him to make up for it by giving him Lucy. Still, if something had to be made up for, then something truly was lost. Something he did not know.

A strange apprehension hovered around his trips to Woodlawn as well. Nixon and the dog would often ride Lucy to visit Grandfather and Franny. Franny was her usual self. She was generally employed helping Grandfather read or write but always took time to serve Nixon a nibble of something sweet.

Grandfather, in comparison, was diminished. John Black was not much taller than Nixon now, curling as old people do, and with blindness causing him to hold his head at an odd angle, his stature had disappeared. His ears were still keen, and Nixon thought his grandfather must lie in wait for sounds. The old man never failed to know when Nixon had arrived and beckoned the boy close to him. The clutching hands Nixon first noticed at his birthday party had only grown more rapacious. Grandfather seemed unable to keep from touching him, plucking at him, and holding him close as though he were being inspected for some unknown fitness.

More often than not, Grandfather told him long stories and insisted Nixon travel with him through the many rooms of Woodlawn as he showed the boy his "treasures." Grandfather Black could not see well enough to make his way through these rooms alone, and Franny always disappeared during these sessions, so Nixon ended up towing the old man behind him, his grandfather clutching his suspenders for guidance. In this awkward way they toured from chamber to chamber, with Grandfather imploring Nixon to open and close cupboards and desk drawers, looking at endless objects secreted within. Grandfather Black was happy to allow the new dog inside his house, so the scruffy pup lolled on fine carpets and limped up the beautiful elliptical staircase, as tales of the "treasures" were passed from grandfather to grandson.

Some of the tales were exciting. There was a miniature painted portrait of George Washington that had been given by Washington himself to Nixon's great-grandfather, David Cobb. His grandfather allowed him to hold it, and as Nixon cradled the smooth gold-framed oval with Washington's impassive face painted upon it, he was told the story of David Cobb, who was one of Washington's generals in the Revolutionary War. Nixon never realized someone in his family had known the first president!

Nixon was disappointed to learn there were none of David Cobb's swords or uniforms hidden away at Woodlawn, but Grandfather Black revealed, with great pride, a deep barrel-shaped chair once used by Great-grandfather Cobb when he was Speaker of the House in Massachusetts. Nixon could not quite grasp what a Speaker of the House was, something to do with lawmaking evidently, but pale and bloodless compared to George Washington and the Revolutionary War.

Old John Black droned and clutched, but Nixon suffered through these afternoons doggedly, grappling with fatigue and struggling forward with his arms in a kind of swimming motion as he tried to pull the old man along faster behind him. Sometimes it seemed his brain would burst with irritation.

It also made Nixon uneasy. Why was he being shown these things? He didn't think, for instance, that Henry knew about their relation to George Washington, or surely he would have spoken of it while building their fort. It seemed to Nixon like he was being tested.

"Where'd you git that dog?"

The cracked voice out of nowhere, barely audible over the rattling yellowed leaves of the birch tree above him, made Nixon's backbone shiver.

He stopped sorting through the scraps of wood and turned slowly in the direction of the malign voice. Two wharf workers probably employed by his grandfather were sitting on a pile of box shooks that they were presumably loading. An empty wagon lacking a team sat nearby.

Nixon had not seen the men, as they were nearly invisible in the dim spot of shade where they sat eating. They must have watched him for a while, silently, as they ate the dinners they'd brought with them, tied in bandana squares, spread across their laps.

One of the men was lath-thin and had a shiftless, clever face. Nixon guessed it was he who had posed the sinister-sounding question. The man was grinning, but his eyes were full of hate. The other was plump and thick-thighed. His broad, swollen face suggested he was probably half-witted. He held a wad of food in one pudgy fist and chewed animatedly, while the other meaty hand occupied itself in the repetitive activity of raking his hair over his scalp where it promptly fell back in greasy strings around his face.

Nixon decided it would be best to behave without guile, standing before the men and widening his eyes in purposeful childishness. The little dog hung directly at his feet. Nixon ignored their question as though he hadn't heard it and posed one of his own.

"Are you loading or unloading?" he asked the men.

"Unloading," the thin one replied, "and off to the mill for more as soon as Jack brings a new team."

"Box shooks?" Nixon inquired, knowing full well they were the bundled slabs of thin wood used to construct boxes.

"Not just any shooks," the thin one said, inflecting a false pomposity in his voice, "but Blacks' Best Box Shooks." He elbowed his fat sidekick who giggled stupidly at this, revealing a chunk of his lunch protruding through missing teeth.

"You didn't ever say," the thin man questioned as though he were laying a snare, "where'd you git that dog?" Another breeze moved through the birch leaves sounding precisely like the rattle of a snake. Nixon's ears felt hot, and he hoped they weren't showing red.

"He came from here," Nixon replied.

"That dog come off the *Comet*," the fat man mumbled, speaking with his mouth grinding in slow satisfied circles like a cud-chewing cow. "They wuz lookin' around for him a few months ago."

"I guess they didn't find him," Nixon pushed back, in a low, even voice.

"Then that dog ain't yours," the thin man said accusingly, stuffing his dinner cloth in his back pocket and picking at a tooth with his index finger.

Nixon looked down at the canine subject standing so close it'd placed one furry foot on his shoe. He felt panic rising in his chest, and the sudden urge to grasp the dog and run. But as quickly as the panic rose, it seemed to harden inside him, and he looked squarely at the two men with what he hoped was a devilish grin. "He sticks to my leg like a burdock, so I haven't much choice," Nixon said.

The half-witted man chuckled and nodded, but the thin man wanted blood and would not bite on Nixon's joke. "Is that so?" he hissed. "Well I see you haulin' that dog around in a little sack on your horse, so I think he has a pretty good livin' with you. You better not fall too hard in love. That dog's sick. It ain't gonna live. It's got a bunch on its neck."

Nixon felt his throat go dry. How did this man know about the lump on the dog's neck if he'd never touched him? Why had he been watching him riding Lucy? Nixon understood in his heart the dog would probably not live a long time, but did not understand the delight this wharf man took in being so cruel. It would seem that adult's vices were as ordinary as those of boys his own age. Nixon suddenly remembered that he was, supposedly, a child, and this adult man was as delighted in hurting him as he would be one of his own fellows.

What the man wanted was the pleasure of his pain, and Nixon knew he must not give it to him. The man wanted to frighten him with the news of the dog's illness and hoped for a reaction. A rage passed quickly somewhere in Nixon's brain. He bit the insides of his cheeks and willed his chin not to wobble. To his own surprise a reply rose out of his throat, delivered in a cold sneer, a reply he was not even wholly conscious of thinking. He placed a flat gaze on the thin man's eyes.

"Well, it won't be any job to bury him. I could dig a hole for this dog with a teaspoon."

The fat man laughed again, this time quite loudly, and flinched slightly when his thin partner glared at him. He was definitely slow-witted and he stood up heavily, wiping his food-stained hands on his abundant thighs. He'd let his suspenders slide off his shoulders, either by carelessness or desire, and they dangled around his legs as he moved, making him look like some great dumb beast standing in a harness. "That dog's a runt," he offered, raking his stringy hair futilely again, trying to appease himself back into the thin man's favor.

"And damned ugly too," the thin man snorted. "What name do you call an ugly dog like that?"

"He doesn't have a name," Nixon answered, knowing he could not let up. "He's going to die. No point in naming him."

"Well," the thin man spat back, "it's the ugliest dog I ever see." Nixon noticed the man's mocking, snooping eyes slide away from the dog and to his own body, where they appraised him up and down. The man's lips curled in a sneer. "And odd," he added, snarling. "That dog is one odd job."

Nixon made several more trips to the scrap pile at the wharf that fall. He always made sure the dog came with him. The men were usually there, snickering.

"Here comes that odd job," they would say, jeering and cackling, poking at one another. They never again even looked at the dog. The dog had been forgotten. When they said "odd job," Nixon knew they meant him.

The Know-Nothings
1854

It had been two months since the Ellsworth Catholic church was bombed with gunpowder. The resulting fire was contained, but the explosion, which could be seen and heard from their house, left George with the unpleasant task of explaining to his children why a local gang was trying to destroy a house of worship.

A year earlier a Jesuit priest had come to Ellsworth. Although George had not met the man personally, he had seen him on the sidewalk. Said to have come from Switzerland, the priest had, nonetheless, spent recent years riding the circuit in northern Maine, ministering to the Indians and Irish and French-Canadian immigrants. George knew the priest must have learned the Penobscot Indian language, but when he overheard the priest speak it was in oddly accented, broken English.

The priest was named John Bapst. He had brown hair going to grey and a long straight nose. Small and frail-looking though he was, he had warm brown eyes with a fierceness behind them and a sprightly, purposeful step. Accepting with approval any man who could withstand the rigors of life in the Maine woods, George thought of Father John Bapst as an upright soul, if he thought of him at all. Good, educated, reverent men were always needed, in any town. George was little interested in the man's religious beliefs.

Others were not inclined to such tolerance. When Father Bapst was given a residence by local Catholics and then succeeded in building a new church a few months after his arrival, most held their tongues.

When several young ladies of the town took an interest in Catholicism after having attended Bapst's lectures, dissension began to take root. In their suspicions, the residents of Ellsworth were hardly alone. The entire United States was swept up in the fear that the large numbers of foreigners, mostly Irish, who were immigrating were going to change their lives forever. In response to this fear a new political party had formed, and by 1854 there were hundreds of thousands of newly registered "Know-Nothings" in America vowing to vote for and support only "native" Protestant candidates. This new party, originating from several secret societies, was named the Know-Nothing Party because its members claimed to know nothing about it when asked.

Things may not have gone badly in Ellsworth had it not been for the newspaper and its hot-headed owner, William Chaney. Back in 1852, Chaney had clerked for George in the store, then drifted off, and after repeated lateness, ceased coming to work at all. He was uncommonly bright but bellicose and erratic, and George was not unhappy to see him gone. Will had recently resurfaced and purchased the local *Ellsworth Herald*. At last he had a pulpit for his penchant for argument, and although his editorship began mildly, by the spring of 1854 he was in full dudgeon, "defending the virtues of the land and its natives against immigrants, and Roman Catholics." At first, George judged Will's rantings to be the harmless, clever speech of a man striving to increase his readership, but now he was not so sure.

As George saw it, the Bapst pulpit and the Chaney pulpit had collided last November when young Bridget Donahoe was expelled from the public school for refusing to read the King James Bible. Both Bridget and her parents considered the Protestant Bible sinful and were instructed against reading it by their church. The Catholics wanted the school to allow their children to read their own version of the Bible. George did not believe this request would be granted, but any chance of its consideration was thwarted by the wording of the petition sent to the school committee by Father John Bapst. In the petition Bapst pronounced the Protestant Bible "the counterfeit word of God, and the most pernicious of all poisons for the corruption of the faith and morals of the faithful." When George read this, he knew it would cause trouble. He wondered if the priest's poor English could be the cause of his insensitivity. Regardless, Chaney seized on these unwise words and made headlines of them.

Bridget, who was about Marianne's age, and most of the Catholic children in Ellsworth left the public school and joined Bapst's new Catholic school. Lawrence Donahoe, Bridget's father, responded by suing the Ellsworth school committee for his daughter's expulsion and requesting her reinstatement or compensation for the costs of attending Bapst's school.

As Chaney railed ceaselessly in the *Herald* about the suit, the case moved swiftly through the minor courts and arrived in the Maine Supreme Court in Bangor. Two local lawyers stood for Lawrence Donahoe, while the Ellsworth school committee went all the way to Boston to find a man for their defense. They hired Richard Henry Dana, known to George as a man from a powerful family and active both in Boston and national politics. Urban and self-confident, Dana's presence was expected to intimidate his opponents before he even encountered them. Yet no matter how menacing the big city lawyer could be, he still required an assistant familiar with the local landscape. Much to George's disquiet, the lawyer chosen to stand at Dana's side was John Peters, his wife's brother.

In the early days of June before the case had even begun, the Catholic church was bombed and set afire. The windows in Bapst's nearby house were broken by a mob wearing white sheets. The *Ellsworth Herald* accused Bapst of breaking his own windows to gain sympathy. Fearing for his safety, the diocese bishop ordered Bapst out of Ellsworth to Bangor, where he was assigned another position with a vacant parish.

George thought the absence of Father Bapst might cool the air, but tempers were so hot as to be unreasonable. It seemed everyone wanted the blood of the Catholics. A small group of prominent Protestants tried to resist and petitioned the town selectmen for a special town meeting to denounce the violence directed at the Catholic church. This group, led by Charles Jarvis, the husband of George's eldest sister, asked the townspeople to meet "to denounce the outrage, assuring our Catholic fellow-townspeople the burning of their school was an act of ignorant bigots, and that all respectable Protestants held such conduct in abhorrence." In his heart George was in full agreement with Jarvis' group, but he was disinclined to place himself in another family feud. His own brothers were still angry at him for supporting their father's marriage, and he did not relish taking sides in a disagreement between his family and his wife's. He also paid heed to his own father's caution about entering the world of politics.

"It is best to stay out of politics," George remembered John Black saying, "and keep your opinions of public affairs to yourself."

The more thought George gave the matter, the more he decided his father was right. The Peters and Jarvis families had appetites for politics, but he did not. What point was there in risking his family's suffering or his business concerns to arson or damage? What he did not expect was just how evil the outcome of Jarvis' meeting would be.

Charles Jarvis and his supporters were so outnumbered they simply gave up and left the town hall without protest. The next edition of the *Herald* gleefully reported word-for-word the resolution passed that night. Printed on the front page were the sentiments of the men who remained at the meeting.

Whereas we have good reason to believe that we are indebted to one John Bapst, Catholic Priest, for the luxury of the present lawsuit now enjoyed by the School Committee of Ellsworth, be it therefore resolved that should the said Bapst be found again on Ellsworth soil, we will manifest our gratitude for his kindly interference with our free schools, and attempts to banish the Bible therefrom, by procuring for him and trying on an entire suit of new clothes such as cannot be found at the shops of any tailor, and when thus appareled he be presented with a free ticket to leave Ellsworth upon the first railroad operation that may go into effect.

Not only had the men refused to denounce violence against local Catholics, they'd encouraged it, and threatened the priest John Bapst with bodily harm in print!

A week later the Catholic church was set on fire again, and then the school committee won its case in Bangor after one day's argument. Lawyers Dana and Peters barely had to clear their throats.

In the weeks following, George was consumed by thoughts. On this hot August day, he stood alone in his store so disturbed he felt paralyzed. It was humid, and George wiped his face and brow with his handkerchief. He stepped to the rear doorway to get some air. Tall enough to reach the granite lintel above him, he placed his hand on it for support and felt its pleasant coolness in his palm. Briefly he rested his shoulder against the door frame and placed the side of his face against its chill stone.

An argument he'd had with his wife the night before had cast him adrift. Their marriage was built quite sturdily on understanding and polite conversation, and they had the agreeable habit of pulling together and thinking alike. The anger last night was a product not of words said, but of what neither dared to say, or even to conceive of: How much longer could they live in this town?

George stood in the doorway of the building, his building, solid and brick. Here was a row of windows with a view of the river. The heat persuaded him to step outside and sit on a keg of nails delivered that morning. The sound of the rolling river came into his ears, its beauty like a mockery and just as quickly spoiled by a clattering wagon passing in a cloud of dust across the bridge nearby. It had all seemed like a paradise once.

Now his searching eyes saw nothing but a boomtown. A few fine houses attested to the spoils of the timber trade, but the town was largely a muddy crossroads teetering on the edge of an undesirable frontier. For years a brisk business was done here, but common civility had been lost.

Even the prospects of continued good business seemed shaky. The crews had to go deeper and deeper into the woods for good timber, and harvests cost more each year. Competitive lumber was pouring into the markets from elsewhere in New England, from New York, and as far away as Michigan. With national troubles like the fugitive slave act boiling, George wondered if the whole country might soon be at war. Any footholds gained in Ellsworth were now threatened with destruction by this foolish local violence. Let other men play at politics. George had a businessman's blood and bones, and in them he felt the chill of decline. Ellsworth was one reversal of fortune away from disaster.

It was then George remembered he was outside his store sitting on a keg of nails, a somewhat unusual place to find him. His elbows were resting on his thighs, and he was rubbing his hands slowly and repeatedly together, a nervous habit he knew he possessed. A discomfort passed through him at the thought of a bystander seeing him thus, idle and possibly troubled.

Mary had given him a pocketful of radishes from the garden that morning. He pulled one out now, grateful to have something to do with his restless hands. He rolled the scarlet ball in his fingers, retrieved his pocket knife from his waistcoat, and sat for a while longer, peeling the ruby skin away in small curls and enjoying their spicy taste on his tongue.

"Ho, George!" a voice saluted from behind his right shoulder.

Coming toward George, down the slope from his elegant riverside house, was Seth Tisdale. Seth was mounted on his black stallion, Ambler, probably the finest riding horse in the county and certainly the most showy, of a breed uncommon in the area, a walker. The horse possessed an unusual running walk and could be ridden for long distances. Seth had brought him from far off, somewhere in the southern states, and was quite proud of him.

Nowhere near as handsome as his mount, Seth was a dog-faced man in his early fifties, with a disapproving glare and a mouth whose corners turned down even when he smiled. He was one of Ellsworth's big men, made wealthy by real estate, carpentry, and shipbuilding. Some of the finest houses in town, including Woodlawn, had risen under his supervision, and rumor was that Seth would soon begin construction of a huge ship of over 1800 tons, the likes of which Ellsworth had never seen before.

George suspected Tisdale who was the head of the embattled school committee, of being a deep-dyed Know-Nothing despite employing Irish servants in his house. Having known Seth all his life, George had learned to be measured with him, and was always careful what he said. Whenever George spoke with Seth, he felt he was being questioned for information and tested for weakness.

Seth rode up beside George's nail-keg seat, propelled by Ambler's distinctive, flat-footed gait.

"I never expect to find George Black sitting idle," Seth said in his nasal twang which contained every inflection of self-assurance. Perhaps he'd seen George's nervous hands.

"Radishes," George replied, holding aloft a small red sphere balanced in his fingers.

Seth regarded him quizzically, tilting his head until he finally understood. "Ah, a riverside picnic," he said.

"Just so," George replied, "and it is close in the store today."

"Yes, the hottest day of the year, I think," Seth answered.

Ambler shook his lovely head, rattling the costly bridle Seth had specially made for him. George noticed for the first time Ambler had a white blaze on his forehead which resembled the letter T.

"Your brother-in-law is a fine lawyer, George," Seth said.

George felt himself characteristically and uncomfortably being tested. He popped a radish chunk into his mouth and chewed it while he replied, hoping to disguise any emotion in his face.

"Yes, the family have high hopes for his successful career," he said with radish on his tongue.

"Well, he will be on the supreme court himself one day if he keeps on as he did in Bangor last month," Seth said.

George toasted Seth with another radish pierced on the tip of his knife. "God willing," he replied.

George felt a sickness of the soul watching Seth Tisdale and Ambler stride away. How could his family remain in this town? He thought of his children. Marianne's beautiful red-cheeked face glistening with fever. Might doctors in a larger city be able to help her? If she did recover what would become of her here, or of fierce little Agnes as she grew into the strong-headed woman she was sure to be? Are they to marry Seth Tisdale's sons? What too of Nixon? The boy had already lost Henry because of the discord between himself and his own brothers. Even if Will and Alex ever came around to speaking to him again, that ice would never fully thaw. George bought Nixon the horse Lucy so he would not be so alone, and blessedly the boy had come across that ugly white dog at the wharf. It wrung George's heart to think of Nixon riding Lucy in the street with the tiny dog dangling in the sack his son had devised for him. Nixon was a good boy. Would he stay good in this raw place? With gangs of men burning churches and fighting on Water Street?

The night before, while arguing with Mary, she'd placed a dish down on the table with enough force that it broke.

"These troubles have nothing to do with us," she said over and over. "We are not involved."

George reminded Mary that her own brother, John Peters, had admitted to them what happened when he and Dana had finished arguing the school committee defense in Bangor. When the courtroom was empty the judge invited both men into his chambers, wined and dined them, and told them they'd won their case. Before the verdict was announced publicly!

Mary reminded George it was his brother-in-law, Charles Jarvis, who stirred up the cause for Father Bapst that led to the lawsuit to begin with.

Both husband and wife knew what was happening, and neither wanted to face the obvious changes being thrust upon them. They were involved, unwillingly, in the center of a storm. Out of fear of the unknown they were clinging to the familiar, but the familiar was wreckage.

The rain has not survived in the stories that remain of what happened that night. Perhaps it is because the rain was the least of the evils to descend on Ellsworth. Or perhaps, to remember the rain would imply a person had either been a witness or a participant in the atrocity, and of course most people "knew nothing" of what had gone on. In any case in the telling and retelling, the rain, like much else, has been erased.

It had been a misty, dour day with a sky the color of yellow lead. That evening, when Nixon carried the dog into the stable, a faintly luminous haze surrounded his lamp, though it dangled inches from his hand. Once inside, he set the dog down in the hay and lay down beside him. It was his habit to talk over the events of the day with the dog, who always seemed so interested.

While they lay together the rain began, tapping at first like many sets of nervous fingers and finally forming a sloping liquid sound as it ran down overhead. Nixon covered the dog with his customary hay blanket and turned the lamp flame low, and the two drowsed there quietly in a warm pile. Lucy too joined in. Thumping her hooves, she turned to press her body against her stall, where the hay pile lay, and leaned the full weight of her hips near to the boy and dog to close the circle.

Nixon's closed eyes flickered at the sound of the sputtering lamp. He'd dozed off and the lamp was running out of oil. It flamed out suddenly, leaving him in darkness. Thinking he'd better get back to the house, he rose from the hay, brushing off the seat of his pants. He ran his hand along the warm little skull of the sleeping dog, and stepped around the corner to feel for Lucy's gentle head in the darkness. Fishing a small chunk of sugar from his vest, he held it to Lucy's soft bristly lips and listened as her square solid teeth chewed. "Good night, Lucy," he said, as he removed the spent lamp from its peg and slid the stable door open.

Outside in the raw air, the rain fell. It was as dark as a pocket, and from up-street he heard sounds of men shouting and laughing. He shuddered a moment with the change of temperature, but saw ahead of him his mother's figure in the lighted window of the kitchen. She was folding a towel, her movements intimate and deliberate and comforting to Nixon as he approached the house in the gloom.

From a distance he heard the sound of running feet. As soon as the figure rounded the back of the house, Nixon saw it was Ann, the house-maid. This was her night off, and Nixon supposed she'd come from the Galway Green section of town after visiting her mother as she usually did.

Nixon was unprepared for the look on Ann's face this night. Meeting her on the back steps, the light of the kitchen window made clear something was very wrong. Ann's chest was heaving from her run, and her wild hair was flattened in black wet strings against her forehead. Her shawl lay askew across her shoulders. Her familiar hands, large, red and scaly, clutched her lamp and one ribbon of her dislodged bonnet that dangled against her sodden skirts.

Nixon's heart turned inside his chest with pity. "Ann?" he said, the single word both address and question.

Her nose flared like that of a horse and the whites of her eyes lolled as she regarded Nixon for a brief moment with a look that contained both horror and fear. Then she pushed past him and through the door, sobbing, and Nixon saw through the window Ann and his mother in each other's arms.

It took a moment before the voices of the men up the street registered in Nixon's ears. What his mind had dismissed earlier as the sounds of a group of men on a Saturday night spree, he now realized were many more voices. He ran to the street and looked up at the corner.

The crossroads of Main and High Streets were filled with people, maybe a hundred, maybe more. Burning torches were being waved and the sound of shouting became a roar. What was happening? He looked over his shoulder at Henry's bedroom window, which was curtained and dark, and back to the light from the kitchen in his own house before turning up his collar and running up the street.

Nixon's imagination raced as he made his way, barely noticing how many men were shouldering past him quickly in the opposite direction. Was it a fire? An accident? When he reached the corner there was little to see, but he was surrounded by people he knew. Shopkeepers, wharf workers, men who came into his father's store. Most were jeering and shouting curses at something the entire crowd surrounded and he could not yet see, but even the quiet ones were gawking and grinning. Some were even throwing stones.

Unexpectedly the crowd surged forward, and Nixon was propelled within it, barely keeping his balance and momentarily panic-stricken at being trampled or crushed. Fighting his way back out of the tangle of arms and legs, he staggered and found himself pushed into the dooryard of Watt's house, where he leaned a moment on the fence in relief. The crowd gasped and cheered and Nixon gazed in amazement as the hideous object of their interest was made clear to him.

Rising in the morass of the mob was a thin man, bleeding, disheveled, and stripped naked, straddling a hoisted fence rail as though it was a horse. As men on either side held the poor wretch in place, the men bearing the rail on their shoulders bounced it up and down, causing the victim to moan in pain and the crowd to laugh in delight. One of the men bearing the rail was a great brute who worked at the shipyard; he had tied an American flag around his shoulders, where it hung down his back like a cape.

"We are Americans!" the flag-wearer shouted, over and over, to great cheers from the crowd.

Insensible to the soaking rain, the mob ridiculed and mocked the naked man. A shoe was tossed into the air and Nixon watched in disbelief as the man's remaining clothing was torn and shredded by the onlookers passing it from hand to hand.

Nixon's mind reeled as he gazed at the familiar, ravenous faces around him leering in the torchlight. Was it really Mr. Jordan who sold him licorice hurling rocks at a bleeding naked person in the street? How was it that fussy Mr. Linn who sang in a squeaky voice at church could now so strongly bellow swear words? Why was the big man from the shipyard wearing a flag on his back? Nixon shuddered at the evil in the eyes of men he'd known as neighbors all his life. Who was this naked man? Would nobody stop this?

The knot of men bearing the rail moved slowly down High Street away from Nixon's house, some of the crowd following. The naked man slumped forward on the rail, moaning and trying to cover his head with his elbows as a shield from the stones thrown at him, but his captors pinned his flailing arms behind him and kept bouncing the rail.

Nixon dared not get too close, lest he get caught again in the mob, but it was thinning quickly, the spectators disappearing into the dark. Nixon kept the men and their torches in view and, by knowing these dooryards and fields with the precision of a child who plays in them, he managed to follow unnoticed, darting from the dim illumination provided by one lamp-lit window to another.

By the time the men reached the corner of Elm Street, the group had dwindled to a dozen. Nixon crouched behind bushes near the Loring house and watched as the men dumped their captive off the rail. Without a crowd to amuse, they became impatient and rolled their victim into the scraggly grass of the Elm Street field, just behind the Catholic church.

"Let's drag the bastard behind the church," Nixon heard one of the men say.

"Yeah, nail him to his cross," another shouted while the others laughed.

"He ain't dead is he?" a third questioned in a quavery voice. "We wasn't supposed to kill him."

"No, he ain't dead," said a man who stepped up and kicked the naked man's prostrate body, "he's just out."

"Well, wake him up."

"How we gonna do that?"

"You flunkies!" the great man with the flag cape complained and stepped forward, pushing the others away. "Piss on him!" He rolled the body of the victim with one foot until the naked man was sprawled with his head thrown back and his face exposed. The big man then laid one heavy boot across the man's body, straddled him, fumbled at his own pants, and aimed a stream of urine at the unconscious face. The others clapped and hooted, with one distinctive laugh rising above the rest.

"Haw-haw-haw-hee-haw!"

Clutching a branch from the bush at Loring's, Nixon fell to his knees. The mule-man! His stomach swirled. Nausea crawled up his throat and it was only luck and fear of discovery that kept the contents of his stomach down. He had to try and get help for the naked man.

The naked man stirred, coughing, and struggled upright, crying out, swinging and flailing at his captors with the best of this strength, but he was outnumbered. The kidnappers hoisted his writhing body and began to trundle it across the field toward the river.

"Maybe we'll bring him back to his church," the big man's voice crowed as the group stumbled away bearing their victim. "When we get through with the good father, he's gonna need a priest."

"Haw-haw-haw-hee-haw."

Nixon stood up. It was the priest! The one chased out of Ellsworth this summer. John Bapst. What could he do? Anyone who wanted to help wouldn't be able to, and the rest would not want to. Nixon was on the edge of panic. He tried to imagine himself in the future, looking back at this night as something gone and long past and no longer important, but this thought was impossible and frightened him even more. He remembered the mule-man lifting Henry into the bloody face of the wharf worker. He remembered his own grandfather's men calling him "odd job." He knew now who these men were and where they were taking the priest.

He needed to get ahead of the men. They were going to the wharves. He didn't dare follow them directly across the open field, but if he

75

crossed behind the house where he was hiding he would have to pass the Milliken house. There was a bad dog there, and although Nixon thought he knew how long the animal's rope was, he could not be sure of it in the darkness. He feared too the dog would start barking and alert everyone. He ran his hand across his forehead as he tried to think, wiping the rain from his eyes. Then he cocked his head.

The Millikens' dog was barking. He'd been barking all along. Nixon raised his head into the rainy air, closed his eyes, and listened. Every dog in the village was barking. Near and far, on this side of the river and the other. Dogs on ropes, dogs in stables, outdoor dogs and indoor dogs, wild and tame, an ancient canine chain letter was being dispatched. Nixon rose and tore down Elm Street to the wharves, keeping an eye on the single torch bobbing across the edge of the field. The Milliken dog cried out a long wail, answered by a dog on the river with a moan like a ghost, and answered again by a pair of voices near the sawmills that sang like wolves from a forest where men never walked. The people could pretend nothing was happening, but the dogs knew.

Sliding through the wet slippery leaves that lay on the slope between two houses, Nixon crossed the corner at Water Street and lunged into the relative safety of his grandfather's wharf. Here he tucked himself under the cluster of birches where he'd been observed by the sneering workers last summer. Leafless now, the trees were silent and offered little protection from the rain, but here he could wait for the kidnappers to appear.

No sooner had he achieved his hiding place than the evil band came into view. Dragging the priest by the ankles, they rounded the corner. The beaten man appeared insensible, and his torso and arms were covered with mud and blood. He still had one shoe on, and a strip of shredded clothing slithered behind him. The men were pulling him up the rise along Water Street, in the direction of Tisdale's shipyard.

Again Nixon would not risk following the men along the muddy roadway and instead climbed the rise beside grandfather's wharf. There were two houses here, but staying close to the river edge of the hill, he could pass at a safe distance from them. From the top the view would be straight down on Tisdale's shipyard, where Nixon was sure the men were taking Bapst. Climbing the hill was more difficult than Nixon expected. He was wet to his skin, and the tall grass and weeds were hard to wade through. His pants stuck to his legs at every step. Passing the first house on the slope, he crouched low in the weeds along the bank. The windows of the house were dark, but he did not want to be seen.

The next house loomed ahead and Nixon squinted to see if any light showed in its windows. It was lived in by the family of a man who worked at Tisdale's shipyard. The thought of being discovered by the men of this house made him feel queasy inside. He wanted to put this house behind him, and if he climbed the slope fifty feet farther he would be able to see the shipyard. Nixon's eyes followed the peak of the roof where it emerged from the bare branches of the tree growing next to it. He could follow the chimney and make a guess where the windows were. He wiped the rain from his forehead again, and stared into the darkness.

There was a quick snap which sounded to Nixon's ears like the crack of a gun, and a light so bright he felt blinded. A scream shot up his throat and quelling it caused his body to start and his teeth to chatter. He slid quickly to the ground. A man's face was perfectly illuminated in the darkness less than a dozen feet from where Nixon lay, and it immediately disappeared back into the murk. The man had struck a match, lit a cigar, and now sat on a tall horse, smoking in the darkness. Nixon had been concentrating so hard trying to see the windows of the house, he'd almost blundered into what was right before him: a horse he recognized with a rider he knew.

Now he lay a few feet from discovery. Instinctively realizing his up-turned face was the most visible part of him, he slowly lowered it into his sleeve. He was grateful the sound of the falling rain disguised the gasp he'd surely made when the match was struck, but he feared now his heart must be audible too, and willed himself into calmness as he lay still. Of course, it was only now he began to notice how cold and wet he was. His hair was plastered to his head and cold seemed to seep through every part of his clothing. He began to shiver, and he had to pee.

Waiting beneath his cigar-smoking mount, the horse shifted his weight from one foot to another. Nixon knew from that sound the horse was impatient, had been waiting for some time, and was tired of standing still. This horse, Nixon knew, was not a horse for standing. Two summers ago Nixon saw this horse downtown, its owner showing it off, demonstrating the animal's celebrated running walk in front of the Ellsworth House. The horse quickly covered a quarter of a mile in its distinctive gait, with its owner astride him holding a filled teacup that never spilled a drop.

That the horse was aware he was lying in the grass, Nixon also knew. Even in the murk, Nixon could locate the tiny glimmer of the horse's eye. The horse could smell him too, just as easily as Nixon could smell the expensive cigar smoked by the rider. Nixon met the horse's gaze with his own, pleading with his eyes for the horse to continue to conceal him. Nixon had spoken to this horse many times when he saw it hitched in the street, praising his fineness and beauty, and this Nixon knew a horse did not forget. Their eyes engaged each other, in the near darkness, but they were already acquainted.

It was then Nixon remembered something else about the summer day when the horse was being made to show off his teacup skills. The horse had a distinctive blaze on his forehead, one which Nixon could make out even now, in the shape of a white T. While prancing in front of the Ellsworth House, an onlooker chided the owner about his fine new horse. "Hey, Seth," Nixon remembered the local wag teasing, "when you got this horse down South, did you have him monogrammed?"

The horse did not give Nixon away. It remained impassively bearing its owner in the rain and sharing an occasional glance with the boy in the grass. Seth Tisdale also sat placidly, drawing in slow breaths of smoke, exhaling with a lingering sigh. The entire time, Seth's face was turned in the opposite direction, his eyes fixed on his shipyard below. Nixon knew the cigar was not the only thing being savored. What horror was Seth watching? What were those men doing to the priest? Pounding him? Drowning him in the river? Nixon could not imagine. He laid his head on his arms and let the full measure of the cold and wet swallow him. He lay there for a long time. In following these men Nixon had followed something else to its end. There was no going back now, and when he looked, he found his fear had subsided. It had vanished. Suddenly bereft, he sought for it, but it was entirely gone. Perhaps this was bravery, he thought, but he did not feel brave. He did not feel anything but the pulse beating in his head.

He did not even feel relief as he heard the squeaking leather of the saddle and the soft nicker of Seth's voice urging the horse to turn. Seth and the horse simply moved away, unhurried, a flick of the horse's tail, and the sound of the animal wading through the grass toward the house and back onto the street beyond. When enough time passed Nixon stumbled to his feet. He waited for a moment for tears and realized he did not want to cry. Limp and shuddering, he knew he must continue to the crest of the hill to look down into the shipyard himself. He staggered the last thirty feet to the top and strained to see the wharves below. There was nothing to be seen, and nothing to be heard. No men, no torches, only darkness.

Returning home should have been difficult. It was darker as every minute passed because there were fewer lighted windows remaining for him to use as beacons. It had taken no time at all for the citizenry to vanish from the streets and melt away into the blamelessness of their darkened homes. Barking dogs were reprimanded into silence or bundled into barns or stables to muffle them. Curtains were tugged closed. Lamps were extinguished.

Unafraid now, Nixon chose the most public route home, but the streets he crept through seemed to belong to a different and more complicated place than those he had known earlier in the day. Two piles of garbage smoldered at Dutton's wharf, spewing a low foul smoke. Across the street, the Eagle was a graveyard. Never had Nixon seen it so still. Its lone lamp dangled over the winking eagle, which no longer seemed comic, but sinister. The Ellsworth House on the corner had three lamps hanging outside, but its lobby was empty too.

It was on this corner Seth Tisdale had shown off his horse's steady gait. Nixon turned his eyes farther up the hill on State Street in the direction of the Tisdale house. Nixon could not resist crossing the street toward it. Feeling his way along the brick wall of the darkened commercial block where his father's store was, he came to its end and looked up at the great white house. There was a low light in the front hall and another upstairs, but no one seemed to be about. Was Seth Tisdale inside? Had he put his horse away? It was impossible to tell.

The house was stately and very beautiful. It had handsome windows along the front and a distinctive hexagonal cupola on the roof. Nixon had never been inside, but once last summer he had walked carefully outside it, counting the windows and committing the details of the cupola to memory. Another day was spent with his knife and a wood scrap trying to shape it accurately. The Tisdale house was was one he'd chosen to make a small model of, and cutting the six sides of the cupola evenly had been a challenge. Now, closing his eyes, he could remember the precise feel of the shape of the earnestly carved wood in his hand, as though he were turning it over and over in his fingers. Now he would never be able to think about the carving or his models again without remembering this night.

He began to trudge home. *Once one knows something,* he thought, *it can never be unknown.* While playing with Henry one day they'd both cut their fingers and rubbed the cuts together. They were blood brothers, they said. Together forever. When Seth Tisdale struck the match and revealed himself, a different sort of wound had opened. On the dark hillside overlooking the shipyard some sort of malevolent magic bonded the boy and the man together. Nixon knew it was this awful magic that now occupied the place in him where his fear had been.

Only when his feet touched his own step did Nixon remember the trouble he was probably in for being out on the streets. Yesterday he would have been filled with trepidation at the punishment that awaited him. Tonight he passed unconcerned through the door into the kitchen, where his mother and Ann still sat at the work table in the light of one lamp. Both women raised their eyes and stared at him in stunned silence, as though barely recognizing who he was.

"Why wouldn't I look different?" Nixon told himself, and as he crossed the room to the stairs, calm was all he felt.

Waking the next morning, he first believed he was swimming in a great murky body of thick water. There was nothing to see but swirls of dark colors, and as he paddled with his arms the surface seemed far above him. Gradually he sensed an object he thought must be a great stone he could grasp and use to hoist himself out of the water.

He broke the surface of the heavy pool and gasped for breath. He ran his arms along the sides of his body and moved to see if he was intact and uninjured, for he felt something terrible had happened to him. As his eyes and brain began to focus, he saw the dark object was his father sitting upright and stern in a chair beside his bed.

Now comes the punishment, Nixon told himself and looked into his father's eyes.

"Don't tell me you were not out there last night," George said flatly.

Nixon's heart scoured his soul, seeking the voluptuous safety of his fear, but he found again, as he had last night, it was gone. A strong, determined voice came out of his throat from another place inside him, sounding to his own ears like a stranger's tongue.

"I was not going to tell you I wasn't out last night," Nixon's new voice replied.

George had not expected this reply or the maturity of the voice that spoke it. He softened inside with pride at the temperament of his son but felt a sharp horror imagining what the boy may have witnessed. Nixon was a mystery to him, both the softest and the hardest child he had ever seen.

"Your mother saw you coming in," George said

"Yes," Nixon replied, "but she did not come up here with me."

"Of course she went up to you," George answered with some sharpness. "You fell directly to sleep."

Nixon then glanced at the empty place on the floor where he'd left his wet clothes last night.

He softened too, with shame. His mother must have sat many hours terrified in the kitchen.

"Is that priest dead, Father?" Nixon asked softly.

Oh God, George thought to himself and replied truthfully to the boy. "No, he is beaten and burned, but it is thought he will survive."

"Burned?" Nixon questioned.

"He was tarred and feathered, son. The tar burns the skin."

"What?" Nixon asked again, clearly not understanding.

George felt great relief that his son had not witnessed this event. "The brutes that got hold of Father Bapst took him to the wharf and poured a bucket of hot tar on him and broke a bed pillow over him."

"Why?" Nixon asked in disbelief.

"It is meant to humiliate, and to make scars. It is a terrible, terrible thing," George said, shaking his head sadly.

"Where is he?" Nixon asked.

"Ann came home and told us a mob surrounded a house up in the Green where Father Bapst was visiting. They threatened to burn the house and Father Bapst came out into the crowd to prevent this. He was quite brave. The mob rode him on a rail to the wharves. When I heard the news I went to your Uncle Jarvis's house. A group of us searched the village. We found the priest in Tisdale's shipyard, but it was too late. He'd already been tarred and was unconscious. He is in the safety of your Uncle Jarvis's house now. Your aunt and others are trying to remove the tar from his body. They have had to shave his hair and eyebrows."

Nixon closed his eyes and turned his head into his pillow.

"What did you see?" George asked softly.

Nixon sighed and turned to face his father directly. "Half the town was watching, but only a few men carried the priest to the river. I followed them as far as Grandfather's wharf. They were dragging him then, and he was naked. They kept on up Water Street hill. I didn't dare follow any farther."

George flattened his lips and drew his fingers across them and down his chin.

"Nixon," George asked the boy even more gently, "who did you see?"

All his life Nixon had told his father everything. Eagerly he offered up all his thoughts and observations. Now this could no longer be. Telling what he had seen would not make it unseen.

"It was a bunch of those that work down at the wharves. I don't know them by name." Nixon replied, and thus created in his heart a place where, for the rest of his life, he kept things to himself.

George placed his hand on the quilt covering Nixon's feet and patted his leg.

"Would you like something to eat son?" George asked.

"I am ready for breakfast," Nixon replied with some bravado.

"Nixon, it is past noon. You have been sleeping for hours. I think there is some soup for you in the kitchen."

Then George did something he'd not done for many years. He helped Nixon dress, laying out some clean clothing and putting a jacket over his shoulders.

"I would not have known you were missing last night had it not been for your dog," George said while Nixon was lacing his shoes.

Nixon did not speak, but looked at his father with questioning eyes.

"When I left the house for Jarvis's I passed the stable and your little dog was barking madly and tossing himself against the door. I've never heard him bark before. I hushed him, went back inside, and saw you were gone. It was the dog who gave you away."

"So Mother did not know I was out until she saw me come back?" Nixon asked, relieved he'd not caused her any fear.

"No," George said.

"I've never heard the dog bark either," Nixon said. "I didn't think he could."

Nixon smiled to himself. His own small dog had been part of the outcry. Years later he too forgot about the rain that fell on Ellsworth that night, but he never forgot the priest or the voices of the dogs that mourned him.

Later that week, Nixon passed his father's desk in the parlor. He noticed there a clipping from the Bangor newspaper, the *Mercury*, neatly cut from a larger page. He held it up and read it:

The Outrage Upon
A Catholic Priest in Maine

By a dispatch from Ellsworth we learn that the Rev. John Bapst, the Catholic Pastor in this city, was, on Saturday night, tarred and feathered and ridden on a rail in Ellsworth. Mr. Bapst was on a visit to Ellsworth when the outrage was committed.

He was formerly pastor there, and was there engaged in a controversy about the school question.

The only thing the ruffians say for themselves in extenuation, is that they had previously threatened to tar and feather Mr. Bapst if he came to Ellsworth again.

He has been pastor of the Catholic population in this city for a few months. Since he has been here he has done much good among the Catholic population, and has brought about many useful reforms, winning commendation on all hands.

We have not terms strong enough to express the indignation uttered by all classes in the city on hearing of this dastardly outrage. The shameless cowards who have done it should receive the highest penalties of the offense, and the town of Ellsworth should be made to respond in damages for this foul wrong to a visitor who could not be protected within her gates.

Ellsworth has long been noted for the low, rowdy, vulgar proceedings of a portion of its population. If the respectable men there cannot stop such proceedings, let them abandon the town and leave it prey to the vile ruffians who inhabit it.

Picnic at Nahant
1860

Nixon draped his left forearm across his head, pulled lightly at the skin on his cheekbone with the tips of his fingers, and drew the straight razor in the opposite hand upward across his face. In the mirror his blue eyes studied his movements carefully.

Every man looks a fool with his face lathered, he thought, dipping his blade in the steaming basin and plowing away another strip of soap along his side-whiskers. He hated shaving; it took all the charm out of the morning, especially a fine summer morning like this where he was able to stand by the open window and watch the breeze shift the curtains back and forth across the sill. Outside, all the sounds of an early Saturday in Boston could be heard. A lone cart and its single horse were rattling up the grade of Mt. Vernon Street, where his family now lived. A peddler drawled in slang-filled conversation with the kitchen maid in the yard behind. A workman on the opposite side of the street was removing a shutter that creaked on its hinges against the brick wall of the house that held it.

Perhaps his dislike of shaving was what led him to grow his side-whiskers in the first place, but he was secretly vain of his lustrous dark hair. As he passed through his teenage years his hair had become more thick and curly. The side-whiskers made him feel older, and oddly more safe, in this new urban world. Marianne and Agnes teased him about his new "chops," and his mother never wasted an opportunity to suggest how much better he looked without them. It was his father, though, who scowled the most, but his father was scowling more anyway, ever since the family had moved from Maine.

Today Nixon was in a hurry. He was to meet Rob Perkins at the steamer wharf in an hour. He splashed a handful of cold water on his face and quickly rinsed out his shaving tools, which smelt like sandalwood.

Nixon had put some thought into his choice of clothing. Boston was a very different world from Ellsworth, with much communication made without speech. He had previously decided on his grey sack coat, with lighter grey trousers and a linen shirt with a turndown collar. He hesitated, though, when he pulled on the waistcoat he had laid out the night before. It had the tiniest thread of mauve woven in it, like the color of a pale spring violet. The color was all the fashion, but usually for women's clothes. He wondered if it was masculine enough, though to his eye it was a beautiful color.

There would be young ladies at the picnic, Nixon was sure. Each one prettier than the last, floating across the lawns like colorful bells encased in the crinolines of their ever-widening skirts.

Nixon did not go unnoticed among the young ladies of Boston. Gossip had made them fully aware of his wealth. It was his surname that gave them pause. They'd never met anyone named Black before. Where did he come from? Who were his people? Nixon sighed, buttoning the waistcoat, and then chose quickly among the neckties coiled in his drawer. Around his collar he looped and tied a loose knot in a silk tie of darker violet. He fastened it with a simple stickpin and snatched his straw hat from the hook where it hung. Ladies liked mauve.

"Are you Black?"

These were the first words spoken to Nixon by Rob Perkins. It had only been weeks since Nixon and his family moved to Mt. Vernon Street, back in the spring of the year. The question was addressed rather impertinently to his backside, and when Nixon turned to see who asked it, he laid his eyes on the smallest bully he'd ever seen. Nixon's first thought was how closely the young man on the street resembled the little dog he had in Ellsworth, who died in his hay bed the summer Nixon turned thirteen. The young man and the dog were both clearly the runts of their litters, both unlikely to back down from a fight. The young man's face was even marked as the dog's had been, spattered with freckles across the bridge of his sneering nose, just as the dog's had been spattered with brown fur.

Nixon surmised he was in the presence of one of his neighbors, since a family named Perkins with sons his age lived in the townhouse next to his. Nixon smiled and held his arms out away from his body, gazing theatrically at himself.

"Black and blue, I'd say," he replied, "I've just come from a tutorial."

Perkins cracked a devilish grin. He had a clean-shaven baby face, a pouting mouth, and a double dose of original sin. At least six inches shorter than Nixon, he looked about twelve years old, although he had to be at least eighteen. "So, you're at Harvard then?" Perkins asked.

"No, not yet. In the fall term, if my father gets his way," Nixon replied.

Perkins' grin grew even wider, and he stepped forward and grasped Nixon's hand. "Then we are in the same boat. Robert Perkins and Black, future delinquents of the class of '64."

"You'd better call me Nixon," he replied, returning the handshake and laughing.

"Who's your tutor?" Perkins asked.

"Today it was Lovering."

"He's a gargoyle," Perkins said, wrinkling his nose.

"Yes," Nixon agreed. "I have Lane too, on other days."

"Old Fish Ball!"

"Fish Ball?" Nixon questioned. He had no idea what Perkins was saying, or what it could possibly mean. Day after dreary day, his father insisted he spend every waking hour studying Arnold's *Latin Prose Composition,* when he hadn't even mastered the mysterious language of the city of Boston.

Perkins began swaying on the spot where he stood and singing in a lively mock tenor, as Nixon watched him in disbelief.

The waiter roared it through the hall,
We don't give bread with one fish ball.
Who would fish balls with fixins eat,
Must get some friend to stand a treat.

"You don't know that one?" Perkins asked goggle-eyed. "Lane wrote it. It's famous. The 'Ode of the One Fish Ball.' You'll hear it often enough at Harvard. Where are you from, anyway?"

"Maine," Nixon answered glumly. He could scarcely imagine his Latin tutor writing a song about a fish ball, but had to concede George Martin Lane did possess more humor than Lovering.

"What does your father do?" Perkins asked. It was a question, Nixon was learning, significant in every Boston conversation, where ancestry had to be ascertained somewhere in the first paragraph of any introduction.

"He's a lumber merchant, now branching into real estate," Nixon answered.

"So, it's real estate for you after Harvard?" Perkins asked in a query less question than statement.

"I suppose so, yes," Nixon answered, realizing for the first time Perkins was right. He would be expected to follow his father in real estate. Harvard was just a dressing.

Perkins tapped Nixon on the chest in jest and familiarity, "Then we are in the same boat! My father is an importer, jute mostly, crammed by coolies into ships in Calcutta. After four doubtless ignoble years at Harvard, I shall be engaged in supplying American citizenry with gunny sacks."

Nixon could not help but snort with laughter at Perkins' caustic wit. "That's true enough. My own future is secured with the sale of box shooks."

The two aspiring Harvard students parted, with promises to meet again in the future. Nixon was amazed. Here he'd met a member of the Boston elite, who was the son of neither a judge nor a lawyer, nor a politician, nor a man of letters. By Maine standards the difference between a Black and a Perkins was undetectable, but in Boston the difference was obvious. A Perkins had been responsible for cramming cargo into the hold of a ship for six generations, a Black for only two.

Four months later, on a mid-August morning, freshly shaved and wearing his violet tie, Nixon found himself again with Rob Perkins, leaning on the rail of the steamer *Nelly Baker* en route to the seaside resort of Nahant. Rob was invited to a chowder picnic at the Crowninshield cottage and asked Nixon to join him. Through a complex catalog of cousinship, which Nixon knew he was going to have to learn to navigate, Rob explained he was related to the Crowninshields through his mother's people, who were Amorys, via another set of cousins who were Mifflins.

As the trim little steamer paddled away from Liverpool wharf, Nixon could see smoke rising from far-off Hull, and the many islands of Boston harbor surrounding them. Little flags flying on both bow and stern, and proclaiming the beloved steamer's name, snapped and riffled in the breeze, sounding like the brisk shuffling of playing cards. In the wake of the churning paddles bobbed a group of melodic oldwife ducks, their strange voices murmuring, and a half-dozen seagulls followed above hoping for some tossed scraps from the gay-spirited day-trippers standing on the deck.

Rob leaned against the rail, and Nixon knew his friend was sizing up the other passengers. Diminutive though he was, his capacity for mischief was massive. There was no sort of trouble he would not go looking for. Still, Nixon found him to be good company, and when they were together life was indeed more dangerous and fun. Rob understood the lay of this complex land, and thus Nixon was happy to ignore the young man's razor tongue. He knew if he could avoid being stung by it, Rob would be an ideal guide.

"No celebrities aboard today," Rob announced.

"Are there usually celebrities?" Nixon asked.

"I've seen Longfellow signing autographs on tickets and even handkerchiefs right here on the deck. The great man stayed one summer in the very cottage where we're going."

"Who else comes?" Nixon said.

"Fanny Kemble, half the professors at Harvard, and a raft of royalty from England."

"Harvard and Fanny Kemble?" Nixon questioned. "Somehow I can't see the professors mingling with a stage actress."

"Even the Magi come alive when confronted with the female form," Rob said dryly.

Their fellow passengers were an assorted bunch. There were several picnic parties carrying their own baskets, including members of the Universalist Church on an outing, boisterous groups of young people, large families with their Irish nursemaids, and a pinched elderly couple sheltering in the indoor cabin.

"Let's circle the deck and see if we've missed anyone," Rob suggested, and the two wound their way among this odd assemblage. Finding no one familiar below, they climbed the steps to the upper deck and the promenade at the stern. In fine weather, as today, most passengers stood outdoors, enjoying the view for the forty-minute ride.

"John Blanchard!" Rob shouted as he spotted a young man in the lee of the bulkhead between the big paddle wheels. Blanchard had dark curly hair and wore a thick-edged pair of pince-nez spectacles on his nose. Standing with his weight on one leg and the other bent against the wall for balance, he was reading a book. He smiled as he saw Rob, allowing the spectacles to fall away from his face and hang on their cord.

"Here's the bookworm." Rob chided. "The most beautiful day of the summer, and he's grinding pages."

"As you, my little toad, are grinding axes," Blanchard replied, clutching Rob's hand with recognition and delight.

"This is Black, George Nixon Black, known to all as Nixon," Perkins explained, gesturing in Nixon's direction. "Are you off to Crownin-shields'?"

Blanchard nodded in the affirmative, placed a hand on Perkins' shoulder, and turned to Nixon. "So, Nixon, how is it you have made the acquaintance of this limb of Satan?"

"We're neighbors, I'm afraid," Nixon replied, smiling. "My family moved to Boston last spring."

"So, you're at Mt. Vernon then, and living near this devil. My own people have just moved as well. We're at 58 Beacon," Blanchard said.

"With a view of the Common. Very nice," Nixon replied. He knew the house, as he'd made a careful survey of the buildings in the area the last few months.

"It pleases my father," Blanchard replied, laughing.

As the steamer passed around the Winthrop peninsula, the landmass of Nahant came into view. Even at this distance, Nixon thought Nahant looked charming. It was almost an island, tenuously connected to the mainland by what appeared to be a long curved sandbar, and dotted with delightful cottages and gardens. The cliffs and headlands were dramatic and chiseled with deep fissures and hollows. He knew it was the summer retreat of choice for Boston's first families.

Nixon had never visited a cottage used only in the summer months. He'd gone to summer hotels in New Hampshire, where his family spent the month of July. New Hampshire was cooler than Boston and idly pleasant, but Nixon felt the only reason his parents chose it was for its resemblance to Maine. Nixon soon tired of the starchy hotel suppers and the piazza prattle. In contrast, a private cottage on Nahant seemed fashionable and romantic, set against the stunning backdrop of the open sea.

As the *Nelly Baker* eased aside the wharf, Nixon and his fellows joined other passengers at the rail, and the crowd began to move down the gangplank. The smell of baked fish and charcoal wafted through the air from a cart where an enterprising local was offering skewered and roasted "nippers," baked potatoes, and lemonade. The Universalists loaded themselves efficiently into a large wagon, and one of the girls of the youthful parties wailed and wiggled dramatically as her beau pulled her bonnet off with a tug.

"Most of this crowd will be headed to the Fandango," Rob said, as the three men stepped off the steamer onto solid ground.

"Fandango?" John asked.

"Frederic Tudor's built an amusement park on his front lawn and invited the public for five cents a head," Rob replied.

"Good Lord," John said, raising his eyebrows.

"The Ice King?" Nixon asked.

"The same," Rob answered. "Now that he's made his fortune cutting and delivering Massachusetts ice to the parched tongues of Bombay, Tudor's turned to Nahant to make improvements. He calls the place Maolis Gardens. It's near Auntie Mifflin's cottage.

"We've shipped him plenty of sawdust for his ice from our mills in Maine," Nixon said.

"I imagine you have," Rob replied. "Tudor seems to know what the public wants. Hundreds of pleasure seekers with nickels in their pockets drive out from Lynn on the weekends. There are pavilions, bubbling springs, and something called a Witch House said to be complete with decorative satyrs."

"I bet your Auntie Mifflin loves that," John said to Rob with a wry smile.

Rob grinned back. "There's talk of building a fence."

The Crowninshield cottage was one of a group situated a short distance from the steamer landing, far from the Mifflin cottage and Maolis Gardens. While walking, Nixon noticed the great beauty of the area. Surrounded by the sea in three directions, the view was of the unobstructed horizon. Overhead, huge white bales of clouds floated in the sky, casting shadows on the sunny hill. Nixon thought these were the sort of clouds one was supposed to lie in the grass as a child and gaze at. He did not recall ever having done this in his own childhood, but here in Nahant on a day such as this would be the place to do it. Nixon felt compelled to say something about how wonderful he found this setting but knew to keep such sentiment to himself in the company of other young males. He would be teased and tortured into shame for revealing any such tenderness.

The modest cottage rose on the edge of a marvelous headland. Snug and unpretentious, the appealing structure was built on a mound amid a large meadow grown with sweetbriar, juniper bushes, and wild roses. A roofed porch surrounded the first floor like a ribbon around a hatbox. This roof was supported by posts fashioned from the trunks of cedar trees, their bark peeled and their branches shortened but intact. The effect was as though the entire structure was surrounded by a group of rustic hat racks. The gable end of the second floor boasted two pointy windows. Was this perhaps the room where Longfellow slept one earlier summer? A circular driveway abutted the front steps and contained a few empty carriages. In the fenced field beyond, the horses belonging to these vehicles grazed, along with the cows brought in for the summer to provide for the family's dairy needs. Beyond lay the sea, its glass-green waves and low roar a constant presence, with a dozen white sails speckling the water.

Nixon could see about twenty people on the property. Some were clambering on the rocks, others pitching quoits on the lawn or sitting in groups in cane chairs on the piazzas. A clutch of children and a spotted dog crouched over a broken kite in the driveway, making repairs to a snapped crosspiece. Tables for the picnic were being readied near the building and the lawn beyond. The work seemed to be under the supervision of a woman who was quite tall and stood very erect.

"We ought to make ourselves known to our hostess," John suggested, indicating the tall woman in the distance. "That's Mrs. Mountford," Rob explained to Nixon. "It's her cottage. She was the most beautiful of the Crowninshield sisters in her youth, but she married a penniless minister."

"Perhaps she meant to devote her life to God," John quipped with a smile.

"Perhaps," Rob replied, "but Reverend Mountford is a dozen years younger than his wife."

"Here is Mrs. Mountford," Rob said, extending his hands to take both of hers in his own and modulating his voice to the titillating tone he always employed with older women. Nixon could not imagine such a false-sounding tone could be taken in earnest but noticed it rarely failed to be appreciated.

"Robbie!" Mrs. Mountford said in greeting, "and is that you, John? You are all so handsome and grown now, not the awful boys I last saw. Are you just off the steamer?"

"I remain delightfully awful," Rob replied, "and yes, we've just arrived; John, my friend Nixon Black, and I, hungry and looking for trouble."

"Well, you'll have no difficulty finding it, as all your relations will be here today," Mrs. Mountford said, raising her eyebrows. That she'd been a beauty in her youth was apparent; her former fairness still echoed around the edges of a face that seemed more tired than aged. Nixon saw she was fashionably dressed as well, wearing the current bonnet that resembled an overturned soup plate, and a lovely peacock-colored long linen jacket over her dark grass-green dress.

"I need to get the food mustered," she continued, noticing a kitchen maid holding a tablecloth and looking confused. "Welcome, Mr. Black, John, and Robbie. I expect a full report from you about Mt. Vernon Street and every other little thing." Nixon thought sure he saw her wink.

"You shall have it," Rob said, laughing, "after the chowder."

While John remained after offering his assistance to Mrs. Mountford, Rob and Nixon went to the cottage to take in the view from the porch, stopping on their way and speaking to a dizzying dozen of Mifflins, Warrens, and Crowninshields. Nixon despaired of ever being able to keep them all straight. The most he could remember was Mrs. Mountford had two other sisters born as Crowninshields, both of whom had married doctors. One was Annie Warren, who was the wife of a famous Boston doctor, Jonathan Mason Warren. The Warrens were a legendary clan of physicians of whom even Nixon had heard. The other was Mary Mifflin, whose wealthy physician husband, Charles Mifflin, never saw patients. Nixon got the idea that within the family, Warren was considered a hero and Mifflin a dilettante, but he noticed Charles Mifflin was also described as being "from Philadelphia."

Climbing the steps, the ocean spread out before Nixon's eyes like a jewel. He'd experienced the sea all his life, but always from the deck of a ship or as a view from a distance. His notion of the sea was of a fickle roadway, sometimes blocking and sometimes facilitating travel or shipping. He never encountered it presented as something to gaze at, as something artistic or pleasant to view. One could sit here all day, satisfied and dreaming.

An elderly man was seated on two chairs drawn up near the edge of the porch. He was a spindly creature, twisted like a barren branch, but with large hands and huge feet. With one of these feet shoeless and resting on a cushion placed on one chair turned to face him, he lolled back in the other chair with a spyglass pressed firmly to his eye.

"Ehhhh, you boys," he muttered, acknowledging he'd noticed them and then pointing to the sea. "There's the *Malay,* out of Salem, with her studding sails out."

"Eben knows all the ships," Rob said, rolling his eyes. "He spies them with his glass. How is your health, Eben?"

"Poorly," Eben replied, poking himself in his stomach region. "Dyspepsia. I can't eat a thing."

"Well, sir, I am sorry to hear it," Perkins continued, "and the gout?"

Eben shook his head slowly, "At my age, a healthy soul is all that matters."

Nixon was no longer regarding Eben. From their raised position the three men could look down at the gravel path circling the cottage and running to the edge of the sea. Walking slowly there was a woman who reminded Nixon of Franny. Of course, it was impossible it was her. Franny had remained at Woodlawn after his grandfather died, despite pleas from his family to join them in Boston. Nixon often thought of her alone in the big empty house. Whenever he thought of her, he pictured her sitting before one of the large triple-hung windows at Woodlawn, with the incoming sun obscuring the details of her face into a silhouette of her curved mourning bonnet and large black bow tied beneath her chin. She had a fierce dignity, combined with intelligence, sobriety, and checked humor. Nixon missed her every day.

The woman on the path wore mourning dress, and this, Nixon thought, was what conjured up Franny in his mind. She was younger than Franny, perhaps around forty. Still, there was some similarity of movement between the two women, something they shared, revealing itself in stature or gesture or some other silent sign. The woman, thinking herself unseen, had removed her bonnet and carried it by its black ribbons. Pausing, she tucked a strand of her dimming golden hair back behind her ear and brought this hand along the crest of her head, smoothing it down and letting her fingers drag slowly down the center parting of her hair. Nixon's throat tightened and he leaned for support on the tree-trunk porch post. The woman replaced her bonnet, tying the ribbons as she walked on.

"Who is that lady?" Nixon asked.

"That's Caroline Crowninshield," Eben said, moving his spyglass off the horizon and fixing it briefly on the woman's receding figure.

"She has three sons," Rob said. "Edward, Frank, and Fred. Edward's at Harvard now, and Fred is still a youth, but Frank will be in class with us. Edward acts the older brother, but Frank is lots of fun. You'll meet them here before the day is out."

"Who is she mourning?" Nixon asked.

"Her husband, also Edward. He was Mrs. Mountford's brother. Brother to all the Crowninshield sisters, Annie Warren and Mary Mifflin too. Old Edward was pretty musty. Collected books and nursed consumption. They say he coughed up a quart of blood on his priceless *Bay Psalm Book* and croaked."

"Rob, good God!" Nixon exclaimed, truly offended. Sometimes Perkins was just too much.

"It's true, though," Eben said. "They traipsed all over Europe for years hoping for a cure, and he died in three minutes in his own library." Eben picked up his spyglass again and trained it on Caroline Crowninshield. She was now standing near an outdoor table, forty years old but slim and supple as a young birch. "She won't be a widow long," Eben said.

Soon they were summoned for food, and Nixon noticed Eben moved like lightning to the head of the line, going back several times for seconds, wearing just his one shoe. Rob had found John again, and the three opted for a blanket on the grass at the sea's edge, rather than a seat at the tables. They ate heartily, clam and fish chowder, corn chowder, fried potatoes and nippers, and a wonderful thin gingerbread. Once they'd finished they sprawled out on the blanket, dozing in the August sun.

"In order to be good, chowder must be made in Nahant and consumed on a blanket," John said.

"You are correct as usual, John," Rob replied, rising from his elbow, "and I must go thank Mrs. Mountford for it. She expects scandalous gossip and I have been inventing some in my mind all morning for her."

As Rob walked away, Nixon watched John remove from his pocket the book he'd been reading on the steamer that morning.

"What do you find so engrossing?" Nixon asked.

"Not engrossing, perhaps, but necessary, given what we're up against next week. It's Aristophanes."

Nixon groaned and lay back on the blanket. "I am terrified of the entrance examinations. I'll fail them miserably, and my father will have the devil after me."

"Aren't you tutoring with Lovering and Lane? Don't fret. We'll all do all right," Blanchard said nonchalantly.

The problem is, I am not we, Nixon thought.

While the "we" of Boston's elite boyhood were likely to have passed their recent educational hours in the halls of Boston Latin School or the parlor of a minister tutor who translated Greek as a hobby, Nixon's experience had been quite different.

For years he and Marianne trudged up Bridge Hill to the rooms of Miss Ellen Hight for their lessons. Overheated in the winter and chilly in the summer, in those two rooms of her own small frame house Miss Hight dispensed education to a class of about twenty children ranging in ages from five to fifteen. Small-boned, sober, and wearing thick spectacles which seemed too heavy for her long nose, Miss Hight examined fingernails for cleanliness, margins for straightness, and handwriting for blots. Never raising her voice, she ruled over a quiet and correct classroom, if not a particularly scholarly one.

On any given day the students sat at four tables according to age, with the front room reserved for the eldest children. In the rear room tables, near the hellfire of the stove, Hollis Joy and the Blaisdell twins would be practicing penmanship, hunched over endless rows of loops and twirls with their tongues extended in exertion. Nearby, at the same table, Celia Lord and Chansonetta Coombs would be writing their tables of twelves.

Eunie Kent and George Eaton would be marking the progress of the sun as it showed through a pinhole punched in a card mounted on a table in the rear room, in order to find "true north" by the sun. Lorena Sprague and Nixon would be "quietly, in a whisper" practicing on one another their memorization and recitation of the Preamble of the Constitution. Even then this was a task Nixon considered spirit-breaking labor and which Lorena mastered in an hour and then rolled her eyes at him as he stumbled over and over. Was it the "general defense and common welfare," or the other way around? He had no talent for memorization. At the table by the front door a wary Marianne and a smitten Horace Toothacher were seated side by side but as far apart as Marianne could manage, concentrating on their essays about particular pilgrims from the *Canterbury Tales*.

Latin, French, or any of the other languages did not appear on the curriculum. Geography was sketchy and limited mostly to the map of the United States, possibly because it was the only large map Miss Hight possessed. Nor was science stressed, unless one counted finding true north with the pinhole, or the time they planted seeds in eggshells and put them on the windowsill, only to have them killed off by being too close to the glass in a late spring freeze.

The entire school day lasted four or five hours and included an extended period of warming milk and eating what they'd brought from home in their lunch tins. On warm days, they were also allowed an outdoor romp, which usually resulted in the girls sitting together on the small porch teasing one another to the brink of tears and the boys being chastised for poking at whichever of Miss Hight's pigs dwelt in a sty in the back of her house. It was one of these pigs, a huge spotted one, that gave Nixon his most ardent memory of his school days.

Miss Hight was building an island from chunks of coal, which were to be doused in ammonia and laundry bluing and from which marvelous crystals would grow, when Lucas Stiles stuck his head through the open window and shouted, "The pig is out!" Faster than Nixon had ever seen her move, emitting a long howl, Miss Hight sprang out the door and chased the pig down Bridge Hill, followed by Stiles and the entire class. The pig was cornered at last, wallowing in porcine rapture in an eddy at the edge of the river.

It wasn't going to get him into Harvard.

Nixon dozed off, and woke alone on the seaside blanket. Rising a bit stiffly, he lifted the woolen square from the grass, shook it, and folded it across his arms. He thought he should return it to the basket on the piazza where they'd found it and take the chance to examine the inside of the cottage.

Stepping inside the cool interior, he realized how warm he'd gotten sleeping in the sun. Here, the walls were painted a soft green, and bamboo and cane chairs were scattered about. The rooms were delightfully simple, almost austere, and his footsteps squeaked across shiny, bare wooden floors. A great white ironstone jug filled with ferns and daisies sat on an old gateleg table in the center of the main room. He could hear the sea, but there seemed also to be a deep silence all around him. Excitement stirred within him as he walked around the room, delighted by the aura of summer, the mysterious sleepy feeling, the sense of something both endless and quickly ending. A few objects sat on tabletops or decorated the walls. They were summer things, gifts from houseguests, unwanted prints, duplicates of articles not needed in winter homes, debris washed in on previous summer tides and then abandoned to an interior decoration unlike any in a less transient home. On a far wall, near a doorway to another room, was a display of small silhouettes framed in dark ovals. Nixon stepped forward to view them, causing a floorboard to shriek and two people in the adjoining room to start.

It was Caroline Crowninshield and a young man who could only be one of her sons. The two had been sitting together in quiet conversation, their bent heads nearly touching, and Mrs. Crowninshield had her hand on her son's cheek. Nixon felt suddenly like a trespasser. What were the sons' names? Ed? Fred? Nixon searched his brain and cursed again his faulty memory.

Nixon saw at once Mrs. Crowninshield's great beauty. It was based, somehow, in her placidity, for she had a languid, defeated gaze and a strangeness that drew him immediately toward her, although he'd not come closer by a step. There was an inscrutability, the sense of a secret, which one wanted to grasp and shake out of her. Nixon swallowed hard; he was sweating. He felt as though he'd just skirted something that for someone else would have been dangerous but for him was good fortune.

"I'm sorry," Nixon said, "I was snooping."

Her brow wrinkled, and she saw she was speaking to a stranger, one innocent and unknown to these surroundings. "Snooping?" She laughed with a short laugh. "These rooms are like a railway terminus. You can't be snooping."

Of course her voice was low, of course it was delicious and fascinating. Of course her laugh was short, indicating she knew absolutely everything.

"Stop shadowing the doorway and come and sit next to us, Mr....?" she said with a smirk.

"Oh, sorry, I, I am George Black," Nixon said, "but everyone calls me Nixon, which is my middle name." Nixon realized then he too had a voice he used with older women, warm and particularly polite.

"Well, I am Caroline Crowninshield, and this is my son Frank." She extended her hand, which emerged from the fashionable pagoda sleeve of an otherwise dour bombazine mourning dress. Eben was right, thought Nixon, she would not remain a widow for long.

Nixon stepped forward to shake her hand. Drawing closer he saw her eyes were blue but in certain light they sparkled with violet. They were uncanny, otherworldly, and very beautiful. He watched, transfixed, the sudden flash of purple that appeared and disappeared with her movements. It was the same color as the stripe in his waistcoat that caused him anxiety that morning. The thought made him smile and relax a bit, as he sat on a chair opposite the sofa. Ladies liked mauve.

"I knew you were Mrs. Crowninshield," Nixon said. "The old man on the porch with the spyglass pointed you out. He seems to know everyone," Nixon answered.

"Oh, Eben Sturgis," she sighed. "When he doesn't have his eye pressed to that spyglass he has it pressed to a keyhole." Frank and Nixon laughed happily.

"Do you know," Frank offered, "Eben's family owned the ship that brought the Siamese Twins to the United States?"

"So he tells everyone," Caroline said, and in a mocking mimicry of Eben continued, "My family has shipped everything it is possible to ship."

"Well," said Frank, "he's wandering outside now wearing only one shoe. Doesn't seem to miss the lost one."

"To be a Sturgis is to be more than peculiar," Caroline said.

"Are you at Harvard, Nixon?" Caroline asked.

"This term, I hope, if I can pass the entrance exam."

"I'm worried about the same thing," Frank said. "Perhaps we can arrange to fail together, or keep each other company at the bottom of the rank."

"You boys! You'll both do just fine. I am quite sure Eben matriculated there, if that gives you any confidence," Caroline said.

"My father's had me entombed with tutors every day since we've returned from vacation," Nixon said. "But I am told I am in good hands."

"Who are you studying under?" Caroline asked.

"The Fish Ball," Nixon answered, and Caroline threw her head on her son's shoulder to muffle her laughter.

After they'd talked for some time in the wonderful room overlooking the sea, Frank and Nixon returned outdoors to find Rob and John. Frank had all the attractiveness and charm of his mother, and as Nixon came to notice, the same flash of violet in his eyes. His face was calm, fringed with crisp gold hair, and gave the impression his thoughts were absorbed somewhere beyond the present moment. Splendid, robust, and red-cheeked from the sun, when he walked through the tall sea grasses along the verge of the cliff, it was with a masculine grace of which he was entirely unaware.

"It was nice to see Mother laughing," Frank said. "It has been quite a while. I think she likes you, Nixon. You are awfully funny."

"She reminds me of my grandfather's second wife, a lady I admire, so it's not hard for me to like your mother as well," Nixon replied. "I'm sorry to hear of your father's death. Rob told me. Consumption is a terrible thing."

"Yes, thank you," Frank answered. He tugged his collar higher up his neck and straightened and smoothed his tie, but said no more.

They came upon the sought-after group, lying in the grass, facing the panorama of the sea. John was reposed on a shaggy hummock, with Rob's blond head resting on his thigh. Nearby, another youth was sketching in a small book, long-nosed, dark-haired, and serious, and a bit younger then the others. Nixon was startled to see in the sketchbook a quickly rendered pencil drawing of John and Rob, so accurate he could identify it at once. He was impressed and wondered who this young man was.

"What a disgraceful crew!" Frank said, throwing himself on the ground among them, and snatching John's hat from his head to place on his own.

"Gorilla!" John shot back, pushing Frank into the grass and retrieving the hat.

Like a litter of purebred puppies, they tussled and scrambled in the grass, living in the happy nonchalance of their lucky birthright, healthy, glowing, and magnificent. Everything that was good waited before them, and they expected to step up to it in due course. The grace of fortune exuded from their faces and bodies, and they carried it without thought. *Am I one of them?* Nixon wondered.

"You all know Nixon, don't you?" Frank said by way of introduction, as Nixon eased himself down beside the others on their seaside perch. "The latest Harvard flunky."

"Not I," said the sketchbook artist, extending his hand. "Hullo, Nixon."

"Bob Peabody," Frank said, indicating the younger man. "The only one among us with any talent, and my third cousin."

"What about Blanchard the Greek?" Bob said. "Word is out you'll all need to follow his example if you have any hope of passing your exams."

"You wait, you fool," Frank hissed back, "you'll be sweating it out in two years when you're in our place."

"Absolutely!" Rob added. "And when you do get in, I am looking forward to exercising my privilege as an upperclassman to abuse a freshman." He punched Bob in the shoulder.

"What if a war comes?" Bob asked, suddenly sober. "What will you fellows do then?"

It was as though the vast open landscape suddenly shrank into a tiny windowless room of absolute silence. Even the pounding of the waves seemed to have stilled. Nixon looked at the empty glasses and the crumpled handkerchiefs in the grass. He looked at the rolled-up jackets, and John's upturned hat, and the open sketchbook on Bob's lap with the drawing of his friends, and realized its pages flapping in the wind as the only sound he could hear. No one spoke. All the young men were staring down at the same ground into a world the question had changed.

"I'd join the army in a minute," Frank finally said, sliding onto his back in the long grass and covering his eyes with his elbow.

"The tide is low! Who wants to go down to Swallow Cave?" It was Frank speaking again, the first words after they all fell silent twenty minutes earlier.

"Not me," Rob said. "I ruined a pair of shoes down there last time."

"Oh, come on!" Frank cried as he stretched and stood looking over the edge of the cliff at the water. "Wade in barefoot with me."

"And give Dr. Warren a cut foot to stitch up in the kitchen? No thanks," John said.

"I'll go," Bob said shrugging, grateful his awkward war question was finally in the past. "I haven't been down there in years."

"What about you, Nix?" Frank asked.

"Why not?" Nixon replied.

Frank wanted to bring a lantern so they could look for sea creatures, and while he went to the cottage to get one, Bob Peabody strolled with Nixon to the top of the cliff path. The meadow on the slope was alive with grasshoppers, pouncing on the boys' legs as they walked. Nixon felt a strange thrill at the thought of exploring the cave.

"You like it here, don't you?" Bob asked.

It was a question that was unexpected, and Nixon answered slowly.

"Why, yes,...I do...very much."

"I sketched you earlier," Bob admitted, pulling his sketchbook from his vest and searching the pages. Finding the one he'd sought, he held it out to Nixon, and Nixon saw himself with Rob and Eben and the spyglass on the porch.

Nixon thought of telling this serious youth how he felt about the clouds, the cottage, and the pale-green room with the ferns in the ironstone vase, but looking at the sketchbook he realized he didn't need to. Nixon turned the pages of the remarkable little book and saw the *Nelly Baker,* the man selling baked nippers at the wharf, and the children hunched over the broken kite, all rendered in lively and vivid pencil.

"You're a fine artist. It's wonderful you can sketch so quickly and accurately. I can tell it is me and Rob, and you have made just a few lines with your pencil."

"Thanks," Bob said.

"Will you try a career as an artist?"

"No, I need to make an income, so I thought I would try architecture." Bob said.

"I once made models of buildings myself," Nixon replied. "I carved mine from wood, as I have no talent for drawing. I had quite an enthusiasm for it for a while, and then..." He let his words taper off.

"Then what?" Bob urged, his grey eyes studying Nixon intently.

"I lost interest, I guess," Nixon said and then smiled. "So you will design cottages like this one," he changed the subject, "by the sea?"

"Yes, like this one," Bob replied.

When Frank returned, they removed their shoes, rolled their pant legs, and began to descend the steep rocks to the mouth of the cave.

"Are there swallows?" Nixon asked.

"Not that I've ever seen," Frank said, "but there are anemones, in all colors. The roof of the cave looks like the ceiling of an Italian church!"

At low tide one needed to crouch to enter the cave through a void which resembled an open mouth. The sea, having retreated, appeared thick and unmoving, like an undulating blue-black syrup, separated from the lighter sky by a dark grey line at the horizon. Bob led the trio into the cave, and once inside the ceiling was higher. It was rough and irregular, and a feeble light eighty feet away at what was obviously a second entrance gave evidence this was more of a long tunnel than a cave. Water ran somewhere with a hollow gurgle. Crabs scuttled underfoot, and pinkish starfish were scattered across every surface, as random and lovely as their sisters in the sky. A cold drip of water from the ceiling landed on his cheek, and Nixon realized he was barely breathing. He felt reckless and ecstatic.

The passage narrowed, so the young men continued along single file. The seawater never drained away fully here, collecting along the edges and leaving a narrow center strip on which to walk. Ten feet farther and the cave opened up again into a space like a room.

"Look!" said Bob, raising the lantern above his head to reveal the ceiling. Here were hundreds of sea anemones clustered together in their colony across the top of the deepest part of the cave. Nixon had never been inside an Italian church; to him the spectacle looked more like a garden, or the pattern of an oriental carpet. That such bright color could exist in darkness was almost incomprehensible, and the colors were various: orange and purple, pink and brown and ivory on the walls of this barren place like a strange miracle.

"You see, I told you so," Frank said, raising his blue eyes to the rainbow ceiling. As his blond hair fell away from his forehead and a mischievous smile crossed his face, Nixon knew he was gazing on something consummate, a view to be recognized in the second it was offered and learned by heart forever, for it would not be offered again.

The exit passage narrowed and curved, and the lantern light grew dim as Bob slowly progressed, sometimes bracing himself against the rock wall with his free hand. The footing became more precarious as the floor was now studded with smaller, rounded stones. Although most were coated with barnacles, others were slippery. The sight of the anemone ceiling and the effort of tilting one's head backward to look at it made Nixon light-headed, and it was only a moment between this thought and the sick panic of feeling himself falling. He reached out for the wall, and tried to find a stable spot for his flailing feet, but he knew he was going down.

Then he felt the rough scooping of a pair of hands seizing him, one beneath his underarm and the other on his left elbow, and he knew Frank had hold of him. Bob turned around at the sound of the scuffle, the cave wall suddenly illuminated by his lantern. Frank's back was braced against the wall where he'd caught Nixon's arms before he had fallen to the ground. Nixon was dazzled by the lantern light, spellbound at being held in Frank's arms, at the thought of Frank's touch and his warm skin through his shirtfront, and of his own body being supported. He was shattered with joy and fear as he felt his face brush across the roughness of Frank's chin and Frank's breath against his forehead.

As he regained his balance, putting his own hands on either of Frank's broad shoulders and drawing in a loud breath, Frank grasped his arm in sympathy and said good-naturedly, "Don't they teach you how to walk on slippery rocks up in Maine?"

Nixon was surprised at the surge of emotion he felt. What the emotion was, he could not say. Embarrassment? Anger? Frank tilted back his head laughing, his violet-tinted eyes sparkling and crinkled at the corners. His cheeks were flushed and his mouth was as red as a wound. Nixon saw the porcelain squares of Frank's teeth glisten and part, with a thread of spit extending from the teeth to his alive, wet tongue. His throat was exposed, white and vulnerable, and it was all Nixon could do to keep himself from thrusting forward and biting it with his own teeth.

When the moment passed, Nixon dropped his hands at his side. His heart was thrashing against his chest and his bones were shaking, but he hoped he appeared calm, if sheepish. Frank raised one hand to his throat and with the other touched the side of the cave wall and began to pick his way carefully toward the exit. Only Bob stood still, holding the lantern by his side. Nixon met the young artist's eye to see what it ascertained. Bob held his gaze on Nixon perhaps a second too long, but otherwise, his glance betrayed nothing.

The following morning, in his room at Mt. Vernon Street, Nixon awoke to find an ugly bruise on his left elbow. It was green and purple, the very same purple that had distressed him the day before, the purple of his waistcoat and of the eyes of the Crowninshield clan.

Distinguishable within the outlines of the large bruise were two dark circles of deepest injury. They were Frank's fingerprints, where his thumb and forefinger had pressed. Furtively, Nixon poked at these bruises with his own fingers. His regular world was disturbed. Before this, his only fear had been passing the Harvard entrance exam, but now some new worm was gnawing at him.

On this first day, he quickly put the thought away, but on later days, whenever he dressed, the bruises were there to remind him. He understood he had somehow been transformed, but the impression of those moments in the cave troubled him, and the memory of the episode was tenacious and reappeared incessantly in his mind.

Sometimes he felt proud of the bruises, as they meant Frank had marked him, had chosen him somehow. Other times he shuddered at the thought of such a possession, and what it might mean.

More often the bruises comforted him. Without understanding why, he felt consoled, and it was in consolation he let his mind rest. As the week before the exam gave way to days, Nixon began pressing the bruises with his fingers to feel the comfort of their soreness and to make sure they were still with him. Sitting in his new black coat in the hot airless room at Harvard, and parroting his hard-learned recitation, he rested his elbows in the palms of the hands, gently rubbing the left one to stay steady. He passed the exam. His grade was poor, but he passed it.

The next night, after an evening of his father patting him on the back and his mother arranging for a celebratory supper, he undressed, exhausted, and sat on his bed. The bruises, which had been growing distressingly fainter each day, had disappeared. He felt bereft, as if now he belonged to no one. He was sleepy and did not allow himself to consider his loneliness for long. All that Nixon let himself acknowledge on this night was that he was going to Harvard.

It was September 21, 1860, the sort of early fall day full of gilt and sunshine, but with a low whistling wind that foretells winter. The members of the freshman class were to gather before the steps of Harvard Hall to have a photograph made on the first day of their classes.

Nixon and Rob Perkins went together, inspected the rooms they were assigned, and then stood with a hundred other young men before the slab-faced facade of Harvard Hall. Some of the high-spirited students gathered to pose sitting in the open windows of the lower floor, but the remainder spread out near the main entrance, fiddling with their top hats and uncomfortable in their requisite black coats as the sunlight quivered like gold water across the red brick walls. A photographer and his assistant bustled to and fro, leaning behind the camera and peering into it, dramatically swirling a black sheet of silk to hide the light.

Nixon thought it unnaturally quiet, given the presence of so many men clustered on the sparse grass. He supposed they all felt, as he himself did, that destiny was unfurling; there was a seriousness to the proceedings that Nixon believed had to do with the threat of the war. Even if being a soldier was incomprehensible, where would they or the entire country be next year if it came to that? Would it even be one country by next September? Nixon had his doubts.

He looked for Crowninshield and Blanchard, who had both passed their exams, but he could not see them in the crowd. There were so many faces here, most of whom he did not know. Panic rose in his heart. Ever since the triumph of passing the exam, he had doubts about his chances. He felt out of place. So many of these men were real scholars, or had fathers from the top ranks of Boston society. Many possessed both attributes. Nixon swallowed hard and tried not to fear he was making a mistake.

Rob pushed a small stone in the gravel walkway with his toe. A quartet of large crows shouldered one another on a branch of one of the elms in the yard, occasionally barking a menacing croak in the direction of the students.

"I don't like the look of that sinister group," Rob said, indicating the crows.

"Do you think them a bad portent?" Nixon asked.

"Everything these days is a portent," a bearded student beside them remarked.

"Well, they do seem ominous," Rob said.

"I had an old Welsh nursemaid who sang a song to me about crows. The number of them had an ascribed meaning, as I remember," the bearded student offered.

Nixon wished they would all stop talking. He lifted his face into the sun and closed his eyes. Something important was happening. The wind was weak but blowing from the west, and now and again it lifted his hair a bit, a pleasant drowsy feeling. He'd always trusted chance to bring him to the right places, and even though age added some anxiety to this perspective, he was not yet ready to abandon it. Harvard felt false to him today. He did not think it was going to be his true direction, but as he was here posing for the photograph, a member of the freshman class, it was to be his first step.

"A boy!" the bearded student said suddenly. Nixon and Rob looked at him, not understanding. "Four crows means a boy, or a birth, or the birth of a boy...something like that."

Rob shrugged and shook his head. Nixon spotted Crowninshield at some distance from them. Frank stood slightly apart, with his hands in his pockets, composed and solitary, smiling slightly to himself. *That is as it should be,* Nixon thought. Frank's self-containment added to his dignity. A young Boston prince, awaiting the best of everything.

Rob coughed and continued to worry the stone in the gravel. One of the crows squawked and fluttered on its branch. The photographer flourished his silk square and signaled the moment for posing had arrived. He crouched behind his camera. Nixon blinked once, and faced the west wind with his eyes wide open.

"Gentlemen!" the photographer's assistant shouted, as the group in one large rustle adjusted themselves and stood silent. "No movement, please."

The Undertow
1861

Francis Welch Crowninshield stood in the chill February air of his dormitory room at Harvard, staring into the mirror hanging from one nail above the washstand. He loosened his tie, which he'd wrapped tightly around his stand-up collar, and peeled away the square of cotton wedged beneath it. He winced as it pulled from the dried edge of the suppurating sore beneath it. He touched the hot, angry skin around the sore, bathed it gently with a wet cloth, and replaced the small square with a fresh one cut from an old handkerchief. Back in the summer this lump above his collarbone had been merely swollen and tender to the touch. Today it was open and oozing, and Frank knew exactly what it was.

In some dim corner of childhood memory Frank thought he remembered a similar sore on his father's throat. Doctors had come and gone, plasters had been applied, and his mother began spending long hours in his father's room talking in low tones. It was probably then his parents decided to go abroad.

While Frank couldn't recall the actual sore itself, he remembered clearly the ugly scar it left. For he could see his father now, in any one of his sickrooms in Lausanne, Madeira, or the south of France, with his head thrown back against the chair or headboard. His dark hair would-be plastered to his forehead, his shirt or bedclothes loosened and soaked with sweat from fevers. The scarred, healed hole in his neck was then visible, deep and awful; evidence of the first fistful of flesh his disease had taken from him, which was only one of many more.

At first Frank was excited at the prospect of traveling abroad with his parents. Europe! The sea voyage on the great paddle-wheel ship! Fred, his younger brother, who was too young to go, and Edward, the eldest and at a critical period in his schooling, were to remain behind, a great misfortune for them both, Frank thought. When they waved good-bye at the wharf, Frank believed he was the luckiest boy alive. Only thirteen years old and about to see the world.

The reality was much different. Shuttling seasonally between one set of grim little rooms and another, rooms that smelled like other people and had other people's furniture, Frank began to miss Boston and his brothers. The food was strange, the schools he was obliged to attend full of sneering and unwelcoming boys, and there were always the fetters of his father's illness. Attuned to every shift in the weather, his parents sought out the perfect temperature, the purest air. They were nomads on a constant search for a curative climate.

Because it was their first foreign home, the south of France was the place Frank recalled most clearly. The yellow house with green blinds in the village of Pau, where they lodged on the second floor. Here his father hacked his lungs away, sitting facing an open window overlooking the Pyrenees. Here Frank and his parents strolled the steep hillside stairways to the river and along the wooded promenade beyond the great chateau, the former home of one of the old kings of France. Here they would pass other sufferers on their careful walks, Englishmen mostly, faces covered to keep the dampness from their lungs.

Then there was the coughing. Night and day, and so persistent and powerful that often the whites of his father's eyes were blood-red. The sound nearly drove Frank crazy. He covered his ears with pillows at night and escaped outdoors whenever possible during the day. Across the street, in the house opposite, lived Mr. Weston, an old British man not ill, just retired. He had a little walled-in garden and he let Frank work in it with him.

Now that he was older, Frank knew Mr. Weston was simply a good old man, doing his best to show kindness to a boy soon to be fatherless. Frank remembered a day vividly when they had marked rows and set out dozens of tiny green onions. "That's a good lad. Keep the rows straight. Press around the plants firmly, so they won't flop over. Well done." Mr. Weston stood, leaning on his hoe, and cuffed Frank affectionately on his ear. Frank could still see Mr. Weston's gnarled spotted fingers pressing the surface of the dark soil, green shoots, keen and fresh, springing up between them.

When Pau got too warm, they decamped for Lausanne, replacing the long walks by the river with walks around the shore of Lake Geneva. Here the rooms reeked of camphor, and his father dissolved until he seemed like a scrap of paper, pale and boneless, unable to cope with the slightest effort. When Lausanne failed to provide relief, another winter was undertaken in Madeira, but there the hoarseness that plagued his father in the last months got worse, and when he could no longer talk except in a whisper, the family boarded a ship for home. They'd been away two years.

The following February, on a night of falling snow, Edward Augustus Crowninshield sat in his library, reading. Only a few days from his forty-second birthday, and emaciated to a wafer, he was propped up with pillows of all sizes to support him. Frank and the others heard a stirring in the room and a choked moan. Thrusting open the door, they found him sitting upright, stunned and rigid. His shirt and waistcoat were soaked with foamy blood, which ran down his chin and neck. His book and the tablecloth too were crimson. His right hand, into which he'd coughed for the final time, lay limply on his chest dripping with blood. He'd not even had time to realize the terror of his death; the look on his face was the horror of spoiling his book.

His father's death, only two years before, and the half-remembered horrors of his boyhood harrowed Frank's mind as the sore on his own throat grew from inconsequential to unmistakable. He had consumption, and like his father he was going to die. Characteristically, it was his mother who glimpsed it first, at the family picnic at Nahant. His throat had only begun to swell and feel painful then. Seated beside him in the cottage parlor, she narrowed her eyes slightly and placed her hand on his cheek.

"Frank, do you have a fever?"

"Mother!" he replied, in his best imitation of disbelief, and pulled her palm away from his face. "It's just a hot day."

Thankfully, Nixon chose that moment to stumble into the room and into their lives, and Frank was very glad of it. He'd grown fond of his new friend from Maine. He liked Nixon for his shy decency and his gentleness and steady temperament, which made Frank aware he could lean on Nixon if he should ever need to. Tall, heavy-faced, and a bit shaggy, his friend resembled a sort of large fierce-looking dog, which was nonetheless allowed, because of its sweet nature and reliability, to play with even the smallest child.

Frank also admired the way Nixon conducted himself. He knew Nixon was bewildered by his new residence, but he dove in eagerly nonetheless, if cautiously. Charmingly self-deprecating and humorous, his friend was doing quite well. Frank's mother liked Nixon. "That's a nice young man," Caroline Crowninshield told her son, emphasizing the word "nice." It had also not escaped Frank how skillfully Nixon swam both with and apart from Rob Perkins. Nixon apparently knew trouble when he saw it.

Altogether, Nixon was his most sought-after companion in this first term at Harvard, although the two were still getting to know one another. Frank remained unnerved by the memory of the day he met Nixon, when they ventured into Swallow Cave. Nixon had slipped, and when Frank tossed his head back in laughter at the hilarious spectacle of Nixon's clumsiness, he found his young friend's blue eyes fixed on him with such an intensity that even when he turned away the eyes would not let him go.

What had Nixon seen? Frank worried he'd seen the swelling on his neck. He gave no thought to it when he threw his head back laughing, but he was not so accustomed to hiding it then. Frank had a vague feeling that since Nixon was from the country, he would be able to identify such a swelling. Weren't country people closer to such things, doctoring themselves as they often did? Frank also knew Nixon had a sister who was an invalid. Perkins had told him as much, but Rob did not know the nature of her illness, and Frank had not dared to ask. All Rob knew was that she was sick, pale, and very beautiful. Frank feared Nixon was well acquainted with consumption, and had probably guessed his secret.

Frank worried about Nixon too, for as well as he was doing making friends, Nixon was falling behind in his schooling. Frank was hardly a model student, but Nixon seemed unable to complete any of his work. It was as though he were unacquainted with the memorization and recitation the system was based on. Nixon was never tardy, never reprimanded, but again and again his work was incomplete, or abandoned. Frank wondered what would happen to his friend when Harvard notified his father. Now that the second term had begun, Frank expected daily to hear from Nixon the tale of some explosion. Frank shivered at the thought of such a confrontation, for he'd gazed into the hard blue eyes of Nixon's father himself.

It was last October, the day of the Prince of Wales Ball, when Frank met George Black. For months Boston had anticipated this visit from a member of the royal family. A sumptuous ball had been planned, and the spaces on the prince's dance card had been fought over by Boston belles with a savagery usually reserved for actual combat. Frank's own cousin, Fanny Crowninshield, was victorious in the battle, wresting for herself the fourth dance with the prince, significantly the first of his unmarried female partners. Most Boston girls, no matter how wealthy, had to settle for buying tickets to the ball in the hopes of catching a glimpse of the future king.

Frank, Nixon, Perkins, and a half-dozen other Harvard undergraduates found themselves caught up in the party spirit of the day. Piled into the back of a farmer's wagon, they made their way that night of the royal fete to a more humble feast at the Fresh Pond Hotel.

Located on the east side of Fresh Pond in Cambridge, the hotel had been witness to years of Harvard students skating, swimming, and shooting ducks. Here the young men planned a riotous night toasting the prince, the queen, the proprietor, and one another, working their way from champagne to milk punch.

At dinner, Frank knew Nixon was in trouble before the game course. The rims of his eyes and his cheeks were red but his forehead was white, and he was holding himself stiffly as he ladled glass after glass of claret. Hours later, when both the candles and the conversation had burned down, Frank was afraid Nixon was going to pass out. Nixon sat silently blinking his eyes, as if discovering eyelids for the first time.

Rob Perkins, who could drink them all dead, was still wide awake and lively and suggested they drive into the city to a house where another party was ongoing. He was negotiating with a man with a carriage for a lift back to Harvard Square when Frank implored him to help move Nixon, who seemed unable to walk.

Insisting he was fine, and brushing their hands away from his shoulders, Nixon made it to the carriage with Frank balancing him and Perkins tugging on his cuffs.

"Suit yourselves," Perkins said, taking leave of Nixon and Frank and riding away in a hired hack to join the downtown party. They'd slid Nixon onto the street at Harvard Square, where he stood unsteadily with his head on his chest while Frank called another hack to take them home to Beacon Hill. It was nearly two o'clock in the morning. The air carried the feel of the coming winter, but the atmosphere was uncommonly festive as they drove into Boston. The streets were active, and lamps burned in windows that on a normal night would be dark.

On the way, Frank did what he could to tidy up Nixon. He retied his tie, straightened his collar, and even ran his fingers through his friend's thick hair to smooth it down. Nixon slumped in the seat and smiled. Reaching the house on Mt. Vernon Street, Frank paid the driver and enlisted him in helping Nixon onto the street. Then he threw Nixon's arm over his shoulder and hoisted him up the front steps to the double front doors. Frank prayed a woman would answer their knock.

When one door cracked and lamplight filled the opening, Frank saw a raised eyebrow cocked over an icy appraising eye.

"I-I, I'm Frank Crowninshield, sir, and I've brought Nixon home." He hiked Nixon up on his arm a bit, so he would appear more upright. Frank was more than a little drunk himself.

George Nixon Black Sr. said nothing, but opened the door fully and indicated the two should enter. Notably, he did not ask them to sit down, or suggest where Frank could lead Nixon. Frank paused to look around, hoping to see Nixon's elder sister. The house appeared empty.

"I am waiting up for my wife and daughter, who are at the ball," Nixon's father said. His voice was dignified and, Frank thought, a little sad.

"The entire city is quite festive," Frank said, noticing Nixon's head was rising from his chest and straightening at the sound of his father's voice.

"Yes," Nixon's father said, offering nothing more.

"We've been at the Fresh Pond," Frank explained. "Nixon's a bit how-come-ye-so. We both are."

"I daresay you are," Nixon's father replied, and Frank noted a thick vein in his temple.

Frank tried to discern whether Mr. Black was composed and furious, or merely inarticulate. He wished he wasn't so drunk, as he wanted to understand this. Frank could tell the man was almost immeasurably hard, but he also knew he had no cruelty in him. Joyless was the word which came into Frank's mind at that moment. Nixon's father was a joyless man. When he finally indicated to Frank, with a gesture of his hand, the sofa in the parlor where he could unburden himself of Nixon, Frank noted a flicker of apprehension cross his face. Emboldened by this sign of emotion, Frank found his voice.

"I'll come by in the morning, before nine, to collect him," Frank said. "We'll be at the college in time for the Prince of Wales."

"He'll be up," Nixon's father replied, and Frank hurried off, anxious at what seemed like the abandonment of his friend, who, at last view, sat immobile on the sofa, his head in his hands. Shaking, and relieved to have the door closed between them, Frank made his way down the hill to his own home on Beacon Street, where he knew he would find a softer reprimand.

The following morning Nixon awaited Frank on the steps of 81 Mt. Vernon. Though he was a bit sallow and his eyes reddened, Nixon seemed fine. He was well shaved, his hair was combed, and there was no evidence of whether he'd spent the rest of the night arguing with his father. Frank thought it better not to ask.

"Is your head bad?" Frank asked, while they climbed into a horsecar bound for the college.

"Yes," said Nixon, wincing, "but my stomach is worse."

The horsecar was even more crowded than usual, and people were already lining the procession route in order to see the prince. The young men were jammed against other passengers and Frank kept a nervous eye on Nixon.

Stepping down into the fresh air of Harvard Square, and hastening to their rooms to get their top hats, Nixon remained silent, and Frank was unsure if he was sick or angry. Frank wanted to say something to Nixon. He wanted to make some gesture of friendship but did not know how. Such gestures could sometimes make things worse.

They retrieved their hats and raced to Gore Hall where they lined up with their fellows and awaited the arrival of the Prince of Wales. When the royal personage finally appeared, an hour late, in a grand barouche pulled by four sleek black horses, the students were disappointed. The prince was their own age, somewhat runty, and more than a little debilitated from the previous night's exertions.

"Good Lord, Nixon, he looks more fagged out than you did last night," Frank said.

"I didn't have to dance with your cousin Fanny," Nixon rejoined, winking.

Frank felt a warm rush of relief. With Nixon's characteristic joke, things were simple again. The foreboding world of the night before was gone. Frank hooked his arm through Nixon's, and they tossed their hats in the air along with hundreds of others and gave three cheers for the silly little prince as his carriage passed by. Nixon was his friend, and everything was going to be all right.

Now, replacing his bandage in his dank room, Frank knew everything was not going to be all right. He was still hiding the wound and had not screwed up the courage to tell his troubles to anyone, even Nixon. Nixon had troubles of his own. When his father found out about his unsatisfactory scholastic performance, who knew what would happen. Perhaps Nixon would join the army with him.

Joining the army was all Frank thought of. There was little doubt now, the Northern states were going to need one. Since Christmas, seven states had seceded from the Union and formed their own government, calling themselves Confederates. A man from the West named Abraham Lincoln had been elected president and was about to be inaugurated. Curiously, the son of this future president was one of their class, Robert Todd Lincoln. A good enough fellow, Frank always thought, but like Nixon he'd been a perplexed outsider here in Boston until the election of his father. Now young Lincoln's popularity had made a great rise, especially with his professors, who paid him little notice prior to the election.

It only seemed a matter of time, even here in Boston. The abolitionist rally at the Music Hall last month had turned into a riot, and most of the class from the Southern states had not returned after the winter break. The aura of war permeated everything.

Everyone understood something momentous and unstoppable was set in motion, but for Frank the events swirling around him held a possible salvation. Frank had lived long enough in a house of consumption to know its every nuance. The stilled behavior, the calculated diets, the false periods of remission, and the spirit-breaking days when a sudden coughing of blood meant the symptoms had returned. Once afflicted, one was an invalid with no future except the vocation of finding a cure. There were only two avenues to possible restoration. One was to remove the illness from the climate that bred it and seek out warmer, purer air; this was the futile path his father had pursued. The other involved exercise, exertion, and manual labor undertaken in the open air. Frank heard whispers of men who'd gone into farming, signed on as sailors, or spent months in the West on horseback, returning from these efforts with their lungs cured.

He would not remain in college. The rooms were damp and the food was poor. Nor would he put himself or his mother in the position of the desperate travel and constant nursing again, only to die in a chair in a closed-up room. No. He would become a soldier. He could then at least try to regain his health, outdoors and under canvas, physically active and in the company of other men who would look after him as well as any brothers. Perhaps he could help preserve the Union, perhaps he would get better. At least he would have made a mark.

"Richard's here!" fourteen-year-old Agnes cried as she tore herself away from the parlor window where she'd been on the lookout. Jolting Belle, the household cat, from her favored cushion and setting a tabletop vase teetering, Agnes dashed up the stairs, where she almost collided with Nixon.

"Slow down!" Nixon warned her, gripping her shoulders, but Agnes lunged away from him, made a face, and disappeared into Marianne's bedroom, where Nixon could hear her being admonished to hush.

Marianne had risen from her girlhood sickbed alive but in a state that would forevermore be described as "delicate." Evincing no symptoms of illness Nixon could detect, other than occasional shortness of breath, Marianne's doctors nonetheless declared her very ill. Her heart was damaged by the childhood fever, and thus she passed over the glad diversions of maidenhood directly to the dreary lifelong occupation of "keeping her health." The word *invalid* was not spoken in the household, but Marianne was clearly under the obligation of, if not improving her health, at least not furthering damage to her heart. To this end she was compelled to avoid exercise, alacrity, anger, or overexcitement. Nixon often speculated on the nature of his sister's restrictions. If Marianne felt resentment at having her life shackled by a disease with no cure, she showed little of it. Instead she seemed to progress through her days calmly and uncomplainingly. Only rarely did Nixon see the flash of injustice cross her face. Those times were often concurrent with visits from Richard.

Nixon descended to the front door, which he opened to reveal Marianne's suitor, Richard Willard Sears. The September day was dreary, promising rain, but nothing could darken the young man's face as he made his accustomed ascent, two steps at a time, to the door of 81 Mt. Vernon St.

"Hullo, Richard," Nixon said, feeling better himself in seeing Sears' genuine smile. He marveled how some people could carry with them such a happy atmosphere and looked with satisfaction into his friend's warm brown eyes. No wonder Marianne was so smitten.

"Marianne is home?" Richard asked, turning the brim of the hat he held in both hands with nervous fingers.

"Yes," Nixon replied, "but I'm on my way to see Frank Crownin-shield off. He leaves today to join his regiment, from his family cottage in Nahant."

"Where is he destined?" Richard asked.

"Maryland, with the 2nd Massachusetts."

"Give him my best," Richard replied, "and wish him luck."

The two men crossed in the doorway and Nixon hurried down the steps in the direction of the State House, where he could hire a hack. As he walked, Nixon imagined the scene taking place in the parlor at home. Solid and robust, with merry eyes and dark, center-parted hair, everything in Richard Sears' countenance suggested joy. Laughter erupted easily from him, and his face was so ruddy it seemed he was always blushing. In no time at all the women of Nixon's home would assemble. Chairs would be drawn up around the tea table; Tigo, the family dog, would move to a position somewhere at Richard's feet; tea would appear from the kitchen; and a long session of talk would commence.

Nixon had known Richard for nearly two years, in fact he'd introduced the young merchant to the family. Before they all made the move from Ellsworth, Nixon was sent ahead to Boston to begin study with his tutors and had spent a few months in the boardinghouse of Mrs. Nathaniel Plympton. Richard had a room there too, and it was at Plympton's the two men first met, although Richard was five years older than Nixon and already engaged in his own business.

As chance would have it, George Sr. knew of Richard too, as the young man was a commission merchant deeply involved in shipping. Since the bulk of Richard's business involved moving cotton from the South to other markets, Nixon knew the Union blockade of the Southern states enforced last May must have caused his friend a heavy loss. Richard, jovial and gregarious, with manners too perfect to allow him to talk shop with the women, had never alluded to it and seemed in good spirits in spite of the war.

Choosing the liveliest-looking cab at the State House, Nixon directed the driver to the steamer wharf. By now he knew his mother was pouring the tea, the corners of her eyes crinkling in laughter, in the way he remembered from Ellsworth but saw less often now. His mother and sisters had infrequent visitors as they were not yet known in Boston society, and they rather doted on the ones who did come. Cakes and savories would have arrived on a tray, and Richard, who had a huge appetite he restrained with difficulty, would be reaching out graciously for the first one. He would be fluent and generous, flushed and happy, and drawn like a moth to Marianne's flame.

When their tea was over, and the quartet settled into gossip, Agnes would spiral around the table wearing her crush on Richard boldly on her sleeve, while Richard would sink lower in his chair, allow the cat to climb into his lap, and tell his stories. Nixon's mother would rest her hands idly in her lap until some particularly amusing tidbit was exchanged, when she would clap them together and laugh in her soft voice. Marianne would glare at her sister, fuss invisibly beneath her cool demeanor, and glide about the room with her head held high, under Richard's furtive and appreciative gaze. Only Nixon knew the two had little chance of ever marrying.

As Nixon's hack rolled its way to the Liverpool wharf he saw the unmistakable stern of the *Nelly Baker* moving out into the harbor. He'd missed the steamer! But how? He was on time, as far as he knew. He fumbled with his watch in his waistcoat and checked it. Bidding the driver to pull over and wait, Nixon leapt from the seat and ran across Broad Street to the booking office, dodging the heavy wagon traffic that passed endlessly along this way. Once inside, the sailing placard announced his error with the words "September Schedule" chalk-marked across it. How had he done it? It never occurred to him the schedule would change with the season. He would miss Frank! They would all think him a fool. He might never see his friend again.

His heart racing, he thought he might yet reach Nahant in time if he took the railroad to Lynn and hired a cab to take him across the causeway. It was his only chance. Threading back across the street clogged with wagons and carts loaded high with bales and barrels, he asked the driver to take him to the train depot as quickly as possible. Climbing inside the cab, Nixon heard the first spatter of the raindrops promised by the dark skies all morning hitting the canvas of the roof. It was not far to the eastern depot, and although the driver reacted quickly and urged the horse on with a crack of his whip, they were at the mercy of the slow-moving teamster traffic surrounding them. All the cargo from the wharves crept by in these large wagons, and ahead of them all Nixon could see was a mass of wet black tarpaulins and wagon roofs.

Nixon had retrieved his handkerchief to dry his brow, and now realized he was twisting it in his hands as his hack slowly passed the granite buildings that faced Broad Street and serviced the wharves. It was in one of these buildings that Richard Sears kept his office, which caused Nixon to remember his argument last week with his father.

The argument had grown, as they all recently had, out of Nixon's insistence he join the army with Crowninshield. Since Nixon had failed at Harvard and had no taste for working in real estate, he thought joining the Union cause was a good idea. Nixon couldn't imagine that he might die in combat and relished the idea of leaving the family and being tested in the company of other men.

"You must be out of your mind," was all his father would say when Nixon broached the subject, or, "I would never allow it."

On this most recent occasion when Nixon insisted, his father had exploded. "You have responsibilities here!" the older man shouted.

"I cannot see what they are," Nixon replied. "I seem to be pretty useless."

"Mrs. Crowninsheld has three sons. One lost will not affect them. If something were to happen to me, who would care for your sisters, or your mother?"

"The girls will be married, I suppose," Nixon stammered. "Marianne and Richard..."

"Marianne will not marry Richard Sears!" George Sr. bellowed.

"Why not?" Nixon argued.

"Richard Sears has asked me to back him with a loan."

Nixon closed his eyes. He did not for one moment suspect Richard of being an opportunist. One only had to watch Richard gaze at Marianne to know that. Nor did Nixon feel Richard's request was so outlandish. This war was unprecedented. Richard was honorable. The shipping interests of both men could be combined. Still, Nixon knew, as Richard did not, that he'd stepped on the one trigger that would cause George Sr. to distrust him. Richard could have been foreign, he could have been ugly, he could have been in every way unsuitable, and George Sr. may have accepted him. The one thing he could not do was ask for money.

"Grandfather helped you," Nixon continued, determined to fight for Richard and Marianne, and in some way he'd not yet thought out, for himself, "and you have helped some of Mother's family."

"That is none of your affair," George snorted. "Let him go to his own father then."

"You know very well his father is dead," Nixon answered.

"Then let him go to David Sears," George Sr. replied with deep disgust.

"Richard is in no way closely related to David Sears," Nixon replied. He'd heard his father talk disparagingly of David Sears before. David Sears was the richest man in Boston. Nixon knew his father had bought land from David Sears but did not know why his father disliked him.

"Then let him go to the devil," George replied softly, not as though he really meant it, but simply as a way to shut down the conversation.

Once Nixon's hack crossed the broad cobbled space before the domed and columned Custom House, the traffic cleared. It was not a market day and the streets here were narrow but quiet. The railroad depots sat side by side, and when Nixon saw the clock tower of the eastern depot come into view, he readied his driver's payment and jumped out of the cab into the cold rain.

Luckily, he had only fifteen minutes before the next train to Salem, which stopped first at Lynn, and he tried to compose himself and still his pounding heart by pacing under the covered platform. The rain slid off the awning in a straight, unbroken downpour, hissing on the stone sidewalk. By the time he boarded the train through the cloud of steam rising from its boilers, he found his heart quieted, but a sharp pain settled between his eyes. As the train departed, Nixon leaned back in his seat, his fingers pressed to his forehead. Small black cinders from the engine pasted themselves to the wet window-glass of the car, rain streaming between them.

It had been a terrible year. His failure at Harvard, the panic of the war, and most of all the leaden weight of his father's disappointment. Nixon knew he'd not measured up to his father's hopes. As he feared from the start, he was unable to complete the work required by the college. No matter how he tried, he could not do it. By the end of the term he was the only student in class asked to repeat the year. He could not go on as a sophomore. It was useless for him to continue at Harvard at all.

Nixon knew his failure was not the only cause of his father's bit-terness. George Sr. had been on edge since the family had moved to Boston. There were deeper disappointments at which Nixon could only guess, other worries which revealed themselves only as lines of pain across his father's face. For more than a year now, the older man had been complaining and critical. He was also, Nixon thought, unnecessarily antagonistic toward his classmates. Rob Perkins kept his visits short, and since the bad night when he and Frank returned from the Fresh Pond drunk, Frank had given his father a wide berth. Nixon never discovered what his father said to Frank that night, but he knew Frank had fled the house quickly. That night, Nixon expected his father to berate him, but he'd showed no signs of temper. He was strangely distracted, as if Nixon's drunken appearance was the last thing on his mind. His father only stood over him and said in his coldest voice, "You are forming the habits of your life, and you had better think about that."

His father was right, of course. Nixon never intended drunkenness. Still, he could not come to a conclusion about his father's feelings. Something in the old man was extinguished. He seemed uncomfortable. It was as though he was homesick.

When the train lurched into Lynn depot, Nixon stared in dismay at the curtains of rain sweeping across the dirt lot beside the station. Here, nearer the ocean, the wind had picked up, which meant an un-comfortable ride across the Beach Road causeway. Not many convey-ances were lined up to meet passengers. Some carriages were already spoken for, and the few that remained were without cover, mostly wagons, or traps with scanty roofs. What a fool he'd been for not checking the steamer schedule! He was not even sure which steamer Frank had planned to take when leaving Nahant. They'd just agreed to meet in the morning.

Near the end of the depot Nixon spied a man with a neat little gig. Was the vehicle for hire? The man looked foreign, with a strangely shaped hat tugged over his head and tied around his chin with a scarf. He wore a grey beard and no mustache. A small horse was in the harness, and unlike other horses waiting in the lot it was covered with a square of waterproof cloth. The man, wearing a coat of the same material, was talking to the horse when Nixon saw them, and stroking its face. His hands sported fingerless gloves. He had the air of a gypsy, or a mendicant, but the gig was in fine shape and its axle was stout.

Always warm to a person who showed care for animals, Nixon crossed the lot with his hand clamped on his hat, and approached the man.

"Are you for hire? Can you take me over to the Crowninshields' on Eastern Point?"

"Aye, but it's rough out there," the man replied, looking at Nixon with some disbelief and betraying his Scot heritage with his accent.

"I'm desperate to see someone before they leave on the steamer," Nixon explained.

"You'll ride up front with me," the man said, both as statement and question, because the little gig only possessed one seat. Nixon knew the driver was unaccustomed to sitting side by side with a gentleman customer. Nixon was unsure if the man was even in the business of taking customers.

"Of course," Nixon replied.

"No baggage, son?" the man asked with smiling eyes as he uncovered the horse and folded the waterproof blanket.

Nixon shook his head no, and the man laughed as he climbed into the gig.

They were nearly a mile along before Nixon realized what the man meant when he described the causeway as rough. Huge waves pounded the narrow strips of sand on either side, and Nixon saw the roadway might become impassable at a higher tide. The little horse made quick time and ignored the roaring beside her with little more agitation than the laying of her ears back when spray from a close wave splattered the gig. The man had a small whip tucked into the corner of the seat, with red ribbons around it and a little bell that tinkled, barely audible, as they raced along. A mile farther, and they were met with a great gust of wind pushing a wave over the roadway and rain that whipped the gig side-ways and caused the horse to stumble and slow.

Both men breathed more easily once they'd entered the relative shelter of the landmass of Nahant. Here, trotting along the main road, the man allowed himself the only words he had spoken since they left Lynn. "Which steamer?"

"I don't know," Nixon replied, pressing his clenched hand to his mouth. He tried to push down in his heart the awful fear rising there. "Can you hurry?"

The little whip with the bells tinkled over the horse's ears, and she picked up speed passing the cottages along the road and up the final hill to Eastern Point. Nixon noticed there was no steamer in the harbor, or at the dock. The Crowninshield cottage appeared, in the wind's eye, with its surrounding pastures lashed and wet. Nixon thought briefly of the long-ago picnic when he and the other Harvard-bound men lay in the summer grass. He'd wondered if he was one of them that day, and later, when riding with them again to the party at the Fresh Pond hotel last fall, he'd realized with joy that he was. He remembered with happiness the companionship, the agreeable feeling of drunkenness, and the recognition of friendship as Frank steered him safely home. He even remembered the strange pleasure of Frank's fingertips as he ran them through his hair, trying to make him presentable. Frank had stood by him. Now he must see him off too.

Drenched and blown, Nixon thanked the man with the gig and of-fered him payment for the harrowing ride. After the man tucked the money away in his pocket he grasped Nixon's shoulder.

"Give that lassie a kiss for me," he said with a wink, his Scottish eyes sparkling.

Nixon narrowed his eyes at the man, uncomprehending. "What?"

"The one you're seeing off, son. It's written all over your face."

Battered by the worry of missing Frank's departure, and uneasy from what the gig driver had said to him, Nixon ran with shaking legs up the steps of the cottage. The wind cut along the side of the house, lifting the fastened shutters and pushing them back against the walls of the structure, making a snapping sound like a command. Dead leaves had blown up in corners and gathered in sodden piles. There seemed to be no one about.

Pushing open the door, Nixon saw the familiar gateleg table, covered with three short stacks of books and a small blue vase with yellow flowers. The beautiful pale green of the room was washed away by the sunless day, and the walls seemed the color of cement. A wood fire smouldered in one of the grates and the house smelled lightly of smoke, forced by the howling winds back down the chimney. There was no servant to greet him or take his coat and hat, so he slipped out of them himself and draped them over the back of a cane chair inside the entrance. The hair at the back of his neck was damp from the rain, but it still rose with a shiver when he sensed that Caroline Crowninshield had stepped into the room.

She stood in the doorway, near the wall of silhouettes where he'd first met her. Her hair was brushed back from her brow, and she wore a dress of dark red. Nixon stiffened to comprehend what he knew she was going to say. He could tell by her face, she was already set to the task of recalling her son.

"He's gone," she said, and turned back into the other room. Nixon followed her and saw she shared the space with her other sons, all gathered to say good-bye to their brother. Fred, who was now sixteen, was seated at a table with a sketchbook, and Edward, Nixon's elder by a year, stood at the window.

"The steamer is out past Winthrop Point by now," Edward said. "We can't see it any longer."

Nixon felt large and awkward for the room, and he had the awful sensation that his hands, which should have been holding something, were improperly empty. He wanted to weep. Anger, humiliation, and love rushed through him, one by one, giving him no time to do more than name these feelings.

"I'm sorry you missed him," Caroline said. "We all assumed you were delayed by the weather." Nixon noticed her purple-tinted eyes were the only color in the grim oval of her face. A familiar misery began to fill his heart. He gazed around the room. Books, furniture, and pictures remained motionless in the sad grey light as the storm tossed outside. More than a person had left.

Caroline Crowninshield stepped up to Nixon and placed an arm around his waist. With the emptiness of his arms suddenly answered, he placed them around her shoulders and held her. He'd never embraced an adult woman before. He'd never been so close to anyone to whom he was not related. She was so small. Her ribs like a little cage. He could feel her heart beating deeply within. His father was right. Of course he would remain at home where he could care for his mother and sisters.

Nixon knew what he had to do. He knew what he had to say. The language was easy for him now. He had rehearsed this line, intended for Frank initially, all week.

He stroked Caroline Crowninshield softly between her shoulder blades as he released her from their embrace, letting his hand slide down her arm and rest in her palm. He looked at her and smiled with the dog-like gentleness that she was coming to know.

"Some people will do anything to get away from Greek conditional clauses."

She smiled faintly in return and squeezed Nixon's hand, her face a puzzle of shifting emotions.

George Nixon Black Sr. sat at his desk with a blank sheet of writing paper before him. He had plucked a pen from its holder and uncapped his inkwell. He did not want to write the letter he was going to have to write.

Nor, for that matter, did he really want to write it using the pen he'd chosen, one of the ubiquitous steel pens, mass produced and used by everyone these days. Gone was the flexibility of the quill, which allowed flourishes he was unable to replicate with the scratchy stiffness of steel. The new pens lasted longer and never needed trimming, but George missed the ritual of cutting the quills to suit himself. Gone was the comfortable act of collecting one's thoughts while paring the feather with a penknife. With the steel version there was no distance between lifting the pen and getting right at what you had to say. Like everything else in his current world, it just seemed wrong.

There was the war, of course. He'd seen it coming for years, but things are always different at distance than they are up close. After the attack on Sumter, Nixon and every other young man talked of joining the army. George assumed Nixon got the idea from his classmate Frank Crowninshield, with whom Nixon was so thick. Initially, George thought it a reasonable idea. Neither young man was very successful at college, and a year in the military could mature them both. His wife had begged him not to allow Nixon to join though, and after Bull Run he realized the war was likely to be long and bloody and cost thousands of lives.

Nixon had failed miserably at Harvard. He was at the bottom of his class and his instructors voted not to allow him to continue on to his sophomore year. He was the only student thus judged. In order to remain at the university he would have to repeat his first terms. This was a disappointment George found hard to accept.

If only the boy would just push himself, George thought, but perhaps it was he who was pushing too hard. Nixon had not received the years of classical education given most of the other youths, and his tutors had all reported that although Nixon worked well, he was unable to memorize and recite.

In one of their many arguments on the subject, Nixon one day cut closer to the bone than he realized when he noted no other man of the Black family had gone through university. It was true. Neither George's father, nor any of his brothers had endured the rigors of college, especially Harvard. They were a family of merchants, after all, and perhaps the wisest course of action would be to take Nixon into business with himself.

It was Boston that disheartened him the most. George felt so minimized here. He missed Maine and dearly wished he could have made a place for his family in Ellsworth, as his own father had done. It was not to be. As he'd predicted, business there was diminishing, and the town had not reformed. Know-Nothing violence was still prevalent. By some miracle, Father John Bapst had survived, but he had left Maine too. George also dreaded the job of equally dividing his father's estate as his will had dictated. The task would take years, travel to Maine was long and tiring, and his brothers were no friendlier to him than before he'd left.

In Boston, business was more successful. The war brought booms and busts, but these waters were easy enough to navigate. It was his vanity that suffered here, though George tried not to show it. In Maine, he belonged to the most prominent family in town. His opinions were sought and respected. He gained much credence from being his father's son. In Boston, he was nobody. Another rich merchant. His wife and daughters were not visited because they were not known or accepted. "From Maine. Not one of us." No one cared how his son fared at Harvard, least of all his professors. Another rich merchant's son from the hinterlands, "not one of us."

In the short time George had lived in Boston this attitude was personified in the figure of David Sears, the richest man in the city. David Sears was a bit flamboyant, as given his position, but George believed him to be an upright man. George had real estate transactions with Sears, and he was businesslike and cordial. That was as far as these relations went. David Sears did not know George Nixon Black. He'd merely done business with him. This diminution rankled George, and despite his better efforts to curtail it, this bitterness entered into every part of his life, and so he began to feel it at every turn. George had no problem living as a modest man, but he found it difficult to live as an inconsequential one.

As if to vex him further, and puzzle him in a particularly devilish way, George found that members of Boston's most admired families did find their way to his Mt. Vernon Street door, but in a way he'd never expected: they came with Nixon. A steady stream of Blanchards, and Perkinses, and Peabodys, and Crowninshields came visiting, all laughing and friendly and apparently happy to be spending time with his son, Harvard failure or not. Nixon knew their schedules and addresses; and for a young man who could not manage to memorize a stanza of Greek poetry, he knew these Bostonians' complex genealogies and family connections as though he had a street map. To George, it was a mystery as unfathomable as it was complete.

George had not come to this realization until the night of the Prince of Wales Ball, when one of the Boston scions dropped by, not to visit, but to deliver Nixon, draped over one shoulder. George had been waiting up for Mary and Marianne to return from the ball, an entertainment he did not entirely approve of, but Marianne had begged to attend for months. When the front door rattled he thought mother and daughter had returned, but on opening it he found Nixon and Frank Crowninshield on the doorstep, both of them drunk.

Tempted to laugh but equally outraged, he was stern with the youths, who'd clearly been on a spree. He did not like the idea of Nixon drinking, but George knew from the look of him he'd gone over his head in innocence, and he suspected the sickness that would come the next morning would be punishment enough. He also could not cast stones. George remembered returning home himself from a similar night when he was Nixon's age, asleep in the back of a wagon, his legs dangling over the edge.

George wanted to hate Crowninshield for his influence on his son, but in the long run he could not. Crowninshield had done the right thing, in fact, the brave thing, and brought Nixon safely home to whatever censure awaited them. He was angry that a member of the "tribe of Sears" had acted properly when he so wanted him to act improperly. Still, the episode made him think. Crowninshield would make a good soldier. Nixon was a good son. The world was shifting, life was less familiar, and he was getting old.

George picked up the undesirable steel pen and dipped it in the inkwell. The day before he'd received a letter from Harvard requesting Nixon's status as a student in the fall term.

Dear Sirs,
My wish is that my son should not return to the university.
Respectfully yours
G.N. Black

Nixon's Nightshirt
1862-1863

◉◞◦ Were it not for the tobacco, Nixon may never have come to know Caroline Crowninshield so well. Certainly he felt awkward this first time delivering it to her, stomping the sticky February snow from his boots at her doorstep and tucking the package deep in his coat so no neighbor would see it.

As no good tobacco could be found at his camp in Frederick, Frank desired a pound of it. No lady of breeding could be expected to enter the shop of a tobacconist, so Frank suggested Nixon buy it and give it to his mother, who was preparing a box of necessities to be sent to him.

Nixon thought to include a box of cigars and a few copies of the humorous illustrated papers, but decided in the end to forgo this idea and do only what was asked of him. Instead he tucked the latest letter he'd received from Frank in his vest pocket. The mails from Frederick were erratic, and Mrs. Crowninshield may not have received a more recent one herself.

> *Friday, January 31, 1862*
> *Dear Nixon,*
> *I received your letter of January 20. Having a bit of time I am prepared to give you a few more particulars on my manner of living. Reveille beats at a quarter to seven, when we all turn out of bed and attend roll call. It reminds me very much of prayers at Harvard, with this exception, instead*

of going to a nice warm chapel, we have to stand for ten minutes up to our knees in cold, wet mud. It is perfectly diabolical. Other than meal times and roll call, we do little except drill.

Meals consist one day of cold meat and bread and the next of bread and cold meat, and so on, day after day. Dinner is the best meal we have. Yesterday we had three first-rate turkeys. We never have a pudding course, except occasionally some cake. After dinner we have no duty to perform until roll call at 8 ½, at which everybody has to be present. After tattoo all lights in the men's tents have to be out. As officers go to bed when they choose, I generally turn in about 9 P.M. Lately the band plays just behind my tent every evening and I sit smoking in the doorway of my tent and listen to it. If you could get me a pound of Green Seal tobacco it would be a perfect Godsend. Bring it to mother and she can include it in the box she is packing to send me.

There is nothing very appalling in this soldiering business except guard duty. The guard is relieved every 24 hours. At 9 o'clock each day a new guard consisting of 60 privates, 1 sergeant, 3 corporals, and a commissioned officer goes on guard. The sentries are relieved every two hours, and each of these reliefs has to be visited by the officer of the guard, which at night is not very good fun. The officer is obliged to keep awake all night, and if he is caught sleeping he is dismissed from the service so they say. I have been on guard regularly and some nights almost die trying to stay awake, and whilst going the rounds sometimes am sleepwalking.

I have a pass to go to Frederick tomorrow night to attend a concert given by our band. I will give you particulars in my next. I must close.

Your friend,

Frank

Standing by the door of the Crowninshield house in the mild winter light, Nixon tried to imagine Frank letter-writing in his camp: the single flickering candle behind the open tent flap or lighting the canvas roof. He could bring himself, in his imagination, all the way to the endless A-shaped tents, the soggy grey ruts, the raw smell of wet canvas, horses, fire, ashes. Nixon could see the shadowed outline of his friend listening to the camp music around a low fire. Frank would be resting his elbows on his knees, seated on a box or a log, and cradling the bowl of his pipe in his hand, with his jacket thrown open and second lieutenant straps curled stiffly across its woolen shoulders. Was Frank mindful of his peril? Nixon could not know. As easily as he could imagine Frank's person he could not bring himself to Frank's presence, for the Beacon Street doorway where Nixon stood belonged to another world.

Heavy wood doors faced him and a low fog lay around the shriveled ivy hunkered beneath snow in the small iron-edged, street-front gardens flanking the tall steps. The Crowninshields lived in a modern house, recently built on the new land being filled in to the west of the Common. Done up in the French Antique style, it was much different than the sober swell-front brick home of his own family on Beacon Hill.

Inside were astral lamps in glittering rings of crystals, rich and curved French chairs, books behind glass doors, and Brussels carpets. After he pulled on the knocker, a housemaid would answer and show him into a room adorned with an ornate mantel and a pair of brass firedogs. A feminine face, anxious and lovely and so much like Frank's, would lift itself up to him. She would hold motionless her hands, which a moment before were busily engaged beside a little worktable with a lyre base. A small crease would form between her eyebrows as she assessed the meaning of his visit, and once the danger of any bad news associated with his presence had passed, she would remove her fancywork from her lap and rise to take his offered hand. Straight-backed and resolute she would stand before him, accustomed to her own peril in a way only one who has been a sickbed awaiter of death can be, both fragile and virile at the same time. *Here is another sort of stoicism,* Nixon would think, and as he slid the tobacco from under his arm he would realize they were more than friends, they were, somehow, accomplices.

It seemed to Caroline Crowninshield she had always been waiting. Waiting for her father to return from his workday, waiting for the mumps to get better, for the snow to arrive and bring coasting and skating, for the snow to leave so new slippers could be worn. Waiting for the fancy dress ball, waiting for the wedding, for the births of each of her boys. Then came the waiting for their mumps to get better, for her husband to survive or die, and now waiting for the end of this terrible war. Even today, she was waiting for the arrival of young Nixon Black, Frank's best friend, who'd sent a message he would be bringing tobacco for Frank's box.

He appeared at the door of the parlor, looking as she knew he would. Fixing her with his tender, almost absurd smile and his clear blue eyes, she could not help feel a fondness for him. He clasped her hand for a moment, and then with a gesture of affecting diffidence withdrew the parcel of tobacco from under his arm and placed it on the table as if it were an unworthy offering. He was so young, and so obviously devoted. One could assume his experience was limited, Caroline thought, but there was something else. He was not a handsome youth, as her own sons were, but he possessed a circumspection she did not find in them, a sagacity barely contained in his modest bearing.

With the same caution as he'd removed the tobacco with, he now revealed an envelope with the familiar handwriting that never ceased to make her heart leap. "I've had a letter from Frank, day before yesterday," Nixon said. "I thought you might like to read it."

"I have had one as well, in this morning's mail," Caroline confessed. "Perhaps you would like to read mine too?"

They arranged themselves cozily, each in one of the French uphol-stered chairs on either side of the table in the center of the room. An overhead gasolier reflected golden light in the large plate mirror hang-ing over the mantel. Jed, the Crowninshields' comic little bristle-haired bulldog, joined them, and was soon snoring noisily, lying with his black feet pushed against one of a pair of China vases on the hearth. They talked for hours in low familiar voices like a long-married couple dis-cussing their household. Swirling snow collected in the casements, writ-ing a white letter L in each pane.

February 6, 1862

Dear Mother,

I received yours of January 30 last evening while sitting in the guard tent thinking of you, and the comforts of home. The officers, guard tent is the worst in the regiment, it is all torn and has no floor. It has a miserable stove that refuses to give any heat. The only time I long for a warm bed and a carpeted floor is under these circumstances. I suffer considerably from cold feet.

Last Friday evening, having obtained a pass from the colonel, I went to Frederick to the concert given by our band. I enjoyed myself very much. The ladies dressed in the most peculiar style, black skirts to their dresses most of them, with red or white flannel shirts, just exactly like mine, pocket and all, instead of tight fitting waists. As for beauty, there was not much there, all of them were rather in the bony line. After the concert four other officers with myself went round to Mrs. Sly's to have supper. We had some perfectly glorious oysters that tasted doubly fine after our camp fare.

I have been busy this last week or I should have written sooner. Recitations have been added to my list of duties. I study quite hard, a thing you will say I never did before. (I see Ned shake his head.) I am studying skirmishing and outpost duty, quite important things for a young lieutenant.

Could you send me another pair of trousers made of light blue cloth. I find several officers have them in this color. Also have them made extreme peg top, very large around the knee, and small round the bottom. The mud is such here that the trousers I do have are a perfect potato bed.

Ever your affectionate son,
Frank

As mindful as Caroline was of Frank's chance of death by a bullet, she was even more disturbed by her suspicion he might be sick. She'd always watched anxiously for the glint of fever in his eyes, the same oily shimmer that dulled the spark from her husband's when he was ill. Everyone knew consumption ran in families. Of all her boys, Frank was the weakest as a baby. His youth, however, was unclouded by illness, and although thin and slight he seemed healthy. Now he was a soldier, exposed to innumerable dangers and deprivations she could only guess at; her only information was gleaned from the newspapers and stories of those who visited the camps.

Only a fortnight before she'd been in the shop of Bent & Bushes to purchase some epaulettes Frank had requested. After stepping outside and pausing to open her umbrella, she stood aside to let another patron enter the shop. As the door opened and the shop bell tinkled, she heard the trailing off of the voices of the clerks within who'd waited on her: "just like his father..." Those were the only words she overheard, but they were enough. The men were talking about Frank and Edward, she was certain of it.

There were often more direct assaults. At tea last Friday, her cousin Caroline Abbott, herself the mother of two boys in Frank's regiment, posed her own indelicate question. As a small gurgle and wisp of steam emerged from the spout of Mrs. Abbott's teapot, she asked, "Has Frank quite recovered from the gripes he suffered at Edinburgh? Fletcher wrote that Frank was physicked for several days and given opium." Caroline willed her gloved hand holding the teacup to stay steady and tried not to show any panic.

"He is perfectly recovered, thank you," she replied smiling, although she was entirely unaware of any report of illness.

At night, Caroline lay sleepless while Jed snored in his little pallet near her bedpost. It was not the many hazards Frank faced that kept her awake. It was not the possibility of telegrams, or wounds, or even consumption that tore at her heart. It was something else.

When nursing her husband in his last days her feelings abandoned her. Everything she had previously known was altered. His mouth, which she once so ardently sought and kissed, became bitter and alien. His body, against which she once pressed herself in desire, could then not be thrust away fast enough. She let him see none of this, of course; she continued to bathe his forehead and sit up with him during his night sweats. The repulsion was hers alone, the odd reflex to distance herself from his destruction. She understood this was a form of self-preservation, but that did not wipe away its awfulness. Never again, she'd vowed as she stood by Edward's grave, would she allow her heart to collude with such a negation. Now, with Frank's life-courting risk, she feared she would find herself in the same state again. The awful evasion. Intolerable for a husband, unthinkable for one's child.

Nixon experienced Frank's absence as a void. It was impossible for Nixon not to picture Frank in his glittering surroundings. The privilege, the pedigree, the perfect clothes, and the easy way he lived among it all. Nixon felt, in meeting with Frank's approval, he'd somehow been chosen. Now with Frank gone, Nixon was deprived of this picture of the world through Frank's eyes. No other of his college friends was quite the same. John Blanchard was pleasant but always the student. Rob Perkins, owing to his penchant for bad behavior, had predictably gotten himself expelled from class for a term and had been sent abroad by his family to cool his head.

Since his own failure at Harvard, Nixon had been working with his father, in a world filled with mortgages and brokers. The hours of tedious college recitations were replaced by the requirements of commerce, and bookkeeping, and attending to clerks and businessmen with an eye to second-guessing them. The loftier goals of memorizing classics gave way to scrutinizing lumber scalers, bartering with tradesmen, and learning which days of the week rents were most easily collected.

Only Frank transcended it all, both soldier and scion, dwelling in a place so impeccable, his uniform and manners perfect and his smile so munificent, one nearly forgot he'd known it all from the hour of his birth. So, Nixon thirsted for him. He talked endlessly with Frank in his head and haunted the mail slot for envelopes addressed in Frank's hand. Nixon knew he loved and admired Frank. What he'd not worked out was why Frank reminded Nixon of something he could not have.

"Is he well, Nixon?"

It was a wind-lashed day in early May when Caroline Crowninshield put this question to him. Since Nixon began to work with his father and ceased to declare he was going to join the army, George Sr. and son had drawn up a truce of sorts. The old man pressed Nixon into all the duties expected of him, showing irritation only when Nixon's attention either wandered or refused to attach itself firmly enough to detail. But by early afternoon on most days he set him free, rarely raising his own head from his ledgers and never questioning his son's plans or activities. Quite often, Nixon walked directly from his father's offices to the Crowninshields'. Here Jed the bulldog was reliably posted, his leering smile appearing from parted curtains in the first-floor window. He knew treats resided in the pocket of a young man who arrived several times a week.

"I have no reason to think he isn't," Nixon replied, sliding a bundle of illustrated papers onto Mrs. Crowninshield's table. "He has written nothing of any illness to me."

"You would tell me?" Caroline questioned firmly.

"Of course," Nixon replied, running his fingers through Jed's brushy coat and fumbling in his pocket for the dog's anticipated biscuit. Nixon knew the rumors. It was said Edward Crowninshield's consumption was passed to his sons. Many speculated Frank would be unable to stand a soldier's life. John Blanchard even confessed to Nixon that Frank's captain had spread the word Frank looked like "last year's run of old shad, and it was only a matter of time before either illness or a bullet finished him." Nixon was not so sure. He knew how much Frank wanted to be a soldier.

"My sister is an invalid," Nixon said, suddenly.

Caroline only let the pause of her surprise last a moment before resuming her stitching. She'd heard this, of course, but Nixon had never spoken of it. "What is the nature of her illness?" she asked.

"Her heart is damaged, owing to the scarlatina she had as a child," Nixon explained. "My parents say she cannot marry."

"Yes, I understand," Caroline said, coiling a thread around her finger and breaking it away from its spool in a deft motion.

"Well," Nixon asserted rather more candidly than he intended. "I don't understand. Why can't she marry? Why can't Frank be a soldier, whether he is ill or not?"

Caroline studied the young man's face until she was satisfied he really did not believe Frank was ill. "Nixon, if your sister marries, she will likely be in a condition to bear a child. If her heart is weak, childbirth might kill her."

Nixon sank back in his chair with the slowness of dawning comprehension. He sighed and pushed Jed's head, resting near his knee, gently away. He'd always assumed it was the money. He'd never considered childbirth.

"Well," he said, with the hope of intoning kindly, "then why can't Frank be a soldier?"

"Unfortunately, I cannot conjure a single unselfish reason," Caroline answered, smiling slightly and shaking her head sadly.

May 7, 1862
Dear Mother,

I have just received your letter dated May 4th, and am very sorry you have been troubled about my health. I can't imagine who could have given you such information. I was never better in my life than at the present moment. Dear Mother, I wish you would rely on what I write myself and not put any faith in reports. I have had some sickness, of course, but not more than the average of officers have to go through. Such a complete change of life as this will affect almost any one. My illness at Edinburgh was chiefly owing to the unhealthy situation of the camp. There were 6 other officers beside myself unfit for duty. I hope you will feel easier about me and not trust again what people may say. As for my not taking care of myself I think you are misinformed also. I try my best to be careful, but will strive still harder. The position of new officers in this regiment is very trying, the old officers can do things which if we should do, would be thought shirking. If for instance I had not reported for picket duty when I did, I should have been regarded as a shirk, and any officer who tries to escape disagreeable duties is disliked by everybody. So you see I am not always at liberty to give up duty when I feel unwell. I am glad however you wrote as you did about your fears about my health, as in future I shall be more explicit in my letters, so you need not be worried by reports. I promise you if I find I can't stand this life to resign and go home, but I don't think there is much chance of your seeing me before the end of the war.

Ever your affectionate son,
Frank

PS Send me some more needles if you can. Everyone borrows them and that is the last I hear of them.

As Nixon returned home across the Common, he noticed the spring wind had knocked blossoms and twigs all along his path. Some of the early flowers, stripped of their heads, lay bent and battered along the edges of their beds. In the parlor of his home, he was greeted by the smile of Richard Sears, who'd apparently overstayed even his usual overstaying, and gathered with everyone, including George Sr. around a lengthy tea. The sought-for letter sat atop a table inside the doorway, and Nixon snatched it up, anxious to be away with it and out of the presence of these people who made him feel impatient and trapped. *I suppose Marianne and Richard are to have a visiting marriage,* he thought snappishly, and hurried upstairs with Frank's missive.

May 9, 1862
Dear Nix,

I am glad you wrote and gave me the advice you did, although some of it is not necessary. The whole report is entirely untrue. My health is excellent, I would not say so, if it were not. I have tried to convince Mother of the fact, but whether I succeed I can't tell. Do all in your power to render her mind easy about me, for I know how terribly that rumor must have worried her. How much trouble is caused by false reports! And people saying what they know nothing about. I suppose some officer wrote home that I could not stand the life and in that way Mother heard about it. That is the only way I can account for it. Several officers said when I first came out I couldn't stand this life a month, but they have owned their mistake, and admit I am a good deal tougher than I seem to be.

The only real danger I had at Edinburgh was from bullets. I was on picket at the most advanced point of our lines, and on alert all the time as the enemy fired at us considerably. Towards dusk, while making rounds I had two shots fired at me, the first I have ever had, and the bullets came altogether too near to be comfortable.

Our work is over in this valley, and it is reported we shall remain at Strasburg. The regiment is in an awful state at such a dreary prospect, so we have determined in sending a petition to the Secretary of War asking to be put some place where we can meet the enemy.

I hear Fred is beginning to shake in his boots as examination day draws near. Do you remember how we dreaded it? I can say now, I would rather face bullets than another examination at Harvard.

The weather here is getting hot, and I shall be thankful when I get some thin clothes. I have had my hair cut short to my head, filed, I believe is the proper term for it, and I feel much more comfortable. The nights are still very cool.

Now dear Nix, I must close. I hear you are getting very friendly with little Jed. I think of him every time I rub my hand over my filed head.

Hoping to hear from you soon,

Your friend, Frank

PS. Tell Marianne her injunction to dodge the bullets is unnecessary, one can't help it. You do it by instinct.

When later that month word came from Winchester, Virginia, that Frank was wounded and unable to walk, brother Ned was sent to fetch him home to Boston.

Locating his brother in an army hospital in Frederick, Ned wrote home immediately describing Frank's wound as not dangerous but very painful, since a bullet had pierced the calf of his leg, nicked the bone, and traveled down toward his ankle.

Thus when the train bearing the two brothers was due in from New York, Grandfather Crowninshield sent his carriage and two stable boys with a long board to carry Frank.

As the carriage pulled up to the Beacon Street door, it brought consequences Nixon had never considered. A small white face floated like a crumpled wraith in the square window of the carriage. The door popped open and a worn boot unsteadily met the step. An argument about the use of the board had clearly happened at the station, and the stable boys remained on their seats. Ned held back too, clutching a knapsack Frank must have thrust in his lap. A black cane emerged, followed by a splinted and bandaged leg. Gripping the frame of the carriage door, Frank slid carefully down onto the street. His uniform hung on him like a father's coat on an awkward son. His belt was pulled to its furthest notch, and the signet ring he wore on his smallest finger had spun around with its engraved initial turned inside his palm. Frank blinked and gazed disbelievingly at the doorway where Nixon and the Crowninshield family awaited him.

Caroline swayed slightly on the top of the steps, clutching her skirts with a slender white-knuckled hand. In the window, Frank's younger brother, Fred, stood with Dr. Warren, the brother-in-law physician Caroline had called to attend her wounded son. Frank spun the crook of the cane clumsily in his right hand. No one moved as he lurched with a grimace toward the steep steps to the house. His face was a mask of pain, the cane an unfamiliar object.

Nixon could not simply watch his friend struggle, so he skipped quickly down the stairway. Before Frank had a chance to protest, Nixon slid his arm around Frank's bony shoulders, scooped up the cane, and swung his friend's arm over his own broad back.

"I owe you a favor on the use of a shoulder," Nixon said, winking at Frank.

Frank lifted his chin and looked directly, then mischievously, at Nixon.

"All right," Frank said, nodding, allowing the corners of his mouth to rise. "As long as we don't find your father behind that door."

There it was, as it always was, as though it had never been otherwise. The guilelessness, the boyish blond head, the endearing smile. Just like the first time.

Frank's homecoming tired him, so the two friends said little else. Although Nixon did not think Frank looked as bad as rumor had it, his friend was changed. Most notably, he'd lost flesh, but his eyes were darker in a way that compelled Nixon to stare into them. The capricious violet he remembered so fondly had entirely vanished. Could eye color change? What had Frank seen? Certainly his friend was no longer young. Something more than weight had been wrung out of him. Something Nixon recognized the absence of. Something he himself had also lost, long ago.

Frank did not return home unaccompanied. The morning of his arrival a letter came too, slipping its way silently through the same door Frank was to limp through only hours later.

Hagerstown, May 27, 1862

Dear Madam:

I am happy to state your son is doing very well, and in a few days will be able to go home to Boston.

He was hit while the regiment was retreating down the hill, where we had been in position, under very heavy fire, the ball inflicting a painful, but not life threatening wound. He was got into an ambulance and brought safely off and is now in a house in Williamsport.

It affords me the greatest satisfaction to tell you that his conduct throughout was perfect, even so much so I was obliged to once or twice command him to seek a shelter when he was needlessly, though bravely, exposing himself.

The preservation of any portion of the regiment was Providential, we being the last off the field and passing through the town when it was actually in possession of the rebels.

With the most sincere sympathy for your anxiety, I remain

Yours very truly

Captain Richard Cary

Caroline passed this letter to Nixon, with her face turned away from it, letting it hang from two fingers of her right hand after Frank had retired to be examined by Dr. Warren.

"Frank has distinguished himself," Nixon said, refolding the note, "as we knew he would."

"Yes," Caroline said, the one word hard like a cold stone on her tongue.

On that day Nixon could not have vocalized what bothered him about the letter either.

This wound from the battle at Winchester was destined to be only the first of the combat injuries Frank would receive in the sobering string of defeats suffered by the Union in the sad months of 1862. The summer after Winchester, much of his convalescence was spent on the porch of the cottage in Nahant, where Frank occupied his time napping with an open book on his lap whose pages were never turned.

He read nothing except the newspapers, hungrily seeking mentions of his regiment, desiring to be back in the field with them. By early September he returned to Maryland. He'd not been there a fortnight when he was again shot, this time in the opposite leg, during the ferocious battle at Antietam.

Frederick, September 21, 1862
Dear Mother,

I suppose you have received the telegram informing you I was wounded at Antietam. The ball, a minnie ball, entered the thigh of the opposite leg from the one wounded at Winchester, so I guess I am to be unlucky about getting hit. I suffer little, sleep well at night and have a fine appetite.

I am very comfortably situated, far better than most, and am located in a private house where I manage to be carried daily out to the parlor where I can recline on the sofa. I do not know if Ned will be able to move me right away when he arrives. The city is one vast hospital. I suppose there are 3500 other wounded men here.

I am longing for home, but live very much in dread of Dr. Warren, and also in the scrubbing I am bound to get from you.

Ever your affectionate son,
Frank

The Christmas season of 1862 was a chastened one. It had become generally understood the war was not going to end quickly, and as news from the disastrous defeat at Fredericksburg began to filter in, it seemed the bloodshed might never end. Nearly everyone in Boston had a loved one in uniform and in harm's way. Despite the shouts of jubilation that echoed in abolitionist circles with the announcement of the Emancipation Proclamation on New Year's Day, it was the sober reality of the black-bordered telegram announcing a soldier's death that was in the forefront of most people's minds.

Frank, whose Antietam wound was healed, had been able to walk without crutches since Thanksgiving and was anxious to rejoin his regiment in January. In the few weeks between the holidays, he and Nixon went about Boston enjoying the entertainments available. Tempted by lavish posters pasted on the exterior, they viewed the "Mammoth Hippopotamus" on display at the P.T. Barnum Museum. Afterward, standing on the sidewalk, Frank said, "It was a mighty puny beast when compared with 'seeing the elephant,'" soldiers' slang for the experience of battle.

Nixon was drawn to the thought of spending an evening at the theater, and as a gift to Frank secured tickets to attend a special farewell appearance by the celebrated actor Edwin Booth appearing as Hamlet one evening just before Christmas. The performance at the Boston Music Hall was a delight, but the two young men were soon to enjoy more traveling time together. It was planned Nixon would accompany Frank back to his camp at Stafford Court House in Virginia, stopping at Washington on the way.

Nixon had never traveled so far south before. The streets of the capital were filled with soldiers, far more than Nixon had ever seen in Boston. They were everywhere, their coats and trousers two shades of blue, and in every state of wear from crisp to tattered. Clustered in the saloons; gathered in raucous, jostling groups around the paymasters' office; traveling to and from camps and the train depot; many were missing limbs or bearing the symptoms of illness.

Washington was essentially an armed camp, a grid of unpaved streets lined with spindly newly planted trees, shops, and warehouses. The buildings had the air of having been thrown together and sidewalks were piled with garbage. The city was presided over by the unfinished dome of the partially constructed Capitol building and ringed with hastily built entrenchments, batteries, and rifle pits. Fortunately, as this was January all seemed cleaner owing to the cold and frost. Nixon could not imagine the scene in the heat of summer.

When they first arrived and Frank applied to the provost marshall's office for a pass to his regiment, he was met with the unwelcome news he was to report immediately for duty at the convalescence camp across the river in Alexandria, which meant that his trip with Nixon would end would end the next morning. The pair had expected at least a few days together, but since there was no help for it, Frank suggested they secure a room for themselves at the Kirkwood House and spend their last night "making Rome howl."

Carrying their belongings up the carpeted stairway to the third floor of the hotel, they discovered they'd been given a room so small the door collided with the dresser on opening and the two small beds within were jammed tightly in the opposite corner. Hunting for the washstand so they could clean up, they discovered it stood alone in a closet-like chamber, just beyond the much-abused dresser and completely hidden from the rest of the tiny room.

"Spacious," Frank commented dryly, "compared with my accommodations tomorrow night."

Frank wasted no time and headed directly to the dining room downstairs, where he supplied their tabletop with a plate of raw oysters and a round of cocktails. For his size, Frank could eat oysters in enormous quantities. Nixon was hungry too, but found his appetite tempered by his anxious dread of parting from Frank. Until the discovery of the order at the provost marshall's office, their farewell lay somewhere in the future. Now their parting had been assigned an hour, and Nixon could think of nothing but it.

After two plates of the delicious bivalves, they left the Kirkwood and sauntered up the street, Frank pointing out certain sights and describing the various uniforms on passersby. They entered another oyster saloon and then another, slowly eating their way up the avenue as the shadows slanted and the sky grew dark. For small chunks of time Nixon found himself caught up in their revelry, but then he would catch a glimmer of Frank's flaxen hair or his silhouette against a lit window on the street and think, *I may never see him again.*

Nixon fought to contain and hide his mood. At one point they passed a photographer's studio. Small tin photographs of soldiers with youthful but serious faces hung pinned on a string in the window. Nixon was tempted to suggest they have their photograph made together, but he was ashamed to say it, and seconds later Frank tugged him along the street in high spirits laughingly drawing his attention away from the dangling photographs to a knot of men struggling on the far corner. Here two soldiers who had snuck into the city without their required passes were being arrested, with great commotion, by the ever vigilant provost guard.

Eventually, Frank and Nixon found themselves back in the dining room of the Kirkwood House. Here, before another empty platter of oyster shells and backed up against the grate of a deeply banked fire, Frank radiated exuberance.

"Did you see the faces of those fellows the provost guard had cornered?" he asked and hooted with laughter. "That runty one still had his fists flying even though the guard had him lifted by the scruff of the neck!"

"They did look surprised," Nixon assented, "and not too sober."

"Of course, they were foolish to even enter a theater. It's the first place the guard look," said Frank, shaking his head as he placed his crossed arms on the table and leaned forward. He lifted his head and looked directly at Nixon.

Frank's eyes seemed to grow larger and glisten. Suddenly shy, Nixon dropped his own gaze from the boldness of them. Looking into Frank's eyes that moment was more than he dared to do. Nixon curled his hands into loose fists, so Frank would not see them trembling.

"I've done it myself," Frank said, pausing entirely for effect and then continuing, "come to Washington without a pass." His eyes were brazen and full of mischief. "All it takes is a little cheek, an article I possess in larger quantities than you perhaps suspect." The words were delivered in a manner that at one moment suggested teasing, and in the next suggested nothing at all.

Nixon swallowed hard and fixed his eyes on Frank again. "Were you ever caught?"

"No, I invariably escaped," Frank said slyly. "You think I am always good, but I can be a devil." Indeed, there was something fierce and smouldering about Frank. His friend's face was shining with moisture, flushed and red. The air seemed to crackle between them.

Frank laughed his familiar laugh and slowly lifted his arm to run his hand through the hair that had fallen against his forehead. Pushing it back from his brows, Nixon watched as the damp spikes of hair passed through his friend's fingers and sprang back to life, like blades of wet grass. "I know I am devilishly warm right now," Frank said.

"Perhaps you are too close to the fire," Nixon found the presence of mind to answer, not really knowing what his answer meant or what question it was a reply to.

Back inside their tiny room, Nixon was unsure what to do. A single lamp burned on the dresser, keeping the room in a dimness Nixon was grateful for. He fiddled with his buttons, undressing slowly, but Frank showed no such compunction and slid out of his clothing easily, folding away what he did not require and laying his nightshirt on the bed nearer the wall. Nixon sat in a chair near the window, removing his shoes, with his shirt opened and pulled out from his trousers as Frank padded by, completely nude, on his way to the washstand in its separate room.

Nixon watched Frank furtively. He supposed in the army men got used to such close contact, but he'd never been alone with another man naked before. He removed his own shirt and folded it away in his valise, listening to Frank splashing in the unseen room. Not wanting to seem shy or unsophisticated, he made sure he too was standing nude, folding his trousers as Frank reentered the room carrying the lamp, which he returned to the dresser. Frank then pulled his nightshirt over his head, and Nixon glanced at him again in the moment his friend's face was covered. Nixon was surprised at how strong Frank's body looked, despite its thinness. He looked too, at the scars of the wounds on Frank's legs. One a small sunken puncture the other a healed, reddened slash.

Following Frank's lead, Nixon laid out his own nightshirt and walked into the washstand room. He washed his face slowly, his hands still trembling as he rubbed them together. Why could he not steady them? He thought again of Frank's nude body passing beside him and felt a quickening somewhere in the base of his spine.

He loved Frank, that he knew. But it wasn't a womanish thing, or was it? He dried his hands on the towel and ran it down the front of his chest. He was embarrassed at the actions of his body's desires. They were nothing like what his mind intended of them. Nixon felt he wanted to reveal something to Frank, to make his true self plain to him. At least he ought to say something to let Frank know he cared for him. It seemed only right. After tomorrow, they might never see each other again. If his love were womanish, though, he could not see anything to do but to be silent about it. He buried his face deep in the comfort of the towel. What had Frank meant by saying he was devilish? He wondered if his friend was even still awake, but as Nixon lifted the lamp he knew he was, as he could hear Frank coughing in the other room. Nixon reached for the key on the lamp to put the flame out. He needed the darkness to say what he wanted to say.

"Nixon." It was Frank's voice that spoke out from the shadow of the other room, causing Nixon's hand to jump away from the lamp key he was turning. Measured and tremulous, Frank's voice was both insistent and not, and Nixon could not interpret it. He was unsure if he was being beckoned, but a sudden impulse implied something was wrong.

Stepping through the doorway with the lamp flame wavering, Nixon faced the beds. Frank sat upright against the headboard staring down at his own bloody hands on his lap, palms up, as if in some sort of strange benediction. The front of his nightshirt was spattered with blood, and when he raised the back of his hand to wipe away a scarlet strand hanging from his mouth, his eyes, which were fixed in the shape of a terrified alertness, looked beyond Nixon, beyond the walls of the room and into some distant place.

Clarity is capable of inflicting the most savage kind of pain. As Nixon's consciousness took in the complete vision of his friend, his mind shuffled through a crowd of memories and made sense of them. The sparkling eyes, the uncommon sweating, the consumptive father, the rush to join the army, the rumors, and, most horribly, the memory of Captain Cary's words that Frank was "needlessly though bravely exposing himself" in the battle of Winchester.

Nixon felt seized and thrust downward by a great force of inevitability, and the space between himself and the bed seemed to change from distance to time. Frank was lost. He was far away and could never be followed. Nixon was not sure whether the howl of fear he then heard came from his own throat or Frank's, but it caused him to fight against the relentless force pressing him downward, to raise his head and look again at the bed. Small and pale among the blankets, Frank was only at arm's length after all. One step and Nixon found himself back in the direction in which he had started. Two steps and Frank was in his arms. As Nixon knelt in the bed rocking him, blood and tears smeared across both their faces.

Frank was perfectly still in Nixon's embrace. He did not resist him. For a long moment Nixon rested his own face on Frank's chest beneath his raised chin. Frank's skin was damp from the fever, and he appeared weak and dazed. He assented readily to the suggestion Nixon fetch the basin and a washing cloth and help him to clean up. Frank sat passively as Nixon pulled the bloody nightshirt over his head and tossed it on the chair, rinsing the cloth in the soapy water and cleaning his face and chest. Nixon's hands no longer trembled. As he braced Frank's shoulder Nixon noticed another healed wound on the young soldier's body. A deep scar, much like the bullet wound on his calf, lay an inch or so above Frank's collarbone. It was just the size and shape of Nixon's thumb. Nixon wondered how this wound was acquired and assumed it was inflicted in one of the battles. So close to his own hand, the wound put Nixon in the mind of the thumbprint bruise Frank had made on his own body, preventing his fall in the cave at Nahant. As Nixon held Frank firmly by the shoulder and ran the washing cloth along his neck, he could not resist letting his hand slide forward and placing his thumb into the spot. *How much we never know about one another,* he thought. Frank had kept his illness secret for months, maybe years. Now it was Nixon's secret too. A danger at least as fickle as a bullet stalked his friend. No wonder Frank longed for the less invisible risk of war.

Once the washing was complete, Nixon offered his own nightshirt to Frank, who allowed himself to be dressed in it and tucked into the bedclothes. With the lamp finally extinguished, Nixon sat for a moment on the edge of the bed. He let his eyes rove the shadowy corners of the dowdy rented chamber. It was like any other. There was no chance of his assessing what he had gained or lost here. He was too far away from himself. All he could sense was oblivion, whose presence he gave thanks for.

Nixon slid into the bed with Frank, and curled against his friend's back, placing his arm around his waist. He then fell asleep with his lips touching Frank's hair, writing for the shabby hotel room another history for it to silently keep.

The voice was melodic, rising in a disembodied swell from the street outside the hotel. The strangeness of the sound woke Nixon completely from his sleep, and he found himself chilled, twisted uncomfortably under a thin sheet, and unable to do anything but listen.

Prolonged and dreamy, the evocative howl resembled no language and seemed to contain no meaning. Consisting of two major keys and several minor ones, it was repeated at long intervals; faded away as the singer moved into the distance; picked up by a different, closer singer; and begun again.

It was very early and the sliver of dawn entering the room was grainy and grey. Frank, already risen and fully dressed, sat by the window in this sallow light. He looked perfectly healthy. He'd changed into his uniform, and a slight luster reflected on the buttons of his sleeve as he reached out and opened the interior shutter with the smallest finger of his right hand, seeking the source of the haunting sound. Nixon let his eyes run across the beloved profile, the disordered hair feathering the brow, the patient mouth, the small straight nose. To imagine his death was impossible, even now. Nixon knew Frank had outlasted pain, and he understood how fixed his determination was. He knew too that nothing was going to be discussed between them. The events of the night were inviolate. With daylight the events became memory.

Another long, lovely chant interrupted his thinking. Nixon rose from the bed, pulling the coverlet around himself and stepping across the cold floor to the window. Frank who had already satisfied his curiosity as to the sound, sat idly, scraping at a small corner of frost which formed overnight in a lower pane.

On the street below was a large herd of cattle. Hundreds of them, appearing ghost-like from a bank of frosty fog, their individual faces becoming clear only just below the window as they passed. Their collective breath steaming above them was indistinguishable from the winter pall as they ambled along the main avenue of the capital in near silence, flicking their tails and swaying their heavy necks. Their horned heads and moving backs filled Nixon's vision in every direction, so thickly were they packed, shoulder to shoulder in the street. Singing to them were their drivers, some walking, some on horseback, flailing their goads and poking at stragglers or those beasts who veered from a forward direction. Nixon's mind journeyed from the hotel window down to a single beige cow. He could imagine the smooth wet hair on her stout neck, the coarse ridge of poll between the horns, and the velvet ear laced with pink veins, and he could see into the long-lashed brown eye, sparked with life by the tiny square of light that resided there, reflecting back the shape of the window he stood in.

"To feed the army," Frank said, turning away from the window and placing a brief ambiguous gaze on Nixon's face.

How brave he is, Nixon thought, not to describe Frank's endurance of battle or illness, but his silence. All his life Nixon expected love would feel like joy, but now he was not so sure. Perhaps love, like death, was a thing one suffered.

Frank had surrendered his trunk at the provost marshall's office the day before, to be shipped directly to the camp in Virginia. He'd retained his knapsack, however, which carried his wool and India rubber blankets and an extra pair of shoes. As with nearly every soldier's bundle, Frank's pack had a tin cup fastened by its handle to it. The hollow echo of this cup sounded as Frank shifted the knapsack from the floor to his lap and tightened its straps.

Outside in the raw cold, tangled in the mist, the herd of animals plodded along, their dragging hooves and rattling rings now audible along with the beautiful voices singing them to their deaths. Nixon sought again the cow he'd studied the moment before, but realized with near-panic he could not tell them apart. With this, his self-control slipped away from him. Tears formed behind his eyes, and he lifted his hand to his face in an instinctive gesture to check or hide them.

"For God's sake, Frank," Nixon pleaded, "you must preserve yourself."

Frank let the knapsack slide down and rest on the floor between his booted ankles and set his eyes openly on his friend once again. "I intend to," he replied. And Nixon believed him.

One day in late February, Jed's bulldog face did not await Nixon on his usual visit to Caroline Crowninshield's. Rather than finding the little pup peeping from the window curtains, Nixon instead found him dancing on his hind legs around the skirts of another visitor.

A young woman near his own age was calling and was stooped in the vestibule with her arm outstretched toward the playful dog. She was attired in a fashionable dress of pale green that contrasted strikingly with her russet hair. Caroline Crowninshield stood alongside, with Katy the housemaid bearing the overcoat of the visitor who appeared to be departing.

Nixon had the discomforting feeling he was about to be the object of an attempt at matchmaking. Although not a common occurrence, it always made him awkward. As a single man from a family of substantial means, he was sometimes coaxed into the presence of daughters or asked to fill the empty place at a dinner that needed rounding out. Because he was the male heir of a family not well known in Boston, usually the daughters were plain and the dinners of a modest sort. Caroline Crowninshield's visitor was not awfully attractive and Nixon silently sighed.

Women were a puzzle. Often full of affectation and silliness, they never said what they really meant, yet once a woman had your arm you were suddenly under a compulsion to find out. There was always an unspoken obligation. It was oblique and tiresome, and in time Nixon managed ways to resist their entreaties. Mothers, however, were a persistent lot, and he occasionally found himself the target of the shy girl thrust into his presence at a dance, or the elder sister with yellow teeth plopped next to him at a long supper. It was through this invisible insistence he learned another lesson about life.

Disappointed, because Caroline Crowninshield had never subjected him to this sort of thing, he approached the women and readied himself for their pounce. As he stepped close enough for speaking, the young visitor rose from her attentions to Jed. In rising she made a small gesture Nixon was quick to notice, placing her hand at her lower side and cupping her abdomen slightly. She was pregnant, Nixon was sure of it, and thus married, an opinion quickly confirmed when he noticed the flash of a wedding ring on her fluttering left hand. He noticed too, as Katy slipped the overcoat over the lady's shoulders, the waist of the striking green dress had been taken out a bit more than was fashionable, by a talented seamstress. He was safe.

Despite her probable pregnancy, the young woman was tiny, as thin and insubstantial as a whisper. She was not beautiful, nor even very pretty, her greatest flaw being a crooked little mouth that looked bitter even when she smiled. Yet her small stone-white face had a pair of lively eyes, which suggested a fierce inner life and a nimble mind.

"Mrs. Gardner," Caroline Crowninshield said, "may I introduce Mr. Nixon Black." Nixon stepped forward and extended his hand. "Mr. Black," she continued, "is from Maine but now lives in Boston and is a great friend of Frank."

"I see." Mrs. Gardner spoke for the first time, in a pleasant voice. The corners of Mrs. Gardner's mouth curled upward in a barely perceptible mirthful twist, but her eyes raked Nixon from head to toe, in a way that made him feel he'd been struck. He stepped back on one heel and bowed politely but felt flustered and exposed in this woman's gaze, which remained warm and amiable. Somehow, this diminutive stranger had effortlessly lifted him to her eyes in examination, as though to get a closer look at him, as an object of curiosity, amusement, or merely something new. Was Mrs. Gardner mocking him? He studied her pale face, her carefully chosen clothing. No, he decided, she was not.

"Frank's friend," Mrs. Gardner said with a playful smile. "Then I had best be on my way, as you two have a subject you are both eager to talk about."

Once Mrs. Gardner had taken her leave, Caroline explained her.

"Her name is Isabella. She's Jack Gardner's wife and lives just across the street," Caroline said, offering Nixon a chair at the tea table the two women had just left. "She is to have a child soon."

"I discerned that," Nixon said.

"She visits often, quite spontaneously. I think she is lonely."

"She does not seem lonely," Nixon answered, still squirming from the young woman's mysterious scrutiny.

"Perhaps it is because I have no daughters," Caroline said, puzzling the question herself.

"I do not take your meaning?"

"She comes from New York. Do you know how many Boston girls had their hearts set on Jack Gardner?"

Nixon relaxed at Caroline's words. She'd answered his discomfort for him. What Isabella Gardner recognized in him was that they were both outsiders.

"At any rate," Caroline said, erupting in a smile as mischievous as that of Mrs. Gardner, "she was correct, I do have something to tell you. Frank has confessed his use of your nightshirt."

Nixon's heart jumped, and for a convulsive moment he fought back panic. In the month since his return from Washington, he'd suppressed the shame he felt in keeping Frank's illness a secret from his mother. He had not even noticed his missing nightshirt himself, until unpacking on his return. He'd given it no thought on the morning of his parting from Frank in the Kirkwood House. What could Caroline Crowninshield possibly know of it, and why? His brain scrambled for an explanation as Caroline slid a folded letter from inside a book that lay on the table. She searched through Frank's handwriting, seeking a certain passage, and snuggled down into her chair, beaming with delight as she prepared to begin reading. Why ever could she be laughing? What did Frank write? Nixon wondered, squirming in dread in his seat.

Dear Mother,

We arrived at General Slocum's headquarters, which we have been ordered to guard, at a rather unfortunate time as far as weather was concerned. It has snowed three days and rained two, so I have had rather a disgusting time of it. I managed to hook (we never steal in the army, we hook or take) a stove from General Slocum's quarters, which I put in my tent and for a day or two got along tolerably well, but the wicked never prosper. On the third day, in the midst of a snow storm, it caught the tent on fire and burnt the whole front off. Misery stared me in the face, and cold also, but I managed to remedy the evil by means of a nightshirt of Nixon's which by some means or other I managed to bring away with me. I'm afraid he won't see the joke when he learns it also caught fire and was consumed, but by the time that second misfortune came upon me the weather had cleared. I immediately returned the stove whence it came, and concluded to lead a better life and steal no more."

Nixon's heart felt raw. His hands, which he'd folded across his chest to conceal their shaking, were clutching at his ribs. His palms were itching. Caroline Crowninshield laid her head back and covered her mouth in laughter.

"Nixon! I think Isabella Gardner has turned your head as well," she joked. "You haven't stopped blushing since you stepped inside the house."

A Bad Place to Grow Good In
1863-1865

Frank had been away for nearly three weeks before Nixon received his own letter from him. During this period of silence, Nixon's mind was kindled into a thousand imaginings, the worst of which involved Frank's rejection. Perhaps too much had been revealed. The long days seemed blurred and ill-defined, and he moved like a sleepwalker through them. When the letter finally arrived Nixon did not open it at once but sat holding it a long time, so sure was he that its contents would undo him.

> February 14, 1863
>
> Dear Nix,
>
> I received your letter just after I arrived and should have answered it sooner, but I have been busy looking after my company which has been in a beastly state of intoxication ever since pay day. The men were inclined to take advantage of me when I first came back, but I rather think I have convinced them it won't do. At least I hope so, they have been very quiet all day.
>
> Since I returned we have been having a pretty rough time. There was a great deal of picket duty and the very worst of weather. The thermometer went down to zero or thereabouts which is very cold for these parts. But now our regiment has been chosen bodyguard to Major General Slocum. I was much pleased at being chosen for this as it relieves me from all picket

and guard duty. There will probably be some provost and fatigue duty to perform but that will be nothing to speak of as it calls for no night work. It is altogether too cold for that sort of thing.

You have heard, I suppose, that Captain Rob Shaw is to take command of a Negro regiment. It took us all by surprise. I know it did me. Bill Perkins, brother to Rob of our class, will take a place in my company. I think I shall like this arrangement very much. He is, as you know, much more reliable than his brother.

Just think, I found my old brandy flask! One of the officers found it after the battle of Antietam and kept it for me.

Your friend,

Frank

Nixon refolded the page and replaced it within its envelope. He then doubled the envelope once again, pushing the crease tightly between his fingers. He stood, crossed the room, and dropped it into the fire. It was the only one of Frank's letters he'd ever burned. Otherwise he knew he would never give up trying to read something between the lines.

In what had already been a year of astonishments, another was about to come. In late March, on the first day of warmth when one could smell the thawing earth, and clusters of small birds began foraging in the grass on the Common, Caroline Crowninshield came calling at 81 Mt. Vernon Street.

Entering the front hallway, she gave Nixon a sly smile, enjoying his surprise at her appearance. Although she'd known Nixon more than two years, hosted his visits to her home, and encouraged his friendship with her sons, she'd never become acquainted with Nixon's family. Social custom dictated she make the opening gesture to newcomers, and Nixon understood the favor she was paying him by making this call. He wondered briefly if her visit had been requested by Frank, but it was no matter. Once Caroline Crowninshield passed their threshold, the rest of Boston would follow. His mother and sisters would now have visitors in abundance.

By chance, the women of the household were out shopping, and Caroline arrived to greet only Nixon and his father, home from their office early. As introductions were made, Nixon watched with wonder to see his father shrivel in Mrs. Crowninshield's presence. The elder man spoke with uneasiness, and Nixon knew at once he would have to lead. For the first time in his life he saw his father at a loss, and Nixon stepped ahead to take charge.

After a few moments of small talk and promises made for a future call to meet the women of Nixon's household, Caroline Crowninshield said good-bye and left. George Sr. dropped himself into a parlor chair and faced the small, bright fire glowing in the grate. An hour later, Nixon found his father still sitting there, the tips of his fingers placed together just beneath his nose, in a sort of praying gesture, opening and closing them slowly.

Nixon was pleased Mrs. Crowninshield was finally introduced to his family and felt a measure of pride in having been able to provide his mother with this success he knew only he'd been capable of gaining. He was, however, less pleased with the visits themselves, preferring to have Caroline Crowninshield to himself. His visits to her home on Beacon Street continued, but he made himself absent from many of the calls she made to his mother and sisters at their home, leaving the girls to devour her alone.

He'd fallen into a habit of spending afternoons and evenings in a new way. Finding his time at home stifling and remembering the wonderful evening he and Frank spent at the theater, Nixon began to attend other performances. It was no time before he began frequenting the cultural district. The Boston Museum and the brand new Tremont Theatre each had a unique allure, but he found the most comfort at the Howard Athenaeum. Sitting in the darkness, he could hear the beautiful voices of the opera they called *bel canto*. Here alone, for the price of a ticket, he could close his eyes unobserved and listen, dream, or weep.

Other pleasures beckoned in the picture galleries around Washington Street, at William and Everett's or at the artist's receptions in the Studio Building nearby. There he found another sort of passion on display, frozen moments of a thousand emotions, requiring no explanation or solution, only contemplation. Nixon marveled at the skill and beauty of the many paintings, which he found soothed him and gave his heart a place to settle.

On such a solitary excursion he stepped into a gallery on a rain-splattered spring afternoon. The drab light did little to illuminate the two ponderous rooms, whose walls were painted a dark crimson and whose high ceilings crowned rows of paintings stacked tightly upon them. Wooden floors creaked and gas lamps sizzled in a stale air that smelled of turpentine and varnish. Nixon brushed against a broad table piled with ribbon-tied folios of proofs and etchings, accidentally knocking one out of its alignment of display. After returning it to its place he noticed a young man in the far gallery standing before a large canvas.

The man resembled Frank to a striking degree. Although the stranger had his back to him, there was no doubt he was a soldier. Nixon recognized the way the man held his body, with the straightforward set of the shoulders and every readiness for movement, but the inclination to conserve it. He could see it in the resigned curve of his torso, forever shaped by the hard lessons of exhaustion. The man even possessed a soldier's brashness, his overcoat draped with studied indifference over his shoulders.

As Nixon moved closer to the man he saw he was pondering a large painting of a Union drummer boy, a cherubic dark-haired lad with one arm raising a drumstick. He noticed too the young soldier's soft blond hair curling over his collar's edge, lovely in this gentle light. Nixon remembered Frank's hair then, the smell of it against his face, and shivered with the intimacy of the memory. What would be the sequel to their night at the Kirkwood House?

In his reverie Nixon stepped too close to the man, and realizing his presence the stranger, caught unawares, startled and stepped back.

"I'm sorry, sir," the young soldier said, "I didn't mean to crowd the view."

Nixon did not speak but made a gesture with his hand of unconcern, and then noticed with horror that the overcoat was not draped gallantly across the man's shoulders for effect. The sleeve that seemed to dangle nonchalantly contained no arm, and a scarred and furrowed trail of flesh crept up the man's neck and across his jaw to a puckered, sightless eye.

Ashamed, Nixon stumbled back, stuttered an apology, and hastened away. What would be the sequel to the night with Frank? What would be the sequel to any of this?

When Frank returned to Boston in July, after receiving a third wound during the battle at Gettysburg, Nixon was surprised at the insouciance he displayed on his arrival. Ranked as a captain now, Frank had his right arm bandaged, but his left hand clasped a lit cigar. He stepped down from the train jauntily, at least twenty pounds heavier than he'd been in January, and gestured, lifting his sling like a flapping bird's wing. "I begin to think they mean to kill me in the end," he said with a smirk.

He headed directly to Nahant, where he occupied the porch chaise once more, apologizing to his mother for troubling her again during the summer. Despite his dismissal of his injuries, they were the most serious he'd incurred yet. The bullet in Gettysburg had entered his arm just above the wrist, spiraled around the bones inside and burst out near his shoulder, leaving him unable to move his fingers. Frank listened carefully to Dr. Warren's admonitions that he keep the limb still and elevated on a side table next to his chosen seat.

Here Nixon visited Frank, finding him splayed in the comfortable chair like some magnificent beast which, having run for miles in the forest, had then thrown itself down in exhaustion. Frank's good arm was laid across his chest in a vulnerable curve, and his face tucked in his collar was soft with sleep. An open book lay on Frank's lap and the light seaside breeze occasionally turned its pages. Nixon leaned over him and retrieved the book as Caroline Crowninshield brought over a tray with glasses and a pitcher of lemonade.

Frank sensed the movement and opened his drowsy eyes to Nixon and his mother standing indistinctly beside him. He closed them again and listened to the sea scouring the rocks far below the cottage. The sound comforted him, as though something were being cleaned with each wave. He counted these waves for awhile, thinking of Nixon, pleased his friend was sitting with him, pleased Nixon knew to be quiet and let his nearness replace speech. For a moment Frank thought he heard Nixon's voice, but the sound was insects—bees, he supposed—crawling in the white flowers that climbed the trellis on the end of the cottage. Caroline gently closed the porch door, and Frank heard the soft shifting of the melting ice in the pitcher.

Nixon found everything to admire in Frank's silence. He'd heard the rumor that Frank had suffered greatly after Winchester, how his friend had lain undiscovered in an ambulance for two days after the battle, pinned beneath the bodies of other dead and dying men. Nixon would never know if this was true. Frank would never speak of it. Still, small confessions sometimes emerged. "Shells do make a fiendish noise," Frank once said, and Nixon knew Frank preserved a bullet that had struck him harmlessly in the chest at Chancellorsville after being deflected by a tree. "Had it not been for that tree," Frank would say, turning the bullet over and over in his fingers, "it would have been all over for Captain Crowninshield."

Nixon wondered if Frank dreamt of the war or had nightmares as soldiers were sometimes said to do. Nixon set his empty lemonade glass on the table and watched as Frank's chest rose and fell in its deep, healing sleep. In the corner of his eye, he noticed Caroline's figure inside the house, pausing by the window to look out at them with an expression of peace and longing.

Frank found his way to his dreams through a pathway of pain. Today, his sleep took the route of a corkscrew tunnel, moving up his arm and sliding out of the hurt as if it were a too-tight jacket entering a colorful, singular world where sensation of that kind was muted.

He emerged, disembodied, into a great bafflement of white air. It hovered like fog or swirling snow, but Frank knew it was a low-slung bank of war smoke verging a battle. Peering into its depths he perceived a shadow that wavered like a dark flag, and despite hesitation Frank could not restrain himself from walking forward.

It was not a good decision. He found himself in a dense undergrowth. Briars seized his boots and ankles and branches lashed his face. He heard the shifting and breathing of men all around him, fumbling with cartridge boxes, nestling themselves in readiness. What was a dim fog now became an acrid smoke hiding furtive shadows in the woods, revealing their presence only with small orange flashes which he understood were aimed at the skirmishers. He studied his own position and found that he and his men were immediately under the flag in the most exposed place possible. They all seemed to know it and lay quiet, some chewing the discarded ends of their paper cartridges as they brought their hammers to full cock.

The enemy came in a great seething, with wild shrieks, driving in the skirmishers. Bullets whined through the thin trees, shattering them to pieces and spewing bark and leaves. Frank had never heard such a fire in his life. It was a perfect din of musketry, and the way the bullets and grape hummed was a caution. From behind, the leviathans of their own artillery were growling like a host from hell, pitching screaming shells into the enemy distance. Not all the cacophony was from weaponry. The air was filled with cries of men, appeals, oaths, prayers, and cheers. Frank drew his sword and ran along the lines of the men, hoping they could hear him as he spat out commands, his throat burning with salt-peter, doing all he could to persuade and preserve them.

Another regiment appeared, to their relief, running at the dou-ble-quick through the thickening smoke, and Frank saw two of the men shelled into extinction, dissolved into bits. He'd seen many men die, tossed to the ground like groaning sacks. He had seen their faces after battles, this one looking indifferent, this one angry, this one surprised. At first, he prayed such deaths were merely random, that there was no plan or reason for them. Later, when he let himself consider they were not random, he stopped himself thinking about it. Making war was one thing, but such speculation was unendurable.

Frank prowled the line, coaxing and encouraging the men, their faces running with sweat and blackened with soot. They pounded cartridges into their rifle barrels, loading and firing, ramrods clanging like the workings of some devilish engine. At all times he kept his own eyes vigilant. Grass was burning in several places, in some spots smouldering blankets and in others sheeted flame. This grey cloaking made it nearly impossible to see, creating endless darkness. Hours passed, or minutes, one never knew which. Light shifted, nothing stood steadfast, distances lengthened or entirely disappeared. Bullets blasted clots of dirt around him, or flew so close they left a ringing in his ears. The authority of the sound was such that it almost became silence.

He saw the puny sapling explode at the same time he felt the sharp jab in his chest. It felt no different than the poke of the bony finger of a punishing schoolmaster, but the force of it sent him tumbling backward into the turbid air. He wondered, indifferently, if he would be trampled, and then, if he were dead. He fingered his jacket front and found the hot bullet buried harmlessly in the fabric. A moment later, another soldier slid down on his belly next to him, rustling the leaves around his head. Frank could see the man speaking earnestly, reassuringly, but he did not know what he was saying.

Focusing his eyes on the soldier's face, he found familiarity. It was Lars from the 3rd Wisconsin, the best baseball player in the camp. He was a gangly Swede with hands big enough to conceal a whole baseball, and Frank had never been able to understand his heavily accented English but felt the sting of his tag-outs many times. Now, in a language foreign to Frank's ears, the western farm boy was telling him he was unhurt. A fact he already knew, clutching the spent bullet in his quivering hands. The situation suddenly struck him as comic and he started to laugh. He could not stop, lying on his back and howling at the beautiful sky, which could be seen now in the thinning smoke, patches of grey torn from the air to reveal the light.

Nixon pulled his eyes from the glittering horizon in Nahant when Frank stirred in his chair. He watched Frank's elbow slide to his side and his sleeping hand pluck awkwardly at his shirt front. *He must have nightmares,* Nixon thought. Frank sighed, opened his eyes lethargically, and adjusted his bandaged arm to a more comfortable place on the table. He smiled broadly and stretched the rest of his body like a pleased cat.

"I think I'm cut out to be a soldier," Frank said.

Nixon smiled in return but was puzzled. He wondered if Frank truly liked being a soldier, or if he loved the war because thus far, he had cheated death.

Ellsworth seemed smaller than when he'd left, dreary and hard-bitten, a place of disappointment. The distance between one end of the town and another, which in childhood had seemed so large, now was a short walk. Passing his old home on Main Street, Nixon imagined its interiors, allowing himself to linger in memory. Here was the window where he talked with Henry late on summer nights, there were the stable doors that closed every evening on Lucy and the little dog asleep in the hay. Instead of nostalgia, however, detachment grew as he looked around him. He was no longer from here. Even the chamber at Grandfather's house, where he was staying, seemed foreign, as he'd rarely slept there before.

The weather this early October was warm and generous, though, and Franny as dear as ever. Perhaps she was a bit thinner, and certainly older than in his youth, but a more affable and composed woman would be difficult to find. Nixon supposed Franny was nearly the same age as the century, somewhere in her early sixties, but he nonetheless found an easy sympathy with her, and they chattered and gossiped at length without noticing the difference in their years. He knew she was a safe repository for any confidence as she had the great gift of good sense and an unflinching quality that made him easeful.

These days his father often sent him to Maine to check on lumber inventories, or to get papers filed or signed. As these trips required staying with Franny at Woodlawn, where she'd lived alone since his grandfather died, Nixon generally looked forward to them. Still, he suspected he was sent so his father could avoid confrontations with his brothers, who still nourished their dislike for him. Nixon saw these uncles—Alexander, Charles, and William—infrequently, but during their inevitable encounters on the streets of Ellsworth, their attitude was sullen enough that Nixon spoke and behaved carefully. Though none of these uncles pursued careers of their own with any vigor, Nixon realized that news of his father's successes in Boston would be met with further bitterness. It was awkward, and Nixon admired Franny for her determination to live in a town where she was treated by many as an outcast. He even went so far as to consider her brave. Ellsworth was not the place to be an outcast.

After an afternoon at the mill assessing lumber, Nixon came into the great brick house and found Franny in her accustomed spot in the library. It was not as grand a library as those in some Boston homes, nor did it house nearly as many books as the shelves at the Crowninshields', but it was an intimate, comfortable room perfectly suited to Franny. She often sat there reading, her mind concentrated on the Bible or one of the other volumes, or writing letters at the pretty French desk between the windows overlooking the back fields and barns.

Today she wore a dress the color of pewter and a fringed square of jacinth-toned challis wound around her shoulders, despite the heat from the low fire in the grate. Her hands, resting in her lap, held a loosely folded paper.

"I have a letter from Agnes," she said. "It seems your sister is enjoying her singing lessons."

"She has a beautiful voice," Nixon assented, "which, of course, I do not tell her, lest it go to her head."

"Perhaps her new interest will replace Richard Sears in her thoughts. Until today, her letters were full of him. You'd think she was Richard's sweetheart rather than Marianne."

"Her smash on Richard is quite complete," Nixon agreed. "But the poor girl sees him nearly every day. I confess I don't understand why Marianne and Richard don't marry."

"Marianne has her health to consider," Franny said, placing the letter in a corner of her desk.

"Mrs. Crowninshield says she could be in danger if she were with child."

Franny raised her eyes above the spectacles she wore for reading and regarded Nixon with the quiver of a smile. "You and Mrs. Crowninshield are on very intimate speaking terms, I should think."

Nixon rolled his eyes and sighed. "She is much like you, Franny. I find I can talk to her. I just wish Marianne and Richard would make the leap. Marianne's fate is not written in stone. We all love Richard as much as Agnes does. Even Father seems to have warmed to him."

Franny absorbed this information with interest. "And your mother?" she asked.

"Oh, you know how silent Mother is, but she's delighted with Richard's visits. Everyone looks forward to him."

Franny sat quietly for a long moment, fingering the watch attached to the long chain around her neck. "I daresay your parents feel more comfortable with the entire family together in these times."

"We can't all live at home forever," Nixon grumbled.

"How is Mrs. Crowninshield?" Franny asked, tucking her spectacles into her reticule and notably changing the subject.

"Fretting over Frank, who is in a rush to return to his regiment in Tennessee and reenlist for three more years."

"Is his arm well enough?" Franny asked.

"He says so, though I know he cannot yet stretch it out straight."

"He is determined then," Franny said.

"Yes, which makes me feel all the more useless," Nixon replied. Franny frowned in question, but Nixon continued. "Frank did little better at Harvard than I did, but he's at least spent the last years bravely. I have spent the war talking with women in their parlors."

"Nixon, you are engaged in your family business, just as Frank's elder brother, Ned, is."

"It is hardly the same," Nixon scoffed. "Ned makes his own decisions. I do what Father tells me, and go where I am sent. I've been all day counting lumber that could have been counted by any of the men here."

"You are acting as your father's eyes and ears," Franny said.

"As though I even know what I am looking or listening for," Nixon complained.

"You are the only son, following your father's wishes, and our victory depends on business," Franny answered. "No one expects more of you."

"I expect more of myself than that," Nixon said.

Nixon saw Franny's impatience with him. She stiffened and raised her chin. Outside the leaves on the trees swayed heavily, awaiting the first cold wind to drive them to the ground. Even now, the room was darkening, foretelling months of early night. Franny's eyes were fastened on him, fierce even in dimming light. She sat forward in her chair and with her long fingers pulled the shawl tightly around her, its deep orange color like the fire's glowing coals. The moment felt like some kind of enchantment.

"You must know yourself, Nixon," Franny said quietly. "What you wish to do and what you can do will almost always be different things.

If you know yourself, you will make the right choices. In my own life, some people have said I am one thing, some another. If I'd not known myself, I would have lost my balance long ago."

Nixon knew Franny was not giving advice so much as recounting a lesson from the sharp edge of her own experience. He watched her in admiration; she seemed so still and complete. A burning log collapsed in the fireplace with a soft crystalline sound, and Nixon saw her eyes had grown very tender.

"I should tell you," she said. "Henry has joined the army."

Nixon's heart twisted in fear and then in shame. Henry, who still lived in his mind as a boy, was to be sent off and possibly killed. Images of his cousin on the riverbank at the log drive and building their snow fort filtered through his mind. Nixon leaned forward and placed his fingertips over his closed eyes. "When?" he asked, not moving his hands from his face.

"Last month, as I understand. He signed on as a substitute for one of the Greeley boys, into the 3rd Maine Infantry."

"What does Uncle Alex think of his son doing this?" Nixon asked.

"I don't know that Alex had any say in it. Henry's been farming downstate in Belfast all year."

"Farming?" Nixon questioned, raising his head from his hands. Henry was such a clever boy, Nixon always imagined his cousin would be more successful than him. Perhaps off to Bowdoin or another college by now. Signing on as a substitute meant Henry received extra money to enlist. Did Henry need money?

"Hasn't Uncle Alex seen to Henry's future?" Nixon asked.

"I don't know," Franny answered. "I would be the last to know."

"What is wrong with Uncle Alex?" Nixon said loudly. "I cannot understand him."

"Let me tell you, Nixon," Franny began in a tone that implied a long explanation. "When Henry was born, his mother died as a result of having him. It was childbed fever, and she suffered terribly. Alex was bereft, and left alone with newborn Henry and his sister, who was only four. It was more than any man could handle alone, and Alex came back here to Woodlawn and lived for a time with your grandparents. John and Mary were glad to care for them. Alex became close to his mother. She helped him through his crisis and grief."

"And he hated you when you replaced her?" Nixon asked.

"It is the reason I have given myself to explain him," Franny said.

Nixon snorted in disdain. "What of Uncle William and Uncle Charles then? What are their reasons?"

Franny shrugged and shook her head. "Your father was always the most capable of the brothers."

"Is that a reason to shun him?" Nixon sneered.

"Evidently," Franny said sadly.

When supper was cleared, the lamps extinguished, and the house lay in the hush of night, Nixon stood by the windows where his grandfather once kept watch. He knew the view by heart, even in the darkness, across the broad lawn and to the river. A movement on the grass suggested a deer had come out in the moonlight to feed, but it was only a dog loping in his long moon-shadow, returning from some tracking excursion to the town. For a moment the dog paused, and Nixon imagined it looked back with canine eyes to the front of the darkened house, but it continued trotting along, random and indifferent.

Would Henry and Frank survive? Would he forever regret not joining them? It seemed impossible that peace would ever return or the world again be righted. A bit of Franny's rectitude had rubbed off on him. Every man had to choose, he supposed; and once the choice was made, one thing perhaps warded off another.

He watched as the dog reached the stone wall at the edge of the property, leapt over it, and disappeared into the brush. Now Nixon knew his father had made hard choices too, and Nixon pondered for the first time what those choices must have cost him.

April 12, 1864
Tullahoma, Tennessee
Dear Nix,
We are still at Tullahoma, and I think we will remain here sometime longer. There is a great excitement about the change in corps commanders. We are to be consolidated with that cowardly Eleventh Corps who dis-

graced themselves running away at Chancellorsville and did not do much better at Gettysburg, though they got credit for a great deal. The two corps united are to be called the 1st Corps. It was the greatest relief to us to know we are not to be called the 11th. There is also a report we are to be consolidated with the 33rd Mass. which made us feel very blue, but with these and what other recruits we get, we will at least retain our officers and organization. Many of the new men are a horrible set of fellows, but in order to fill quotas they take what they can get. It is not what it was when we started out.

General Slocum is to leave us, and we look upon his departure as the worst thing that could happen to us. He was especially well regarded in our regiment from the fact he would have nothing to do with newspaper reporters and such men.

Last week the officers of the second went with the brigade band and serenaded him. We were joined by nearly all the officers of this post. The general seemed much overcome, the tears actually came to his eyes when he spoke about leaving us. He then invited us into the house where he had drinkables of all descriptions. I passed a very pleasant evening.

The consolidation of the corps will probably cause a change in the divisions and brigades but what that is to be, nobody knows. Could you buy and send me another star such as I have worn on my caps? We do intend to keep the old badge.

Just think, in another month I shall be twenty-one years old. As mother would say, "I am old enough to be better." It is true enough, but the army, I am more and more convinced, is a bad place to grow good in. If you hold your own, you are lucky.

Your friend,

Frank

Everything was different since the 3rd Maine Infantry had transferred to the 17th in June of 1864. If they had enough men they might have kept on as before, but since so many of the early volunteers had served their time and mustered out, too few were left to to sustain it. Moses Brown, who had joined less than a year earlier, was one of the 129 men required to switch.

In the month before the transfer it seemed the government had every intention of getting its money's worth out of men with only days left to serve. Moses and his fellows in the 3rd Maine had done nothing but march, dig, and shoot, passing through the terrible battles at the Wilderness, Spotsylvania Court House, and Cold Harbor. Huddled together night and day, fighting from wet stinking ditches they'd hastily dug—sometimes turning up bones of soldiers who'd fought on the same ground years before them—the men prayed the battles would end. Now, as members of the 17th, they may have regretted what they prayed for.

Moses was a lumberman from Bangor, twenty-four years old, who before the war worked winters in logging camps and summers in the sawmills. Born in New Brunswick, his father was an Irishman, but his mother was of French stock and came from Quebec near Three Rivers. It was she who passed on to her son his good spirits as well as his thick head of dark brown hair. She named Moses after her grandfather, a famous voyageur. His mother had died of typhoid fever when he was a boy, and though he tried, he could not recall her. He was named for a man he never knew by a woman he could not remember.

Now, as far from the Maine woods as he was from the memory of his mother, he felt nothing but dread. After an order to march to Petersburg, they had blundered their chance to take it, and Moses and the other men grumbled as they saw what could have been a great victory thwarted because they were poorly managed. Now in the first part of July 1864, Moses found himself at the center of the Union lines along the Jerusalem Plank Road, south of Petersburg, digging and dodging bullets in the blazing Virginia sun.

Here the 17th Maine was digging zigzag trenches and building dugouts and bombproofs against an enemy who were so close in their own trenches Moses could hear them talking. Sharpshooters in both armies plied their deadly trade. Exposing any part of your body above the parapets was imprudent in the extreme. The heat was intense, and the dust suffocating. The landscape resembled hell. No wind stirred and heat rose in waves from a barren desert, denuded of any plants or trees. Shovel handles and gun barrels left in the sun would burn your hands. Rest, when possible, was interrupted by swarms of ticks and biting flies. Water of any kind was a long walk away.

It was during a water run Moses noticed something wrong with Henry Black. Moses and Henry mustered in the army on the same week and in the same place. Moses liked Henry and felt like an older brother to him, as there was some innocence left in the younger man. Henry had a gentle face, curious and boyish, somehow unspoiled by all he'd seen and done.

Their kinship was also based on what they had in common. Although they'd not exchanged much in the way of confidences, Moses knew Henry had lived in Ellsworth, and although he was farming when he joined the army, Henry could talk to Moses about logging. On the long evenings of the past nine months of their service together, they'd swapped tales of what they knew of the lumber camps and the river drives of home.

Early on, Moses wondered if this Henry Black in uniform was a relative of the famous John Black, the legendary Midas of all the lumber trade in Maine. When Henry admitted he was a grandson of the great man Moses could not help but ask the obvious question.

"Why didn't you buy your way out of this contention?" he asked, genuinely curious.

"My grandfather is dead," Henry replied succinctly, "and my father and I don't have that sort of arrangement."

Moses never pressed the point. It wasn't his place. Nor did he really care. He and Henry looked out for one another. Their conversations about home relaxed them both. Neither man wanted a confessor, just someone to talk with about how things were.

The nearest stream was half a mile off. The men, by their own agreement, took turns fetching filled canteens for the entire group. It had been an hour since Henry loped off, just after noontime, hitching through the dusty warren of trenches with a dozen canteens looped over his shoulders. He should have returned by now. Moses, who was playing cards with Ben Clifford who cheated, and Jere Atkins who didn't, found his eye wandering more frequently to the angle in the trench where Henry should appear than watching Ben.

When Henry did stumble around the corner, he looked lost. The trenches were a maze, but Henry suddenly slumped to the ground. The canteens he carried were still empty and Henry's clothing was wet with more sweat than even the terrible heat of the day dictated. He was shivering and would not speak.

"He's got the shakes," Jere observed. "Shall we fetch the doctor?"

"They'll just dose him with quinine, and that will make him deaf for a week," Moses said. "Let's get him under cover and let him rest."

In their area the men draped their shelter tents over scantling that spanned the narrow width of the trench. It afforded at least some shade from the sun, and with it a degree or two of coolness. Ben set off again with the canteens, and Jere helped Moses move Henry under these shelters nearby where they'd been playing cards.

Most of the digging was done at night. Had they attempted it during the day, too many men would have been exposed to picket fire and snipers. During the day the men rested as best they could, read, talked, made minor repairs to their works, and waited. The sun withered everyone into a state of inertia, and things were generally quiet in the afternoon. Their card game broken up, Jere and Moses curled on top of their blankets for a nap.

It was about three o'clock when Moses was awakened by a beam of sunlight, burning through a tear in his canvas roof and striking his eye. Jere had apparently already woken and gone off. Moses rose and walked to Henry's shelter to check on him. Henry was sleeping fitfully and sweating heavily. To Moses' disgust, he saw Henry's closed eyes were covered with a dozen flies, feeding off the moisture gathering there. Moses always covered his own head beneath his cap with a square of wet cloth to help keep cool. He now removed the square and wet it from his newly filled canteen. He placed the damp cloth over Henry's eyes to protect them from the flies. Then he walked slowly to his shelter and removed his shirt. While sleeping he'd been bitten by insects under his arm. He sat cross-legged in the dust, picking lice from the seams of the shirt and killing them between his fingernails.

After a short while, Moses sensed movement beneath Henry's shelter. He saw Henry rise slowly, pull at the cloth covering his face, and cast it on the ground. His eyes were filmy and perplexed, his face muddled. Moses watched as Henry dug deep into the side pockets of his coat and withdrew, with a curious lingering and reverent gesture, two round white objects, one in each hand. They were the onions from the Fourth of July! The ones sent especially to their regiment in barrels from Maine. Moses could not believe Henry had kept them so long. They were distributed only five days before, but most of the men who'd each received a share had gobbled them up by now, greedy for the taste of anything fresh. Moses had eaten his own days ago. *Good,* thought Moses, *Henry must be feeling better and has his appetite again.*

Henry had woken to a delicious cool sensation. Every hair on his body was alive and shivering, little bumps of flesh prickling like ice marching on a hundred thousand places on his skin. A great whiteness blinded his eyes and, realizing they were covered, he reached up and wiped the blanket of snow from his face. He'd fallen asleep in the snow cave! Around him he saw deep snowbanks and tunnels, the blinding sun in the vast sky. On the parapet the blue flag of Maine hung tattered on its pole, and he knew it was the Black Fort and Charlie Perry and Tom Stimpson were just across the field preparing for battle. He smiled and relaxed because he had his own snowballs ready. He'd saved them carefully, snowballs from Maine, hidden in his pockets. Cold and clean. He reached in to pull them out and look at them, to make sure they were still there. He handled them carefully, so they would not fall apart or melt, and he felt great joy lying back on the walls of the fort waiting for the signal for battle. He closed his eyes and allowed himself to take in the deep cold air through his trembling lungs, his head cradled in the soft arms of the snowbank, the delicate tickling feeling of snowflakes gathering on the lids of his closed eyes. But he must go. Nixon cannot do it all alone. Charlie and Tom were waiting. They were bad boys and needed to be beaten. His lashes flicked open, scattering the snowflakes that had fallen in his closed eyes as he leapt toward the wall of the snow fort.

>‑•‑<

Henry moved faster than Moses would have ever believed. He lifted his eyes from his delousing chore and Henry had already sprung to the edge of the scarp and was climbing it. *Henry is out of his head* was all Moses could reason as he dashed toward his friend shouting his name. In seconds Henry was gripping the firing step and in seconds more was thrusting himself above it. He climbed using the strength of his left arm; in his right he was clutching one of the onions he'd removed from his pocket. Moses pulled himself up on the firing step and grabbed Henry by the only thing he could reach, the hem of his pants leg, which was so rotten it promptly tore away.

"Henry! Goddammit!" Moses cried. He could not understand what Henry was doing as his young friend stood atop the parapet, one foot balanced on the headlog, with his right arm drawn back clutching the onion like a baseball he was about to pitch into the Rebel lines. Moses stared at Henry and bellowed his name. Poised to hurl the onion, Henry's face looked grim but triumphant. His lips were pulled back from his teeth like a growling dog, his skin glistened with sweat, his short hair damp in spiky wet tufts. His wiry body was poised but strangely calm, and as Moses reached up again to get ahold of a higher portion of Henry's trousers he thought he heard Jere's voice rise above the group of men gathered in the trench beneath him.

"Sniper!" someone cried. It sounded like Jere, but the sizzle of a bullet made the voice indistinct, and Moses jumped in horror as Henry's thigh came apart before him. A splash of hot blood and sharp splinters of bone splattered across Moses' face, and as he reached instinctively to ward it away he saw he was drenched with it. Henry slid down the inside of the trench on his back, headfirst to the bottom.

Henry lay still and felt his breathing coming on fast. He must have slipped or lost his footing, as his leg just seemed to give way. There was a commotion around him, but his mind could not get a fix on it, and he did not care. There was a lovely warm liquid running from his waist down his back toward his neck, slowly between his shoulder blades, as one felt water in the bath. When he squinted into the sky above he saw the clouds and the blue framed in a black rectangular box. He wanted to keep the sky and the clouds and the blue, but the box kept getting smaller. He hung on to his snowball tightly but it was getting late. Charlie and Tom must have won.

Goldsboro, North Carolina,
March 25, 1865
Dear Nix,
I am afraid I have been a poor correspondent of late, but I must plead what I have been through as an excuse.

These past campaigns are the hardest I ever went through. My leg has stood it well. At first it troubled me a good deal, but after a week on the march out of Atlanta, it ceased to bother me at all. Marching in deep mud behind wagons and cattle is not what it is cracked up to be. I footed it every inch of the way from Atlanta to Savannah to here.

We have in these campaigns accomplished wonders, and literally wiped out part of Georgia and most of South Carolina, nearly every house has been burned and everything eatable taken. We worked the whole way tearing up track and destroying fences. I couldn't help thinking how I should feel were Massachusetts treated the same way. It is a hard thing to go into a house full of women, take everything and burn the house, but we have to do it. The first time I tried it I nearly gave in to the entreaties of the women, but I have grown hard-hearted of late. I think especially that South Carolina has paid well for the trouble she has caused this nation, but not too well.

At first we had an abundance to eat but since we have been in the Carolinas we have not fared so well. We have lived on meal and ham and I am sick of the sight of both. Now we are at base, if anything can be bought I shall buy it. I am particularly in want of drawers. The pair I have on, my only ones, I have worn for a month. To say they are torn is nothing, they are ragged, and as for dirt, I can give you no idea of it.

I wish you could see me now just as I stand, I don't think you would recognize me. I will try to give you some idea of my appearance. In the first place imagine a cap, once blue now brown, with the back of it covered with grease, surmounted by a star or what was once a star, now a dingy piece of red velvet with shreds of gold lace around it. Next comes the face. Well!

It is the same old face, badly begrimed with pitch pine smoke, and badly in need of shaving; an old time-worn blouse turned from blue to a rusty brown, but still whole. Next comes trousers. If it were a possible thing I should like to send them home as a curiosity. They are covered with spots, smoked completely black, and as for tears and mends, there is no end to them. The back of the legs I burnt badly and was obliged to take them in considerably, which gives them a rather unique appearance. They have been mended partly with white and partly with black thread which adds to their remarkable appearance. I was going to describe the look of the seat of them, but unfortunately there is very little left of their original structure, it being mostly composed of odd pieces of cloth. A pair of partially burnt government shoes complete the "tout ensemble."

I shan't in this letter undertake to give you much idea of this great unparalleled campaign, but thank God it is over at last and we shall get a little rest. I suppose it will all be over soon enough. I can hardly realize there will come a day when I will go home for good and hang my sword up on the wall never to draw it more. I expect when the time comes, it will be terribly hard for me to leave the old flag that I have fought under so long.

Your friend,

Frank

It was the day of the Grand Review of the Army in Washington, but Nixon could not revel in it. It was for Frank a glorious moment, and he begged Nixon to travel south and see it. There were to be two days of triumphant parades, brass bands, heroes, and speeches. Thousands of the soldiers who'd fought so ardently were to march down Pennsylvania Avenue, rejoicing in their victory. The Union deserved such a day, and it was hoped the celebrations would begin to heal the wound left by the shocking assassination of President Lincoln last month.

Yet Nixon could not make himself attend. He knew he would stand in the street and gaze at the mute windows of the Kirkwood House. His mind would race up the stairs to the room he knew to be there, and throw open the door, but the rude beds and the battered dresser would have nothing to say to him.

Worse would be watching the soldiers. Frank would pass by and toss a wink, but to face the 17th Maine as it marched would be to see only the empty space in the row where Henry should have been, for his cousin was no longer anywhere in the world. Utterly gone, with only his name on a crumpled black-bordered telegram, and all the secret hand signals, the snow fort, and the delight of youth were gone with him.

Nixon could not join Frank, he could not rejoice or mourn with men who'd been soldiers, he could not claim any wound from the awful war. He could only continue to bear the weight of recollection.

When evening fell on that day Nixon believed his only solace could come from obliterating his memories and shrouding himself in sleep. After lying in bed for some time, he turned over on his stomach. As he'd done in childhood, he covered his back with his pillow, and discovered there was no relief in it, just as there would no longer be any relief in tears.

The Grand Tour
1865-1866

John Blanchard stumbled across the great saloon in a zigzag path to the mahogany table where Frank and Nixon sat playing cards. The three friends had set out on the steamer *Africa* five days before and had fine sailing to Halifax, but were now in the deep ocean where the waves were growing taller. Earlier in the day, the waiters had put out the table guards, which kept Frank and Nixon's card game from sliding away, and long arcs of spray could be seen through the rows of windows on either side of the elegant paneled room.

"How about a game, John?" Frank asked. "I need more players to teach euchre to Nixon."

"God, no," John answered, pushing Nixon aside and plopping beside him on the crimson velvet sofa. "I'm having adventure enough just walking."

"You do look a little fishy," Nixon observed.

"I am regretting my heavy supper," John said, "and coming to warn you the cabin stewards brought sideboards for the berths in our stateroom."

"This is good news," Frank said. "When I made this voyage as a youth, my mother was obliged to wedge me into my berth with pillows and rolled up petticoats."

"I wager you were still tossed on your head," John teased. "I have also come to warn you of something I've just read." He brought out from his pocket a small volume, marked with a delicate ivory bookmark. Frank propped his elbow on the table and covered his smile with his fist, directing his laughing eyes to Nixon.

John opened his *Murray's Guide Book* under the lamplight and cleared his throat. "When a steamboat reaches its destined port, the shore is usually beset by a crowd of clamorous agents from the different hotels, each vociferating the praises of that for which he is employed, stunning the distracted stranger with their cries, and nearly scratching his face with their proffered cards. The only mode of rescuing himself from these tormentors, is to make up his mind *beforehand* to what hotel he will go, and to name it at once." John put his book down on the table. "Don't you fellows think we ought to decide on a hotel before we arrive in Liverpool?"

Neither Frank nor Nixon immediately spoke, but Frank stifled a laugh and glanced at both friends. "I believe I'm long past the day when I worry about getting my face scratched," Frank said, "but you could consult your book and choose one for us, John. What do you think, Nixon?"

"Absolutely," Nixon said, smiling wryly at his earnest friend. "You have my complete confidence, John."

"Lights out in the saloon in half an hour," a passing steward announced, as John slid from the couch and staggered along the wall, clutching the gilt edges of the wainscot, his feet wobbly but his mind at ease.

Seeing the Cunard steamer *Africa* before boarding last week had taken Nixon's breath away. A year of delight lay before him as he anticipated the foreign tour ahead. The war over and travel resumed, he, Frank, and John were encouraged to make the grand tour most young men of their class enjoyed. Nixon felt especially fortunate to be allowed the journey. Frank was a hero of the war and John a successful graduate of Harvard, and both were expected to take a respite from their labors, but George Sr. understood the advantages of such world experience and was glad to have his son take part with other respectable young men. Nixon would return, George Sr. hoped, ready to take his own place in the adult world of men.

So it was with the thrill of anticipation Nixon walked the gangway of the *Africa* that September of 1865. In the harbor, she resembled nearly any large sailing ship, with three masts and the usual rigging retained despite her steam engine for safety and extra speed. Nearly 270 feet long, she was an elegant black ship with tiny touches of gold paint on her side paddle wheels, and the signature red and black Cunard funnel.

For Nixon, all eleven days of his journey were wondrous. While poor John was struck by seasickness for half the trip, and even Frank had to admit to little appetite until a week out, Nixon was a lucky sailor and woke daily in his narrow berth well rested and eager for his breakfast of toast, Irish stew, mutton chops, crimped cod, eggs, and coffee.

He delighted in all of it, the rolling and swelling of the sea, the strange mix of the 150 entirely observable passengers. Nixon savored the overheard bits of shipboard gossip, and the long evening twilight when one could read a book in a deck chair until as late as nine o'clock.

Nixon especially enjoyed exploring the ship, and before docking in England he'd seen it all, snooping his way through the boatswain's store, the wine cellar, and the cooking galleys where each morning the baker turned out 200 hot rolls in minutes. He even visited the cows in the cow house, responsible for the legendary bedtime mugs of hot chocolate the Cunard steamer passengers enjoyed.

One of their last nights at sea, after a rather festive supper with ample champagne, Nixon joined his friends on the deck. No smoking was allowed in the ship, so men would gather there, in the lee of the funnel to enjoy pipes and cigars. It was a beautiful night, moonless and full of stars. The waves of the deepest ocean had subsided, and the paddle wheels stirred up brilliant flashes of the mysterious blue-green light sometimes given off by the sea, trailing it in the shape of their own passage back to the faint glow of the western horizon. The men watched, mesmerized, hands in their pockets and collars upturned, the churning sound of the water a pleasing lull. Nixon did not want any of it to end.

When the time came for disembarking, the trio found they'd planned needlessly for the clamoring hotel agents. Instead they were engaged in a long search for Frank's valise, which had gone missing at the customs house and was finally located beneath supernumerary ladies' hatboxes.

Then they endured an unusually long inspection from a scrupulous customs man who sifted through their belongings with relish, if not neatness, searching for contraband.

Once released from these official clutches, they emerged to rain and an area empty of other passengers, hotel agents, or conveyances. Rather than overzealous agents, only one sullen ashcat remained. Despite their requests to go to the Adelphi Hotel, this unsavory youth led them instead to a place called the Palace, which it most definitely was not, though it was sufficient. Here they took possession of two rooms, laid their overcoats out to dry, and sprawled on the beds, exhausted.

"Say what you will about Latin," John quipped, "the Romans showed they fully appreciated the nature of luggage by designating it by the appropriate word: impedimenta."

The friends had previously agreed to part in Liverpool. John was to remain the year in England and, eager to visit the Lakes District, he would be heading north. He'd packed some stout boots and intended to do some hiking. Frank, declaring he'd hiked long enough courtesy of the Union Army, could not wait to get to the streets of the great cities. Nixon, inclined to museums and theaters himself, was to remain with Frank. John thus boarded a train to Keswick with his walking gear and his beloved volume of Wordsworth, while Nixon and Frank headed to London.

Nothing prepared Nixon for what he was to discover in the largest city he'd ever seen. London was like a great machine, rich, powered with steam, blackened with coal, abundant and earnest. Picture books led him to expect the great dome of St. Paul's; the sinister, secretive Tower; and the arches of the London Bridge. Nixon followed the trails of all tourists, gazing at the windows in the arcades of Regent Street, standing in the foggy glory of Nelson in Trafalgar Square. As many before him, he too walked reverently through the gloom of Westminster Abbey. He sauntered, drowsily, through the vast rooms of the British Museum, looking at, but not seeing, the glass cases of artifacts, the stern-faced portraits of famous personages, the displays of venerable stones. On his many forays, Nixon even discovered his own London in the lure of the

Strand and the theaters in the West End; in the many ships berthed in the rat-worried, wooden docks of the Thames; in the broad streets, the crowded horsecars, the crooked, squalid lanes that often led to a comfortable chop house and porter.

What Nixon did not expect to find in London was Boston, but the city he'd left behind was everywhere. He and Frank put up at Maurigy's Hotel. In the lobby as they arrived they met Mrs. Appleton. They collided with people from home at every turn. There were Chadwicks in Chelsea, Sohiers at Windsor, Bradlees strolling in St. James' Park. He and Frank arrived in England with an obligation to make several visits. Frank had, for instance, promised his mother they would call on his aunt and uncle Mifflin, who were en route to Italy. Yet each visit fostered two more, friends and distant relations eager to fete the young war hero, and soon the young men found their nights filled. They attended dinners and entertainments of every description, and before they boarded the steamer at Folkestone bound for France, Nixon was better known in Boston society than he'd been when he left Massachusetts.

Nixon thought Paris delightful. Here, he and Frank committed themselves to inexpensive lodgings on a quiet side street, still close to the major sites. In a matter of days they'd walked the boulevards from the Palais Royale to the Place de la Concorde a dozen times. They wandered the endless *salles* of the Louvre among the statues and old masters and enjoyed the splendid table at the Cafe Voisin.

With calm satisfaction Nixon realized he had Frank to himself. Without intending to, they had developed a fixed routine. Rising at about eleven, Frank took an hour to dress, trying on and discarding many shirts and ties before finally deciding, while Nixon drank slowly from a cooling cup of coffee. They read the papers together for another hour, and then sauntered to some cafe and breakfasted on whichever wonderful French dish Frank chose from the *carte,* teaching Nixon how to read it. Frank was partial to concoctions that included mushrooms, and for the rest of his life, whenever he confronted a French menu Nixon remembered the first word of French he'd ever learned: *champignon.*

One day as he watched Frank close his eyes, point to the menu, and choose their breakfast by blind chance, he had the startling realization that he and his friend were different. Nixon had never considered that they were not entirely alike. Now Frank seemed so taut and restless, as though he were holding a confined energy in check. While Nixon was content to stroll and observe, Frank craved action and spent afternoons at dancing lessons and making visits whenever he could. Frank's absurd sense of fun revealed itself even at the opera, a spectacle that held Nixon spellbound. One evening as three hundred actors dressed as hussars danced on stage, Frank elbowed Nixon out of his trance to roll his eyes up toward the aristocratic women in the private boxes above them, cupping his hands in front of his chest to indicate breasts. It was true the women's dresses were very low cut, but Nixon had only noticed the costumes on stage.

"They might just as well wear no tops at all," Frank joked.

Nixon knew Frank might feel dogged by his illness and eager to enjoy life, but as far as he could tell, Frank had been well since the night at the Kirkwood House. Nixon longed to ask him about his health, but the thought of confronting Frank frightened Nixon considerably. Perhaps his friend only wanted to make up for what he'd missed in the army. Separated by the war, Nixon knew Frank only as he'd envisioned him, and it was different when his friend became familiar.

While Frank danced his afternoons away, Nixon succumbed to the lure of the Parisian streets. They were, at this time of year, enchanting. Winter mists slipped through the trees and the flagstones gleamed with frost as the days leading to Christmas progressed. The boulevards were lined with small booths selling every sort of food: cheeses, balled and blocked and veined with ashes; stacks of oysters and bushels coiled with glistening eels; little chestnuts, their skins scored with an X, roasted on street corner braziers.

Most charming were the displays of *santons,* little clay figures both homely and elaborate, representing the holy family and the manger. In the twilight of Christmas Eve, Nixon was passing under the arcades on the Rue de Rivoli, peeling and munching chestnuts and gazing in the windows of the shops where these *santons* were displayed with tiny candles. Pausing before a jewelry shop, his eye fell on a window of cameos in a pretty array. He'd wanted to buy something for Frank, a gift to show how valuable his friendship was, and here were some scarf pins of exceptional workmanship. Nixon left the shop a half-hour later, stepping into darkness and a light snow, and when he entered their small hotel, it was with a small velvet box in his pocket.

On Christmas Day, after a jolly dinner and an afternoon consuming champagne frappe and bourbon whiskey punch, Frank beamed as he opened his gift.

"Is it Apollo?" he asked, running his hands over the delicate carving mounted in the little pin.

"Yes," Nixon answered. "He seemed right for you."

Thus the days in Paris slipped through their fingers, and as the calendar turned they began to think of continuing their journey. They decided to meander through France with a stop at the city of Pau, where Frank once lived with his parents while his father sought a cure for his illness.

A new railway had just opened to Pau, and as soon as they stepped down from the train, Frank led Nixon to the Haute Plat, to take in the spectacular view.

"I never expected to see snowy mountains and palm trees in the same view," Nixon said as his eyes scanned the outline of the Pyrenees down to the river below.

The following day they went on horseback to see the places Frank had known in his youth. Overnight a swirling fog descended on Pau, remarkable in the way it obliterated views and snaked like a living thing through the streets. Nixon rode a few paces behind his friend, observing the ordinary buildings, the doorways, the lace curtains. There was no past visible to him, but he watched the flickers of feeling moving beneath Frank's face. They lingered before the school Frank had once hated, and Nixon watched the warmth of pleasure on Frank's features as he pointed out a small garden where he'd helped a neighbor. When they located the house where Frank had lived, it was, he exclaimed, exactly as he remembered it, yellow painted with familiar numbers on the door, and a mist-shrouded sign still offering it for let: *Appartements meuble a louer.*

"Shall we go inside and take a look?" Nixon asked, but Frank shook his head. He'd lost his heart, Nixon knew, and held his horse back to give Frank the privacy to run his arm across his face, wiping away what Nixon saw were tears.

They followed a long wooded walk that led to the great chateau of Pau, the birthplace of Henry IV. It clung to a steep precipice, resting in the mist like a sleeping bird, weathered trees twisting around it like the boughs of a huge nest. They separated, each taking his horse a different way, Nixon watching Frank as he disappeared behind a wall or pillar and then reappeared, walking his horse slowly through the fog, which obscured the view of the castle walls and river below. Nixon knew his friend like a landmark and had kept Frank's secret so long he supposed there were no other secrets. They came together again, Frank approaching from behind a somber wall, the tail of his horse lashing. He was handsome and pale, with the little Apollo stickpin resting in the fabric beneath his throat, and Nixon felt the same old flood of adoration on seeing him.

Nixon turned his horse behind Frank again, but Frank circled his animal and the two began following one another in a tight circle. The moment was completely inarticulate, time vanished, traceless, leaving nothing except their rotation. The only sound was the breath of the horses and the muffled thuds of their hooves on the grass. Then Frank began to speak.

The horses moved counterclockwise head to tail, as Frank told his story. His childhood winter in Pau, the bloody death of his father, Frank's own first bleeding in the army camp at Edinburgh, and his fear of an early death. Everything he'd kept hidden at the Kirkwood House. Just as suddenly his story ended, leaving them in the finality of silence. Frank extended his hand and grasped Nixon's, and they continued circling the horses for many minutes in this way, both holding one another in their gaze, something shifting and trembling between them.

They would be changed. Nixon knew it then, but he did not know whether to pray for a different fate or feel blessed for the gift of this one.

When Nixon and Frank clambered aboard the six-horse diligence in the town of Oneglia, the cities of Pau, Arles, and Nice lay behind them. After wandering in all those places, visiting ruins and Roman antiquities, as well as taking daily excursions into the mountains, they were anticipating Italy. A drive with magnificent vistas awaited them and they'd chosen to ride on top of the diligence, which in America would be called a stagecoach. Here was the seat, called the banquette, in the open air, behind the luggage racks and above the passengers who rode under cover, inside in the coupe.

For the first few hours they jumbled along, enjoying one of the finest rides in the world. The road ran high along the edge of mountains that descended steeply to the sparkling sea. By afternoon, they discovered just how uncomfortable the banquette could be. Outside Savona, Frank vomited over the side of the coach, rifling in his jacket for a handkerchief to wipe his mouth. Complaining of a violent headache an hour later, he asked Nixon if he could lie across his lap, as his head was bursting. The rest of the journey was misery to him, and when he finally climbed down from the diligence in Genoa, all the strength had gone out of him. Nixon believed Frank's symptoms were like those of the seasick passengers on the *Africa,* and supposed his friend was made ill by the hours of bumping on the coach, but the following morning he was no better. Nixon ordered toast and coffee for them both and questioned Frank as to what he wanted to do.

"We had better push for Rome," was all he had to say.

While Frank slept in their Genoa lodgings, Nixon sought out the ticket offices of the Messageries Imperiales to secure passage on the steamer to Rome, and a hotel once they arrived there. All was confusion and commotion at the shipping offices, people resting on their trunks, pushing queues at the ticket windows, with all manner of business being transacted at each and no organization. Children played on the benches, women cradled bawling infants, old men who seemed not to be traveling at all lurked against walls. The Italian language bewildered Nixon, and it was some time before he understood there would be no steamer until late that night when the *Pausilippe* would sail for Civitavecchia, the closest port to Rome. No berths were available. He and Frank would have to travel on the deck.

Arriving that evening at the quay they saw, as Nixon had feared, the steamer was quite full, and a diverse crowd would be accompanying them to the Eternal City. Frank was weak and shaky. He'd not eaten anything except the toast, and after Nixon found him a rare place to sit on the deck, he sought out an official to see if he could get Frank a berth. The steam whistle sounded, the paddle wheels began to churn, and the *Pausilippe* began moving away from the harbor.

Nixon obtained one of the berths after offering a steward some money, but they were appalling, little more than long sofas where one slept elbow to elbow with strangers, even ladies. Frank, who'd slept in far worse conditions, threw himself gratefully onto the padded platform, while Nixon sat on the floor beside him and tried to sleep.

Sometime in the night Nixon awoke, rubbing his neck, which had been in an awkward position. Frank was coughing blood, a great deal of it, into several handkerchiefs.

The following forenoon, docked, clear of the ordeal of Customs, and after a quick meal of soup, Nixon helped Frank into the waiting room for the train to Rome. The same sort of confusion that harried the steamer offices in Genoa reigned here, but by noon they were on their way. Nixon left their luggage in the hands of an agent, who claimed he would deliver it to their hotel in Rome, but despaired of ever seeing it again. The train moved away from the coast and entered a vast and lonely area, which Nixon decided, after consulting his map, was the northern Campagna. It was a wilderness of scrub plants, ravines, and occasional flocks of sheep guarded by foul-looking dogs.

As Frank slept on his shoulder, Nixon fidgeted on the cushionless seat and tried to think. He wanted to make sure he knew where he was and followed the rail line on his map as they moved along. Near Santa Marinella where there were some orange trees hanging with fruit, he remembered the Mifflins were in Rome. Mr. Mifflin was a doctor, and Nixon relaxed a bit as he realized there would be someone who could help, if Frank would accept it. The train rounded a high place marked on the map as Il Truglio, and from here a line of beautiful purple hills appeared. The Alban hills, his map said, dotted with peaceful-looking white buildings. Nixon admired their beauty and wondered what it was like there.

Outside the train station in Rome, Nixon and Frank found a one-horse carriage to carry them to the Hotel d'Angleterre, at the cost of fifteen 15 *baiocchi*. Nixon fumbled with the foreign money, perplexed by it, while Frank struggled to climb in.

"I'm weak as a cat," he said.

Nixon watched with curiosity as the carriage moved away from the station. Rome! He did not know quite what he'd imagined—something put into his head by Professor Lane, his Latin tutor, probably, a city of marble and grandeur. But, the glory of Augustus was not what lay around them. The little greasy-heeled carriage horse pulled them through narrow, gloomy streets without sidewalks. Here and there were buildings of some magnificence, but they were crowded alongside yellow-tinted hovels with crumbling roofs. Vines crept over the buildings, appearing in some cases to be holding them together, while emaciated dogs rooted in piles of garbage swept up against their walls.

The February sun overhead was as bright as midsummer in Boston, and there was much activity in the streets and piazzas. Roman men with wide cloaks and peaked black hats strode the pavement, barbers sat under archways cutting hair, and a pair of priests in long robes and hats like platters appeared from one crooked lane and disappeared into another. Dozens of tiny shops were crammed together in buildings close to ruin. There were cobblers' stalls and shops selling nothing but crosses and rosaries, a window of cakes covered with sugar flowers right next to a stable. They passed through a large piazza with a huge fountain shaped like a merman blowing a shell horn, and a large ox lifted his head from its waters. On many corners flowers spilled into the street, artful bouquets for sale. Equally numerous were the groups of men clustered and peering into the windows of offices marked with signs displaying gold coins and announcing the Lotteria Pontifica.

As they moved onward the streets grew increasingly crowded, and finally the carriage came to a stop before a festive crowd mobbing a row of carriages and tossing flowers into them. The vehicles were trying to move from the side street onto a larger, equally congested thoroughfare.

"Questo e Corso. Carnivale," the driver turned and said to them, as a bouquet of flowers struck the roof of their carriage.

"Hotel d'Angleterre?" Nixon asked.

"Impossibile," said the driver.

"Hotel d'Angleterre?" Nixon questioned again, gesturing for the direction. People were now surrounding their carriage, blocking them in. The driver pointed forward and gestured to the right. "Hotel d'Inghilterra," he said.

"How far?" Nixon questioned, worried whether Frank would be able to walk through this horde.

"La strada e chiusa," the driver said, shrugging.

Nixon had no idea what the man had said. It was clear they were going to have to find their own way to the hotel.

"Can you walk, do you think?" Nixon asked Frank.

Frank smiled and stared at the spectacle before him as though just seeing it. His face showed every sign of fever.

"This is the Corso," Frank said. "It's Carnival."

Frank clung heavily to Nixon's arm as they entered the Corso. The street, wider than most they had driven on, was crammed with carriages and people. Spectators, chiefly women, packed the balconies overhanging the street catching the bouquets of flowers being tossed by masked men standing in the open carriages below. Some of the carriages were filled with flowers waist deep. Rascals ran amok, pelting the unsuspecting with balls of colored powder, flicked from little tin horns. It would be impossible to pass the street without getting dusted, and the two were already being pelted by flower-tossing merrymakers from every direction. It was marvelous, and for Nixon, frightening. Frank was enchanted, and leaned with all his weight against Nixon, smiling up at the balconies. Women, who always found Frank attractive, threw little bouquets in his direction.

"Bello, bello!" they cried, covering their mouths and giggling. *"Ubriaco!"*

"Hotel d'Angleterre?" Nixon shouted up at them, and they tossed him a flower and pointed farther up the street.

Masked merrymakers crowded and pushed, their laughter and shouts shrill and foreign. Blossoms and powder rained down from the balconies above. The pavements were set with small reticular stones which were difficult to walk on, as they were continuously jostled. Frank lost his footing and slid to the ground laughing, nearly pulling Nixon down with him. He was in no condition to be out here; they were lost and Nixon felt panicked.

"Put your arm around me," he commanded, and as Frank did, Nixon hitched him up securely around his neck and shoulder. Suddenly a reveler in a lurid wire mask appeared before them and pelted them with colored powder, shaking his finger at them in mock disapproval. *"Ubriaco!"* he hissed and ran away, laughing wildly.

Nixon then understood that people thought he and Frank were drunk. Pressed and crushed in every direction, Nixon felt frightened but pushed his fear away. This was a party. People meant no harm, but he must get Frank to the hotel where he could lie down.

"Hotel d'Angleterre?" he asked over and over, and masked strangers kept pointing and pushing him onward. They were directed to a side street, still packed with people and lined with jewelers and cafes where Nixon began to see some signs in English. A few more staggering paces and they reached their hotel. *"Carnivale,"* the desk clerk said when he eyed them, shaking his head and laughing.

Later, after he'd helped Frank unpack and climb into bed, Nixon sat and faced his friend directly. "Do you think it would be wise to send for Dr. Mifflin?" Nixon asked.

"Yes," Frank answered, turning on his side and pulling the covers tightly around himself. "I suppose we should."

After sending the message to Dr. Mifflin from the hotel, Nixon stood at the mirror preparing for bed, combing blossoms and colored chalk out of his hair, feeling a sick dread at the terrible inevitability of what was happening. Swept into a chaos against which he had no power, he could only watch. He found a tiny flower that had lodged in his collar and held it in his fingers, spinning it by its slender stem. What a maelstrom it had survived to arrive here, intact, in his hand. When he threw it in the wastebasket, he felt like a murderer.

Dr. Mifflin and his wife arrived the following morning. They looked the same as Nixon remembered them from the day of the Nahant picnic before the war. The older man was still balding and inclined to monologues. He was kind, but a life of ample means had fostered in him the tendency, which he concealed with some effort, to pomposity. Mrs. Mifflin, whose given name was Mary, was Frank's aunt, the sister of his father. She was a person of more subtlety, and Nixon decided she was clever enough to have mastered the trick of esteeming her husband without really listening to him. Frank, who'd spent a miserable night, seemed relieved to see them both.

Nixon watched Dr. Mifflin examine Frank. The physician peered into Frank's throat, lifted each of his arms, and listened to his chest, all the while making little murmuring sounds that Nixon thought were meant to assure patients he was thinking.

If he even had any patients. Nixon thought back to the picnic when the family were gossiping about one another. He remembered someone said Dr. Mifflin didn't see patients, and Nixon was left with the idea the family had little confidence in Mifflin, especially when compared to Dr. Warren, who had treated Frank's war injuries.

Dr. Mifflin then stood before Frank and announced in a histrionically sage voice the same exact thing old Dr. Mason had said to Nixon's sister Marianne, back in 1852. Frank was to stay quiet, not excite himself, limit walking, and ride when he could.

At that moment Nixon lost any confidence at all in Dr. Mifflin. The old man knew nothing, and Caroline Crowninshield would have to be notified.

Mrs. Mifflin, who'd remained poised in an armchair in the sitting room, then suggested they send their carriage around every few days, so Frank could ride out and take the air, a suggestion, as far as Nixon was concerned, that would do just as much good as any of Dr. Mifflin's other prescriptions.

After Nixon saw the old couple to their carriage and ordered Frank a midday meal, he flung himself out on the street. He had never felt more alone or ineffectual. He began walking, faster with each step, shouldering the pedestrians idling before the cafes and thrusting himself out into the aristocratic sweep of the Piazza di Spagna. He had no objective and did not know his direction. The feet rushing up the famous Spanish Steps were someone else's feet, the mind that realized he was walking below the apartments where Keats had died of consumption was some other mind. He felt drunk and clumsy, and was aware people stopped and stared at him as he passed. Not caring what he looked like and with eyes raw with tears, he stumbled blindly onward, with blurring vision, down crooked narrow streets. He walked until at last he came to a dead end and stopped, his chest heaving.

Leaning on a wall, Nixon rested until his breath steadied and his mind slowed to a pace where he could think. He became aware he was standing near the doorway of a church. The people entering and exiting were clearly worshippers, and following them, he stepped through the plain door and across a bare atrium, into a surprisingly elaborate main interior, the nave separated from the aisles by granite pillars.

He shivered, as it was cold inside, vast and echoing. Grim old women wrapped in black clothing knelt and murmured, fingering beads. Banks of candles burned, and there was the scent of wax, incense, a close and human smell. Nixon thought for a moment he ought to light a candle, but did not because he did not really believe in it. He walked instead up the right side and passed through a door flanked by black and white columns, into a smaller chapel where he took a seat.

Quite dim inside, it was a moment before his eyes noticed the mosaics around him, first as a glitter illuminated by the tiny candle flames, and later as fantastic as anything he'd ever seen. Apostles, saints, swirling halos, in glowing colors varied and magnificent, came into his view slowly, as though they had been hiding in the dark. He slid his face into his hands.

He was only beginning to learn that death often came in chapters, and it was sometimes not until the end that you discovered when the first page was written. Frank had been right. The anemones on the roof of Swallow Cave in Nahant looked like the ceiling of an Italian church.

When Caroline Crowninshield arrived in Italy to be with her son, it was the time of the violets in Rome. They grew in great carpets around Villa Borghese and in parks, and people went out to gather them and to enjoy their perfume. Young girls sold them in charming bouquets from straw baskets near the Spanish Steps.

As Nixon stood at the metal railing of the quay in Civitavecchia awaiting the arriving steamer, he held a gift bouquet of the diminutive flowers. It was only as he saw Mrs. Crowninshield disembark that he recalled the violet flashing in her eyes the day he met her, when he was young enough to be worried about nothing but the color he was wearing.

Both felt easier on seeing the other, for as long a pilgrimage as Nixon had shared with Frank, he'd gone ever further with Caroline Crowninshield. As smoke from their train stretched out behind them over the lonely Campagna, and streaks of clouds tore through the sky, the thing which had been shredding his heart finally quieted.

When Caroline Crowninshield first saw Frank he was out of bed, had dressed carefully, and was having his soup. He had grown fond of a local one called *capelletto,* which contained little pasta caps filled with spiced meat. Frank always had his breakfast downstairs in the hotel but usually took his midday meal in his room, which he'd barely left since the end of the carnival.

The last time Frank had gone out it was the night of the Mocoletti. He had rallied somewhat from his bleeding episode on the steamer but remained quite weak. Nonetheless he longed to see more of the carnival, the one event he'd most desired to attend on his tour of Europe. The Mocoletti, the procession of the little candles held in the Corso on the last night of the carnival, was said to be wondrous.

In the Piazza Venezia, Nixon and Frank purchased their *mocoletti,* small candles mounted on long sticks, and wire masks with which to disguise themselves. The Corso was indeed astounding. Lit almost to daylight by thousands of candles carried by revelers, one could see the faces of people on balconies three stories above. The effect was mesmerizing. Pinpoints of flickering light running the entire length of the boulevard, it appeared as though the tiny flames were moving on the currents of a river. Less of a procession than a joyful melee, Nixon noted with some trepidation the chief goal of those on the street was to extinguish the others' candles.

Frank immediately fell into the spirit of the game, and Nixon could see the Union soldier in his friend revealed as Frank dodged and whirled, protecting his lit candle from passing runners wielding batons tied with rags for extinguishing lights. He noticed Frank did not attempt to extinguish others' lights but expended his limited energy preserving his own.

"If we had candles to waste like this during the war, we'd have been overjoyed," Frank shouted, as he ducked into a doorway to avoid an outstretched baton.

Everyone in the street was jostling and laughing; confetti and bouquets were being tossed. Shouting and singing rose from the crowd, and the smell of cooking food drifted from the side streets. A groom led a pair of black horses that had been raced down the Corso earlier, their still-moist flanks streaked with color from the powder that rained from the balconies above. Groups of men ran by wildly putting out candles, which were just as quickly relit and carried on. Sellers of *mocoletti* weaved in and out of the crowd singing the praises of their wares and replenishing candles as fast as they could be sold.

Below one balcony, which was draped with a fabric crest and held a group of especially aristocratic and well-dressed Italian ladies, a band of local Romeos hooted and yelled, tossing bouquets to which had been tied live goldfinches. Nixon watched in horror as the struggling little bundles sailed through the air, some being caught by the laughing women leaning over the rails, and others plunging to the pavement below where they were quickly ground to bloody feathers and blossoms by the hundreds of feet passing over them. That such barbarity could exist side by side with such beauty unsettled Nixon's mind.

He was glad, then, when they reached the safety of the farther end of the Corso and turned back to the hotel. Noting one of the tables at the Cafe Greco was empty, Frank darted inside and claimed it.

"Let's have coffee and something sweet," he suggested, grinning.

It turned out to be a moment that would never leave Nixon, an image of his friend as he would always remember him. Frank had pushed his mask to the top of his head as he rested in the chair, shielding his candle flame to the very last, his shoulders and one cheekbone dusted with confetti, beaming with triumph and breathing like a hard-panting dog.

The following morning he was sicker than ever.

When Caroline Crowninshield entered the hotel room in Rome a month after carnival, she let her eyes skim over Frank's thinning frame as he rose from his dinner soup to embrace her.

She did not allow herself to notice the basin under the bed where Frank coughed blood on his bad nights. She did not see the dressing gown on the door peg and the street clothes that remained folded in the closet. She ignored his coughing, his gulping for air, and the pile of pillows on his bed, which indicated he had to sleep sitting up.

Nixon watched her as she took in these sights and skillfully dismissed them, and realized he was watching the moves in a game that was familiar to her. *She learned this game nursing a dying husband,* Nixon thought, as he excused himself from the two so they could be alone.

What Caroline did let herself notice was the wire mask and candle stub propped on Frank's dresser. "I thought the rumors of you tossing confetti on the Corso were entirely untrue," she said to Frank with a smile.

Her son shrugged his shoulders and smiled back at her. "Would you like some soup, Mother? It's delicious and Dr. Valeri says it's the best meal I can have."

Frank's learned the game's rules too, Nixon said to himself, closing the door and leaving mother and son together.

Thankfully, Dr. Mifflin had seen fit to call Dr. Valeri to Frank's aid. A small, rumpled Italian, Dr. Valeri was the physician to the great charity hospital of Rome, the San Spirito. He came to examine Frank as soon as he was called, stepping into the hotel with his waistcoat undone. Nixon liked him immediately, noting something haunted and yet resolute in his dark-circled, intelligent eyes, which moved slowly across whatever they were observing. The doctor spent two hours with Frank, carefully noting each of his symptoms, counting his pulse and listening to his heart and lungs; he scrutinized Frank's war wounds too, leading Frank to recall the occasion for each in return. Dr. Valeri had seen birth and death, murder and disease, and was well acquainted with them all.

He pronounced Frank an invalid, forbade his smoking and Nixon smoking around him, and prescribed total rest and a removal to living quarters in a higher climate. To that end, Dr. Mifflin sought out a villa on a sunny slope in Albano. What Dr. Mifflin lacked in medical experience he made up for in his knowledge of Italy. They were not to worry. They were to get Frank packed and ready to travel thirty miles distant. Servants were retained to cook and do chores. Dr. Mifflin had seen to every detail; his own carriage would transport them. They were to head for a rented villa in the purple hills Nixon had admired from the train on the first day of his arrival.

Seeing the Villa Luscinia from the windows of the Mifflin's carriage, Nixon glimpsed a noble seventeenth-century home of unremarkable architecture but sited as only an artist could have imagined. Built before an old grove of laurels and stone pine trees from which trickled the mellifluous whistles and trills of a particularly musical bird, it was fronted with a broad terrace and surrounded by a carpet of mosses and tiny blue flowers, mixed with the famous violets which had now faded back in the city.

Once Nixon had walked the pathways of the property he found the place beautifully picturesque. The villa itself, now used only seasonally and sparsely furnished with an air of pleasant abandonment, had many highly decorated and nearly empty rooms that seemed perfectly right for the warmer weather. One could linger for hours, conjuring the lives of the former occupants. The gardens had gone to ruin, and small but fantastic fountains that once spouted water now existed as elaborate planters for all manner of beautiful ferns and vines. The change from the dirty streets of Rome was so complete and reviving, Nixon could not imagine that Frank would not feel better here, and for a few weeks his friend did improve.

Frank took great heart in the disappearance of his cough and his bleeding, and attributed this miracle to the hours he spent resting on the terrace during the strong heat of the midday. He was quite often chilled and relished the time he sat there, accompanied by his mother or Nixon, visited frequently by Dr. Valeri and the Mifflins. He was still very weak and plagued by a persistent chest pain, which made his breathing difficult.

The view from the Villa Luscinia was exquisite. From its stone prominence one could see the broad plain of the Campagna, the far horizon of the Mediterranean, and in clear air, the dome of St. Peter's, which one evening near Easter they'd all come out on the terrace to find inexplicably and beautifully illuminated. At the time, it had seemed like a wonderful portent, but after that Frank began to falter a bit more each day.

One night, Nixon discovered Caroline Crowninshield on the stairs, tucked into one of the empty niches on each landing that had once displayed a sculpture or vase. She was frozen in place, leaning back against the barren, curved walls with her arms folded tightly across her chest and her head lowered like some dark Madonna trapped in an apse. Nixon knew she was crying quietly, with few tears, and that these few tears lay in little star-shaped splashes on the dusty marble at her feet. He knew she had already cried herself past all consolation, and understood that having reached that point, one never goes that far again.

He touched her elbow, and she lifted to him her beautiful, unbearable eyes. She was dissolved in fear, a dissolution so complete Nixon also felt the force of it, its physical pull like a wind that sweeps two people clinging together off a cliff. It was absolute, like desire, and Nixon imagined suddenly touching her forehead with his mouth, and running his lips down the warm curve of her cheek. But he only tightened the grip on her elbow to steady her and to ward away from himself the terrible power of the precipice on which she was teetering.

She pulled away from him, farther back into the recess, and gazed indignantly on his clutching hand, recoiling at his insistence.

"I cannot go back up there. I cannot go into Frank's room and see him like that," she said.

"But you must," was all Nixon replied.

"Why can't he be spared?" she exclaimed, her voice rising with grief. "After all he has suffered and sacrificed?"

Nixon knew better than to answer. There was no answer. He'd asked himself the same question. Instead he said what he ardently felt. "You cannot keep away from him."

She knew he was right, she'd promised herself as much after Edward died, but she did not want to be told so, especially by a boy. What was it about Nixon? She was never able to explain it fully to herself. He possessed some utter goodness, a calm without smugness, a strange wisdom she could not fathom the root of but which drew her to him. Yet, he'd not loosened his grip on her elbow, as though he were keeping her from falling.

"Let yourself be frightened," Nixon said almost in a whisper. "If you follow the fright to its end, it will disappear."

Nixon's eyes were soft and tender, glowing with emotion. *Some woman is going to lose herself in those eyes someday,* she thought. He was right about the fear, she knew that too. What she could not work out was how a young man understood horror so well. What had happened to him? Still, she could not control her derision, and she scoffed at him.

"I know this," Nixon said quietly. "You must try."

She twisted away from him, pulling her elbow roughly out of his grasp. "You are twenty-three years old. What can you possibly know of anything?" she sneered and stepped aside, pushing him away.

"Caroline!" he said loudly, grasping her arm again, this time clutching her wrist and pinning it. Her small body was trapped behind his against the wall.

My God, what am I doing, he thought. *I have called her Caroline. I am probably hurting her. I am attacking the mother of my dying friend!* Yet he continued to press her tiny wrist against the cold plaster and felt the little sinews in it, the rapid pulse in the blue veins that curled just beneath its surface. He felt her ragged breathing against his face; she felt his trembling on the wrist he held tightly. A current like lightning ran through her, and she heard him sigh. He released her, dropped his arms to his sides, and stepped backward away from her.

"You do not want to love what you are losing," he said, in a tone freighted with failure.

She stepped toward him, with her marvelous eyes fixed on him, with every sort of emotion running through them. She raised her hand and Nixon waited for it to strike him, he waited for the impending shame, for his expulsion from the house, for his loss of her and Frank forever.

Instead she rested it on his cheek, held it there for a long moment, then walked slowly up the stairs to her son.

Frank did not die as his father had, sequestered behind coal-smutted casements in the icy snow of Boston in February. Frank died by an open window through which large squares of sunlight cast themselves across his bed. Outside, breezes rummaged through the grove of ilexes, whose branches wove together above overgrown thickets of cistus and genista and from which rose the familiar whistling crescendo of birdsong. Blossoms loosed from almond trees tumbled among the hedges in these soft whirlwinds of late spring. Frank died in a landscape that seemed to be begging him to stay.

Sometime in the night Frank's world shifted, as though the picket-rope to which he'd been tethered slackened, its ground-pin, once driven in firmly, now slipping from a softened earth.

At least he believed it was night. He was accustomed to gauging the time by listening to the birdsong, but they seemed to sing at all hours, so he was no longer sure. He only knew he had slipped but not yet fallen and was in some in-between place, without suddenness and without fear.

Old half-recognized ghosts gathered around him, touching him as he passed; his cousin Louisa's baby blinking at him from its basket, and old Mr. Weston from Pau cradling a box of seedlings under his arm. The nameless girl in the white dress forgotten these many years who had drowned in Conway when the whole town was out strawberrying the summer he was eight stood by the foot of his bed. Her head, which rested on his bedpost, had wet locks hanging in tangles, and a blue sash come undone from her waist curled in a damp swath on the floor, but there was no horror in it. Memories clustered around him the same way the people did, but he did not reflect on them, and things he regretted, or felt proud of, were all the same.

Frank was conscious of the pain in his chest but could not feel it, in the same way you knew the surgeon was digging a ball out of your leg but the whiskey you'd been given made you not care. He could hear his breathing, but then found the sound was indistinguishable from the noise of the breaking of waves at the cottage in Nahant, and found himself there.

He pulled on the flimsy boathouse door that stuttered open on each tug. The interior he already anticipated, the coils of rope, folded sails, and window glass clotted with cobwebs. Creosote and dust. There would be a pile of soiled cushions, a bucket of rusty shutter dogs, and a ruined paintbrush hardened in a cup of solidified paint left by some careless cousin. In front of the listing workbench he would find his own small dory lying across two old chairs with ruptured caning. He was going to paint it next summer. Its red oars were tucked overhead in the rafters.

What he did not expect to find inside was Sam Storrow. Glamorous Sam Storrow, with the high forehead and the cleft chin who dazzled all the girls. Saucy Sam Storrow, quite brashly enthroned in Frank's dory, his lanky frame nestled in the bow and his long legs draped over the gunwales, smiling at Frank as if daring him to complain about his choice of seating. Frank's heart rejoiced at seeing his friend, for the last time he'd gazed on Sam's face it was as he threw a shovelful of dirt across it.

Sam, a fellow officer, was killed in Averysboro in 1865, by one of the last bullets ever hurled at the 2nd Massachusetts. Wanting to see a comrade decently buried, Frank took on the task himself, and now approached Sam eagerly. He wanted to tell him he'd buried him the best he could. Frank had taken careful note of where the grave was; he'd paced it off and noted the landmarks nearby, in case Sam's family wanted to locate it. He stood by the dory and recounted the ordeal, yet Sam only smiled. Sam didn't care where he was buried.

Frank felt himself slip again, this time into something inscrutable. He could no longer follow his thoughts that moved from the past to the future. He found himself flailing, objecting to this transcendency. He should say good-bye. He wanted another glance. He pushed hard against something measureless and opened his eyes, hearing again the birdsong and realizing it was afternoon. His brother Frederic was there, but how could that be, as he was in Boston? He wanted Frederic to know he was not afraid, but felt he'd already told his brother so, in some other life-time. Nixon was there. His finest friend, sitting with his hands knotted in his lap, and Frank saw Nixon's eyes questing for him. He wanted to speak to Nixon, to tell him something he now understood about love, and about the forgetting of love, but he knew Nixon was too far away to hear him.

Frank saw his mother with pity. She seemed so afraid, with her fist drawn to her mouth and a deep furrow between her eyebrows. How he loved her. He wanted to tell her not to be afraid, but these words were far away too, useless now.

Nixon would tell her. Frank closed his eyes. He could count on Nixon to tell her.

Sam Storrow stood before him on the rocky beach at Nahant in his officer's uniform, the red oars of the dory thrown over his shoulder.

"Come on, Frank," Sam said, hailing him with a toss of his elegant head. "I'll do the rowing."

The next morning, in the clear light of the first sunrise Frank would never see, Nixon looked into the room where his friend's dead body lay. Caroline was moving around the chamber slowly, touching things, folding clothing. When he entered the room her hand was resting on the face of the wire mask from the Mocoletti, a mask that once covered the silent face now draped beneath the sheet. Nixon felt something cold and raw twist in his stomach.

He recalled the scene from yesterday. Caroline Crowninshield sat by this same bedside biting her hand, he and Frederic with her. The symptoms of restless panic caused by Frank's writhing and gasping for air, which had so unnerved Caroline days before, had passed. Dr. Valeri said Frank's heart was enlarged and there was no hope. He was unconscious, clammy-skinned; occasionally his body twitched. Nixon was amazed then, at the end, to see Frank open his eyes.

They fluttered drowsily, and focused uneasily, not falling on anything in the room but on something inaccessible, something important. A great desire to know what Frank was seeing overtook Nixon, but before he could begin to solve that mystery, the eyes closed and Frank was lost.

Now, on this desolate morning, standing in the terrible empty room with Caroline Crowninshield, he wished he'd looked at Frank's eyes differently. It was the last time Nixon would ever see them and he was terrified he would forget.

He was too young to understand the power of the mind's eye, which would never erase someone it had so often struggled to fix there.

The family healed as Frank had, on verandas. Having sent Frank's body to England, Nixon and Frederic and Caroline Crowninshield ventured first into northern Italy, and finally into the cool mountains of Switzerland to pass the summer.

They settled, at last, in the town of Vevey, on the northern shore of Lake Geneva, at a hotel called the Trois Couronnes. Here they rested, fed the swans crumbs of tea cakes, and tried to recover. One day they even went shopping in town and Mrs. Crowninshield helped Nixon choose gifts for his family: enameled earrings with little Swiss scenes for his sisters, a music box inlaid with an edelweiss for his mother.

Frederic, who had rushed to Italy days after his graduation from Harvard, joined a classmate from Boston for a hiking trip in the Jungfrau, but Nixon had no desire to leave Caroline Crowninshield. Their days were much the same as during the war. As in Boston, they sat together with Frank elsewhere, speaking of him often but not of the reason for his absence. They conversed easily, but not of anything that would wound. Bundled in the black clothing of mourning that mercifully protected them from the attentions of others, they strolled the lakefront and read books late into the evenings. They loved each other because of what they had survived together.

In the lobby of the hotel hung a marvelous map. It was very large, and represented a nearby section of the Bernese Alps. Constructed of hundreds of layers of thin wood, glued in a stacked manner to show the elevations of the entire region, Nixon admired it and never tired of studying it.

On a hot July morning that threatened a torrid afternoon, Nixon, awaiting Mrs. Crowninshield's arrival at breakfast, found himself facing the map again.

"Cherchez-vous quelque chose?"

The voice, behind him, was like syrup, in each of its syllables warm, but the effect on Nixon was one of having ice water dripped along his spine. He shivered and turned to meet it, bringing his eyes to rest on a young man with the face of an angel. Near Nixon's own age, the man had a halo of curly bronze-colored hair, the tip of each lock with an area of a lighter blond so his whole head seemed full of light. His face Nixon recognized from the marble statues in every museum, handsome in every aspect, and in the tiny twist of the beckoning smile, irresistible.

"Do you need directions?" the man asked again in a lightly accented English.

"No," Nixon said hesitantly, stepping away from the questioner, feeling a slight discomfort in being placed between this stranger and the wall. The youth was no gentleman. He was smoking, too early in the morning, a small sort of European cigar, and his clothing, although correct enough, was somehow a bit brazen.

The young man circled him, moving to Nixon's other side, inhaled, and smiled again, lifting his beautiful head to exhale the smoke away from their faces. Nixon saw the man's muscled neck, its swallowing movement, and he was seized by the terrible grip of memory. Frank in the cave. Frank circling him with the horse in Pau. Nixon was terrified by the urgency of the desire he felt, the barely contained impulse to touch the handsome man.

"I am Philippe." The man took his cigar with his left hand from the grip of his right, and lifted the free fingers to his mouth. He extended his tongue, fixed his eyes directly on Nixon, and with a deliberate slowness picked a small flake of tobacco, with his ring finger and his thumb, from its wet, pink, surface. "I am known here," he continued, "if you are ever...looking for directions."

The thing that for all these years had only whispered or stirred inside Nixon, now revealed itself with all the swiftness of a certainty. What had been unimaginable when he woke that morning now became more than imaginable. It became a fact. A fact, which was on one hand welcoming, but on the other, terrifying. Only now did Nixon realize the trouble he was in, the trouble he could easily be in, both with the world and with young men like Philippe.

"Thank you, but I think I know where I am," Nixon said politely as he walked away from Philippe, scrupulous about not looking back over his shoulder, and heading for the figure of Caroline Crowninshield, who'd just come down the hotel stairs.

Philippe nodded and smiled wryly. There were two men in the lobby who knew Nixon was lying.

"Who was that man?" Caroline asked, her violet eyes blinking over the rim of her breakfast teacup just before she took a sip.

"The man by the map?" Nixon answered, knowing full well whom she meant. "I haven't much French, but I believe he was advertising himself as a tour guide." It occurred to Nixon then that he was twenty-four years old and concealing for the first time something he would now hide for the remainder of his life. The thought exhausted him.

After breakfast, as they sat on their customary lakeside bench tossing crumbs to the swans, Caroline asked him another question. Nixon could feel the question coming before she even vocalized it; he saw her stiffen and straighten her spine. He knew she had prepared what she was to ask. He swallowed hard and listened.

"Nixon?"

"Yes?"

"Do you think Frank loved you the way you loved him?"

Nixon closed his eyes for a moment but did not let her see it. He wondered if the question came because of her glimpse of Philippe. He wondered how much she knew of such things. He was quite sure his mother and sisters were ignorant, but Caroline Crowninshield was worldly. She had three sons. At least he could answer her truthfully.

"No," Nixon answered. "Frank loved everyone. I rather wanted to keep him to myself." He watched as Caroline's shoulders relaxed, with the answer she'd hoped to hear. She then smiled and said, "That you did quite well. I envied all the time you spent with him on the porch those summers at Nahant."

"I admired his bravery," Nixon said. "I often sat with him in awe."

"Still, if Frank possessed valor, then it was you who possessed discretion," Caroline said. "You've never told me what you two talked about."

"We didn't talk about much of anything," Nixon replied.

They sat silently for a while, watching the swans shoveling their black beaks in the mud of the lake bottom, their sinuous necks both strong and graceful at the same time.

"I will always be ashamed I didn't take an active part in the war as Frank did," Nixon said. "It is true my father wished me not to, but I will never live down the fact I spent all those years completely safe."

Caroline took Nixon's hand. "No one who waits for a soldier has a heart that is safe," she said.

That September, nearly a year to the day since they'd set out for Europe, Nixon and Frank both returned to Boston. They sailed aboard the *Cuba,* with Caroline and Frederic Crowninshield, in the only voyage Nixon ever made where he was overcome with illness. Although the others attributed Nixon's confinement to his cabin to seasickness, the actual cause was grief. Nixon could not endure the knowledge Frank was traveling as cargo.

A long line of carriages sat along the grassy verge of Oak Avenue in the Mount Auburn Cemetery in Cambridge. Horses dozed and hung their heads or rattled their harnesses to scatter flies as the group of mourners who'd come to bury Frank gathered around the grim obelisk in the Crowninshield plot.

Nature had put forth another mocking day to accompany Frank's burial, this one drowsy with heat, the fields and trees of the surrounding farmlands lush with hay and fruit, the sky scrubbed of clouds, and not the least foothold of fall.

Nixon was glad to have found someone to stand beside whom he wouldn't feel much obliged to speak to. He'd been pressed for details of Frank's death by curious acquaintances since the day he returned. At the cemetery he noticed Bob Peabody waiting on the slope across the roadway near the graves. The two men shook hands and remembered each other, Nixon noting they'd met in Nahant on the same day he first met Frank. Nixon recalled Peabody's skill at sketching and wondered if a sketchbook was in his pocket even now. Peabody had just graduated from Harvard and was planning further studies in architecture in Europe as soon as he could muster the funds. They agreed to meet again for supper in the coming weeks.

Frank's casket, which had traveled all the way from Italy, was lowered into the ground; resting upon its lid was his wartime sword he'd so cherished. Frank was given the rank of major posthumously. Caroline stood with her sons, and though both she and Frederic appeared exhausted, it was Ned's countenance that caused alarm. Hollow-chested and pale-faced, Ned held his arms across his chest as though he were freezing and gazed at his brother's casket with undisguised horror.

"Poor Mrs. Crowninshield has borne so much," Nixon said.

"It appears her troubles are not yet over," Peabody replied. "Is it true what everyone is saying about Ned?"

Nixon did not reply at once. He did not want to be a gossip or a liar. He recalled Peabody's sensitive drawings, considered his demeanor. He had to judge.

"Yes, Ned is dying," Nixon said bitterly. "I imagine he will be the next one buried in this ground."

A year later, he was.

A New Jerusalem
1872-1882

◉〜◎ "There is a huge fire burning in the warehouse district."

These were the words of Richard Willard Sears as he stepped through the Blacks' front door at 10:00 P.M. It had been unnaturally warm that Saturday in early November, and Richard's face was shiny with exertion as though he'd just hurried from some distance. George Sr. greeted him and the younger man entered, reaching into his pocket to retrieve the handkerchief he then blotted across his forehead and neck.

"Where is this fire?" George Sr. asked, aware that he had no properties in this district, which was across the Common from Beacon Hill, but knowing Richard would not be at his door if the situation was not serious.

"They say it started near Summer and Kingston, but I've just been there and it has burned all the way to Winthrop Square. The Beebe clock has been consumed."

"Good Lord," George Sr. said, "that's several blocks."

"The flames are traveling roof to roof," said Richard. "I don't like the way it's spreading."

Nixon joined the two men, having overheard their conversation.

"Do they have engines there what with all of Boston's horses sick with distemper?" Nixon asked. Richard was such a fixture in the household, Nixon hardly bothered to greet him any longer.

"That's just it, the rescue is too slow," Richard said. "With so many horses down, they're dragging engines in by hand."

"This is not good," said George Sr. "Those warehouses are packed with winter stock; they'll burn like torches."

"It's like daylight outside!" Agnes exclaimed from the parlor, where she'd been listening to the conversation and thrown open the curtains to search the sky between the roofs of the houses along Mt. Vernon and Beacon Streets. "The sky is orange."

Resisting the impulse to look was impossible, so in ten minutes the entire family had put on their overcoats and walked into the Common. It seemed everyone in the city was out, and the scene was one of complete confusion. It was as if several dozen families had decided to set up housekeeping in the park, and its grounds were filled with furniture, paintings, crates, and bundles. Streams of frantic people poured out from Winter Street and Temple Place, carrying rescued possessions in rude carts or more often by the armload or in bedsheet sacks slung over their shoulders.

The buildings on the opposite side of the Common reflected the lurid light of the burning, the distant fire glowing in the window glass as if they too were in flames. The leafless branches of the trees were luminous, like fingers of frozen lightning.

It seemed the Common was surrounded by fire, but Nixon had no doubt as to the location of the real conflagration. Great billows of smoke rose above the warehouse area, reflecting, in a sinister orange hue, the consummation below. Soot and debris flew far into the sky, whirling with great force, and Nixon concluded that although the air was fairly calm, the fire must be traveling in a hellish whirlwind of its own making.

Richard, who was thinking the same, said, "The fire seems to be spreading against the wind."

"A fire this large can make its own wind," George Sr. said grimly.

Nixon looked at his father as he spoke. His father was nearly sixty years old in this autumn of 1872, and now had scant hair that he combed back over the baldest part of his head, not out of conceit but for convenience. His jowls had softened, along with the rest of his body, but his eyes were still a sharp blue and to dismiss the man in any way as feeble would be a mistake. Still, there was some new mystery in the face of his father tonight. The elder man was pale and vague, his lips pulled into their familiar thin line of thought, but a quiver of emotion lodged in his expression, so private Nixon felt forced to look away.

"Nixon, what do you say we sprint down Milk Street to see how bad it is?" Richard suggested.

"Will it burn as far as our house?" Marianne asked.

"No," Richard answered, a bit too suddenly, but years of the habit of reassuring her were second nature to him now. "I don't think there is any chance of that. It's heading toward the water."

"It seems a good idea," George Sr. said. "We'll have to monitor this until it is safely out."

"We'll wait for you here," Agnes said, and no one objected to her plan. The Common was rapidly filling with crowds coming to witness the city burn, disaster always a spectacle.

As Nixon and Richard reached the corner of Milk and Federal Streets, they saw how out of control the fire was. Elbowing their way through the mass of onlookers they followed Federal Street as far as they could. From this distance they could see the south side of Franklin Street completely ablaze. Flames poured from every window, licking far into the air above crumbling roofs whose eaves were waterfalls of seething fire. Roaring, belching fire engines, which were infernos on their own, smoked and heaved, hurling puny streams of water at the blaze. There seemed to be little water pressure in the hoses. On one corner, a broken lamp leaking gas flared like a firecracker; on another a group of firemen wrestled with a pry bar, trying to move a chunk of chimney that had fallen on a length of hose. A panicked dog ran through the crowd, whimpering and scanning the faces for one that was familiar. There was no chance of seeking the advice of any official. Inquiries to the other onlookers brought the alarming rumor the fire had reached the wharves and was consuming a schooner that had not been moved to safety.

"My God, if this is true then the fire has burned acres!" Richard exclaimed.

"Even if it is not true, it will be," Nixon replied. "This fire is moving fast."

Returning to the Common where the family awaited, Nixon saw the small group appear in the strange semidaylight of the burning city. The profiles of his sisters first appeared as silhouettes, wearing near-identical pelerine cloaks draped over the elaborate back-bustles of their dresses. When the faces of his family became clear to him, Nixon knew what he would remember most about this night was the fire's unholy light. It was fiendish, almost wicked, and he had the strange thought as he scanned the features of these people he knew and loved that not one of them was young anymore. Even Agnes, who'd just turned twenty-five, was past the prime of youth. Marianne was sick, he knew that now too. Ever since he'd sat with Dr. Valeri in Albano and learned the signs of a dying heart, Nixon could no longer deny her illness. Her symptoms were slower and more subtle than Frank's, but their results would be the same.

"Is it worse?" Agnes questioned.

"Yes," Nixon answered. "Franklin Street is all in flames. The fire is burning the wharves in the harbor."

"Perhaps we ought to clean out our offices," Richard suggested. Long since recovered from the losses of the Civil War, Richard had continued his successful ventures as a commission merchant. Since his attachment to Marianne, he'd located his office near George Black's on State Street and made his home at the Parker House, a comfortable hotel within walking distance of Beacon Hill.

"I've been considering the same," George Sr. replied. "Do you think it will spread all the way to State Street?"

"It's spreading every direction except south," Richard said, which was his way of saying yes.

As they walked back to Mt. Vernon Street, up the slope beside Park Street, making their way between the piles of rescued belongings and people, George Sr. listed the items he wanted Nixon to retrieve from the office.

"Fetch the green folio and the tall ledger," he said. "In the Marland safe you'll find the bundles of mortgages. Take those and the notes. The cash is there too, in the grey cloth bag. Mind you're careful with it; keep your head."

"Father, I know what to do," Nixon said, exasperated.

"There's three hundred dollars there, and every sort of ruffian is out on the streets tonight," George Sr. cautioned.

Nixon rolled his eyes and said mockingly, "Do you really think I believe everyone running out of Winter Street is carrying things that belong to them?"

They'd been so engaged in speaking, no one noticed Mary Peters Black had stopped some distance behind them.

"Mother?" Marianne called softly, but Mary did not seem to hear. She had turned away from her family and faced the view of the burning district.

"Mary," George Sr. said, "we should get home."

It was Nixon who walked back to his mother to rouse her. When he looked into her face he was confused, for he did not see fear or regret. He saw triumph.

The office smelled of dust, old baize, and carbonated paper. Nixon climbed the staircase with its ironwork railings from the marble lobby on the street landing. He turned the familiar key in its weighty lock and entered the simple room. He'd brought a lantern as a precaution, but found the tabletop gas lamp attached to the overhead fixture by a small tube sizzled to life easily.

Here was their worktable and slant-top desk, with the cupboard above where ledgers were stored. Here was the cane-backed chair with wheels, which his father had rolled back this very afternoon, slapping the palms of his hands on his desktop to signal the workday was complete. Here was the wire wastebasket, the book weight, the cup of pens, the tiered box of envelopes. Here was the tray that went back and forth daily at noontime to John Dornhorfer's, transporting a veal cutlet or an egg sandwich to be eaten at the desk. The paper calendar from the Superior Insurance Company, suspended by a string, hung beside the window.

Ordinariness was here, and stillness. Only the window through which Nixon often daydreamed gave an inkling of disaster. From its view, in a gap between the buildings opposite, Boston was melting away. Walls tumbling, hundreds of rooms exactly like this one disappearing into flames. By morning, he guessed this building might be gone too, and perhaps even areas beyond it, all the way to the properties he and his father did own, the market blocks beyond Faneuil Hall, where the city's produce and meat changed hands, at Suffolk and Blackstone.

Nixon began to load the carpetbag he'd brought. The tall ledger, in current use, went in first as a flat sturdy base for the rest of the papers. String-tied bundles of notes and mortgages, the green folio, the cloth bag of cash. A small-enough pile for the vastness it represented.

When Nixon returned from Europe in 1866, he'd entered this room and found that George Sr. had placed a desk at a right angle to his. There was no question Nixon was expected to use it. During the war, Nixon had collected rents, kept inventories, run errands. Upon his return, the ledgers were opened to him and it was made clear how wealthy his father was. Nixon gazed with a drying mouth, and an anxious heart, at the long, neat columns of numbers, and very quickly tallied he was the son of a millionaire. He and his family could have anything they wanted. Indeed, George Sr. did not need to work at all.

Nixon knew too the fortune laid before him was not the result of some clever thrust of a gambler's ambition, or the rough jostling of business competition. It had been wrested slowly, doggedly, hand over hand, and with the constant purposefulness of habit based deeper in disappointment than in hope. His father worked painfully hard because he believed if he did not work, he would not deserve what he had earned.

Nixon ran his hand around the baize-lined interior of the safe and the cupboard to ensure both were empty. He opened each drawer of the desks and sifted the contents for valuables. On his father's desk he saw a small felt pen-wiper Agnes had cut and sewn for her father when she was a girl. Blackened with use, it sat near his father's inkwell always. Then Nixon noticed a thin bundle of paper protruding from beneath the blotter.

Sensing it was not for his eyes, he nonetheless unfolded it and read. "Be it known that I, George Nixon Black Sr.," the written words began, in the familiar thick script of his father, dotted with the heavy sweeps of the pen common to older men accustomed to obsolete quills, "of lawful age and sound and perfect mind and memory, do declare..."

Outside the city was burning. In hours this desk would probably be ashes, but nothing could draw his eyes away from the document in his hands, nor compete with his shock in finding it. Nixon sat wearily in his father's chair. The will was a draft, with no official seals, and there was nothing to be discovered in it that surprised him, no dramatic declarations or bitter renunciations. The bequests were based on common sense, fair and soberly dispensed. Yet, there was something awful in its presence. His father had perceived his own mortality, and someday he would die. Nixon never conceived of his father being dead, and a terrible sense of loss seized him.

Nixon was not asked to retrieve this will, so he left it as he found it. He placed Agnes's pen-wiper atop the bundles of mortgages and latched the carpetbag. He turned out the gas, gathered the lantern, and stepped over the threshold of the room, leaving it already in his memory. Let it burn, he thought. It was here my father grew old. He closed the door gently, but not so gently the Superior Insurance calender did not sway once more against the wall.

Once the office papers were safely retrieved Nixon spent the night in the streets monitoring the fire. He would always remember the numb feeling of watching the city disappear behind the curtains of livid flame. The leather and fabric wholesalers were destroyed, and he supposed there would be no way of reporting the news of the disaster, as the newspaper offices and printing presses were all aflame. Nixon thought sadly of the many things that must be lost, particularly of the painting gallery where he'd stood before the image of the Union drummer boy during the war. That building was in the center of the inferno and Nixon imagined fire crawling up its crimson wallpapers, eating away at the old creaking floors, curling the paintings into ashes. Paint would blister on the canvases, which would pull away from their frames and become transformed in moments from beauty to debris.

He and Richard helped others struggling with rescued belongings, carrying bundles and moving them to places of safety. In the early hours of the morning, they came upon the familiar figure of the Reverend Phillips Brooks of Trinity Church handing armloads of choir robes from the old church that was threatened on two sides by the fire. Brooks was tall and hugely built, and his commanding voice could be heard over the roar of the destruction. Nixon was accustomed to hearing that voice during the Wednesday night sermons his family had begun to attend. They had not forsaken their Sundays at Emmanuel Church, but all of Boston had taken notice of Brooks, and George Sr. especially enjoyed the midweek sermons.

Now Brooks was directing the rescue of objects from the church, handing items to faithful parishioners as calmly as if he were handing a lady down to dinner.

"May we help?" Nixon shouted to him.

"Nixon Black!" Brooks replied. "Yes, we'll take all hands. We thought she was safe but it appears the old church is going with the rest of it."

Nixon and Richard stepped forward and were passed candlesticks wrapped in curtains.

"We're taking things to the corner of the Common where the apple lady sells. Mr. Curtis is there watching over our pile."

After several trips back and forth to this rather distant point, efforts were abandoned. The windows of the church were exploding with the heat of the enveloping flames.

The fire did not burn itself out until noon the following day. As a last-ditch defense the firemen dragged forty of their horseless engines and lined them along State Street, directly in front of Nixon's and Richard's offices and poured water on the buildings in an attempt to staunch the blaze. It worked. The inferno petered out, and Nixon and Richard, sooty and exhausted, went home to sleep.

George Sr. did not return to his office until three days after the fire. The building survived the blaze, but he was stunned when he rounded the corner on Milk Street. The Old South Church where Sam Adams had conceived of the Boston Tea Party was still standing, but everything beyond it was wiped out. Acres of streets were leveled, looking more like Roman ruins than the city he knew. Among piles of still-smouldering bricks and debris, teams of men and a few horse wagons scavenged what they could. Property owners poked through rubble, trying to locate safes and recognizable valuables. Twisted metal and spires of chimneys exposing fireplaces where now no fire would ever burn rose into the smoky air.

When George arrived at the building where his office was, he paused on the stairway. This would be familiar, not like the grotesque scenery of the street. The landing would be checkered squares, the handrail a polished sweep of iron. Above the wainscot on the plaster, a sooty hand print smudged the wall. As there was soot coating everything in the city, it could have been placed there by anyone who'd climbed the stairs. Was it Nixon's? George held his own hand against the print to judge it for size. It was much larger than his own. What size were his son's hands? He did not know. Setting down the carpetbag of papers Nixon rescued the night of the fire, George searched his vest for his handkerchief. Carefully, he rubbed the hand print clean before continuing his ascent.

George wanted to come here alone today. The office was as he'd left it. Sunlight fell across his desk chair as it always had, the safe stood mute, the pens sat in their cup at the ready. He knew much water had been pumped against the face of this building, but there was little evidence of it. A small amount had seeped though a crack in the window casing and made a brown stain on the wall below. Half the city destroyed and he had suffered only four inches of wet plaster.

The calendar was askew, and as George moved to straighten it his heart went sick with astonishment. The view from the window was completely changed. Through the space between buildings across the street he could now see all the way to the shipping in the harbor. A water view, once blocked by other structures, now revealed itself, the sunlight glinting on the waves beyond the blackened and collapsed wharves. It was, George thought, as empty a landscape as that seen by the old Puritans' eyes. Federal Street was gone, Congress Street was buried in rubble, Pearl Street a memory. Destroyed were the old homes he'd first seen as a young man. Gone forever was Betsey Lekin's boisterous boardinghouse, where he'd stayed with his own father when they first traveled to Boston on business. George was a young man then, not yet wary and grave. Often not even quite sober. After how many splendid meals had he walked this once fine neighborhood with his father, already taller than John Black although he was just twenty-one? He remembered how they had ambled along on the cobbles, talking of their plans. He'd loved the lumber, the ships, the wharves, the eating-houses, the other businessmen with their heavy gold watch chains. One day he would be his father's partner. He couldn't wait to begin.

Nixon was wrong in his assessment that his father had grown old in the State Street office in the long years of toil before the fire. George Sr. grew old the day he could see the harbor from the window.

Time passed and the Superior Insurance Company calender was exchanged for another. March winds were blowing the day Bob Peabody took Nixon on a tour of the building site of his first great project.

During a luncheon of sausage pie and beer at Jacob Wirth's, Nixon relaxed with pleasure as he listened to his friend. Peabody's life had been a whirlwind of good fortune since he returned from his studies and apprenticeships in Europe in 1870. He'd joined in partnership with the brilliant and industrious John Stearns, who studied at the Lawrence Scientific School and whose engineering talents were the perfect complement to the restless and artistic ideas that rushed from Peabody's pen. Bob had recently married the delightful Annie Putnam of the vast and well-connected Salem-area Putnam clan, and they had a pretty baby girl they named Ellen.

The opening of an architectural office so soon after the fire was fortuitously timed, but Nixon could also see that Bob Peabody was a man suited for the times. His eye was on the future just as it had been during his Harvard years. He spoke hopefully of progress and advancement for the city of Boston. He and Stearns had lost the competition for the newly planned Trinity Church, but they were among the finalists of the contestants for the new Museum of Fine Arts, to be located adjacent to the church. Peabody was overjoyed to be already in competition at such a high level. Meanwhile, he and Stearns had won the job to build the structure whose foundations he and Nixon were visiting today, the Providence Division railway station, which when built would be among the biggest in the United States. Bob Peabody was not yet thirty years old.

As Nixon and Bob picked their way through the vast site of the future station across from the Common in Park Square, Nixon was enthralled to hear Peabody describe it. Standing on the site of the future doorway,

Peabody raised himself on the tips of his toes describing the design of the iron gates. Bob's coattails flapped as he ran, or danced rather, down the imagined lengths of the huge building, describing brick-faced walls and Nova Scotia sandstone trim.

"Modern Gothic," he said, spreading his arms to indicate the future location of an arcaded porch and 150-foot tower. He tugged the sketchbook from his pocket and quickly rendered the clock face, the weather vane, and a group of picturesque gables. Slashes appeared representing waiting rooms, small shops, and offices. Nixon soon realized in admiration that his young friend had built every inch of the structure in his head as though already standing. It was endearing, and impossible for Nixon not to be impressed.

When Bob's description wore itself down to a quieter pace, the two men rested on a pile of lumber in the midst of what was to be the train shed. As Bob described the size of the arched iron roof that would shelter the platforms, Nixon felt suddenly inadequate.

As a boy, Nixon might have tried to carve a model of such a building, but today he sat beside the man charged with its actual construction. That man, younger than himself, would somehow piece together bricks and cut stone, iron fabrications, bearing loads and lintels, piers and belt courses, piles and trusses and slate, to create the place where the thousand miles of railway tracks south of the city would find their end or their beginning.

There was the pain of the knowledge that this sort of talent was beyond him, followed by Nixon's even graver distress that he had no idea if he possessed any talent whatsoever. Those were pains enough, but they were accompanied by the more persistent suspicion that his wealth made any talent he might have irrelevant.

The cold spring wind blew gravel from the building pit, which stung Nixon's eyes. Time felt closer to him that morning, life a little less limitless. Perhaps the world was beginning to move beyond him. He rubbed the grit from the corner of his eye and squinted to the far end of the works where the corner of the train shed was staked out. Peabody would already know the long row of arched windows, the louvered roofs that would stand here, but Nixon could imagine something different as Peabody described his plan.

Soon enough, in this very spot, Nixon knew there would be platforms. He could hear the shouts of the porters and the clatter of the timetables. Great engines would heave away their steam, and clusters of pigeons would startle in flight to the arched trusses overhead. Inside, in the vast oaken waiting rooms, a new immigrant would cower in bewilderment, standing beside a Boston merchant consulting his watch and counting the minutes until his train for Providence. A husband would abandon his family here, a young bride begin her journey to a home away from her mother; a freshman scholar would arrive for his first term at Harvard, a soldier be waved away to a future war.

Thinking of the place this station would occupy in the millions of hearts that passed through it, both profound and mundane, made Nixon feel something like reverence for the structure, as though there would be something holy in its existence. Who knew what square of parquet or which wooden bench would remain forever in some private memory? Which missed train or which caught one would alter something irrevocably?

Sensing some deep-felt sentiment stirring in his friend, Peabody clapped Nixon lightly on the shoulder to rouse him and said, "It will be up to our generation to build up Boston."

Nixon scoffed and shook his head. "Not me, Bob, I haven't your talent."

"Nonsense, man!" Bob replied, genuinely surprised. "Why, we architects are mere scribblers without clients. Look at the new museum and the Trinity Church. Entire projects are being completed by men of our age, the builders and clients. I can draw all day, but nothing rises without a patron with vision."

Walking across the Common later, Nixon's imagination quickened. The landscape was still pale and cold, not giving an inch in this raw dry March, but each day it was lighter for a few minutes longer, as though some veil was being lifted.

Peabody's words had stirred Nixon, speaking as they always did of possibilities. One day last year, before the fire, Nixon and his father had passed a parcel of vacant land. Suggesting they might someday consider building a structure for commercial rental, Nixon felt the sting of George Sr.'s immediate disapproval.

"Buying a tenanted property for speculation is one business," George Sr. said succinctly. "Building and seeking tenants is quite another."

At the time, Nixon accepted his father's wisdom on the matter. Now he was not so sure. Nixon hoped to find the right hour and broach the subject again. Life was passing, and the word "patron" reverberated incessantly in his mind.

"Frances Wood Black—died February 14, 1874." Agnes Black looked on as her brother penned these words on the timeworn page. Nixon formed the letters as elegantly as he could, but his own dark, coarse handwriting contrasted greatly with the delicate, feminine swirls of Franny's earlier entries.

Agnes had just entered the library at Woodlawn with a pot of tea and two blue and white cups. She found Nixon bent over Franny's Bible, dipping the dead woman's pen in the pot of ink to complete the record of births and deaths that Franny had kept faithfully all her life.

"I will not have her forgotten," Nixon said, rather sternly, and Agnes understood. Though Franny had died three months before, Nixon still grieved her.

Brother and sister had come to Woodlawn this May of 1874 to finish sorting Franny's things. Nixon was named the executor of her will, a task he took quite seriously, and he asked Agnes to help decide what to do with Franny's clothing and feminine possessions.

Agnes poured the tea and placed the steaming cup beside Nixon before settling herself rather gracelessly on the velvet sofa in the center of the room. She was no more a handsome woman than Nixon was a handsome man, but the siblings shared dark, thick lustrous hair, which Agnes wore in a shiny twist high on her head. She had a lively figure, but not a small one, and large hands of which she was embarrassed and which she frequently tried to hide. Witty, unstudied, and a bit artless, she often shocked people when she spoke, as her voice, improbably, was strikingly beautiful.

Nixon remembered how he and Franny had sat in this room on another day which now seemed a hundred years ago, when she told him

Henry had joined the army. That day the trees outside were rich with color, but today the sky was grey and branches still frozen in leafless bud scratched at the windows like little claws.

Agnes looked toward the subtle sound and grimaced. "I don't know how Franny stood living alone here all these years," she said.

"She paid a high price for the privilege, if privilege is what it was," Nixon answered.

"Yes, defiance might have been enough reward. She never came to live with us in Boston, no matter how often we asked," said Agnes. "I think she was brave."

"Braver than either of us," Nixon said with regret, placing between them, quivering in the air, their conspiracy, the fact, known to both brother and sister, that they shared more than dark hair.

Agnes studied her brother, his inert hands in his lap, sitting awkwardly at Franny's desk. He was over thirty now, looked all of his years, and as an unsuccessful scholar and tepid businessman must be a disappointment to his father. Unmarried, he was certainly a disappointment to his mother. Yet he was dutiful, and almost preternaturally kind. He also possessed beautiful eyes which had an appealing sadness, which Agnes felt accounted for his popularity with older women like Franny and Mrs. Crowninshield. Indeed during the war he had seemed obsessed with the Crowninshield family and more attached to Frank Crowninshield than was natural. He still visited Mrs. Crowninshield regularly, although she'd since remarried, and to a much younger man, an event that set Beacon Hill's female tongues chattering.

Agnes, who often used humor as a weapon, could not find it in herself to belittle Mrs. Crowninshield. Caroline Crowninshield admired Nixon and was kind to their entire family, praising Agnes' singing and encouraging her in the practice of it. Agnes learned from watching Mrs. Crowninshield as well. If that lady, who nursed a husband and two sons through consumption and their deaths, decided she wanted to marry a handsome, healthy younger man who made no demands on her, then Agnes thought she deserved to do it.

I am the misfit of the family, Agnes told herself. Her outsider status in Boston ensured she was paraded before the same type of second-rate marriage partners as Nixon had been, and perhaps worse. First the runty and scoundrel younger ones, the wastrel Brahmin scions, then as she aged, the awful gang of widowers.

Marianne, because of her illness, remained safe. No one had any expectations for her, and if her future was grim, it could be no grimmer than my future, thought Agnes. There was no pressure on Marianne because she was ill, and no pressure on Nixon because he was the only son. No mother would risk alienating her only son.

In the past, Agnes could rely on her father to be her champion. If not exactly indulgent, he was fair to never urge her to marry. Since the fire, though, George Sr. was different. He was milder now and more fragile. Their mother made more of the decisions these days. None of this was spoken of, and no one was accused of being a disappointment, but when Mother's temper ran short, it was always directed at Agnes.

Thus the siblings were united. They had both failed to live up to their parents' hopes.

In these early years of the 1870s, Nixon and Agnes grew closer, and the city of Boston, as Bob Peabody had presaged, grew rapidly around them. There was a financial panic in the fall of 1873, which made George Sr. even more cautious, but Boston continued to expand nevertheless, and to Agnes and Nixon it was as if the world had cleaved wide open.

Their shared interests made companionship easy. Agnes suffered no compunction in dirtying the hem of her skirts while Bob Peabody toured them around the raw, dusty building site of the new Trinity Church. It was not his project, but Bob enjoyed watching its progress and explaining the difficulties of erecting such a massive superstructure on spruce piles driven into the newly filled earth of the Back Bay. Nixon was delighted to join Agnes in gawking at the curiosity of a female store clerk working at Gilchrist's department store, or to ride with his sister in one of the novel swan boats that had replaced the rowboats in the lagoon of the Public Garden.

Their love of music incited their attendance at every sort of performance both high and low, and they found they agreed on the strange, emotional beauty of the unknown Russian composer Pyotr Ilyich

Tchaikovsky's piano concerto, which premiered in Boston, as well as the charm and engaging silliness of the new Gilbert and Sullivan musical stage play, *HMS Pinafore*.

When the Museum of Fine Arts opened in the summer of 1876, Nixon and Agnes became frequent visitors, and they could often be found arm in arm crossing the black and white marble floors of the entrance, climbing the open filigree ironwork staircase, and spending time in the galleries with the Etruscan carvings, Mesopotamian reliefs, Greek statues, paintings, and plaster casts. Everything enchanted, everything was fresh and unexplored.

During that same hot summer of the nation's centennial, Nixon and Agnes decided to travel to Philadelphia to witness the Centennial Exhibition. They stayed at the United States Hotel, a newly built structure close by the fairgrounds with fountains and flag-topped mansard roofs, and spent a week visiting the exhibits. Here within several massive structures were thousands of platforms and vitrines displaying the goods and products of both the United States and the world, everything imaginable, from corsets to carved walnuts. They ascended the elevator three hundred feet to the top of the Sawyer Observatory, wondered at the spare beauty of the Japanese house, and recognized the more familiar objects shown in the Old New England Kitchen: everyday objects used by their great-grandparents, from spinning wheels to fireplace cookers, a quaint bit of history surrounded by everything else that seemed so new.

On their fourth day out, when Agnes' feet finally had to surrender to the blisters occasioned by the new kid boots she'd purchased especially for the trip, Nixon rented a rolling chair and pushed his sister around the buildings in it. Thus propelled she was able to continue on, seeing the monster ferns in Horticultural Hall and the much-discussed nude statues mounted by the French and the Italians in the Art Annex.

One exhibit they visited twice. In the din and clamor of Machinery Hall, they gazed on the huge Corliss steam engine. Forty feet high and spinning a flywheel at least as broad, the great pulsing beast silently provided the power to propel all the other machinery displayed in the hall, its massive cylinders driving dozens of printing presses, wool combers, buzz saws, water pumps, and sewing machines. Like the eighty-ton German cannon elsewhere in the building, Nixon found the engine both marvelous and threatening. He thought of the sawmills on the river in Ellsworth, which in his youth seemed full of power and menace. In his boyhood those blades spewed both sawdust and danger, but it took their water-powered teeth as long as five minutes to halve a single log. It was no longer a world in which things were harvested. It was now a world in which things were made.

"It would seem," said George Sr., pushing himself away from the desk in his rolling chair, knitting his fingers across the belly of his waistcoat and chuckling, "that Mr. Carr desires that I kiss his ass."

"What?" Nixon asked, raising his eyes from the ledger he'd been copying. His father was not above ribaldry but usually avoided vulgarity, even when confined to a small office with no one listening but his son.

"The old farm down in Maine, in Otis," George Sr. answered, passing Nixon the letter he'd been reading. "You know the stone wall near the south pasture that Carr toppled? I asked Sam Linscott to suggest to Mr. Carr that he replace it."

Nixon took the letter, which had been folded with dirty hands, and unfolded it. Nixon did not understand why George Sr. held on to these old farm properties. They and the tenants in them were nothing but trouble. His father would never countenance such problems from a Boston tenant.

July 2, 1880
Mr Black
I told Mr. carr about putting back them wall stones he said you was to
cis his ass
from
Samuel Linscott

Nixon rolled his eyes and returned the paper to his father without comment. What his father thought harmless, he considered malevolent.

"I'll see both men up there later in the month," George Sr. said. "Then I will sort it out."

George Sr. was soon to travel to Maine in a trip avidly promoted by Nixon's mother and intended as a vacation to extend into the fall. As far as anyone could remember, George Sr. had not allowed himself a vacation for many years, but it was clear he was looking forward to this one, which would take him into a cooler climate, and where he and Mary could enjoy Woodlawn, which he'd decided not to sell, and perhaps a few days by the seaside in Bar Harbor.

Sometime in August, when the mosquitoes had dried up more or less, his father would take the buggy out to Otis and meet with Sam Linscott and the wall vandal Carr. Nixon had visited these farms himself, many times, attempting to collect rents.

George Sr.'s arrival in Ellsworth would travel up the gossip line to Otis long before he did. As he drove his buggy into the farmer's yard, Mrs. Linscott, who'd just wrung the neck of the banty hen that stopped laying in July, would wipe her bloody hands down her apron front and glare over her shoulder at his approach, stepping quickly into the house with the feathered corpse hung over the edge of an enameled pot, letting the dog-holed screened door slam behind her.

Linscott would wait until George Sr. stepped out of the buggy and walked toward him before he feigned any interest in his presence, and he would then toss his ax with a force just a few degrees less than provocation into the stump he used to split wood, scattered unsplit all over the dooryard, and grunt a greeting.

The men would then talk of heat, horses, and prices of feed and lumber, and George Sr. would drive away satisfied. The stone wall would never be repaired.

Nixon understood, as his father did not, that in the letter sent by Linscott, the messenger was as happy to deliver the insult as Carr was to send it. Nixon knew what simmered inside such men, and what it looked like when their rage boiled over.

A week later, when Nixon deposited his parents at the train depot for their anticipated vacation in Maine, he marveled. Nixon already knew two people could look at the same place and see two different things. He wondered if the same place could actually be two different things.

Beacon Hill was sleepy in August, with so many families away for the hot months. Nixon had little office work to do. Posting rents, paying bills, and opening mail were his chief tasks. There was some painting and a roof being repaired on one of their properties in Chelsea, which required superintending, but Nixon's work hours were short. He often walked home for lunch and stayed there.

A bit more than two months after his parents left for Maine, Nixon was returning home and passed the doorway of the Parker House Hotel, where there was some commotion. A one-horse ambulance from the General Hospital was parked near the entrance, and an attendant and hotel employee were carrying out a body in a stretcher. Hotel guests and diners in the restaurant stood in the windows gawking, some with their hands covering their mouths.

As Nixon stepped closer to take a look, a messenger boy jumped in his path. "It's Mr. Sears, sir!" the youth reported with much gesticulation. "A resident! He was eatin', an' clutched at 'is heart, and fell dead in 'is soup."

Nixon pushed away the boy, who began recounting the same news to the next pedestrian on the street, and stumbled toward the men struggling to load the familiar shape into the ambulance.

Richard! Nixon approached the men and snatched at the tablecloth covering the body. "I know this man!" he shouted, and the attendant did not stop him as he tore the cloth away and recognized the dead face of Richard Willard Sears, distorted and awful, emerging from a shirtfront foolishly covered with bits of spilled peas and carrots.

The attendant then seized Nixon's hand and pulled the cloth from it. "Here, now!" he shouted. "The family is being notified. Step away!"

"I am his family," Nixon said weakly.

"Then you will find him at the morgue," the attendant firmly replied, staring at Nixon in disbelief.

When Nixon came to his senses, he'd somehow walked nearly half-way home and was shambling blindly in front of the Athenaeum on

Beacon Street. He glanced at his watch. Ten minutes past two. The fifteenth of September 1880. The first moment of a coming year in which time was lived and remembered only in fragments. From that day he existed on the edge of himself, viewing his life as a stranger might. His ears hummed constantly, there was a lingering sense of disengagement, memories and intentions collapsed into a slippery numbness.

Nixon didn't know how he made it home that day, but he remembered how Agnes fell silent when he told her. It was Agnes who was brave enough to give the news of Richard to Marianne, but Nixon had no recollection of his elder sister's reaction. He only knew Marianne cried afterward for days, as he lay sleepless, wondering if such grief would sunder something within her, rend the heart that had long labored just to beat. After a lifetime of anxiety over his sister's frailty, he feared Richard's sudden death might cause her own.

As unable as Nixon was to fix himself securely to detail during these days, he latched with effortless desperation to the ironies of the grim situation. He could not rid his mind of the waste of Marianne's sacrifice. That it was the failure of Richard's heart that would finally separate them, after years of denying themselves marriage to spare her own health, seemed to Nixon to be a cruelty beyond measure.

Then, two weeks after Richard was buried, the telegram from Maine arrived. George Sr. had died on his vacation.

Nixon had thought he already understood the strangeness of grief, how it pounces unexpectedly, bearing memory. He'd experienced its incessant seep, a fog that finds its way into everything, even dreams, whispering of the one who is both absent and present. He was the only man in the family now, and he accepted this required of him some measure of courage, but he was unprepared for a grief that came as isolation.

Seated in the sanctuary of the new Trinity Church facing his father's coffin, Nixon listened to Phillips Brooks' eulogy, delivered in the rector's characteristic voice, which was both bold and intimate at the same time.

Agnes sat next to her brother, austere, chilled. Her features were willfully composed and tearless. She'd built herself a protective covering, using a material Nixon could not identify, and he knew he would not be able to find his way to her. They had not lost the same thing.

His mother was more comfortable in her mourning. Her hair had nearly gone to white in these years, but her cheeks and lips retained, unaided, flushes of a young girl's pink. Nixon searched her milky blue eyes for something other than normalcy but could not find it. Mary Peters Black was a conventional woman, resolute but not repelled by pity, and she accepted condolence as a balm. Sympathy seemed to be regarded as a payment she was now due, and she knew, as the widow, she was important on this day. Earlier, before they left the house, she'd fussed about the length of her veil. Each grief had a path of its own.

It was Marianne who was crumbling, and Nixon could see no way to spare her. In the days of two funerals, she faded so completely even her features seemed to dissolve. She alone had lost everything.

One morning, less than a year later, in late August 1881, Marianne simply failed to wake up. In the months before her death, others had spoken of how well she was doing and how bravely she'd "borne up," but Nixon knew such observations were illusory. There had been no final illness, no shock, merely erasure. In the end, Marianne's heart did not fail from any defect, but from emptiness.

On a Sunday afternoon visit, not long after Marianne's burial, it was Bob Peabody who helped Nixon find acquiescence. Peabody had weathered his own sorrows in recent years. His first child, Ellen, died of the briefest of childhood illnesses before she reached her fifth summer, and a son born weak and sickly in 1875 had not lived a year.

"I thought you might want advice on a stonecutter," Peabody eventually got around to saying. "We architects know the best ones."

It was true. Nixon needed this information. The graves of Marianne and his father in the Mount Auburn Cemetery remained unmarked. This troubled him, but ordering a stone was a finality Nixon was not yet ready for. Bob Peabody realized this and, sliding his sketchbook from his jacket, began to console his friend in the only way he knew how: with his drawing pencil.

At the close of the afternoon, after two pots of tea, a final sketch of a tomb lay completed on the library desk. The friends worked together, Peabody taking Nixon's suggestions and making them into pictures, while advising on styles and types of stone with the knowledge of his profession.

That evening, sitting alone at the desk and fingering the drawing of the sober monument, Nixon awoke. A cold year lay behind him, lost like a trail carelessly marked, with footfalls he could never retrace. It seemed as though he had sleepwalked its entire length, but this night he realized otherwise. The desk had been his father's, but the red seat cushion George Sr. always used was removed, and the bundle of old quill pens thrown away. Two steel ones with twisted ivory handles rested in a pretty azure-blue tray Nixon had brought from its former place in the hallway. The tattered paper blotter was exchanged for one backed with a dark morocco, and a cabinet card showing Rome's Spanish Steps leaned against the lamp.

At the State Street office one unremarkable day, Nixon decided to occupy the big desk and the chair with wheels. He pushed his own desk against the wall, where it now often held a vase of flowers along with his dinner tray. The calendar that always hung between the windows was changed for one that rested on the desktop, and in its place Nixon tacked a lithograph depicting *Iroquois,* the feisty little American thoroughbred who'd just won the British Epsom Derby.

More than furniture had been rearranged. Tucked into the corner of the new blotter was a card on which Nixon had written the words "57 Beacon Street," the address of an enticing townhouse that had just come on the market. Perhaps it was time for a new start. Nixon had sold the old tenant farm with the toppled stone wall in Maine. There was no one who needed it anymore.

It could have been said that Nixon took up the duties his father dropped, but George Sr. never dropped anything. Rather, his father had removed his life like the coat hung neatly on its hook. For a year now it had hung there, something in the corner of Nixon's eye. On this day, Nixon discovered the coat where it had been all along. He lifted it with the care one would give to a relic, and with great hesitation tried it on. The lining still smelt of his father, the color was faded, and its style had passed, yet Nixon was surprised at how well it fit him.

He ran his hands down the face of the coat, along the corded lapels, across the stiff buttons, arriving finally at the flaps by his hips where he burrowed his hands in the openings beneath them. Grief carries a thousand things in its pockets. One of these things is liberation.

There was a small but active crowd on the sidewalk in front of the Music Hall as Nixon and Agnes passed by, returning from shopping together. A posted sign in the street announced: "Sensation of 1882! The Boston Music Hall has the honor to announce that Oscar Wilde will deliver an address this evening at 8 o'clock. Subject: The English Renaissance. Tickets $1.00."

Nixon had read of Oscar Wilde and noted with interest that many members of the crowd were men he'd come to recognize. Front and center were the clumps of hooting Harvard students, wearing flowered buttonholes and regaling ticket buyers with parodic poetry delivered in mock-lilting voices.

"A thing of beauty is a joy forever, its loveliness increases..." one young fool recited as he pranced about on his toes. Pushed away roughly by one of his fellows who quickly finished the stanza, rolling his eyes and flapping his hands with limp wrists, "...it will never pass into nothingness, but give ridiculous addresses." This elicited a great round of laughter from the students and some of their onlookers.

"What exactly is Oscar Wilde famous for?" Agnes asked, looking at Nixon, then at the boys, and then to Nixon again.

"For being himself, I gather," Nixon answered, as his eyes met and turned away from the bold gaze of two handsome men tucked into a doorway, Boston's versions of Philippe. "It seems Wilde himself is the main attraction."

"They say he carries a lily wherever he goes and wears purple knee breeches," said Agnes.

Lurking on the edges of the crowd and pretending to examine store window displays were other boys Nixon recognized too. Glum and shy, they skulked about, hands in their pockets and eyes on the ground, hoping that by coming here they would learn a thing about themselves they already half suspected.

"Well, good luck to him tonight, if those Harvard students have tickets. They'll give him a hard time."

Nixon would never think of attending such an entertainment. He was wary of what such an attendance would say about him, what clue it might pass to others, who, given enough clues, might hazard a guess about him. He knew the danger of his position. Given his wealth, any contact with a man like Philippe could lead to gossip and trouble, even blackmail. Nor could he consider an association with a man from his own class. He could count dozens of young Boston men from good families whom he suspected of being like himself, but Nixon knew he was not really one of them. Caught with a Boston scion, Nixon knew he would be cast as Philippe.

"Ag," he began as they continued along their way, "do you regret never having married?"

Agnes laughed. "Don't count me out of the game. I may yet surprise you."

"Pffffft," Nixon sputtered, "You'd have had a dozen husbands if you wanted them."

"Yes, maybe so," she replied. "If I'd wanted them."

"Why didn't you want them?" Nixon asked, genuinely curious about his sister's motives.

"I'm different. I don't know why," she said, tucking her arm through his right elbow and gesturing toward the steps of the Park Street Church nearby. "I'm different because I can be."

Brother and sister stepped arm in arm across the traffic of Tremont Street, heavy and noisy at this hour. Wagons, carts, and pedestrians moved in all directions. On the steps of the church an elderly woman wrapped in a light shawl sat beside her display of potted spring narcissus. Some yellow and some white, they looked both bright and vulnerable amid the tumult of the winter city.

"These look happy beside all the grey snow," Nixon said, smiling at the flower seller and fingering his waistcoat for the few coins needed to pay her. "Because of the money, you mean?" he asked, looking directly at his sister.

Agnes had turned and was leaning over to choose the pot of flowers she had in mind. She lifted it, clamped it in the crook of her left arm, and tucked both gloved hands inside her muff. The flowers quivered on their tall stems, and against the dark ground of her seal-trimmed coat, they appeared like small shivering stars in the night sky.

"Yes," she answered. "Because of the money I don't need to do anything I don't want to do."

Agnes thanked the flower seller, and the pair began a slow climb up Park Street. "I'm not sure marriage is all it is praised to be anyway." Again she gestured, but this time it was toward a brick townhouse just ahead of them. "Think of that house," she said.

"Lawrences'?" Nixon said incredulously. "They've been married for years."

"So they have," Agnes said flatly. "He lives on one floor and she another. Take Sally Codman too," she continued. "You think she missed the whist game last week because she was ill? They brawl like sailors. He's blackened her eye more than once."

Nixon thought for a moment. He imagined the Lawrences on different ends of the long table in their dining room and recalled the face paint he'd noticed on Sally Codman from time to time.

"Why not an older man? A gentleman?"

"Oh God!" Agnes said and heaved a loud sigh. "Now I'm over thirty, everyone keeps after me to marry this old man or another. Well, I won't be a nurse, or look twice at a widower so his children can make faces at me forever. I won't end up like Franny."

"I agree with you there," Nixon said nodding. He placed his arm around her shoulder as they came to the top of the sloped street just before the State House. "I think we're both a disappointment to Mother."

Agnes rolled her eyes. "I wager I hear that sentiment more than you."

"No doubt," he answered. "Sons don't get much complaint."

"If one is an only son especially. I envy you! I wish Father had let me do the business."

"Lord knows, you'd be better at it than me, Ag. You've always been the quickest one, and more like him than the rest of us. Believe me, I'd hand it to you in a minute if I could."

"But I can't engage in real estate, or business, or anything that would interest me. A woman like me can't even sing in public." She stomped

233

her foot lightly on the walk. "It's so unfair. Don't you see the only thing I can do for myself is not to marry?" They'd come to a halt at the corner of Joy Street. Nixon felt helpless to do anything for Agnes, but he too wished they could change places. As much as she envied him, he would rather have been her.

"I would have liked to have a child," Agnes confessed, staring down at her boots and digging nervously with one toe into ice on the sidewalk.

"That would fulfill Mother's dream, certainly," said Nixon. "She won't get a grandchild from me, I'm afraid. I can't imagine being a father."

Agnes shifted the small pot of white flowers directly in front of her and clutched it tightly to her belly with her muff. She smiled at him. "Precisely! Who are you to be talking to me about this subject anyway? You'd rather have any stray horse than a wife."

"Perhaps," Nixon said sheepishly, "but not just any horse."

"Oh, no," Agnes replied pointedly. "It would have to be a stallion."

Nixon's shoulders jerked slightly and his forehead felt suddenly too warm. His eyes darted quickly to look into hers. Agnes' mouth was completely impassive, but her eyes were dancing and laughing like the little flowers beneath them. She knew! His sister knew, clever girl! She knew and she loved him anyway. Nixon reached out and touched her nose with his fingertip.

"You devil," he said. "Let's go home."

Nixon was half an hour early for his appointment. He'd lingered part of the morning in the Common until he was driven into a restaurant by the chill, where he poked with little appetite at a sandwich and eschewed the desired glass of wine for a cup of tea. It had snowed overnight, a weak March dusting which the bright daylight melted immediately on the pavements, resulting in the damp passing through the soles of his shoe leather. Finally, having nothing left to take up his time, he slipped through the doors of Trinity Church, hoping to spend these last minutes unseen.

The church was a wonder, praised by all. Nixon never tired of studying its rich decoration. Luminous murals of biblical tales and angels adorned the ceilings and gilt leather and oak timbering enhanced the walls, which already seemed ancient and echoing.

At times Trinity reminded Nixon of the cathedrals he'd studied with Henry. At other times, he recognized with the sudden insistence of memory some similarity to church towers he'd seen from train windows in France, glimpsed over Frank's shoulder. More often, sitting in the vast, expressive space, he recalled the great Corliss engine at the Centennial Exposition. The powerful machine and the bold church were alike somehow, American brothers, ambitious and confident, captivating and menacing too. For there were traps and snares everywhere, even within a house of God, and Nixon was preparing to avoid them.

Trinity Church was not yet complete this March of 1882 as Nixon entered its doorway before his meeting with Phillips Brooks, the rector, and Robert Treat Paine, the man who headed the building committee. Even though the church was in active use, not all the windows were fitted with the stained-glass panels planned for them. Plain glass filled the openings temporarily, strange patches of blankness amidst the lush textures and color.

A call had gone out for donors, and with his mother's approval Nixon responded. The Black family would be pleased to donate one of the large windows in memory of George Sr. and Marianne.

It was suggested to Nixon that the artist John La Farge, who'd painted the stunning murals on Trinity's interiors, be considered for the design, as the already famous La Farge had recently added stained glass to his broad field of artistic talent. La Farge was already awarded the commission for the prominent set of windows on the west wall of the church. Nixon had met La Farge once years before, when the artist and his team were climbing scaffolding and painting the murals on the ceiling of the unfinished church. Peabody introduced them when he and Nixon visited the construction site. At the time, Nixon thought La Farge seemed a bit rabbity, wearing a shabby coat whose pockets he fumbled through before appealing to Peabody for a cigar.

Meeting La Farge again recently, this time over supper to discuss the subject of the Black family window, Nixon found a cultivated man with a brilliant mind, full of excitement about his ideas for a new type of window using novel glassmaking techniques and a new glass he called "opaline." Nixon wanted a window whose theme represented a hopeful future. The church was new, Boston was expanding, and he wanted a memorial for his father and sister that reflected this hope. John La Farge wanted a window that could showcase all he believed his new glass could do. With their complementary visions, Nixon and La Farge shook hands. The artist was to have free rein in interpreting Nixon's theme and would send his proposal drawings to the rectory.

Today the drawings were to be revealed. Nixon walked slowly up the aisle of the church, lightly touching the tops of the pews and noting each was carved with a different sort of leaf. Nixon knew in this initial meeting, where the window design was to be presented to Phillips Brooks and Robert Paine, he was a competitor in a field of well-to-do Bostonians who wished to furnish their church and leave their own names within its walls. The meeting was, in many respects, an interview.

Nixon was not concerned with the sanction of Phillips Brooks. He believed he already had it. Phillips Brooks was an inclusive man. Within the church community he was an adored figure, and his ideas and preferences were already written into the design of the structure. He was unmarried and possessed soft, patient eyes, enough for Nixon to believe they either shared a sympathy, or that it would be unimportant if they did not.

When the time for the appointment came, Nixon exited the church through the north transept, momentarily eyeing the arch-topped opening where the Black family window was proposed to be installed. A soft light spread through the plain glass there, coloring the pews the hue of dark honey. He stepped onto Clarendon Street and walked the short distance to the rectory where Phillips Brooks lived.

Entering the rectory up a short stairway sheltered by a marvelous brickwork archway that Nixon admired each time he saw it, he stepped inside the silent interior. From the adjacent study Nixon heard the confident voice of Robert Paine.

"I tell you, Brooks, that gentleman thought he had me, but I told him if I have made a million dollars out of a rise in Atchison Railroad there is no reason why I cannot understand a little matter of this kind."

Nixon sighed and bit his lip. His instincts about the direction from which resistance might come had been correct, and he hoped he was ready for it.

After a rather tense introduction, Nixon stood with the two men in the fabulous room, not the usual drawing room but a large study, filled with bookcases and sunlight. A massive fireplace of rough-cut stone sat at one end of the room surrounded by chairs and decorated with small paintings, fanciful tiles, and a large table displaying a cast of President Lincoln's face. Somewhere beneath Nixon's feet, a furnace rumbled.

Phillips Brooks moved quickly to the table, where a cylinder of rolled paper rested, and spread it out with a youthful eagerness. He was perhaps five or six years Nixon's elder, but boyishly happy with the task set before him.

Paine was guarded, examining Nixon openly. He was about the same age as Brooks, but balding, wearing pince-nez eyeglasses and long greying mustaches, which unsuccessfully covered a peevish, pouting mouth. His fastidious features revealed a stubborn character and a broad streak of petulance. Robert Treat Paine, great-grandson of Robert Treat Paine, signer of the Declaration of Independence. In Paine, Nixon saw a Bostonian born and settled in a city perfectly suited to him, where he existed pleasantly, with no idea his good fortune might be other than his own doing.

"I have been tempted to unfurl this before your arrival," Brooks said, while unrolling the large sheet of paper, placing a paperweight and three prayer books on its curling corners and smoothing his hands across the watercolor drawing reverently. A corner of the large scroll curled over Lincoln's plaster nose.

Paine watched Nixon as he leaned forward to look at the drawings he'd commissioned. The younger man had come with his family out of Maine before the war. Like many of these newly rich families, they made their homes in the better parts of the city and bought pews in the churches. Paine remembered the father, George Black, a grim sort but an admirable businessman. Enthused as everyone was with Brooks' preaching, the Blacks joined Trinity about the time the new church was finished. Paine also recalled the sister, Marianne. She'd been sickly and very beautiful. He was sorry he'd not made the effort before this meeting to find out what killed her, and he could not now remember. The subject was apt to come up today as the window was to memorialize her. He would try and steer around it.

Paine noticed too Nixon's thick shiny hair. He wondered if the man was vain, and if he combed something through it. Black was carefully dressed, and awkward. Paine heard he had not finished Harvard. He must not be very clever, Paine thought, taking some comfort in the notion.

"La Farge meant these large windows to be narrative," Brooks said, "and to harmonize with the murals inside."

The watercolor showed a fantastical domed city, built under a rainbow. Below the city, floating on clouds, was a woman dressed in white with her hands and eyes raised, surrounded by angels. The word *IE-POSOLYMA* was penciled in the corner. The drawing and the colors were beautiful, but Nixon knew nothing about it.

"It is beautiful," Nixon said.

"Why, it is marvelous!" Brooks exclaimed. "La Farge has given us something wonderful here! John's vision of the Apocalypse. Just as told in Revelations: 'I, John, saw the holy city, new Jerusalem, coming down from God, out of heaven, prepared as a bride adorned for her husband.'"

"The figure in white is a bride?" Nixon questioned, putting aside all thoughts of the Bible and seized with the unsuitability of this window, a bride, for Marianne. He would have to talk with his mother and Agnes.

"A glass allegory!" Brooks said, smiling. "Isn't it wonderful? A New Jerusalem, in every way."

The men talked for some time, discussing the details of the commission and of plans already undertaken for other La Farge windows in the church. When it came time for their parting, Phillips Brooks said to Nixon and Paine, "In addition to our pleasure in receiving this window from the Black family, I am pleased you two men now know one another better."

Nixon saw his chance. "So am I," he said, carefully balancing his tone between deference and insolence. "My mother has told me, she believes Mr. Paine is one of our cousins."

Paine looked incredulous. His pince-nez glasses slid nearer the tip of his nose and his eyebrows arched into his forehead. He was from Boston. He knew all his cousins.

"Third cousins, is what my mother says," Nixon said brightly. "My great-grandfather, General David Cobb, was brother to your great-grandmother, Sarah, who married Robert Treat Paine."

"Your great-grandfather was David Cobb?" Paine asked, almost furiously.

"Yes. I remember my grandmother, his daughter, when I was a child. She was proud her uncle signed the Declaration of Independence," Nixon lied.

This bit of flattery went a small way to soften the blow Nixon delivered. Paine recovered at the words and puffed his chest out again. "This is extraordinary," he said.

"It is a marvel," Brooks said, clapping both men across the shoulders with his outstretched hands. "I have always said the Trinity family is larger than we can ever know."

A month later, Nixon and Agnes were invited to travel to the studio where their window was under construction. Agnes was not long out of her black mourning clothes for Marianne and was able to wear a pretty blue dress for the occasion.

La Farge himself was away and unable to guide them, but a workman in a leather apron awaited their arrival and took them through the works, explaining the process. Nixon had never seen so many types and colors of glass. Not only was every color of the rainbow represented, but there were so many shapes and forms of glass: glass that looked like confetti, mosaics, nuggets, and puddles of colored custard; pieces of glass cut in chunks; faceted pieces resembling jewels; and entire sections which had been folded while they cooled so they mimicked drapery.

Nixon thought stained-glass windows were simply pieces of colored glass joined with strips of lead, with the features painted on, but here a whole new technique was being employed. Glass was layered to create folds and shadows, grass and clouds, and colors chosen to imitate weather. Two colors of glass were overlaid to create a third color. Balls of glass were placed in the design to replicate jewels. The result was windows of irregular thickness, like the map he had admired years before on the hotel wall in Switzerland.

Part of their own window was being cut and laid out on its pattern, next to another nearly finished window that had been commissioned by Harvard.

Pride was not an emotion Nixon really recognized, having felt it so infrequently in his life, yet it overtook him when the man in the leather apron called him "the client" and he saw his own purchase lying alongside one made by the college he'd failed in. His modesty was such he could thrust such pride away, but his tongue thickened and his heart felt a flutter of sweetness as he watched Agnes.

Wearing color at last and walking dreamily alongside the worktable where their window lay, his sister had removed her glove and was running her hand along the glass pieces assembled like a large puzzle. Her fingers drifted across the lavender squares that formed a band below the city and trailed along the grooves of a piece meant for an angel's wing.

"Are you sure Agnes... about the bride?"

"Yes," she said, laughing and lifting a nugget of blue glass to her eye and looking at him through it. "Yes, yes."

Kragsyde
1882-1886

@✎ "This property has a cave?" Nixon asked.

"Yes, but I wouldn't go scrambling down there in your city clothes," said the old man seated in the wooden chair in the middle of the grassy meadow overlooking the sea. He then laughed and gave Nixon a wide squinting smile. A leonine mane of white hair encircled his face and was complemented by a white beard and side-whiskers. In his black serge clergyman's clothes he looked like a nobleman with a ruff in an old Dutch painting.

The Reverend Cyrus Bartol was sixty-nine years old this August 1882, and he'd ridden out to Manchester, a newly fashionable coastal town northeast of Boston, to show Nixon a property he had for sale. Charming and eloquent, Reverend Bartol, who lived near the Blacks on Mt. Vernon Street, had made quite a prudent investment in real estate in the last ten years. At about the time of the great fire, the popular Transcendentalist, apparently unable to transcend the value of a dollar, bought up acres of the beautiful coastline around this once sleepy town and was now parceling it out to newcomers like Nixon for much more than he'd paid.

This bright, hot August day, the Reverend Bartol sat in the kitchen chair he'd brought with him, enjoying the view, which was unsurpassed. The six-acre parcel was a dramatic headland with few trees and plenty of bay, sumac, and juniper, which flourished right to the edge of a jagged cliff riddled with crevasses, tide pools, and, reportedly, a cave. The open ocean lay beyond it, dark water turning turquoise where it met the distant sky. At the far edge of the property, Nixon could see Agnes in her blue-and-white-striped skirt and her parasol, happily picking at some flower growing there. Seventy feet below, the waves struck ceaselessly, a perpetuity that today seemed like a miracle.

A house built here would dwell in water and wind and would have a life of its own like a silent creature known only by the sound of its breathing. Hours it would spend wrapped in nights and fogs, years of days both long and short. A thousand rains would fall on its roofs. Dawns would creep through its shutters; ships would pass, ringing their bells; trees planted here would struggle to grow amid the salt air and the squalls. Sparrows would flit and sing from the roof ridges and foray into nest building during the time of blossoms. In late summer, the still afternoons would bring insect music until the evening dews washed their songs away.

Regattas of white clouds would cluster and scatter, black walls of thunderheads would bulk up along the horizon. Lightning would brighten midnights and storms bring devastation, favorite plants uprooted, shingles torn off and scattered in the far grass. Heat would come and glitter off the windows and waves and sear the rocks. Gulls and fishing crows would scream and quarrel. The porch would drum with hail and frame the view of stars spilling away from the cliffs, the motionless moon trailing its light path made unquiet by the sea.

In the winter the house would be a sleeper, shutters latched and furniture drowsing beneath sheets. Snows would pile on the pathways and curl in drifts around the chimneys, water would freeze in the eaves. Rust would come, and mold; woodwork would creak and snap in the sunlight and again in the frosts. Spiders would spin their soft white eggs in cornices; books would fox; mirrors would begin to shed their silver. The house would wait, not lonely, for the beings who left the gloves curling in the cupboard, the boots in the pantry, and the coat in the closet that never felt right worn anywhere else.

Underneath it all, Nixon imagined the cave. Cool and dripping, filled with seaweed and shells, feathers and cast-up stones. Holed out in the cliff below, it was like a secret. A small piece of a rescued past, known only to him and savored, like a photograph hidden between the pages of a book. In the winter, the cave would be coated in ice; in the summer the home place of little brown bats who would head out into the gloaming with their snapping wings and squealing voices, wheeling and diving, seeking the bugs that crawled and thrummed against the screens.

"I accept your offer. I would like the property," Nixon said.

The corner of Bartol's mouth twitched slightly, and Nixon watched as the elder man let his eyes run across the horizon dreamily, viewing it for a final time. "You'll be happy here," he said.

Nixon did not reply to this unexpected sentiment, and Bartol began to rise from his chair, which Nixon steadied while offering the old minister an arm for support.

"I knew your father," Bartol said, having risen to his full height and resting his hands on the back of the old chair. "Your investment will be a sound one, even at my price." The smile was again bestowed, this time with twinkling eyes. "The good Lord only created so much shorefront property."

Love is a mystery, about which no one knows. Why it comes, why it does not, what disguise it may wear, what suitability it abjures, what trespass it dares, where it goes. It is perhaps the one thing that looks like everything but remains, nonetheless, singular. There are kinds of love that never will be again, that have disappeared into histories, and there are kinds of love which are yet to come. Love is sleeplessness, argument, laughter, and redemption. One moment, two people are unaware of the existence of the other, the next moment they are bound as tightly as if they had grown that way. Sometimes love is inexorable. Then it has a pulse of joy.

Nixon was already happy the October day he rode his favorite horse, Turk, out to his Manchester property and climbed the small rise where it overlooked the sea. He and Agnes and their mother had only a few days remaining of their summer vacation, which they spent in one of Cyrus Bartol's cottages in a nearby harbor, before they returned to their new house in Boston.

Back in the city the newly purchased townhouse at 57 Beacon Street was being readied for them. During the summer, furniture was moved from 81 Mt. Vernon Street, wallpapers and paints were redone, and curtains and fixtures were hung. When they arrived back in Boston, it would be to a completely new home, elegantly fitted out and facing the trees and green beauty of Boston Common.

Meanwhile, Bob Peabody was working on sketches for a new cottage to be built on the Manchester land. Today the surveying crew was due to arrive to make measurements of the property. Nixon was interested in the surveying. Were he born into a different life he would have enjoyed such a job, making accurate measurements, working in the outdoor air.

Riding around the road that followed Lobster Cove and rose up the hill to Smith's Point always lifted his spirits. On the land side of the road was a charming pond fed by springs where local cows often watered; on the other was the pretty cove, the open sea, and the promontory where his house would stand.

He left Turk loosely tied beneath a grove of spruces and walked toward the highest ridge of his land. The day was almost hot, but the breeze had a bit of autumn in it. In the summer when he'd walked here, the sea winds rushed through the meadow with a whispering, slithering sound. Today the grasses were dry, and pods and husks rattled in the air. The blossoms of the warm months had disappeared except for the purple asters tangled in the faded goldenrod and yellowed timothy. Crimson woodbine and chill-reddened blueberry crawled across granite rocks thrust from the ledge beneath the soil. The gulls were absent today, but two crows chuckled at him from the twisted top of the tree that shaded Turk. Ahead he could see the surveyors, three men and a tripod at the far edge of the property near the cliff by the sea.

Charles Brooks Pitman rested on the ground next to the tripod between the other men with whom he was working. He sat cross-legged on a folded jacket with a long foxtail of grass clamped between his teeth and his shirtsleeves rolled. He was handsome, made more so by his rumpled condition, and sat easily, relaxed, with his lovely forearms draped lightly across his knees. When Nixon first saw him, Charles was speaking a foreign language in a teasing voice to the fellow standing beside him. The other man, who was older, had removed a bandana he'd worn around his neck, and was slapping his back with it to ward away insects.

"Horst, *die Fliegen stört Sie?*" Charles said, laughing. The older man shot Charles an exaggerated, disgusted look.

The third man, who'd been seated on a knapsack writing in a notebook, stood when Nixon approached them. "Mr. Black?" he asked, extending his hand in greeting. "I am Ernest Bowditch, surveyor."

"Yes, I am Nixon Black," Nixon replied. "Don't let me bother you. I've just come out to watch you make your measurements."

"Lovely property here," Bowditch said, "but a challenge to survey, with the irregularities of the coastline." Nixon was looking beyond Bowditch at Charles, who was meeting his gaze with a comic grin, the grass still held in his perfect, even teeth. He had a wonderful smile, with lips that were shapely and sensitive. He couldn't be much more than twenty years old. Was this young man a German? It was certainly possible—his hair was fine-textured and flaxen. The elder man looked German, broad-shouldered with a powerful neck, and red-faced with bristly hair cut in an almost military fashion.

"This is Horst Burkhard," Bowditch said, indicating the older man. "My right hand. There's no better man in the field than Horst."

"Unless he meets up with biting flies," Charles said with a smile.

Bowditch laughed and cuffed Charles on the head. "This clown is Charles Pitman. A family friend and in his second year at Technology, so I assure you he can measure."

Horst stepped toward Nixon and shook his hand, and Charles stood and did the same. Charles Pitman, maybe twenty-two or twenty-three years old, a student at Massachusetts Institute of Technology. Nixon wondered why he spoke German. The young man's hand was small and cool. Nixon noticed the white moons of his fingernails, the agile sun-browned wrist which Nixon could have easily encircled with his own thumb and forefinger. He looked straight at the young man, who was already looking straight back. Charles had eyes the color of the quicksilver that lay in the bulb of a thermometer. Nixon took his hand away before Charles could feel it trembling.

"We'd better get back at it," Bowditch said. "Good to meet you, Mr. Black."

"Er macht uns arbeiten zu hart." Charles said to Horst, but winked at Nixon and translated, "He works us too hard."

"Ja, das ist wahr," Horst replied, slapping Charles on the back and hoisting the transit mounted on the tripod over his broad shoulder.

"It's a miracle I get any work done with you two chattering Teutons," Bowditch said, smiling and stuffing his notebook into his knapsack.

"You're just miffed because you don't know what we're saying about you," Charles teased, standing and shaking out his jacket before tying its sleeves around his slender waist.

Nixon watched for nearly an hour as the men moved around the property with their instruments, peering through the transit and making calculations in the notebooks they carried. He watched Charles especially, moving in his baggy worker's trousers, virile and adept. Who was this young man?

The afternoon was lengthening. Nixon rose from his granite lookout and gazed once more at the sea, mottled with the dark shadows of clouds drifting above it. He turned his eyes to the men again, to Charles, a far-off white shirt bent over a notebook, scribbling. Nixon strode across the headland, wading through the knee-high grasses. In another year on this land, his house would stand. What would it look like? Where would he be? When he untied Turk's reins from the trunk of the spruce, his hands were still unsteady. He knew with certainty this time what he felt.

Love is a mystery. It goes wherever it wants, perhaps especially to places where it is not expected. Nixon's desire was not aware his intellect had ceased to search for it.

On a bleak evening in February 1883, Robert Peabody arrived at 57 Beacon Street bringing summer. Peabody carried, under one arm, rolled in a canvas covering, the stage set for every August the Black family would ever spend again. Tapping the slush from his boots, the architect stepped over the threshold with his drawings of Kragsyde.

Agnes had already christened the property with this name, after her explorations the previous summer along the rocky cliffs, collecting stones and samples of the flowers growing there. Nixon and his mother had adopted the picturesque name, and now Nixon was happy to see it spelled out in a florid hand in the top corner of the large sheet of cream-colored linen before him.

Just as he had done with John La Farge and his creation of the stained-glass window, Nixon was careful to leave the details of the design of this seaside home in the hands of Bob Peabody. The family had specified only a simple cottage, smaller than their Boston home, in which second-best furniture and rugs would be comfortable. Agnes and Mary Black wanted porches. Nixon hoped for a large stable that would give his horses a taste of the country air and perhaps house an additional pair.

Nixon's heart quickened when he saw the masterful results of Peabody's ruling pen and his inky brushstrokes. Before him lay a building in the Queen Anne style but completely encased in rustic wooden shingles. In design, it was like the newly built house he'd rented from Cyrus Bartol last summer, but more wonderful, crafted of rough wood and homely stones, yet ingenious and original. Playful porches and a tower sprung from dark and secret interiors, delightful inglenooks were alongside fireplaces. An imposing archway, included because Nixon had admired the brickwork version on the Trinity rectory, solved the problem of the shallow building site's limited space in which to turn carriages around.

"I consulted with Olmsted on the siting," Peabody remarked, referring to the well-respected landscape architect responsible for the design of Central Park in New York City and a string of beautiful pleasure grounds in Boston. "It was his suggestion to allow the drive to pass beneath a section of the house, giving me the chance to provide you with Phillips Brooks' arch."

Nixon was impressed. The famous Frederick Law Olmsted had been consulted for his mere six acres? But, of course, Bob Peabody knew everyone and was fast becoming famous himself.

"Olmsted has asked if you would consider putting the landscaping into his hands." Bob said. "The great man seems to think there are too many properties in the vicinity that look like public gardens. He hoped you might want to keep the natural character of the place and work it up."

"By all means," Nixon assented, as this was exactly what he had in mind, for in his deepest heart he'd never forgotten the cottage at Nahant. He wanted a similar, casual place with a genuine feeling of nature. He dreamed of a charming structure facing a view of great beauty, a house he could fill with old things and antique furniture. He wanted the green room and the ironstone vase he'd long remembered. The drawings now before him had the desired homespun character, a touch of the new English aesthetic, and the delicacies of Peabody's beloved colonial work: simple small-paned windows, dentil moldings, paneled wainscots. Kragsyde, as conceived by both architect and client, was both ancient and brand new.

"Is this cottage like the one you would have carved?" Peabody asked.

"Pardon?" Nixon replied, not understanding.

"You told me the day we first met at Nahant that you carved buildings from wood when you were a boy. Is this the sort of cottage you would have carved?

"Yes, so I did," Nixon chuckled, remembering. He was astonished he and Peabody had recalled Nahant at the same moment.

The library, that February night, was softly lit. The gas lamps were turned low, and the log fire, banked deeply, flickered its shadowy light across the earnest brow of Robert Peabody. Nixon could see clearly the same face, years younger, illuminated by the dim flame of a lantern in Swallow Cave, watching as he was rescued from falling by Frank Crowninshield.

Nixon placed his hand on the drawings and ran his palm over them. Everything he could salvage from the past and hope for the future was here. "Yes, Bob, this is what I would have carved."

Nixon knew now he had been closely observed, and on this roll of linen, lovingly rendered.

Perhaps because he wanted so badly to see Charles Pitman again, Nixon now saw him everywhere. The student surveyor remained camped in Nixon's heart, and no attempt of Nixon's to forget him would dislodge him. Instead, Nixon's desire seemed to bring Charles into his presence, as he believed he caught sight of him a dozen times a week. Charles would step down from a horsecar or disappear around a street corner as Nixon rushed to catch up with him. Nixon would glimpse his face in a crowd only to have the face upon closer observation dissolve into a stranger's face. Nixon began to wonder if the young man even existed. Perhaps he'd seen a ghost with Bowditch on the day of the surveying. If so, it was a ghost he avidly pursued. Nixon walked often and unnecessarily in the area where the buildings of Massachusetts Institute of Technology stood, unsure of what to do if he saw Charles, but both hopeful and fearful he would. On one occasion, just after waking, Nixon glanced out his bedroom window at Beacon St. and was certain he saw Charles seated in the Common looking up at his window. Rushing down to the front door, Nixon found himself in his dressing gown on the townhouse steps, staring at an empty bench. His very guarded inquiries into the members of Bowditch's staff yielded no results, and he dismissed the two men named Charles Pitman the city directory listed: one was a furniture maker from Chelsea and the other of unknown employment living on Mozart Street in Roxbury, in the working class district of the breweries. Such pursuit was madness, he knew. All he could do was pretend his impulses did not terrify him.

The construction of Kragsyde began with a season of stones. There is not a man of New England who does not know about stones. Open the soil in any place in the region and you will find them, a bony and persistent crop, pushed forth each spring by frosts and laboriously gathered. Once wrested from the soil and dragged off, stones languish forever in heaps at the corners of orchards or in meandering walls built casually to mark boundaries.

Breakers of backs and plows, stones have been the bane of every Yankee farmer, and once these same men had traveled as soldiers during the war, they learned not every part of the United States claimed granite as its most bountiful harvest. There were places in Ohio and Illinois with soil as deep as a man was tall, where crops like corn and alfalfa could get a purchase. Stones sent more than one man west.

Robert Swain Peabody counted on the bounty of such stones when drawing the plans for Kragsyde. Once disrupted, the glorious headland at Manchester would yield tons of raw material for the foundations of

Nixon's cottage, and in the hands of skilled and artistic masons, the stones they overturned would not be a nuisance but the makings of beauty.

Late in April of 1883, the crews from the building firm of Roberts and Hoare began turning over the land. With small charges of explosives and digging tools, the site began to take on a shape.

The Black family rented the Bartol cottage again for the summer, and Nixon rode out daily to the building site, watching the foundation walls rise under Peabody's and Olmsted's guiding hands. Astride Turk's strong back picking through the upturned soil, or dismounted and seated at some distance while the horse pulled and munched the long grasses on the verges of the torn-up ground, Nixon found it pleasant to watch the masons. Working in silence and concentration, these older men lifted the stones freed from the site carefully, bathing them in hogheads filled with water with a strange tenderness that resembled a baptism. Younger laborers tended to the mixing of the mortar, filling endless pails of it, and lugged the stones from their size-sorted piles to the older masons. Trowels scraped and rang in the air as they slathered the stones, snugging them into their appointed places, tapping them tightly with the butt end of their tools. The air tasted of the sweetness of the cement lime and smelled of wet and ancient stone.

The curious thing was, as the house was built, Nixon felt built-up too. As the mortar cured and stones became walls, he felt an exaltation pass through him. Later as the rafters rose in the glinting sun, placed by exuberant, loquacious carpenters who romped fearlessly, with their tools lashed to their waists, on the thin ribs of wood that rose a hundred feet above the sea, Nixon felt an even greater change. He paced through new spaces that were soon to be rooms, gazed through apertures at views never before seen. Kragsyde began to take shape, lying like a coiled dragon atop its cliff, its roofline the backbone, the greying shingles the scales, the sea thrashing and bellowing below. As Nixon smelled the sharp raw wood and stood in the showers of sawdust swirling around him like snow, the part of his personality that had cowered within him stirred, and shuddered, and grew braver. He had become lighter and more full all at the same time.

Charles Brooks Pitman descended the stairs from his rented rooms on Mozart Street and stepped onto the sidewalk. He was twenty-four years old and moved gracefully, folding the pair of gloves he carried and tucking them in his pocket, while allowing his umbrella to hang from its hook on his arm. Any casual observer could describe him as neat, respectable, and clever-looking, but they would be at a loss to offer more. A closer scrutiny might reveal that the young man's mouth almost always held the expression of a half smile, as though he were recalling a joke or pleasant story.

Charles had dressed carefully this evening, since he was going to the theater, but high fashion was not his aim. He was, in fact, attempting to be inconspicuous, dressing well enough not to stand out at the Globe Theater during *The Count of Monte Cristo,* starring James O'Neill, and plainly enough not to be noticed in his neighborhood, where tickets to such a performance would be beyond the means of many of the residents.

It was a short walk to the horsecars from the three-decker house where he lived. The house was a fairly new structure, owned by old Arno Bauer, whose years as a foreman at the Boston Belting Company had resulted in his status as a homeowner, and kept clean by Mrs. Bauer, a rotund and red-faced hausfrau who wore her apron string tied in a bow across her prominent belly as though she were a parcel. Mrs. Bauer was fond of gossip, and Charles was careful to avoid arousing her attention. Still, Charles lived here happily, and the Bauers were grateful landlords. Young Mr. Pitman's rent was paid promptly, and he spoke to them in their native tongue.

For a man of some wealth, Charles Pitman had a difficult time securing a home in this area, though not because of money. He'd lived here for ten months, since he'd tired of his studies at Technology and appealed to his father that he take a year off. Old Benjamin Pitman was not pleased, but consented as long as his son was working in the field of his studies. So Charles took up several jobs, chiefly surveying, with men like Ernest Bowditch. He'd worked a stint with an engineer named Whitman surveying a tract near Suffolk Street for what was to be a charity housing project, and in that time discovered the rooms on Mozart Street. Benjamin Pitman relented after Charles had promised to return to his studies at MIT, and Charles moved from the family villa in Spring Hill in Somerville to his own rooms here.

The district around Mozart Street was clustered with factories, breweries, and the German immigrants who worked in them. Each day brought the clamor of manufacture, the clatter of transport wagons, and the odor of slowly cooking grains and yeast. As Charles walked northwest to catch the horsecar into Boston, he could count five billowing smokestacks in his vision. He was making an early start that evening, for by seven o'clock the brewery workers would pour from the customer rooms where they relaxed after their shifts and fill the streets on their daily commute. Charles wanted to avoid Klaus.

Initially, Charles took up residence in this area because of men like Klaus, men with little education and even less English language, but nonetheless healthy and natural, both plain and passionate, and irresistible to Charles. Here he could know men like this, far from his father's watch. Sometimes Charles wondered if his father could ever be sympathetic to his desires; after all, Benjamin Pitman himself had made what some would say was an inappropriate choice in love, but Charles decided no. His father's "unfortunate" choice had at least been a woman. Charles believed his father could never understand loving another man.

Klaus was a wagon driver for the Vienna brewery and in every aspect a typical German youth. Taciturn to the point of sullenness, shy, and conversant only in German, he and Charles watched one another for weeks before Charles realized Klaus was too frightened to approach. All it would take was one gesture on Charles' part, he thought, and it was true. Charles reached for Klaus' hand in the darkness of an alley outside the brewery on Station Street, and it was as flame to tow. They retired to the third-floor rooms at Mozart Street and Charles did not realize until morning, after Klaus had crept away, that they'd broken a chair. Now, nearly a year later, their encounters, although undertaken more quietly, had not lessened. Klaus was as wanton as ever, but Charles began to tire of his German lover. Klaus' mouth, unless it was kissing him, was full of complaint and tales of home troubles. He was sometimes not clean, and he had a temper.

Charles began to desire a more suitable, cultivated man, one whom he could talk to in his own language, and of more elevated things. Charles had not been unaware of the man, Mr. Nixon Black, whom he'd met last year while surveying with Bowditch. The man had wonderful thick hair and a gentle, slow manner. Nor had he forgotten Black's remarkable, devouring eyes. Had Charles imagined Black's attraction? He did not know. For a long time after, he followed Black secretly, hoping to learn more. He discovered Black was unmarried, that he lived in a huge mansion on Beacon Street, apparently with two women, a mother and a sister, and kept many horses and carriages. Black's wealth and age intimidated him, but Charles also saw evidence of the man's tenderness. When Nixon Black went out, he often took his dogs, which he lifted himself into his carriages, even an old rheumy-eyed terrier that Mr. Black wrapped in a soft blanket on chill days and placed gently on the seat.

Charles stepped down from the horsecar at Park Square, passing by the big train station on his way to the Globe. Black's house was across the Common; he could see its facade through the trees. Once he sat on a park bench looking up at its windows, but thinking he spotted Black in a window he'd hurried away. Arriving in front of the theater, Charles paused by the large poster near the lighted window of the box office, shifted his umbrella, and reached to retrieve his wallet. Mr. Black often attended galleries, musical events, and the theater. If only I could talk to him again, Charles thought, then I would know.

"Don't you want to see the Count?" Nixon said to Agnes, who was seated in the parlor with her forehead resting in her hand. "James O'Neill!" he said, flapping the newspaper announcement of the production over her head and trilling his voice in a singsong manner to indicate Agnes might be more than a little infatuated with the famous actor.

"I said I have a headache," Agnes responded firmly and none too sweetly to her brother. "Go by yourself, and stop being annoying."

Nixon pursed his lips and thought for a moment. It was the third week of October, and Agnes was claiming headache. Although such things were presumably unknown to him, Nixon realized by long acquaintance this must be the week of Agnes' monthly. He tugged lightly at one of her curls and said, "As you wish, O convalescent. If O'Neill is good, we shall go together on another night."

Mellie Fraser, the housemaid, handed him his coat, and he stepped onto Beacon Street with the intention of crossing the Common to the Globe Theater. It was a smoky night; small piles of leaves raked by the street crews smouldered in the gutters. The cool air felt good against his face, like the sea air in Manchester, from which he'd just returned. The Bartol cottage was closed now for the season, and families were returning to the city. Next year, they would stay in Kragsyde for their first summer. The women were already choosing curtains and fabrics. He would visit Woodlawn in Ellsworth and arrange for some of the furniture there to be brought down to Kragsyde. His grandfather's house was shuttered, but some of the old-fashioned things there would look charming in the new seaside home. He supposed they would visit Maine even less once their residence at Kragsyde was established.

His mind wandered thus as he strolled through the crowded commercial district near Washington Street. The street was full of conveyances from which theater patrons were alighting. A lit sign near the box office announcing *The Count of Monte Cristo* glowed in gaudy persuasion. There was a young man standing before it, fishing in his jacket pocket. His hair looked like the student surveyor, Charles Pitman...and then he lifted his gaze.

Neither man moved, because they shared the same fear that if they did, what they beheld might be lost to them, a pair of quicksilver eyes reflected in a pair of blue devouring ones.

Charles had no trouble accepting Nixon's invitation to exchange his seat for Agnes' and join him for the performance. The trouble came in trying to take the measure of a stranger as he sat silently in the dark. Charles made furtive glances at Nixon. He seemed so still and composed. It was perhaps only in contrast to Charles' own agitation, but it seemed to the younger man that Nixon was uncannily passive, inert to the point of torpor. It would not be impossible to conclude he was slow-witted, but Charles knew better and wondered if instead the man beside him was incredibly clever. How much did Nixon Black know?

Charles understood himself from an early age. He'd discovered when he was twelve where his preferences lay. In 1872, his eldest brother, Benjamin Jr., had taken ill. Anxious for his son's health, Benjamin Sr. packed the family off to Europe for three years while young Benjamin was sent to a spa to regain his constitution. The rest of the family lingered first in England and later in Germany, where Charles eventually enrolled at Stuttgart Polytechnic and learned the German language.

While in England the family lived in a fine district in London near the British Museum, in a row of handsome townhouses backed up by a narrow mews of smaller homes for the domestics and the stables. It was here Charles met Harry Tulit, the son of a coachman's groom. The boys played together and fought, made up and played again as young boys do, threading trails through the streets, getting up sporting games in muddy laundry yards, and hiding in the maze of stables.

One such day, a childish slight descended into a wrestling match that propelled the pair, pushing and shoving, into the stall of an indifferent Cleveland bay. Here their pummeling melted into a different sort of fumbling, as they learned with each other a bit of what adults already knew. These gropings continued for a few weeks, until the afternoon when the boys hid themselves in the plush interior of Mr. Montague's ruby-colored brougham. The door to the lavish carriage snapped open, and Harry tumbled out and ran hell-bent for home, leaving no doubt in Charles' mind what he was, and what Harry was not.

All these years later, Charles still thought of Harry. He remembered precisely the horsey stink of him, his dirty fingernails, their conspiratorial huddles. He remembered his thin chest, rippled with ribs, coated in freckles; the brown circles of his nipples; and the wiry, rust-colored forelock that dangled across his brow. Poor Harry, his world was to go no further than the confines of the mews, but he remained with Charles forever, always conjured with fondness, even though the last thing Harry did to Charles was to hit him in the face.

Charles, who normally delighted in the theater, could not recall when a production had dragged on so long as this one. Consciously trying not to fidget and trapped in a fever of apprehension, he still managed a few more glimpses of Nixon. His observation was rewarded, for one scene seemed to affect his companion, though Charles could not guess why. The curtain rose to a darkened stage where several dozen players carrying lit candles joyously reenacted the streets during the Roman carnival. The visual statement was stunning, but it did not account for Nixon's shifting in his seat, clearing his throat, and covering his mouth with a hand that Charles thought was trembling. It gave Charles the idea Nixon might be hiding other things, and if Charles took the chance of reaching out, they might be revealed.

As they emerged from the theater, Nixon was dazed by the flutter of the city around them, carriages swallowing the theater audience, people talking excitedly about the play and their immediate plans. It was just after ten o'clock, so supper could still be suggested, but Nixon began to wish for privacy and his stomach was not well. He'd not expected to be confronted with the sadness of the old ghosts of Rome, especially after the happy accident of meeting the youth who'd haunted his thoughts this past year. He had not expected to be riven with emotion and the need to conceal it all at once.

"Where are you headed?" Nixon asked Charles, for if nothing else, he meant to discover the residence of this elusive young man.

"My family live in Somerville, in Spring Hill, where I'm expected tonight, but I have my own headquarters on Mozart Street near the Stony Brook," Charles replied.

So this was the Charles Pitman the city directory listed on Mozart Street! Spring Hill was a prosperous area, not far from the colleges, but Mozart Street was an odd neighborhood for a young man with an income, as Charles Pitman seemed to be. "Are you a brewer then?" Nixon asked, in jest.

"No," Charles said and then laughed. "I am still studying engineering at Technology. When I met you with Bowditch, I was taking a year off, but I've begun again this term."

"Shall we walk across the Common?" Nixon suggested. "I live on Beacon, at number 57, and you can catch the car to Somerville near my doorstep."

The pair stepped down from the curbing and crossed Essex Street with the Common in view. The remaining leaves hung precariously on the trees, with all the amber gone out of them, and the blurry balls of the streetlamps suggested the presence of the autumn frosts.

"How did you come to live at Mozart Street?" Nixon asked, for his curiosity was more insistent than his upset stomach, and this slim, elegant young man had all of his attention.

"I surveyed nearby with a man named Whitman for a charity housing project commissioned by Robert Treat Paine. Apparently Paine has plans for entire charity villages. I lived at Mozart while I worked the job, found I rather liked it, and never left." Charles answered.

The mention of Paine gave Nixon an unpleasant jolt and sobered his heart. Did Pitman know Paine? If so, it would sour everything. "Do you know Paine?" Nixon asked.

"No," Charles answered. "I never laid eyes on him, but I supposed you might know him. Paine has aims to better the world, as I hear. Charity villages, cooperative banks, and such."

"Yes," said Nixon, who'd heard much of Paine's humanitarian zeal, mostly from Paine himself. "So he does. He has it all worked out."

"You don't believe Paine means to make the world a better place?" Charles asked, his face such a pale moon of earnestness, Nixon understood his answer meant something to the young man. Nixon had to be honest, though he chose his words carefully.

"I think Mr. Paine would like to be taken seriously," Nixon said with a small smile.

Charles wrapped his arms around himself and lifted his head in laughter. "Mr. Whitman thought the same," he related. "He said Robert Paine hasn't a single enemy and none of his friends like him."

Nixon laughed and shook his head. Everything about Charles delighted him.

"So, you don't think it's possible to save the world?" Charles stopped and faced Nixon, looking at him seriously, his question posed with all the candor of innocence. His face was taut and unlined. He was so young.

"No," Nixon said, beginning to walk again. "I don't believe I do."

The two walked for a short time in silence. Nixon wondered how Charles had taken his confession. The Common was dark along this stretch of pathway; the sort of darkness that comes in October and seems so impossible in July. The men walked shoulder to shoulder, hands in their pockets, their coats brushing. Charles' umbrella, hanging from his arm, sometimes tapped on Nixon's leg. The air smelled of brown, with the burning leaves and the smoke drifting.

Nixon was aware of only the briefest movement when Charles slipped a hand inside his pocket and clasped his own. Initially he was surprised and then embarrassed, but no one could have witnessed them; they were walking too closely, the pathway was too dark. It was a pleasant feeling, the interlocking of the dry, warm fingers, the wrapping together of the thumbs. Charles' fingers were strong and soft. Nixon remembered the look of them from the day of the surveying: the small wrists, the square, even fingernails with the half moons, now burrowing beneath his own hand. Nixon felt hot, then giddy, as though his soul had been flung from his body. Nor did Charles remove his hand as they continued walking, but let it linger, tracing his own fingertips down the length of Nixon's fingers, lacing them together tightly. Nixon closed his eyes and allowed his hand to be clutched. It was wonderful, and it was god-awful, and when the two reached the far side of the Common where the light was stronger and Charles had slowly withdrawn his hand, Nixon knew something had happened to him, but he could not give it a name. Nor did he know how to end this night, which he now wished would never end. His voice was dumb, words disappeared, nothing was as he thought it would be.

Charles rescued him. The youth turned in his tracks, smiled broadly, promised to keep in touch, and dashed out into the street, where he turned briefly, waved good-bye, and skipped out of Nixon's sight. It was not until Nixon could no longer see Charles that he realized at once why he loved him. He loved him for something he had almost forgotten. He loved Charles for his joy.

"I won't do it," Charles said adamantly, "no matter how often I am convinced." He stood in his light-colored jacket and straw hat, on the train platform with Nixon. The sun was shining, and other weekend travelers clustered around them, jostling their hand baggage, one of which was a wicker basket containing a small brown dog who peered through the woven slots and bared his tiny teeth.

The entire winter had passed since the night when Charles clasped his hand. That night, Nixon stumbled home and, after the sickness that plagued him finally presented itself, he lay on his bed amazed at the degree of desire that he felt. He was over forty now and had expected an entirely different fate.

Charles had done as he promised. He stayed in touch. By mid-November he'd left his card, accepted Nixon's invitation to supper, and arrived at Beacon Street, immaculately dressed, and suffused with enough wit, youth, and enthusiasm to win the pleasure of both Agnes and Mrs. Black. Not since the visits of Richard Sears had the table heard so much laughter.

Indeed, Charles became a special figure to Agnes, as the two shared a mischievous temperament and a gift for silliness. One time the two had the idea of visiting the new Gaiety theater to visit Baby Alice the midget and the stuffed mermaid displayed within. Nixon asked his sister about their visit to this rather crass entertainment.

"Oh, Charles is the perfect escort to visit a midget," she remarked in her offhand way. "Nothing fazes him. Why would it, as his family history is so fantastical?"

Was Charles' family history fantastical? Nixon did not know. He'd never asked. He never would. Obviously his sister knew things about Charles he didn't, but there was much else about his friend to contemplate. The young man's face, his superior intelligence, his disarming smile that caused something in Nixon's chest to unlatch each time he saw it. Charles was a bit of a mystery. He never talked of himself or his studies. Nixon had not met his parents or been invited to Spring Hill or Mozart Street, but what he viewed as reticence did not trouble him. His heart was sure of Charles, and so his head gave it little thought.

Over and over, he remembered the night Charles took his hand. No matter what happened in the future, that moment would never happen again; it would remain as a singular memory, unique in his history. Nixon often looked out his window to the path where they'd been. Even now, Nixon thought, people are walking across the spot where Charles touched me—the place in my life where I was most perfectly happy.

On this sunny Saturday, the day before Decoration Day, the two men were wedged tightly on the narrow train platform between two groups of ladies with large bustles, a stack of luggage cases, and the wicker basket with the little dog, now barking sharply.

"He doesn't like his cage," Nixon said, observing the furry creature flinging itself against the walls of his basket.

"Nor do I," Charles replied, "I won't go back to Technology again. I am done with schooling." The signal whistle blew and as the train was boarded, Nixon and Charles walked the length of two cars and found their seats.

Nixon sighed. He'd been discussing this subject with Charles for over an hour, halfheartedly endorsing the idea that Charles continue to his final year and graduate with his degree. The conversation made him feel old, as though he were his own father. He well remembered being in Charles' place.

"I feel finished. I want to enter the field and dispense with the classroom," Charles declared. In fact what he really wanted was never again to spend a winter like the last. The schooling was not the problem; it was his predicament. He was in love with Nixon and, worse yet, with Nixon's family. The gentle bearlike man with the remarkable eyes and the soothing voice had invaded him, had found his way into his very bloodstream and traveled through it, like a fever. Charles found he wanted Nixon. Indeed he envisioned himself calmly and safely held in his arms, but safe from what? Charles was unsure where he stood with the man. Surely, Nixon liked him, surely he was attracted, but he'd made no reaction to Charles' holding his hand. Charles wanted to ask him to Spring Hill but didn't dare, fearful of Nixon's reaction to his family, and he couldn't bring him to Mozart Street until he'd settled things with Klaus.

"Settling" with Klaus was months of torture. The German youth had not taken it well, and as gentle as Charles tried to be, Klaus reacted with violence. He argued, he begged, he threatened, he broke a window. Charles locked his doors and avoided the streets, but Klaus followed him for months, alternately pleading and snarling. Only in the last days was Charles sure he was rid of him. Klaus had left his job at Vienna brewery, and his friends said he'd left the state. Charles began to think he might follow Klaus' example and go away himself.

"I'd like to get on one of those big projects like the New York and Brooklyn Bridge," Charles said. "Now that is a grand span. I've even thought to join de Lesseps' outfit on the Panama Canal," he continued brashly. "I can speak French."

"I don't think that project is going well," Nixon said dryly.

"No," Charles admitted, as he too had read the stories of sickness and landslides burying workers alive. "There will be a canal there someday, though, and I won't spend another birthday at Technology."

"When is your birthday?" Nixon asked, to change the subject. He knew Charles was twenty-four, but he'd never learned the date of his birth.

"I was born September 21, 1860," Charles said.

Nixon tried to remember where he was that day, but of course he could not. It was around the time he entered college, fraught with worry about passing his exams, the fear of failure and the war permeating everything.

"That was about the time I was entering Harvard," Nixon said. "I've told you how that turned out. Now I wish it were different, but at the time I was not eager to go."

"So you know how I must feel! You've been there yourself."

"I didn't have your talent. I felt out of place," Nixon admitted, remembering the opening day, when they all posed for the class photograph, the golden sun, how many of those boys were now dead. He was eighteen years older than Charles. "I thought my future was to be decided elsewhere."

"So do I," said Charles, not indicating whose future he actually meant.

When the train arrived at Manchester station, they sought the carriage they'd ordered to take them to Kragsyde. The seaside cottage was complete, and the furniture and fittings delivered in the last months and set in the designated rooms by the carters. All that awaited was the final arrangement of the rooms, and this job Nixon elected to do himself. He'd discussed with the women of the household where each piece was to go, but the actual moving of the furnishings was to be left to the strength of men. Nixon delighted in the thought of doing the arranging, and Charles volunteered to lend his shoulder to the task.

Charles would forever remember the ride along Lobster Cove and his first view across the sparkling water to the great new house on the clifftop, silhouetted in the bluest sky. Charles saved his highest approval for older houses, particularly those that had survived for more than a century, the kind that may have witnessed the Revolution or the Indian Wars, those with quaint kitchens, vast square chimneys, and snug sitting rooms. Yet here was the most beguiling of modern designs, more expansive and elaborate than its ancestors but as perfectly wedded to its site as the mosses and ferns surrounding it. The marvelous structure resembled a placid, mythic beast, come out from its lair to sun itself high above the sea. He'd wondered, on the day of the surveying, what would rise here, and saw now Robert Peabody had designed a great success. There was no doubt Kragsyde was special. It possessed history and romance, but also a taste of magic.

The day was becoming warm and all around the house there was the sound of a strong sea and a breeze from the northeast bearing the great wet smell of the ocean. Nixon had not visited the property for a month and found that Mr. Temple, Olmsted's man, had come and freed the new plantings from their winter covers. Rich dark mulch surrounded the new spirea and mock orange, which in contrast seemed green and vivid. The wild crab growing naturally around the stable was a fragrant blur. The powdery flowers of creeping phlox were blooming and crawling over the edges of the new stone walls along the drive.

Consenting to a tour, Charles first entered the stables with Nixon. Two rows of handsomely finished box stalls lined an alley finished with floor drains and brick pavers laid on the bias. Hay was already down from the loft and lay in nearby mangers. Tack, oiled and polished to gleaming, hung from pegs in its own room with eye blinkers and bridle rosettes worked with the letter "B" in silver. Only missing were the horses themselves, which had yet to be brought from Boston, and the cheerful banter of coachmen and grooms, who in another week would be harnessing and currying their charges in this new shelter, built with every equine comfort in mind.

Nothing stirred when Nixon keyed Kragsyde's lock, and as they entered, Charles listened, but found the house in near-silence, even the noise of the sea muffled. Most of the shutters were closed, casting the rooms in an indoor twilight that only just allowed his eyes to see. The odor of fresh paint and varnish lingered, and furnishings lay under ghostly sheets like strange solemn presences. Rugs were rolled against baseboards, with bales of folded curtains piled atop them, tied in brown paper.

Nixon said nothing as he moved quietly up the short flight of stairs and across the main hall, raising the window and pinning back a shutter, exposing a shaft of oblique and searing light that illuminated a trail of gold on the oak floor from one man to the other.

Charles squinted and stepped into this path of sunlight, removing his straw hat and placing it atop the largest newel post of the stair. Nixon continued to move around the rooms, his footfalls reverberant, tending to the shutters, while Charles stood before the first uncovered window and gloried in the view. The piazza outside was nearly a hundred feet above the sea. He turned again and climbed the paneled staircase behind him, holding his breath, as all the while the light became richer with the opening of each window, and the lovely colors of the walls were revealed to him: pale green, ocher, salmon. Charles felt as though he were stepping inside Nixon himself, a man still mysterious, silent, with all his treasures hidden. On the landing, the feet of a gateleg table emerged from beneath a sheet and a large veiled painting leaned against the wall. Charles entered the room at the top of the stairs, a bedroom, directly above the room where he'd stood below. He paused for a moment in the shadowy room and listened to the buzzing of a housefly thrashing in the window of a shallow dormer, and the sound of Nixon's footfalls coming up the stairs behind him. Charles crossed the room, unlatched the lock, and lifted the casement slowly. He reached outside to the clip that held the shutters, parted them, and brushed the fly out into the air. From this level, he could look down to the edge of the sea, into the place where it boiled and churned against the rocks.

"It is superb, Nixon!" Charles said loudly, intending his voice to carry into the stair landing where his compliment could be heard.

He had no idea Nixon had already entered the room, and that his friend was standing quietly beside the bedroom door, recalling the day when he and Peabody agreed on the placement of this room, a guest room, sketched hastily on the back of an envelope in a restaurant. Charles stood with his back to Nixon, unaware he was being observed, facing the window, his eyes on the astonishing view. He was perfectly dressed for an early summer day, crisp and dignified in a suit of pale grey heavyweight linen. Nixon gazed at Charles' bare head, the short blond hair razor-trimmed with precision, his dark-blue tie threaded through the stiff collar and knotted with care.

Charles lifted one hand then, smoothed his hair over one ear, and brushed his fingertips against the skin of the back of his neck, finding a tiny blemish resting above the collar. Vaguely, he fingered it a moment, discerned its existence, and ran his fingers around the inside of the collar, lightly tugging it upward to conceal the imperfection.

Nixon, in witnessing this, went weak with longing for the ordinariness of the gesture, the self-consciousness implicit in it, the desire to be pleasing from one already so perfect. Falling into a hopelessness of desire so authoritative he had no power to stop it, Nixon pushed thought away and pushed hope away. This was a lifetime hunger that would no longer allow itself to go unfed, and no other part of his being had any say in it.

With a gesture that seemed almost weary, Nixon stepped toward Charles slowly and thrust his face into the blond hair along Charles' nape. The hair was soft, like the fur of a small animal, and Charles' skin felt cool against Nixon's warm breath, which tasted of the tea he had drunk at the railway station that morning. Unprepared, Charles made a low noise in his throat that Nixon felt with his lips, and when he placed his hands on the top of Charles' shoulders, Charles reached up to grasp them. Nixon took hold of the left hand only, slid his right arm tightly around Charles' chest, and drew him down to the floor.

There was a sort of unwrapping, shirtfronts parted and collars loosened. Nixon stripped the blue tie from beneath Charles' collar and whipped it away like a lash, causing some fastener—a button—to skitter across the floor and collide with a sharp crack on the opposite wall. Neither man paused, as they had gone too far to check their frantic divestment. Nixon had gone the farthest, as close as he'd ever been to an edge whose abyss he always feared was destruction. Now there was nothing in Nixon to prevent the rending his hands were doing. His hands knew what they wanted.

Nixon raked Charles' hair with his fingers, clutching fistfuls of it like the grass one grabs hold of to climb a steep hill. Such was Charles: silver eyes which widened and narrowed beneath eyelids which crumpled like paper; his ears, with their delicate tracery, which hear everything except what the past and future have to say; his jaw, firm and resolute, which forms the face sought for months in every street; his tongue, which rivals the fingers as the body's blind explorer, whose taste is true, but whose words might be fiction; his clavicles, slopes of perfect bone where the pleasure of disobedience can easily lose itself; his arms whose grasp encircles and remembers forever the circumference; his hands, whose clandestine searching had brought their bodies to this place. The long back with the voluptuous spine and the tears of salty sweat shed on either side of it. The shoulder blades, the clipped wings of angels, that may or may not carry a warning of sin. The navel, the scar of the wound suffered on the day when longing began. The stomach, which can tell the heart nothing about hunger. The hips, which guard the secret of the hunger the heart already knows. The legs, which clamp, and bear, and climb, and flee. The feet, whose soles have a map of every land they have traveled. Back again to Charles' throat, where Nixon knew his own named lived, and where he placed his mouth often, just to hear Charles speak it.

Charles was a river, and Nixon swam him.

They lay for a long time after, on the floor of the empty bedroom, among the twisted clothing of their transgression, facing one another, startled at what they had done. It was as much the chill of the air as sudden modesty that made Charles finally sit up and pull his jacket across his lap. He picked up his detachable collar, which had rolled beneath the window, and examined it for a moment, running his fingers along its stiff edge before casting his eyes across the room in the direction where the escaped fastener had flown.

"That was my collar stud," he said with a shy smile. He placed the collar around his bare neck, a humorous sight, and began crawling along the varnished oak floor feeling for the tiny object, no bigger than a thumbtack. Nixon rose and joined him, the two men nude, on their hands and knees, searching the perimeters of the empty room.

"I give up," Charles said, lifting himself up and sitting on his heels. "I think it is lost forever." The collar had slid sideways on his slim neck, open at the throat where the missing stud would have clamped it tightly. Nixon was in a far corner, hair wild and tousled, searching with his nose near the floorboards, but on hearing Charles speak shifted to a cross-legged position and pulled his twisted trousers into his lap. They eyed one another and began to snicker. The snicker escalated into laughter that soon had them crying. The laugh was one of joy, of permanence and familiarity. This unplanned passion may have been the long-denied expression of their love, but their laughter was the promise that sealed it.

Nixon quickly learned the appeal of Mozart Street. For the next year he slipped in complete anonymity off the public horsecars and into the tangle of streets, where not a soul would recognize or pay any attention to him, and he could find himself in Charles' little rooms, utterly trans-ported from the life he led on Beacon Hill. Soon it was this secret life that defined him, as he donned a shabbier jacket and moved, ever on the verge of desire, among the clatter of the iron-wheeled beer wagons and the crowds of overall-clad working men. Threading through the streets of cheek-by-jowl three-decker houses joined by drooping strings of drying laundry became a flight from conformity. His path to the white iron bed on the third floor of the house on Mozart Street led him to the outskirts of everything.

Sometimes, awakening after a long afternoon together, they would venture out to one of the customer rooms of the local breweries. One such evening, in early February of 1886, they crossed the bridge over the Stony Brook, in a light snow, to Germania Street. Here was situated the Haffenreffer brewery, an elaborate brick and granite construction with a small unmarked doorway leading to a charming basement room. Here the languages of German and lager were spoken, and Charles could translate both.

Outside, the cold snow squeaked beneath their shoes, but no sound escaped the brick building. The room was a roar of men, smoking, joking, drinking. As was not uncommon, someone had produced an accordion and banjo, and an unofficial band struck up in a corner, with men in their working coveralls singing, the drunkest of them improvising a staggering jig. Large posters peeling away from the walls showed buxom, corseted women balancing steins while seated provocatively astride barrels. Edelweiss flowers were painted along the ceiling plaster, interspersed with German drinking slogans, and the patrons sat at common tables as mug after mug of beer slid down the smooth wooden surface in response to shouted orders.

The noisy customer room at Haffenreffer's perhaps manifested more than anything else Nixon's complete happiness. Here was masculine companionship, however coarse, after years of confinement in a household of women, as well as the privacy of anonymity. It was here too where he could witness Charles' unfettered cheerfulness and revel in his young lover's charm.

Two hours later, boarding the horsecar, he saw the snow had deepened, and what had begun quietly was now blowing up a gale. The horse team plodded forward, tails lashing, the steam of melting snow rising from their backs. The nearly empty car tugged along its rails unsteadily, the twin lanterns dangling from its roof swaying and casting futile beams of light before them. The driver, heavily cloaked, draped the reins over the cowling and stood with his hands tucked in his pockets and his face sunk in his collar. Nixon too placed his gloved hands inside his coat to keep them warm. Staring into whirling snow was dizzying, like being carried down a fast-moving stream. Nixon noticed his hand, which rested over his heart, was not trembling. The old bane of his shaky hands left him the day he'd placed them on Charles' body. There, in the shabby car of the Metropolitan Street Railway, he gave thanks for the love he'd received. Charles' love enclosed his life, pearl-like, smoothing everything, filling the barren place in his heart where Frank had been, covering even the stubborn wound Seth Tisdale inflicted on the night the priest was tortured when he was a boy in Maine. Anything bad could happen, Nixon believed, after that night, especially if you are different and alone. Now, with Charles, he was neither.

Arriving at the Common and looking across it, the unusual sight of many lights blazing in the windows of his house met his eye, even through the blowing snow. He paused for a passing sleigh and began to trudge toward his door.

He could hardly believe love had found him, when he himself had lost all knowledge of how to look for it. His good fortune left him astonished. It was a miracle he had been delivered to Charles, and had discovered in him such tender and steady arms. He would soon need the steadiness, for in the one room upstairs where no light burned, Agnes lay dead.

The moment he stepped inside the overly bright house Nixon knew something awful had happened. Katherine took his coat with weeping eyes, and in the stairway to the kitchen, the cook and hired man could be heard murmuring in low and anxious voices.

He took immediate flight to the parlor, finding his mother slumped on the sofa, in her one hand a crumpled and wadded handkerchief, and in the other the consoling palm of Dr. Pimm. The doctor's explanation poured out, a burst appendix, pain, fever, poison in the blood. Mary Black moaned and shuddered at hearing his words, and Nixon took her into his arms, a strange blank calm overwhelming him as his mother sobbed into the collar of his jacket.

"We did not know where to send for you," Dr. Pimm said, narrowing his eyes.

"No," Nixon replied. "I have been out all day."

Nixon crept quietly down the hall leading to the bedchambers of the house, using the light of a handheld candle. With the aid of Katherine and a sleeping draught provided by Dr. Pimm, Mary Black had finally been convinced into her bed. Nixon had listened for some time as his mother tossed and softly whimpered, and finally fell silent.

The calm of his movements earlier did not mean his mind rejected what had transpired. Indeed, all he could conjure was the terrible new fact. Agnes, his sister, his darling girl, was dead. Her death was only an hour old when he'd stepped through the doorway and passed from gratitude for his happiness to this awful anguish. Now, walking through the hallway to Agnes' chamber door, he knew this very house had been damaged, wrecked in some horrible unrepairable way, as if some part of it was carried off by a sudden storm. He paused before he entered, listening to the gale outside, and realized he was cringing.

Unaccustomed to entering the chamber where Agnes slept, he was struck by its girlishness. A powdery sweet smell of Agnes herself resided there, along with the little objects of her collecting. A wardrobe loomed in the dim and flickering light. Inside he knew her dresses were hung, shoulder to shoulder, arranged in the order Agnes placed them, but to him they were each a memory: Agnes singing at the Eliots', Agnes at the Kragsyde cliffs, Agnes at church.

There was a shelf of porcelain figurines: a dancing couple, a rough-coated lamb, another she particularly favored of a cat playing with a ball of yarn. A table held her many scrapbooks and her pot of glue. She'd pasted things in them for years, cards and clippings, and plants she'd purposely flattened and dried. He'd looked through them once. Everything was identified with its name in her precise, ovoid script. Tucked beneath a table was the tassel-cornered bed of little Billy, Agnes' old blind terrier who'd died last fall. She mourned him still, and kept his bed and ball nearby.

A chair was drawn close to her bedside, and Nixon sat in it, placing his candle on the table. He could not bear to turn on the gas lamps and throw the room into a rawness of full light. Someone had closed Agnes' eyes and folded her arms across one another, but the way the sheets were twisted beneath her shoulders bespoke the hours of painful writhing she had endured. Guilt flooded him, and the thought that perhaps he ought always to remember when leaving someone that it might be for a final time. Still, he knew it was only in the days of death one grieved thus; once life took over, one always expected... always.

He touched her hands, which were grotesquely swollen, the ring she wore almost swallowed by the flesh of her finger. He noticed too, they were formed into little fists, not a symptom of the illness but of her determination. Her face was remote, almost unfamiliar, but its countenance was lucid with the understanding of her fate. To be so full of ambitions and talents that could never be realized, and now would, in the space of a day, vanish! The thought of her coffined and lying beneath the beautiful stained-glass window at Trinity, which would forever be inscribed with the name of her sister and her father but not herself, as though she'd never existed! He knew now, gazing at her stranger's face, that he had watched hope disappear from her eyes for years.

In the pale candlelight, he noticed something else. While reaching out to brush a dark curl from her temple and touch it for the last time, he saw a tiny mark on her cheek. It was the dried trail of a tear, a single despairing drop, which, hours before, had slid down the side of her face and behind her ear. A sob like a cough rose in his throat. His chest ached. He placed his wrist against his mouth and bit it. What awful things the voiceless dead have to say, and how loudly they can speak. He would not forget the tear, or the meaning of its crooked path, as long as he lived.

A few days after Agnes' funeral, Nixon returned to the house from his office for his noontime meal. He'd stayed close to home during these days, taking all his meals with his mother in quiet privacy, but he could no longer neglect his mail or paperwork, which he'd tried to dispose of in a few hours this morning.

The black crepe was removed from their door, but climbing the steps he sensed again a taste of disaster. Mellie anxiously let him in, snatched his coat, and burst out, "You better go up sir," indicating the stairway with her eyes. "It's Mrs. Black. Colleen and I don't know what to do."

Nixon brushed aside the frantic housemaid and hurried upstairs, expecting to find his elderly mother in a state of illness. He rushed into her bedchamber, found it empty, and moved then to Agnes' room, where he heard some rustling. Here he found a scene entirely unexpected.

The room was in a state of destruction. The curtains had been torn from their rings and Agnes' clothes were pulled from the wardrobe and strung about. Mary Black sat on the floor, in a pile of debris Nixon slowly recognized were the torn pages of Agnes' scrapbooks. Her grey hair was undone and hanging in an unruly mass, and she was swaying and speaking in an incoherent groan. Nixon stepped forward to place his arms around her, and beneath his feet crunched the remnants of the porcelain cat, lying in shards around his mother's skirts.

Sensing his presence, she lifted her eyes and gave a short aggressive laugh.

"Mother!" Nixon exclaimed, "What has happened?"

She sat on her heels and eyed him. The face he'd known all his life was gone, replaced by one made ugly with grief. "I have lost everything!" she cried out.

Nixon understood this was lamentation, but it was taken too far, and the disgust in her voice alarmed him. He reached out for her shoulder to help her stand, and she slapped at him, a hissing sound like the threat of a cornered animal escaping from deep in her throat.

"I have nothing," she wailed, rocking back and forth, and Nixon saw that although his mother was nearly mad he felt strangely as though he were the one in danger. He'd heard of such things: derangement caused by grief. He would send Mellie for a doctor.

"You are unwell, dear," Nixon said, turning to leave the room and fetch Mellie. "I am going to send for the doctor."

"I know what you are!" his mother's voice spat after him. If she had thrown a knife, it could not have met its mark with more accuracy, splitting his heart and running like ice through his blood. He paused, stiffened, and stood taller. He knew now what this was about. His mother was not ill. He turned slowly and faced her. She met his gaze with eyes of iron.

"I am your son," Nixon said.

"I want no son of your kind. You are foul, an abomination!" How acid her anger was. Nixon wondered for a moment how long she had nursed it. "You are perverse," she continued, "and I have known it for years!"

Nixon's mind scrambled wildly, grasping for a response that would not be terrible, that he would not later regret. If only he could just say it and have it over with, but there was this barrier, and no obvious path to communication, much less understanding.

"Then why did you keep me from serving in the war?" Nixon asked. He'd not been raised to disagree with his mother, but this question, which had always puzzled him, seemed especially important now. He asked it almost without thinking. She looked confused for a moment. She had not expected the past to have any bearing on the reality of her present. Nixon saw her mouth soften slightly. Mary Black remembered

271

how afraid she'd been for her son's life during the war. The fear of his eradication. Her old premonition—*the unbearable can happen, and then it can happen again*—came back to her. She'd spent her venom and now realized she had to use caution.

"You don't know what it is like to lose your whole family," she cried.

Actually, Nixon thought, *I do*, but his heart bent in pity for her. They'd always engaged in a sort of contest, as perhaps every mother and son do, of her pressing and him resisting. Yet Nixon was not prepared to carry the weight of the demand she was ready to place on him. A flash of anger beset him. Was he wicked? Was he immoral? Or was morality simply another name for a lack of courage? He then did something he would have been unable to do in years before. He walked out of the room and left her behind the door.

Leaving the house as well, Nixon stepped outside onto Beacon Street into a world that was utterly changed. He began walking uphill, then turned and walked the opposite way. It was not his intention to leave his mother without aid or comfort, but he did not know what to do.

The trail from the door of Nixon's house to the door of Caroline Crowninshield had never grown cold. Their old fondness endured, ripened by the joys and sorrows of the many years into the happily familiar. Nixon thought now, as he hurried down Beacon Street, how easy his conversations with Caroline had always been. Just as it had been with Franny in his youth, with Caroline he never felt as though he put a foot in the wrong place. Visiting was equally comfortable whether they were engaged in the latest gossip or sitting together in silence.

The envious chatter of other women went around the city when Caroline married her second husband, a pleasant handsome man much younger than herself. She was Mrs. Arnold now, thinner and paler, in her mid-sixties but retaining the cautious tenderness for which Nixon loved her. She was a woman who accepted that sadness lasted a lifetime. Nixon believed he was the only person who understood that, as pleased as Caroline Arnold was to invite new joy into her life, she would rather have her old life instead. He knew what she had lost.

"Of course, I shall go to her at once," Caroline said, concern in her eyes as she listened to Nixon's description of his mother's condition. Nixon did not know what he expected Caroline to do, nor even why he appealed to her instead of any other, and he brooded as he helped her into her long coat.

He could barely keep pace with her while striding up the street to his house. Caroline's face was impassive, yet deeply attentive to something within herself, and Nixon knew not to speak because her mind was making sentences, rehearsing perhaps, what she was going to say to his mother. What could one say?

Once inside, Caroline let her coat slide into the hallway chair before Mellie could even take it, and tugged at her gloves and bonnet, tossing them down. "Get some tea ready, please," she said to Colleen, who stood wringing her hands at the top of the kitchen stairway, "and don't show yourselves unless I call to you."

"You must go out too," she said, addressing Nixon. "Give us three hours, and come back."

The room seemed dark, and Nixon realized the front door blind was drawn, leaving a single shaft to pour in from the upper hall window and light the room, dimly and strangely, like a vapor curling down the stairs. Caroline, with no hesitation, lifted her skirts and began to climb. Nixon felt a thick pain in his head, a horrible dread as he recalled his mother's state and her anguished outpourings, the things she'd said to him in that terrible room. He felt a suffocating apprehension.

"This is a mistake!" he cried, rushing up the stairs to catch Caroline, stopping two steps short of her and reaching out his arm. She turned slowly toward him, a head taller than he was, her face a regal, resolute calm. "I can't...." Nixon continued but then trailed off as he looked at her, dropping his arm to his side. Her eyes widened, her pale brow glowed like ivory in the unfamiliar light. How fierce she was! Fierce and small like a little wren. She stepped down closer to him. Her nearness was both vivid and inevitable. He could hear her steady breathing.

"Nixon," she said, and she placed her hand on the side of his face with a slow lingering motion before she turned and continued up the stairs.

The Bowl of Roses
1886-1900

Independence Day 1886. Heat draped the coastline like a blanket, the sun shattering the roofs of the houses on Smith's Point into glittering angles, their long grey expanses seeming to be snapped into full billows like sails. Beneath their taut edges lay the refuge of shadowed porches, rough stones, and coarse shingles, all rich textures which suggested the great houses were moving, ever so slightly in the heavy air, as though stirring in a fitful sleep.

Members of every summer picnic party who ventured to the rock-strewn beach at Lobster Cove took a moment, shaded their eyes, and gazed up at the marvelous dwellings. Yet it was always the silvery-sided house with the striking archway that kindled the most curiosity, inviting speculations and suppositions about the lives of those within.

The flag at the Pratts', which regularly chattered away the summer, found no breeze to freshen it and today hung limp and exhausted on its pole. Even the sea was still, a vast and opaque blue-green, like a bowl brimful of paint. The only sound was that of a jangling harness and a working horse pulling the white ice wagon, cresting the steep grade of the point, carrying frozen blocks cut last winter from Ayers' Pond to the kitchens of the area. It passed the front drive of Kragsyde, where a pair of stone plinths marked the entrance. Following a flat grade at last, the hot horse heaved a sigh and the driver allowed her a slower pace as they moved along the road beside the low stone wall to the back drive where deliveries were made. Along this drive the rhododendrons had finished

274

dropping their blossoms, and a gardener raked them in small white piles beneath their glossy leaves. Clumps of lilies were just coming into color, yellow with mahogany spots.

The iceman, Ayers, a descendant of the family for whom the ice pond was named, greeted the gardener, who hailed him in return before pulling into the kitchen yard, sliding from his seat, and tying on his rubber apron. One of the dogs of the house, Mick, a black hunting type, galloped out to investigate and circled the wagon in happy leaps, snapping at the flies the horse brought with her and sniffing at the legs of the iceman. Mrs. Carlson, the cook, flushed and with sleeves rolled up over her elbows, came out to greet him. Will Follett, who worked around the cottage, drew a pail of water for the horse. They talked as Ayers manhandled the slippery blocks with his tongs into the iceboxes in the cellar of Kragsyde.

In the pantry above, through windows facing the kitchen yard, Tena Grant watched the iceman and polished a spoon that came up from the breakfast wash looking tarnished. Newly arrived from Canada, Tena had just been hired as a maid to replace Colleen O'Brien. She was eighteen years old. Tena placed the spoon in the velvet-lined drawer and folded the polishing rag into quarters, tucking it in her apron pocket with the aim of returning it to the cellar laundry on her next trip down. But first she thought to look in on old Mrs. Black on the porch, to see if there was anything she might need. Tena stepped around the folding Japanese screen concealing the butler's pantry from the dining room. This large room was painted a cool blue color, and she glanced quickly around to make sure it was in perfect order. There was so much to learn.

Guests were not frequent or numerous at Kragsyde, so the mahogany dining table was small, with reeded legs. Two Sheraton side tables stood against the paneled wainscot; they were opened end to end in case of a large party. Six vase-backed chairs circled the main table, with six others tucked around the room ready to be pressed into duty. Mellie Fraser, the more senior housemaid, said the silver and paintings traveled back and forth from the house at 57 Beacon Street each season, and each year a different painting hung on the wall in this room. This year there was a portrait of a woman in a blue gown. Tena thought she was the most beautiful woman she'd ever seen.

"Tena," Nixon called quietly to the new housemaid so as not to startle her. The new girl was in the dining room, staring at the portrait he'd bought on Charles' advice at one of the winter auctions. "What do you think of her?"

Tena jumped a bit, despite Mr. Black's soft voice, not having heard him enter the room. She was trying her best at her new job, hoping to make a good impression. "This is a good house." Mellie Fraser told her on the day Tena was hired. "Work hard and see you don't get caught shirkin'."

Mr. Black was carrying a large blue-and-white porcelain bowl that she'd seen in Miss Black's room, filled with dried flower petals. Tena knew Miss Black had died unexpectedly last winter, and Tena was told to clean the room but not to disturb anything within it. Tena wondered if she would be scolded for not emptying the bowl; then her eyes returned to the painting of the beautiful woman, a lady too old-fashioned to be Miss Black.

"I think she is beautiful, sir. Is she a relative?" Tena asked.

"No, but I thought she was beautiful too. Her name was Hannah. She lived more than a hundred years ago."

"It seems a plain name for such a fancy lady," Tena observed.

Nixon placed the bowl on the table and stirred the dried petals with his hand. "My sister, Miss Agnes, saved these roses from the garden last summer." He beckoned Tena toward the bowl. "Can you still smell them?" he asked.

Tena hesitantly leaned over and inhaled, as Nixon sifted the dried petals through his fingers. Amazingly, she could smell the roses, sweet and earthy and a bit like an orange peel. "I can smell them! I can!" Tena was surprised, and her voice indicated as much.

"This is what last summer smelled like," Nixon said, casting his eyes downward. Tena bit her lip and shifted uncomfortably on her feet. She didn't want to make her employer sad, and she could not think of the right thing to say. "I think it is a good tradition, saving the roses from each summer," Nixon said, smiling again. "I am going outside to gather more roses to mix in with these."

Tena brightened, relieved. "So I should never throw them away, sir?"

"No. I think I will keep this bowl on the hall table so we can all smell the summer roses. By the way, are the lanterns unpacked yet?"

"I was thinkin' to check on Mrs. Black first, sir," Tena said.

"I'll do that for you," Nixon said. "Can you fetch me the garden scissors from the pantry? Just put them in the bowl as you pass by, and I will check on Mother."

"Yes, sir," Tena said, moving back to the pantry screen before pausing and turning to speak again. "Mr. Black, sir?" she said awkwardly. "I apologize for the shirkin'."

"Shirking?" Nixon asked, not comprehending.

"Looking at the lady in the painting, instead of working," Tena said, ashamed.

"Tena," Nixon said with a small smile, "look as long as you like."

He chuckled as Tena scurried away, and glanced through the double doors leading to the covered piazza. His mother had achieved her seventieth year last February, only a few days before Agnes died. She wearied easily now and napped often during the day, a circumstance that did not worry Nixon because he knew from the crack of light slipping beneath her door at midnight that she did not rest well after sundown. She was dozing at this moment, her hair swept back from her milky face, her hand dangling from the edge of the chair where it had slipped during sleep. She wore a dress of black fabric so dark it shone blue, like the feathers of a raven, and an oval jet brooch. The near-silent ocean a hundred feet below lapped gently like the waves of a small pond, casting quivering reflections on the porch ceiling. The blue sky had faded to white in the heat. An insect buzzed in a far-off tree.

The family dog that most favored her, a little spaniel she called Teddy, lolled on its side on the wooden floor, in the coolest place it could find, with its spotted legs stretched out and one silken ear fallen backward to reveal its delicate pink interior. Teddy's handsome eyes followed Nixon, but the dog moved not another muscle as Nixon reached out to his mother, unwound the watch chain caught under her brooch, and sat in the chair beside her.

Nixon never knew what Caroline Arnold had said to his mother on the awful day when he'd sought her help. He'd understood Caroline's gesture on the stairs, but nonetheless left the house in a torment, pacing the streets while waiting and vowing every sort of remedy and renunciation, even that of leaving the country in the company of Charles. Raw as the wound of Agnes' sudden death had been, worse was his belief that his sister had perished in a state of unfulfillment, and his only vow from that day on was to not do the same.

When he returned to the townhouse, he found the two women in the sitting room, as placid and unremarkable as on any afternoon visit. The only peculiarity he could ascertain was his mother's hair, which was done up in the same way Caroline did hers, and he guessed Caroline had repinned it. What else she repaired remained unrevealed, and Nixon understood this was a privacy belonging to his mother and Caroline. Mercifully and mysteriously, the day and its repercussions were erased. If any traces of his mother's dissatisfaction remained, they darkened her features infrequently and briefly, in the same way a cloud crosses the summer sun.

Nixon reached out and delicately stroked the back of his mother's sleeping hand, with the intent of waking her. She was utterly strange to him, and entirely familiar. He traced the blue veins that meandered there until her eyelids fluttered, and she woke with a start.

"Oh-ooh," she said. "Is it time for luncheon?"

"Not yet, Mother, but I think the girls would enjoy your company while hanging the lanterns."

General Jacqueminots, the dark red roses; Cristatas, the ones whose stems needed the support of little sticks; Gabriel Luizets, pink and pale, like tiny peonies, drooping over the newly spaded earth. Nixon moved along the path of the garden with the blue-and-white bowl and balanced it carefully on the stone wall supporting the thorny tendrils of a bush of yellow climbers. The bowl was an antique Fitzhugh, Charles told him, nearly a hundred years old. It came from Woodlawn, and Nixon supposed it once belonged to his grandfather Cobb, but what mattered most was its importance to Agnes.

Agnes taught him the names of these roses last summer as she wandered among them, marking each with small wooden tags on which she'd penciled their names. Today he gathered them, remembering his sister with her tags and scissors, wondering if memory was actually a penance and if it would always seem so illusory and just beyond reach.

Nixon could hear Mellie and Tena on the big porch and the happy tones of his mother's voice.

Tonight was illumination night, and as the skies were filled with fireworks in the harbor, the cottages in the vicinity were decorated with strings of Japanese lanterns. Last summer Mary Black delighted in the spectacle, and she'd spent all of one afternoon assembling the paper lanterns while Agnes and Mellie climbed ladders and suspended them. Made of pleated paper and painted in gaudy colors, when the variously shaped lanterns were lit with candles they glowed like happiness in the darkness.

Some of the roses that flourished here last summer were winter-killed. The new La France tea rose for which Agnes had high hopes was gone, replaced by the gardener with a more durable but predictable Catherine Mermet. A year ago Nixon could have asked his sister if they ought to try planting it again, and he grieved knowing the question could never be asked now, remembering all the questions he'd never asked, thinking he could ask them anytime.

Mervielle de Lyon, a pretty white rose, had bloomed in June, leaving only shiny green leaves. Old Blush dangled in the heavy air, carrying the weight of two bumblebees, dispersing its fragrance of violets. Baroness Rothschild, which Nixon had only just remembered shatters at the moment its bloom is most perfect, filled his palms with petals, which he carried to the bowl on the wall. Nixon was pleased his mother was enjoying decorating for the illumination. He was grateful to spend his forenoon with Agnes, trying to reclaim what had once been merely ordinary.

Little brown moths fluttered against the gently rocking, glowing lanterns on the porches. A cooling breeze graced the evening, and all across the rugged terrain surrounding the harbors and coves of Manchester, such lanterns danced, outlining the eaves and gables of the houses where they were suspended. The fireworks launched from a barge in the main harbor rumbled and hissed, throwing color far into the sky like sparks from a distant fire. Charles, who'd spent the day at a picnic sponsored by his camera club, arrived in time for their early supper. He now sat in a wicker chair pulled close to the one used by Mary Black, and together they clapped and drew long sighs when the bursts of color were their most vivid.

Nixon leaned against the porch railing on the side that faced the sea. He breathed deeply, closed his eyes, and listened to the sounds of the summer night. The deep growl of the fireworks, the spattering of insects on the lanterns. At some distance, he could hear the notes of a banjo and a fiddle, boats passing along the shores serenading the houses whose decorations were deemed most beautiful with silly popular songs. Young men in flannel shirts and straw hats, their girls in skirts of cotton lawn singing "Johnny Get Your Gun," "Somebody's Mother," "My Darling Clementine."

The birds of the day had gone quiet. The night was powdered with stars, the waves far below spread in soundless white crescents as they reached the rocky shore, and the Belle Lyonnaise roses crept another inch along the trellis. Kragsyde was never again more beautiful, and no one knew it. The perfection of the day slipped away, as the perfection of many days does, unnoticed. They did not know then, any of them, that only when its image was frozen and reduced to a curling sepia photograph pulled dusty from a drawer would it be yearned for. After all, it was still July, and the September of this way of life was many years away.

The ensign of royalty fluttered from the flagpole atop Boston's Parker House hotel and inside, in a reception room full of flowers, Nixon watched as Charles was embraced by a queen. A plump and bejeweled hand was extended, to which Charles offered his lips, stepping forward with a quick glance at the floor to ensure he was not treading on the white train that curled around her tiny slippered feet. Thus recognized, he leaned forward again to bury his face in the spray of scarlet and yellow feathers that surrounded the royal neck and to exchange kisses on either side of her exotic face. An ample bosom blazed with the flash of a diamond star; a necklace of rare shells rested across her dusky chest. She was the queen of the Kingdom of Hawaii and she was Charles' cousin.

Of course, Nixon had known all this before. Long ago in the room on Mozart Street, Charles confessed with some trepidation the story of his family, fearing Nixon might reject him when he learned of the experiences of his father, Benjamin Pitman. Old Benjamin, who started life as a Pacific trader, had been married three times, his first two wives dying in childbirth. Charles' mother, Martha, was Benjamin's third wife, but his first marriage was to a Hawaiian Chiefess, Kino'ole o Liliha, a rich land-owning woman descended from the Hawaiian kings. Benjamin and Kino'ole had surviving children, and Charles had two half-black half-siblings. It was enough to raise eyebrows in conservative Boston, but Nixon barely reacted. Exhibiting the personality for which Charles so loved him, and which made him such a mystery, Nixon replied to Charles' tale with nonchalance.

"I imagine Kino'ole o Liliha was very beautiful," Nixon said, as he could easily understand a passion for a lovely, high-toned woman.

Charles, unaccustomed to thinking of his father as an admirer of female beauty, cast his thoughts back to the oval wedding portraits of the youthful couple that now hung in his half-brother's drawing room. "Yes," he replied, realizing for the first time, "she was."

"Where are your Hawaiian siblings now?"

"My sister Mary never left Hawaii. She is years older than me. Since I left when I was a baby, I can't remember her. My brother Ben Jr. is in his thirties. I've not known him well either, because of the difference in our ages. He's married a daughter of the family who owns the Hollander Company, the fancy clothier, and lives here in Boston in a townhouse on Boylston Street.

Nixon was silent after this, and Charles fidgeted until he could stand it no longer and finally asked, "Well, what do you think of it?"

"I think," Nixon began, and for emphasis laughed and kissed Charles' cheek, "that Pitman men make good marriages."

Now Nixon knew all the Pitman men seated with him at this private family reception at the Parker House. Queen Kapiolani and Princess Liliuokalani were on their gala tour of the United States, en route to the Golden Jubilee of Queen Victoria in England. Benjamin Sr. was clearly enjoying the party, leaning back in his chair with his short thumbs tucked in the armholes of his yellow waistcoat and regaling his family with tales of Hawaii. Harold, Charles' full brother, was present too, so strikingly handsome he was almost difficult to look at, but oddly abstract, with a personality which seemed uncommonly bland.

Hoary old Benjamin was always interesting, reminding Nixon of his own grandfather. Made rich by his Hawaiian marriage; his plantations of coffee, arrowroot, and sugarcane; and his work as the local customs collector, he was, Charles said, a great champion of the Hawaiian people, eschewing many of the ideals of the missionaries who invaded the islands. He and his brisk, good-natured wife, Martha, were the sort of couple Nixon most admired. Brought together after the deaths of their former spouses, they possessed a mellow affection for each other, born of experience and circumspection. There was no snobbery and little inclination to judgment. Benjamin was aging fast but he knew it; his humor was direct and his speech without falsity. Nixon knew the old adventurer had long ago eyed himself and Charles, sized up the situation, and decided it was not worth the argument. "To hell with it," Nixon could almost hear him say.

"The queen and her party have dazzled President Cleveland in Washington and left the blue bloods of Boston all agog," said Charles. "Now they shall lay siege to New York."

"With London soon to come," added Martha. "How do you think Queen Victoria will find our Hawaiian queen?"

"Queen Kapiolani will hold her own with that lot," old Benjamin said, lifting a rather withered tea cake from a tray on the table and frowning at it. "She has British blood."

"Has she?" Harold asked, with a look of disbelief.

Old Benjamin smiled and lowered his voice to a conspiratorial whisper. "Her grandfather ate Captain Cook," he said.

Nixon stifled a laugh. Agnes had been right. Charles' family history was fantastical.

"You must come and see the new paintings at the Chase Gallery," Charles said, not looking at Nixon directly but instead at the dangling strip of scarlet ribbon he was cutting with a pair of scissors. The two men sat in the dining room at Mozart Street at the small table that functioned more as a desk since Charles had given over his kitchen sink and drainboard to his photography. He was lately in the habit of taking his meals elsewhere now that the kitchen was filled with trays and jars of chemicals, the window covered over.

"Do you mean the ones you and Mother saw last week while you were shopping?" Nixon answered from behind his open *Transcript*.

"Yes, the Boston Water Color Club's 1893 exhibition. There was one group that was quite wonderful, by a Miss Laura Hills. Your mother was very impressed with them. I truly think she would like one."

"She did mention them. We should choose one for her for Christmas," Nixon said. Charles folded the corners of a square of tissue paper around a velvet case containing antique earrings Nixon's mother had helped him choose for Martha Pitman last week. "They're not that sort of paintings," he said, twisting the ribbon around the package. He poked Nixon's newspaper to seize his attention. "Hold my knot, will you?" he said. Nixon leaned forward, crumpled his *Transcript* in his lap, and placed his finger on the ribbon around Charles' gift. "They are portrait miniatures. The artist is seeking commissions. Your mother wants one of you."

"Good Lord!" Nixon exclaimed, as Charles tied the bow across his finger. "I can't imagine anything less decorative."

"Nonetheless," Charles said, smiling and admiring his gift-wrapping and his persuasiveness. "It is what she wants."

"You can't be serious," Nixon said, peering at the display of painted ivory miniatures at the J. Eastman Chase Gallery later that day. "They are all young ladies."

"Of course we are serious. Don't you see how fine they are?" Charles said.

"Fine, yes, but 'Seven Pretty Girls of Newburyport'"? Nixon replied, referring to the title of the exhibit and rolling his eyes. "Don't you think I'm a bit grizzled for this sort of thing?"

Charles ignored his protest and examined the diminutive ivories more closely with a magnifying glass. "It's the same technique as the

George Washington miniature you inherited from your grandfather," Charles said. "But these have so much more life!"

They were amazing, Nixon had to admit: beautiful young women, in frills and bows, and charming little girls with pigtailed locks and calico dresses. The colors were unusual and rich, and the little ovals stood out against their background like small jewels. The sitters' imperfections were smoothed over but not eliminated; freckles still dotted cheekbones and uneven hair ribbons stayed uneven. Charles was right. The George Washington who sat on a small easel in his parlor looked by comparison many years dead. These miniatures seemed both antique and modern.

"I wouldn't be surprised if Miss Hills painted these using a brush with a single hair," Charles said, squinting through the magnifying glass. "The detail is amazing, and the color.... I understand she began with pastels of flowers. She certainly continued using her garden palette here. She must have the patience of Job to produce such results with wriggling children."

"That's just it," Nixon said. "I don't think I'm the sort of subject she is accustomed to."

The gallery attendant, who'd been standing at a discreet distance but listening to every word, stepped closer to the two men, his hands folded deferentially at his waist. "As of Friday last," he said, smiling, "we've taken orders for more than a dozen."

On Christmas Eve, over a delicious leg of lamb and after more than a little wine, Nixon told his mother that he would pose for a miniature painting as a gift to her, if she promised to pose for one as a gift to him. She agreed, but tried to make him submit to posing first.

"Ladies first," Nixon insisted, and closed the conversation.

During the following fall of 1894, posing with a single rose cut from the greenhouse she and Nixon had built at Kragsyde in honor of Agnes, Mary Peters Black embarked on one of the last great adventures of her life. Having her likeness painted was a flattery she never would have indulged on her own, and she secretly delighted in it, coming home after every sitting with tales of Miss Hills' skill and pleasant talk. Finally she returned with a soft and pretty portrait of herself on a thin oval of ivory, wrapped in a pouch of velvet felt.

Nixon felt confident then, the following January, as he climbed the stairs of Miss Hills' Boylston Street studio to take his turn, that the process would be both painless and quick.

Miss Laura Coombs Hills arrived early at her studio. The air outside was winter-sharp, and she wanted to build a fire in the circulating stove in the small room. She already knew the unnatural posture a cold sitter could assume.

Laura was proud of her studio, with its west-facing exposure and roof window. Here she could do good work among her carefully chosen furnishings, which included souvenirs from her travels, her favorite vases, her easel, and artfully draped fabrics. Her routine was to bank the fire, slip on her apron, draw the water needed for her paints, and ready herself for a morning of concentration mixed with light conversation to put the sitter at ease. She knew she was becoming steadily more expert. She'd painted miniatures for clients for a year now, and had settled into a professionalism honed by confidence. Her paintings were in demand, and she was increasingly able to work with certainty and speed.

Today's sitter was a gentleman, Mr. Nixon Black. He was unknown to her, but his mother, who sat for her last fall, was a pleasant elderly lady. Most of her sitters were women and children; men were rare, and she found the prospect of painting them more daunting. They were often rigid and tense, and lent themselves less well to the softness of the technique. She dreaded too the day a bald man would walk in, not entirely sure what she would do with a gleaming or freckled pate.

Laura had not needed to worry in this case, for the sitter who entered her doorway was a man without a single sharp angle. Indeed, Laura was struck immediately by his furriness, dressed as he was in a fine long coat with a luxurious Russian sable collar. It was the sort of coat worn only by the very wealthy, and the rare rust-colored pelts that trimmed and lined it melted into the brush of the man's own side-whiskers, which contained tones of the same reddish hue. Mr. Black was perhaps twenty years her senior and a good ten inches taller, with a kind face and a quiet voice and step, which Laura believed was the countenance of a man who lives with his elderly mother. His face was pale, despite having just come from the freezing cold, and smooth, like the lining of a jewelry box. In fact, nested in his pale face were eyes like gems, the very blue of the summer delphiniums that grow in every Boston garden. Laura knew without hesitation what she wanted Mr. Black to wear while posing, and what color her background was to be.

Nixon valued privacy too much to be comfortable with the close inspection required of a portrait subject, but after his second morning sitting for Miss Hills he found this discomfort replaced by his interest in observing her. The lady artist was a mite, barely five feet tall, with dark hair and even darker eyes. She was a plain woman but suffused with vitality and humor. Her studio was delightful, warmed with a handsome Pennsylvania fireplace, and filled with artistic bric-a-brac and some interesting pieces of old pewter. Several of her paintings lay propped behind sheets in the corners, and a pastel landscape was showcased on a simple easel.

Nixon sat against a bare wall where a window cast soft light into his face. The window was slightly open to keep him cool, as the artist had requested he pose while wearing his fur coat, suggesting the color would go well with his face. Miss Hills sat on a stool on a platform beneath a skylight, holding a thin board to which the small oval of ivory was pinned. She worked, as Charles had suggested, with brushes that had only one or two hairs, soaking them in an old blue bowl and wiping them on a rag draped across one knee. She appeared entirely immersed in the task before her, but chattered away happily and unintrusively as she worked.

Nixon was fascinated with her workmanlike method. He watched her feet, placed tightly together on the platform; her eyes squinting slightly as she leaned forward to study his figure; her dark hair, which she often stopped to tuck behind her ear while holding a brush in her teeth. There was no doubt he was watching a woman who was to make her artistic career a success, so intent and purposeful were her efforts.

It was impossible for him to watch Miss Hills and not think of Agnes. The world of art was opening to women in Boston. Appendicitis was now often cured with surgery. Had she been born in a different time, his sister might have been able to pursue her talents as Miss Hills did.

Until she died, Mary Black kept Laura Hills' completed miniature of Nixon, with its remarkable likeness of her son dressed in his fur coat set against a blue background, on the dresser in her bedchamber. After his sessions with Miss Hills, Nixon, who was already an enthusiastic supporter of the art museum, resolved to remember living artists too.

Charles loved Woodlawn. To Nixon the old house was a place he had outgrown. Like childhood itself, it had faded, brightened only occasionally by memory. As he predicted, the family traveled to the Maine homestead less often after Kragsyde was built, finally settling on an annual two-week visit in midsummer. They kept the property maintained, but it had now sat empty for twenty years, occupied only by the caretaker who lived in one of its outbuildings and cared for the horses Nixon stabled and bred there.

The commercial successes of the town of Ellsworth were long behind it. Lumbering had collapsed, and the ships that once clustered in its river port were abandoned one by one, made obsolete by the railroads. The whole state of Maine had suffered since the end of the war. The farming, the forests, the markets, and the weather were better almost everywhere else. True, some factories on the rivers survived in the southernmost parts, and grand cottages for summer visitors were rising in some of the beautiful coastal areas, but the state was remote and cold, desirable only in the hottest weeks of August. "Far Harbor," some of his Boston friends called the expanding resort on the outer island of Mt. Desert in the same county as Ellsworth. It was far, and time seemed to have abandoned it forty years before.

For precisely these reasons, Charles loved the place. Where Nixon saw an old house standing atop a decaying town, Charles saw a marvelous example of the architecture of the early century. Where Nixon saw the rooms of Franny's exile, Charles saw an untouched trove of perfectly kept artifacts, some in an undesirable Civil War–era style but others passed down from Nixon's grandparents, true antiques from the time of the Revolutionary War and the country's early history. When Charles accompanied Mary Black and Nixon to the house for the first

time in the early 1890s, he was in awe of the beauty of the estate, its so-
phistication despite its remote location, and the quality of its furnishings
and construction.

"You have a treasure here," he told Nixon, and made it his task to
convince his companion it was so.

Nixon knew the miniature painting of George Washington inherited
from his great-grandfather Cobb was valuable. The whole country, especially younger people like Charles, were enthralled by history and antiques. Turning against things that were newly made, they formed clubs
to focus on old china and pewter, and combed attics for articles of their
forefathers. Nor was collecting these artifacts enough. The new rage was
to trace one's ancestors, preferably back to a Revolutionary patriot or a
Mayflower passenger. Nixon thought such family tree climbing might
be more rooted in proving one had a pedigree that did not include
recent immigrants than in seeking John Alden or Paul Revere, but he
began to take an interest. Charles enlisted Nixon to join him on long
drives to study historic houses and coaxed him into antique sales and
auctions. Charles even convinced Nixon to attend a summer costume
party where all the attendees dressed as Puritans, though the irony of
that frolic caused them both much laughter.

Watching Charles drag an old spinning wheel from the Woodlawn
barn and spend an afternoon cleaning it, and hearing him press Mary
Black for memories of her girlhood were irresistible. Nixon began to
recall the stories his blind grandfather told him while dragging him
through the house as a boy, and these histories, only dimly remembered,
took on more importance to Nixon when he saw them reflected in
Charles' delighted eyes.

Before too long, the old Woodlawn kitchen was decorated with
household antiques, and Great-grandfather Cobb's chair from the Massachusetts House of Representatives, which had so bored Nixon as a
child, was given its place of honor in the library. Franny's marble-topped
furniture was banished to the barn, but Nixon insisted her portrait be
hung prominently in the dining room. The finest of the furniture was
displayed in the grandest rooms, and old John Black's extravagant 1824-
era high-post bed was returned to the largest bedroom. Because of

Charles, Nixon began to understand that the past had left him an inheritance unlike any other. He had grown in this place. Woodlawn was the soil his ancestors had prepared for him.

A favorite pastime was to picnic beneath a grove of white pine trees along the side of the drive leading to the grand old house. Here, on a fine day, the family could set up a table or spread a blanket on the ground, and feast in the dappled sun,

On one such day in July of 1897, while Mary Black was away visiting a cousin, Nixon and Charles decided to do just that. Chicken sandwiches were made and carried in a hamper with root beer and strawberries to the pretty spot. Here, beside the old stone walls that lined the sloping drive, Nixon and Charles ate their food and lay back on the blanket, safe in the steep alcove of shadow from the noontime sun. Charles threaded his fingers beneath his head, stretched his elbows against the ground, and closed his eyes. The great ancestral boughs above them filtered the summer light that glinted in moving orbs along the grass. A red squirrel who'd complained to them all through their sandwiches scurried along the tops of the stacked stones and into the branches overhead.

"The Tisdale house is for sale," Nixon said. He'd remained seated upright, with his back against the wall, and one hand draped across a bended knee, turning a plucked blade of grass over and over in his fingers.

Charles lifted his head toward his friend and, squinting, looked up at him. "The white one with the fancy cupola?" Nixon nodded.

"It's a marvelous house," Charles said and laid his head back down, drawing his arm across his eyes. "I imagine the Tisdale who owned it was some local potentate?"

"Seth Tisdale," Nixon replied. "Yes, but he died years ago."

"Did you know him?"

"Yes," Nixon answered.

A slight breeze swam through the trees, parting the long needles, stirring the fragrance of pine resin. Pale feather-like ferns that spread in carpets and smelt of cut hay fretted softly, swaying their delicately curled tops. The air was drowsy and liquid. Somewhere, a woodpecker pounded away at a bark-bound insect.

"Do you think the building could be made into a library?" Nixon ventured.

"Why not?" Charles answered.

"There is no library here, and I have been made to understand, after talking with some of Mother's relatives, that Ellsworth would be open to accepting a library as a gift."

Charles answered this statement by uncovering his face and turning to look at Nixon. "And...?" he prodded.

"Would you be willing to draw the designs for the remodeling?"

The squirrel began scolding again, as Charles lay smiling into the sky.

That October, while the carpenters in Ellsworth checked their measurements against Charles' drawings for the new library in the former Tisdale house, Caroline Crowninshield Arnold was dying.

Her illness had been swift but pitiless, and she was torn away from those who loved her before most of them even had a chance to fear her gone. Nixon stood with the other mourners in the funeral crowd at Emmanuel Church, and again later in Mt. Auburn Cemetery, but could not grieve her in either place. Two days after her burial, he returned alone to the cemetery and stood near the sad rectangle of newly turned earth, which marked a tiny space compared to the one in his heart.

It was a fine October day, but it had rained the night before, and yellow leaves loosened from the trees in the downpour stuck to the nearby gravestones like bright and rustic stars. New oak trees surrounded the site and an older tulip tree from whose depths a dove's hymn sounded: a plangency that caused Nixon's eyes to tear.

Here in this plot lay an entire family, perished. Edward Sr., Caroline's first husband, beneath his chaste spire of tapered stone, the first to die and perhaps the unwitting killer of the sons buried beside him. Nixon well remembered the day, in the early eighties, just before Kragsyde was built, when he woke to read in the morning paper word of the startling discovery. He'd gone immediately to Caroline's home to sit with her, understanding perfectly how she would feel upon reading such news. A

290

man of science named Robert Koch had discovered consumption was caused by a germ. It had long been assumed Frank and young Edward inherited the tendency of consumption from their father. No one realized until then that Edward Sr. had probably infected them with it.

Nixon paused before the brothers' graves, Edward Jr.'s carved with oak leaves, and Frank's with a carving of his unbuckled sword. Thirty years they had been in the ground. Once there was an hour when Nixon's entire being depended on Frank's presence in the world. Now his old friend was a figment he could not quite grasp, a whisper he could not quite hear, spent in the bitter flame of time's passage. Was it enough that he remembered Frank, or had the years made his love even more hopeless?

To think of the people he so loved, buried in orderly rows, saddened Nixon. Yet here, such orderly rows spread in every direction, aloof from the beginnings or endings of any man. In another part of the cemetery his own family's plot awaited, different from this one in only a single respect. Once Nixon's mother passed away, the Crowninshield and Black grave sites would be exactly the same. A father and mother in each, two dead siblings in each, and two living sons left behind.

Caroline Crowninshield Arnold and Mary Peters Black would each have a son spared the caprice of war and illness. Like Nixon, Frederic Crowninshield had survived. An artist, he lived much of his life in Europe, but he'd married and had children, two of which he named after his dead brothers. Against all odds, somewhere today another Francis Welch Crowninshield lived and breathed, his existence perhaps a better tribute than memory.

Nixon paced the edge of the ground where Caroline now lay. Her headstone was not yet placed, and other than a clutch of already browning roses left behind by another mourner, the spot was unmarked. They'd been an unlikely pairing, the slim aristocratic widow and the inexperienced, awkward youth, yet they became yoked together as survivors. He would grieve her forever. A bright star in his heavens had burned out, and although he was no longer afraid to sail alone, he would dearly miss having it to steer by.

Charles never returned to study at Massachusetts Institute of Technology. Although he wavered over the decision for some time, he found he enjoyed occasional jobs with surveyors and architectural offices, and not being bound to any one project for too long a time. Additionally, a few months after the reception for Queen Kapiolani, his father became ill, suffered for some months, and died during the coldest week of the winter. Charles and his brother Harold, who'd just finished his studies at the Lawrence Scientific School, spent much time in assisting their mother, and with their father's death both came into inheritances that settled any question of compulsory employment. They were free to do as they wished.

It was decided the widowed Martha Pitman would be advantaged in living with her sons in the city of Boston, and in the early 1890s a newly built townhouse, patterned in the Federal style on Bay State Road, was purchased for the family. Here they took up residence, although Charles was often with Nixon and maintained his room and camera works at Mozart Street.

Photography was an all-consuming passion with Charles. It appealed to his artistic impulses but also to his love of science and experimentation. He spent many days trundling his equipment around, and even more time perfecting skills in developing, printing, toning, and testing each of the new advances. Photography, along with his sketching and designing and his avid pursuit of antiquities, filled his days.

Charles was not surprised that Nixon asked him to draw the plans for the remodeling of the Tisdale house. Charles loved old buildings, and the notion of giving such a structure a new purpose while preserving its original beauty naturally appealed to him. Moreover, he and others like him were concerned such structures were being left to ruin, or worse, torn down and lost, in the current rush to build bigger and newer. Dreaming up a new interior for the Tisdale house would be gratifying, and he was eager to put his mind and hand to it.

He was a bit puzzled by Nixon's desire for the project. He already knew Nixon's generosity to the art museum and animal charities knew no bounds, but in general his friend was a more measured philanthropist. His standard response to a donation request was to offer ten dollars, no matter who asked. If the Catholics asked for funds for new kneelers,

Nixon gave ten dollars; if the Protestants required repairs to an aging steeple, he gave ten dollars. When members of opposing political parties came begging, he gave each ten dollars, and, as far as Charles knew, never cast a vote for any.

Yet Charles had never known Nixon to take any particular interest in his hometown. Charles was aware some bad blood existed between Nixon's father and his brothers, but only one of these old uncles remained alive, and Nixon rarely spoke of him. Charles himself was very interested in the fortunes of Hawaii, following the recent events of its overthrow and annexation, despite having left its shores forever as an infant. Nixon was far more detached, speaking fondly of his old home but never expressing the enthusiasms of a native son. That he'd taken a sudden interest in this library was unexpected, not the least because Nixon rarely moved with such sudden decisiveness in any situation. Perhaps, Charles hoped, he was responsible for Nixon's growing pride in the place of his birth.

Nixon gripped the handle of the wooden box of photographic plates and held the door of the new library open as Charles lifted his camera outfit across the threshold. The remodeling was completed just before Christmas of 1897 and conveyed to the citizens of Ellsworth by letter a few days later. Charles was thrilled with the results of the construction and hoped to make some photographs of the building. He wanted his images to convey all the reality of a library in use, with books already on the shelves and paperwork in evidence on the desks, so the two men made an unusual wintertime trip to Maine, arriving in mid-February with Charles' equipment.

They made arrangements to work on a day when the building was closed. The rooms were neat and spare, transformed from the former parlors and bedchambers of the Tisdale family to open spaces with shelves, benches, and large tables. Arched windows were added, a small wing and a porch torn away, galleries built. Two lovely false trusses crowned the ceilings of the central room. Both Charles and the builders had done a fine job. Nixon walked slowly though the rooms as Charles set up his tripod and camera in the hallway.

The priest John Bapst had been tarred, feathered, and tortured because of a book: a Catholic version of the Bible that many citizens of Ellsworth did not want to allow in the schools. Nixon entered the front room on the river side of the library. In the 1850s this would have been Seth Tisdale's parlor. Nixon well remembered himself as a boy crouching against the wall of the commercial block below, straining to get a view of the window in this very room. On that awful October night, in the hallway just beyond where Charles now stood fiddling with the camera, a single light burned ominously, giving his shivering self no clue whether Tisdale and his horse had returned. Now Nixon stood in the room that all his life, he'd imagined as stained with evil.

Outside the same grey river roiled, sweeping to the sea, bearing the weight of smoke from the chimneys of the town which slithered over it, and the winter fog above. Nixon overheard Charles grumbling, something about "as bad as wet plates," and watched as his lover dragged his camera to a different position after crossing the room to open the window curtains fully.

It was not hard for Nixon to remember himself, cold and cowering in the grass, hiding from the man mounted on the tall horse, who was smoking a cigar. He knew now that every event which followed in his life had been in some way illuminated by the light that appeared that night when Seth Tisdale struck his match.

Now, Seth Tisdale's parlor was full of books. Books that could be read by anyone who cared to enter. Nixon could smell them, clustered on the shelves, dust and glue and leather. Perhaps some youth would step inside this place and find in some slim volume a paragraph that spoke to his soul. That would be grand, but a future soul was not what Nixon was after.

Nixon could hear Charles' footsteps as the younger man mounted the stairs ponderously, with the heavy load of his camera balanced over one shoulder. Charles had a new camera he could hold in one hand, but he preferred his older, larger one. Charles always had precise ideas. Eager to fulfill Nixon's request, Charles had worked many hours last summer at the large table in the library at 57 Beacon St. on the plans for this building, bent diligently over his drawings with his ruling pen and triangle.

As a boy, Nixon had struggled to carve this building from wood, throwing his efforts away when it became a reminder of atrocity. This year, he had looked on admiringly as his lover laid a sheet of clean tracing paper atop the floor plans of this house of malevolence, and with talent and ink wiped the old rooms away. The home of Seth Tisdale now held books, and had been remade by a man whose habits and heritage Tisdale would have reviled. Nixon was too young that night of the priest's torture to understand that his witness to Tisdale's actions had been a kind of question. Now Nixon was old enough to answer.

Charles' footsteps moved overhead from room to room. Nixon remained by the window and looked out again at the town of his birth. Old snowdrifts had melted into untidy piles against the sidewalks. It was just after noon, and rooms were already lamp-lit. The toneless skies that produced neither light nor shadow hung in thick monotony around the grim frame houses clinging to the sloping streets. These were the same families who lived here when he was a boy, their unchanging histories interlocked in the same lusterless weave. Nixon knew better than to hope for the good intentions of men. He had answered Seth Tisdale, but he had not forgotten that half this town had gathered to jeer at the priest, just forty years ago.

Charles entered the room looking cross and held up his hands in a gesture of defeat. "I can't make any photographs today. There is not enough light. I had forgotten how dark it is here."

"Yes," agreed Nixon. "It is dark."

Half-Interest in a Four-Poster Bed
1900-1914

The sun lit his face even before he awoke. It broke its way through the eastern windows and lay first in a row of burning globes along the baseboards of the quiet room, beneath silver-green walls painted the exact color of the wings of soft moths who fly during the nights of June. It paused a moment, as though gathering strength, and then resumed its banishment of the dark. It crept upward, mounting the slack and somnolent draperies, flickering along the tiger stripes of the maple legs of the lowboy, brightening the rose washstand whose green-rimmed pitcher now held a clutch of blowzy white peonies that had shed petals soundlessly onto the carpet during the night. Not until it had risen above the knee of the wing chair and glinted from the brasses of the secretary did it wake him, and even then he lay still, moving only his eyes from the ceiling, to Frederic Crowninshield's watercolor of an Italian archway, to the rectangular panes of the window reflected in high-pitched brilliance on the fireplace wall.

He listened first, as he always did, for the sound of the sea, irritable today, as though it were tired of forever clawing fruitlessly at the rocks that rimmed it. Yet there was no wind of any kind. The shutters lay fixed, the stairways climbed mutely, no water pipe shuddered. Kragsyde was silent.

Nixon then felt for Charles, who slept pressed against him, his feet twisted among the ankles of his own feet, and his palm nestled in the smooth hollow of Nixon's hip. Charles' other arm was draped over Nixon's back and ribs, where his hand dangled, his sleeping fingers poised such a short distance from Nixon's chest that when Nixon breathed, the tips of them grazed his skin in a drowsy, pleasant rhythm. At the same slow pace, Charles' breath whispered into Nixon's neck, a warm sigh, followed by a prickly coolness, followed by another warm sigh. This was a daily experience, but it always held Nixon spellbound, the sound of the sea and the living warmth of Charles' breath against his neck. If his happiness had a container, it would be this house, this room.

Indeed Nixon was finally accustomed to the belief he'd lived his life in reverse order, with his greatest freedoms and happiness granted now that his hair was grey, and his sufferings meted out when he was young and strong. It was a seventy-two-year-old man who lay curled in the arms of his fifty-four-year-old lover in this July of 1914. When the great desires and furtive passions of his earlier years had scorched themselves into his flesh in the rooms at Mozart Street, he never imagined the impact of time on love. He would not have guessed then that knowing one's way contained all the ardor of finding one's way, or that impulse and intent were both flowers from the same garden of paradise, which simply bloomed in different seasons. He never suspected the hot and frenzied happiness he'd experienced nearly thirty years before would have further warmed into the rapturous liberties of age with its cold, cold flame of joy.

The miracle was in how this happiness was bestowed. It simply came to him, day after untroubled day, which the calendar now measured as the dozen years they had lived together. He and Charles never shared a cross word and drifted from one pleasant thing to another. There were always dogs, books, paintings, friends, and travels. Fate was in an abundant mood, and Nixon could not be faulted for waking each day anticipating the feast laid out for him.

Very little was planned; the pair moved according to whim. Last night they'd discussed taking the dogs out riding, with the aim of further training them. Nixon had purchased two St. Bernard brothers, Boxer and Hub, one beautiful and silly, and the other less perfect to the eye but solid as to brains. Hub followed the horses dutifully, but Boxer was still distracted by any squirrel and required further teaching. In the end, however, the two men decided to go out driving instead, perhaps to the teahouse in Wenham, with Charles at the wheel of the new Buick B-25 motor.

On this day, like most others, they would breakfast slowly. Marmalade and bread, eggs and ham, perhaps potatoes fried in little cakes. By midmorning they would visit the greenhouse. Both men were always eager to step inside it, inhale its earthy smell, and see what had changed in the night. Once inside, one felt as though underwater, submerged in a green and glowing tank where life of every kind flourished. It was a small and copious jungle, threaded with valves and hoses. Water pooled and overflowed and spattered. Leaves and branches stroked clothing as one passed. All was lush here and fecund, and no matter the season, exciting.

A talented gardener, Axel Magnuson, had been on the job for several years now, and each day brought surprises. The behemoth eighteen-foot fern dominated one corner like a pasha beneath its tent of scrim, pitched to keep it shaded. Cactus plants thrust their gnarled branches upward in the dry rooms, sharing space with barrels of pungent fertilizers. Begonias and geraniums by the dozens waited in different stages, grown to fill in any that were damaged in the gardens.

The greenhouse was relatively empty in July, most of its wooden tables bare except for young chrysanthemums, which were weekly pinched and pruned to shape for the coming autumn. Injured plants were being nursed and vines in pots teased to climbing. A few small tomatoes clutched their cages, and salad greens and herbs lay against the east wall alongside rolls of winter burlap, trussed and stored upright.

It was here, a week earlier, where Nixon made a discovery. Fumbling in the wooden trays of the herb table to pluck a sprig of parsley to taste, he noted some marks scratched into the mossy stains that crept up the bottom glass of the wall, the clumsily etched signatures of ENOCH and WILLY, children of the chauffeur and a groom, along with some childish hieroglyphics, unknown in their meaning and yet perfectly understood. Nixon felt a warm rush of peace and familiarity. He knew at once the sort of secret nest onto which he'd stumbled. The long row of burlap would make a perfect fort. Whether the hiding place was active, he could not, as an adult, ascertain, but he backed away instinctively to preserve its innocent holiness.

It was no different than Kragsyde. For these dozen years he and Charles had been tucked together in their own fort, a secret place of his own making. He understood then the miracle he'd been living. He had been gifted in his old age with the thoughtless happiness of childhood. How long he had waited.

Back in the winter of 1902, fate had not yet finished demanding the full measure of its payment. It still had three coins to extract. Nixon's mother died in September of that year, during the first rainy night after weeks of pleasant weather. She loved the summer, and Nixon was not entirely surprised she let go of life when the season was ebbing. The house was full of guests that evening, and thus full of mourners the following day when it was discovered she'd passed away. Charles was there, and a Peters family nephew and his wife, of whom his mother was particularly fond. That these observers were on hand to witness his grief made Nixon uneasy, and he blamed them for his lack of tears. But after the doctor was called and Nixon waited in his mother's room, something different came upon him.

He entered her chamber daunted, fearing her countenance would be a mask of pain or objurgation, but her features were composed pleasant-ly, and despite her advanced age she looked astonishingly young. She'd died in her sleep, with her bedclothes unruffled and one hand laid across her chest. Her white hair lay in a thin braid along her neck. She seemed set down tenderly and intentionally, like a flower on a grave.

He had lived with no person longer. Thousands of words, meals, and gestures had passed between them. He knew every nuance of her sur-face and absolutely none of her depth. His mother was the most familiar mystery of his life.

Nixon rested his elbows on his knees and placed his fingertips on his eyelids. He was the last of his family. He was to live without any of them now. This would be, mercifully, the last deathbed he would sit beside.

Yet tears would not come to his eyes, and Nixon did not understand the strange emotion which flooded him. He felt carved out and hollow. *Why,* he thought over and over, *do I not feel anything?*

After some time, Charles knocked and entered, visibly weeping, and pulled a chair to the dead woman's bedside. Charles still wore his dressing gown, and buried his head in her coverlet, stretching out his arm and clutching the lump of her ankle beneath it. In the curious ways of the human heart, in which fondness often seems to skip generations, Charles and Mary Black had formed a strong affection. She even asked him, two years before, to act as appraiser for her will. "Charles understands the value of old things," she said teasingly to the two men, "and I am an old thing."

As Charles sobbed into the blankets, Nixon reached out to him with love and pity. Only with his hand stretched into the air did he pause with the impulse to pull it back. He'd never touched Charles in the presence of his mother. The two men agreed long ago not to flaunt any evidence of their attachment that might be uncomfortable for her. They'd never in these many years allowed her to witness an embrace. Nixon resumed the motion of his hand and let it rest on Charles' back, where he rubbed it gently. It was not until this hesitation that the meaning of his tearlessness was clear to him. He was now, for the first time in his life, alone and left alone.

Just three months later Charles' mother died, of a lingering cold that became a deadly pneumonia. On the eve of her funeral the two men came together at Nixon's Beacon Street home. Intending initially to spend one night, Charles never left.

Not many weeks after Charles made his removal complete, shifting his possessions from his mother's home at Bay State Road to Beacon Street and bidding farewell to his little rooms at Mozart Street, a new darkness stirred.

Bridget Sullivan, who assisted Mrs. Carlson the cook, had given her notice. Nixon entered the parlor to speak with the woman, as he had long ago adopted the habit of meeting with his household employees while seated with them in the comfortable room. Here he found Bridget, straight-backed in her chair, perfectly attired as always, in her black dress and starched fichu collar and apron. She was ordinarily a smiling woman, well-built, with pretty grey eyes and red-blonde hair that fell in a saucy curl on her forehead. She was a good worker, and he was sorry to part with her. He noticed today her smile was wiped away; she would not meet his eye and held a handkerchief twisted around her index finger. With this he felt a shudder of the premonitory consciousness that first made itself known to him in boyhood and stirred again on the day he and Charles tried to photograph the Ellsworth library.

"Bridget, Mrs. Carlson says you wish to give your notice," Nixon began.

"Yes," she replied, her single word answer taking Nixon aback, as Bridget was a talkative girl.

"Are you sure, Bridget? Have you found another place?"

Bridget sniffed and lifted the handkerchief to her long nose. Nixon believed she may have been crying. He knew she'd found no other place.

"Danny thinks I ought to move on," she said.

Nixon knew Danny. Daniel Sullivan, Bridget's husband, as handsome and as coarse a brute as worked in any household on Beacon Hill. Sullivan was houseman for a family who lived at Louisburg Square, and Nixon had seen him hit a cart horse with a coal hod one day. One only needed to look at Danny Sullivan to see he would use his fists before his brains.

"Has there been any trouble, Bridget? Something I can possibly help?" Nixon tried again. Nixon wondered if Danny had ever struck her.

"No, sir," she said, with her head cast down dejectedly. "Danny and I think I ought not to work here anymore."

Nixon watched Bridget and observed the gathering of her terrors. She was willing herself into her stiff pose, sitting in her chair stone-still but with an unbearable agitation she was not quite able to conceal. Every part of her body wanted to writhe with fear and guilt. A flutter of anger pulsed through Nixon, and it appeared oddly, as a thin smile across his mouth. He knew what Bridget was getting at, but he wanted to make her say it.

Nixon rose from his chair suddenly and took note as the woman flinched. "I must insist on your reason," Nixon began with great gentleness, but he purposely stood over her while speaking these words, and cast her face, which had been lit by the window, into shadow, "or I should never cease to wonder."

"It's Mr. Pitman and.....," Bridget burst out in a voice that sounded almost hoarse, but immediately caught herself and stopped. She stood up quickly, nearly as tall as Nixon herself, and for a moment he admired her. She was a comely woman, and her defiance in standing was brave, almost arch. Danny Sullivan had not struck her yet, Nixon concluded, but he would. Someday Danny Sullivan would believe he had to.

"Have you and Mr. Pitman had words, Bridget?" Nixon continued to press.

"No," she admitted, finally lifting her eyes in which the ugliness of her complaint glowered but focusing them on a place beyond Nixon's right shoulder. They stood in silence for a long moment.

"All right, Bridget," Nixon said returning to his chair and releasing her from the gaze he'd pinned her with since they began speaking. "Be sure to inform Mrs. Carlson of your exact intentions. Don't leave her shorthanded."

Bridget did not answer and fled the room.

Nixon closed his eyes and sighed. Fragments of his life clustered around him in the hush of the darkening room. All his life he depended on observations to inform his understandings. He drifted through the great welter of the things he'd seen and considered them. He sat for a long time, long enough to line the pieces up and make sense of them. Long enough to wonder if one day men like he and Charles would be safe enough in the world to join one another and heap scorn upon some creed that was less safe. Long enough for the fluent sequence of his memories to answer him yes, and to remind him the world did not get better, it merely changed.

Nixon then saw through the window Bridget Sullivan scurrying across the twilit street to join her waiting husband, who'd been smoking and lurking against a tree in the Common, her silhouette beseeching his until the hulking man could be seen lifting her and twirling her around in delight.

It had taken nearly fifty years, but the Irish were Know-Nothings now.

After this, Nixon and Charles drew a careful line around their life together, and their long happiness began. Not all the Irish servants fled, of course, but there was a definite thinning out, and when the need arose they replaced resigning domestics cautiously. The circle the two men built for themselves was porous, however, and always included the admission of trusted friends. Oldest among their acquaintance was the architect Robert Peabody.

Bob Peabody, like Nixon, was hovering near his sixtieth year in 1904, and all the promise of his early manhood lay behind him in a distinguished career. Scores of well-known buildings had emerged from his sketchbook to the reality of bricks and mortar and stood all over the United States, ivy-clad in the yards of a hundred schools and colleges, guarding books in libraries, stabling horses, or housing thousands of offices and hotel rooms. Some of the finest, like Kragsyde, sprawled on the vast acreage or rugged cliffs of the resorts of the Eastern Seaboard. Fame had not eluded him, nor fortune, and in his older years he enjoyed a fine home he designed and built in Boston at No. 22 in the Fenway and a summer cottage at Peaches Point in Marblehead.

Sometimes the men would gather at Kragsyde, enjoying competitive games of billiards on the porch overlooking the cove. Just as frequently, the men would visit at Peaches Point. Here, surrounding his main dwelling, was a playhouse Bob's grandchildren named "Castle Joyous," and a lovely trellised bower with views of the sea. Bob Peabody loved nothing so much as the sea and the ships that sailed on it, and this bower, covered in vines, was supported on its corners by the salvaged figureheads of four old sailing ships. Here the friends often sat, overlooking the sea, under the gaze of three cracked and stoic maidens and one fierce and worm-riddled Indian chief. Meanwhile, the Peabody family sailboats, *Molly* and *Jack Tar,* circled idly on their moorings.

On a breezy Saturday in August 1904, Nixon and Bob Peabody rested in this bower looking on as Charles and young Bob Peabody Jr. readied the *Molly* for an afternoon sail. The two older men settled in their wicker chairs, Nixon on one with large curled arms and Bob on another sized for two sitters but largely overtaken with the sprawling body of Fly, the family's cocker spaniel. Now and again, voices and sounds rose from the cove where Charles and the seventeen-year-old boy were unfurling the *Molly*'s distinctive red sail and pushing out into the open sea. Nixon watched Peabody's aging hand and recalled how he'd seen it the first time, taut and deft with a pencil, but now like his own, loose-skinned and spotted, as it combed rhythmically through the silken swirls of the spaniel's fur.

"Do you remember the picnic at Crowninshields' just before the war?" Peabody asked.

"Yes," Nixon answered after a moment, not wanting to give away just how succinctly he remembered everything about that day. "I remember an old eccentric who carried a spyglass."

"Eben Sturgis! I'd forgotten he was there, but I suppose he would have been, as all the family were there." Peabody stopped speaking and shaded his eyes, squinting at the disappearing sailboat. "They've caught a good breeze now," he said. "They'll be out beyond the bell buoy in no time. I just thought," he continued, "that you and I are the only ones left."

"Not from the entire picnic, hopefully. We can't be that old," Nixon said.

"No, of course. I meant those of us who were in college together. I remember so well sitting in the meadow by the sea. Poor Frank and Edward first, and it must be almost twenty years now since John Blanchard died. He was the last one, other than ourselves."

"John always was a man of the world," Nixon said.

"The Old World at least," Peabody added. "Imagine, after all his travels, dying of typhoid in Italy."

"Rob Perkins too," Nixon said. "So many years dead, and so soon after college. He couldn't have been much more than thirty."

"What a devil he was. Always in trouble and glad of it," Peabody said. "It seemed he had a bone to pick with the world."

"I think he was afraid," Nixon said.

"Afraid! Afraid of what?"

"I don't really know," Nixon replied. "Afraid of measuring up, perhaps, when he was younger, and certainly afraid of dying at the end. You remember we were neighbors? I visited him just a few days before he died. The consumption had wasted him to a skeleton. He could barely hold his head up, but he insisted I answer his question."

"What did he ask?"

"He wanted me to tell him what it was like with Frank, because he knew I'd been there. He wanted me to describe Frank's dying," Nixon said.

"How awful! What did you say?"

"I told him Frank died quietly in his sleep. I lied."

Bob Peabody went quiet but continued to stroke Fly, who stirred, stretched, and pressed his sleepy head further into his master's thigh. "We have been the lucky ones," he said finally.

"Yes," said Nixon as he turned his eye to the sea and picked out the red sail of the *Molly*, like a tiny smudge of blood on the horizon. "We have."

Often another old ghost rose up from the past and appeared around the edges of his life. Sometimes Nixon would see her at a summer tea table at the Essex Country Club, sometimes at one of the Friday afternoon Boston Symphony concerts at the new Music Hall, resplendent in a box opposite his own, exotically dressed as though she too were an Italian Renaissance room. And once in a while he met her in the new art museum recently built near her own fabulous house in the Fenway on what was once the old circus grounds: Isabella Stewart Gardner, stalking in an extravagant gown, with a rope of great pearls swinging, some hair jewelry glittering, and the latest fashionable painter or poet or a handsome and brilliant "museum boy" on her arm.

She and Nixon were not intimates. Nixon knew only too well how fast he would perish in her midst, and how dangerous a lair her friendship would be for him. He'd no desire to expose himself to the sort of intrigue that seemed to exist around her, yet he admired her more than any woman of his age in Boston.

The two had so many common interests that frequent meetings were customary. Both Mrs. Gardner and Nixon were known throughout the city for their splendid horses and carriages, and the care they lavished on their animals. Both were known too for their patronage of the arts, though their methods of support were different. When the Harcourt Studios burned in a terrible fire in November of 1904, destroying the life's work of many prominent artists, Nixon was one of the first men to sign a plan to support the construction of a new building to house the studios of working artists, and within a year the Fenway Studios were born. Isabella's patronage tended more toward personal support, but she and Nixon had pooled resources more than once to buy an object the art museum desired.

Isabella had traveled a long path since the day Nixon first met her in Caroline Crowninshield's parlor, when they were both young and new in Boston. The baby son she was pregnant with that day had not outlived the war, and when more children did not come the young woman embarked on a very different life from that practiced by most of her sex. Calling on a vast and gritty courage she must have found within herself, she became a world traveler, an astute collector, and the mistress of a salon of fascinating individuals who were inordinately handsome, unmarried men whom Nixon recognized immediately.

It was never clear to Nixon whether Isabella was indifferent to the gossip she engendered or whether she invited it, but it was no matter: she was a wonder. Even after her husband's death she continued from strength to strength, directing the construction of an amazing Venetian-style palace to house her collections and her person.

When meeting on the porch of the country club or outside the Music Hall, stepping from their grand carriages, they met in the same way as forty years before in Caroline Crowninshield's parlor. Isabella's quick eyes would recognize Nixon and pass across the figure of Charles, while Nixon would take in the young painter at Isabella's side. The old outsiders knew one another exactly and would exchange the smile of comrades, for they had both, in different ways, passed successfully through the gauntlet that was Boston.

Nixon winced inwardly a bit each time he heard a close report from one of the guns. The men who'd come down to Cohasset on Boston's

South Shore for the shooting party this September weekend often came up quite near the house. The house, White Head, was surrounded by water and sat on less than three acres, pinned to the mainland only by a handsome arched bridge. It was owned by Harry Long and his wife, Susan Bowditch Long, the sister of the Kragsyde surveyor, Ernest Bowditch, whose employment of Charles had brought him and Nixon together.

These were Charles' friends, and friends of his brother Harold: bankers, stockbrokers, and a few artists, all younger than Nixon, a generation of prosperous men born too late to remember the war. They were a small group assembled this late summer weekend of 1912, Harold and his fiancee, Christiana Whitney, along with their spinster artist friend Charlotte Schetter. An old hunting companion of Harry Long named Matt Luce joined them, and the artist Frank Benson and his wife, Ellen. Their interests revolved around outdoorsmanship, music, art, and collecting Americana. Nixon found them vivid and interesting but daunting too, and was pleased he was old enough to use poor eyesight as an excuse to avoid the bird hunting. He had no stomach for watching the helpless creatures blasted from the sky, dropping like stones to the ground and lying in struggling heaps before being snatched up in the jaws of a dripping English setter. Charles too resisted the shooting, which his brother Harold relished, but took eager part in a morning outing of smelt fishing where he'd pridefully outfished Harold. Nixon, for his part, was content to follow Susan Long around her gardens, hunting ripe tomatoes.

"I'm glad to have you alone, Nixon," Susan said, as she rustled among the vines twined up the rows of wooden stakes on the leeward side of the house. "We're overdue for a long gossip."

Susan had approached Nixon lazily, crossing the broad lawn down to the garden in her sweeping dress as though she were a great schooner, tacking in the strength of the wind. She was an earthy wide-hipped woman, broad straw-hatted, purposeful, and industrious. When she was younger there was always a child pressing to her skirts or a dog pouncing, either of which she ministered to affably and efficiently while remaining completely composed. She gardened without gloves, wearing pearls.

"I thought I was here merely to carry your basket," Nixon joked, walking beside her bearing the basket she'd pressed into his hands, now being filled with tomatoes.

"Of course I want to know every detail about Harold and Christiana. How stunning to learn they are to be married!"

"Yes, a year from now, I am told," Nixon said.

"But what do you think of it?" Susan asked. "They must both be nearly fifty years old."

Nixon shrugged, as he'd thought the same thing. "Charles says it's time he settled down."

"Nearly out of time, is more like it," Susan said, laughing. "When did he ask her?"

"Another mystery," Nixon replied, "You know what a sphinx Harold is, but he's a conventional man, so I'm sure he was down on bended knee."

This was true. Harold was conventional. After coming into his inheritance, he found he liked managing money, and drifted into the dull world of finance, becoming a stockbroker. He reveled in the masculine world of banking and athletic outdoor pursuits. He was extremely good looking, always in well-cut clothes, and seemed to lack any sort of curiosity whatsoever. Early in their relationship Nixon questioned Charles about his brother, anxious as to what his reaction to their love would be.

"Oh, Harold knows," Charles had said, "and doesn't want to know. We don't ever need to disguise or mention it." So in twenty-seven years, Nixon never had.

"Bended knee? Harold is so awfully handsome, but Christiana is awfully rich, so you are probably right," Susan replied chuckling. "Christiana does seem so much more warm-blooded than him. She has a devilish sense of humor. I quite like her."

"So do I," said Nixon. "I think she will be good for him."

"Harold has been telling the men here he and Christiana intend to go on a camping trip on their honeymoon."

"Camping trip! Pfffft!" exclaimed Nixon. "Christiana may have warmer blood than Harold, but it is still very blue. She'll have him on a steamer for Europe less than a week after the wedding."

Later, after Susan took her basket of tomatoes to the kitchen for the cook, Nixon remained in the seaside garden. At some distance near the shore, he saw the lone figure of Miss Schetter, with her white sketchbook in her lap. He'd met her once years ago, when Miss Schetter came to see Martha Pitman during her last illness. Charlotte Schetter had known the Pitman family most of her life, meeting them in Germany when she was just a girl, during a time when her own father and young Benjamin Pitman were being treated in the same spa.

As Nixon approached her in silence, he observed her tiny figure. She was a plain, brown-haired, brown-eyed woman with expressive hands, which even at this distance he could see moving across her paper. There was something pitifully alone about her, but infused with a tremendous vital force, so she seemed sad and brave all at once.

Once near enough to speak, he said, "I have watched a number of artists at work, but none any better than you."

"Mr. Black!" Charlotte exclaimed as she turned, smiling and pawing at a strand of hair the wind had caught and blown in her face. "I'm so glad to see you!"

Nixon remembered suddenly her eccentricities, the black velvet choker she always wore around her neck, and the strange compelling quality of her voice, which he could not accurately describe. "Calling me Nixon would be nicer to my ears," he replied.

"Nixon, then," she said, standing and closing her sketchbook. "I saw Charles earlier, and he said you were here. He'd been out fishing in the Basin and was boasting about his smelt. I sent him off. I can't even describe how he smelt."

Nixon laughed. She was an outrageous flirt. He'd forgotten that too. Strange she'd never married. "What are you drawing?" he asked.

"Just lines today. It's hard to concentrate with all the shooting."

"Not to mention the plummeting corpses."

"Not to mention," she smiled.

"Why don't we go up to the house, where you can tell me all about your painting?" Nixon asked.

This they did. The late afternoon was still warm and the windows of the veranda stood wide open. Seated here and drinking a pot of smoky tea, Charlotte told Nixon of her tiny new studio located on Washington

Square in New York City. With the sun retreating and the doorway curtains pushing gently into the room in the onshore breeze of evening, she told him of a painting she'd exhibited at the National Academy, and the work she was doing to earn her way, copying paintings.

Nixon watched her carefully as she spoke and recalled Miss Hills' tiny studio on Boylston Street. It was impossible for him not to regard Charlotte with complete tenderness. She worked so hard, and was no longer a young woman. Even in the cover of twilight he could see the crinkles at the edges of her eyes, her small hands curled softly in her lap. She had absolutely nothing to lean on except talent. He felt the terrible leap of struggles within her and was beset by a sudden urge to place a kiss of consolation on her pale brow. But a kiss would do her no good and likely be misunderstood, perhaps even bringing on some other awful pain, so he sat motionless, allowing his empathy to travel in another direction. When the darkness arrived and he had made his plan to help her, Nixon noted the guns had finally gone silent.

Supper was conducted in a near-foreign language as the excited hunters described their day.

"Why, there were bunches of peeps passing!"

"I bagged one, and then three chickens came and I missed."

"I missed a winter, but saw a beetle in my 'coys, and when he jumped I bagged him."

"Did you see those four summers that went into Yellowleg Rock?"

"Those grass birds passed me high, but two chickens came and I dropped them both."

It was not until the last course was served and the men left the women for their cigars that Nixon felt he could take part in any of the conversation. They'd retired to a spacious room flagged with blue slate and set under deep cove moldings. The decorating hand of Susan could be seen here in the simple curtains, Tiffany lamps, and fine wing chairs, but Harry had his say as well, with Audubon prints and every level surface covered with bird decoys. A wooden merganser floated on the dark pool of a mahogany lowboy, Canada geese crouched in the act of preening with sinuous necks curled so preposterously and gracefully they invited touch.

"How go things at the Preservation Society, Harry?" Benson asked.

Harry Long sighed, shaking out the match he'd used to light his cigar, dropping it into a small glass tray lying beneath the stilted body of a speckled wooden plover. "Sometimes too fast, and sometimes too slowly. I must say Appleton can often be a trial," referring to William Sumner Appleton, the rail-thin, unmarried, and notoriously waspish founder of the organization.

"A bit techy, is he?" Luce asked, with a sly smile.

"Let's just say he has his own ideas," Harry replied.

"Of which he will inform anyone, endlessly," said Benson with eyebrows raised.

"He's a bit of a missionary," Harry assented, "but he has to be. To give Summy his due, he is high-minded and very public-spirited. He's entitled to great credit, but it can be difficult to cooperate with him."

"Say now, Charles," began Benson, still in a mood for teasing, "you love old houses, you're a preservation man, why don't you join the society?" Charles raised his eyebrows, ran his hand through his hair, and stifled a smirk. "I don't think so, Frank. With all those dowagers, and Appleton, I don't think I could stand the pressure." The roomful of men chuckled.

"Nixon, then, what think ye? With a George Washington miniature on your mantel, how can you resist?"

Nixon leaned back in his chair, a fine comb-backed Windsor. "Oh fellows, you ought to go easy on me now. You're all young men. You've no idea how much work it is when you get to be my age, simply to preserve oneself." This brought loud roars of laughter. "I have met Appleton, though, just once, at Harriot Curtis' home. They're cousins." Nixon leaned forward and turned to Charles. "You were with me, Charles, do you remember? We were making Christmas visits?"

Charles shook his head. "No, I don't, but with that house so overrun with widows and spinsters, I don't remember who I saw. I still can't sort them out."

"You were at Harriot Curtis' house?" Harold suddenly burst out, nearly rising from his chair, "at Christmas?"

The men all turned toward Harold, as he was usually quiet and never spoke out in such excitement.

"Well...yes," said Nixon, not understanding what he'd said that agitated Harold. "Not on Christmas Day, but during the general season. Why, is that strange?"

Harold twisted uncomfortably in his chair. He'd spoken without thinking, and was now forced to continue. All eyes were on him, anticipating a wonderful bit of gossip.

"Christiana told me..." Harold said in a hushed voice that came out in an inaudible croak, so he began again. "Christiana told me... that Sumner Appleton delivers an armload of ladies' undergarments to his spinster Curtis cousins every Christmas."

The room was silent, cigars were removed from dropped mouths, legs were uncrossed, and feet planted firmly on the floor. Finally Charles broke out in laughter.

"No-ooo!" Charles said, dragging the word out in a disbelieving tone.

"Lacy nightgowns, petticoats, even step-ins. She said he lays them out on the table and the sisters rather fight over them. Cousin Summy's underwear party they call it. They do it every year."

"Good Lord!" said Matthew Luce. "Do you suppose he buys them himself?"

"In a strange sort of way," Benson said thoughtfully, "this does rather seem like him."

Harry Long was rocking in his chair, shaking his head with delight. "Now I'll never look at Summy the same way again. I always thought he was a dyed-in the-wool bachelor. I guess he does notice the opposite sex!"

Or maybe not, thought Nixon privately, as he said, "Well, we saw no ladies' undergarments on our visit. Thank goodness we didn't blunder into that!"

How strange and quick these younger people were. Free and brazen, but somehow ruthless too. They stirred in him a kind of anxious, inchoate yearning. Nixon could not decide whether they were shocking him, or keeping him young.

The steamer was more than an hour beyond the Ambrose lightship before Charles released Nixon from his embrace.

They'd boarded the *Lusitania* at Pier 54 in a sizzling rain, leaving behind the raw and furious city of New York, whose deep streets cowered beneath the risen hackles of its great buildings. Even here by the river, above the uproar of stevedores and longshoremen, one could hear the grinding clamor of the elevated trains and sense the presence of their subterranean brothers, pulsing under broken macadam and bleak tunnels and across hulking bridges.

Charles and Nixon passed across the gangway, making their way through crowds of other passengers engaged in their farewells, leaning and waving handkerchiefs from the rails. They crossed its wide deck, climbed the thickly carpeted treads of the grand staircase, and stepped into the seduction of opulence. Here, gold-and-black lifts shuttled rapidly in their elaborate cage, stewards awaited beckoning, and a dozen pleasure rooms for writing, dining, and music ran in each direction. The two men followed the familiar white corridor to their pair of en suite staterooms, where they were passed by a steward announcing, "All visitors ashore!"

Locking the cabin door behind them, and finding their "wanted" luggage properly delivered, Charles then found Nixon's mouth, pressing his lover boastfully against the brocade inset on the paneled wall. He held him in place with kisses and ran his hands down Nixon's arms, lacing their fingers together and squeezing them into fists. Another journey! Months ahead, entirely to themselves! Somewhere on an upper deck, a band was playing. Charles pressed his face into Nixon's shoulder, which smelled pleasantly of soap and cigars, and peeled his jacket away, letting it slide behind them against the gray brocade. He then let his fingers rummage Nixon's shirt seeking its buttons.

Outside on the Promenade Deck, a hundred passengers were roaring, the ship's whistle blaring its departing blasts. Charles knew the gangways had been hauled up, and the tugs were beginning to tow the great liner out into the river.

With his hands against the skin of Nixon's chest, Charles paused to look at him in the curtained half-light of the opulent stateroom. Nixon's eyes were closed in pleasure, his head turned sideways and laid against the fabric of the wall. Charles' heart lurched with emotion at this view of him. He loved Nixon. He loved his lonely face, and his kind heart, and especially his reticence, which made the gift of his love so much more valuable. He loved that he had him pressed against the thinnest of walls, with only inches between them and the din of the outside world, the other world, always too loud and still too unready to hear any promise he would willingly vow.

The two men were the same height, but Nixon outweighed Charles by nearly twenty pounds. He was solid, sweating a little, clutching Charles' ribs in a tight embrace. It was two steps backward to the narrow bed, and Charles took Nixon's weight and slid beneath him, surprised at the warmth of his chest, delighted at the twining of Nixon's legs around him.

A small trembling of the ship signaled the fumbling of the tugs as they eased her bow to starboard and set her in the right position in the river. Far away a bell rang, and another shudder as the *Lusitania*'s own propellers engaged, chewing at the waters of the muddy river. Black smoke poured from her forward funnels, and the great workings of her own thews sent her steaming out through the Upper Bay and onward to the Narrows.

Now, with the ship long past the mouth of the Ambrose Channel and racing into the open sea, Nixon sat up on the edge of the bed. The decks outside were abandoned of passengers, and the curtained stateroom was filled with a silty, silvery light. Charles lay face down on the bed, sleeping heavily, with one arm outstretched and his hand loosely clutching the decorative garland in the brass footboard. Nixon reached out and laid his own hand on the skin between the younger man's shoulder blades, and ran it up into his hair. Charles' hair had grown silvery too, little threads of it, nearly indistinguishable from the blond it was, matching now the remarkable color of his eyes. Charles never lost his boyish look. His hair grew soft and close to his head. His skin remained smooth, his face aged but still mutable. His frame was spare and strong, and he wore any clothing he decided to hang on himself like a mannequin. Sleeping, he always looked like a young faun.

Nixon let his eyes wander around the stateroom. Outside he knew large waves leapt against the cutting bow of the great dark ship, and a keen wind carried their spray down the length of her. In a week he and Charles would be conveyed beyond all dissemblance, to places where they were strangers. Theaters and restaurants where others did not know them, houses where even the domestics were alien. Rooms like this one, where their scattered clothing would be sorted and hung away by a pleasantly indifferent steward who had ignored such a scene ten thousand times before. Nixon stood and crossed the room to the unused bed, stripping it of its cover, returning to lie again with Charles, carefully placing himself so he was in touch with the entire length of Charles' body. He drew the cover over them both. He had everything he wanted. His privacy, his lover, and the special pleasure of distance passing beneath him. Distance and departure were the instruments of his passage, but defiance was his destination.

Each year, Nixon and Charles traveled. From January to April they wandered. Each season they embarked on one of the great steamers, the *Mauretania* or the *Lusitania*, to cross the Atlantic Ocean and follow a peripatetic route, which had more to do with caprice than purpose. They visited all the great cities of Europe. The fog-smeared streets of London, where they took long teas and were measured for clothing at Anderson and Sheppard on Savile Row. Music under the great dome of the Paris Opera, and the red-and-gold glories of the Teatro di Carlo in Naples.

Yet always, they were drawn to the small and secret places of the world, and it was never long before they hastened from the grand boulevards to the places where no tourist paced the streets with his Baedeker. They found, once embarked on such a journey, they could completely dissolve in it and let it carry them as recklessly as a river. It was a life untamed, a flight from something nameless, into another something that was inaccessible. They turned to the hot and terrible lands, the places of donkeys and camels and goats. As stowaways in such careworn places they could be what they really were: outsiders, strangers, odd jobs. Adrift in the blistering sunlight, shouldered in close and shadowy alleys by other men who were also mysteries: French soldiers and Zouaves, Moors in beautiful embroidered jackets, turbaned Bedouins from the desert. Here, far from any American or European, they could saunter among the tradesmen, metal-shapers, leather-dyers, and shoemakers, and along the rows of steaming cook shops where grave men sat cross-legged and pulled at their long pipes. Here they could do as the bur-nous-wrapped Arab men did, and which they could never do at home: walk arm in arm in the menacing and fabulous streets.

Italy finally captured them. A small town, on the far southern island of Sicily, named Taormina. Suspended between the sky and the Ionian sea on the rugged cliffs of Messina, the beautiful town possessed Greek and Roman architecture and a climate of perfection. Showers of pink bougainvillea hung over its ancient walls, spilling into the terraces of the old hillside villas where Charles and Nixon rented their rooms, each of which gazed out upon the Mediterranean and the snowy-topped Mt. Etna in the far distance. Trees of beauty abounded, oranges, lemons, figs, and luxuriant palms. It was Taormina that became their most constant destination on their many trips abroad.

On their first visit, Charles lost no time in discovering another of Taormina's exotic occupants. Wilhelm von Gloeden, "Guglielmo," the noted photographer, had his residence and studio here. Wishing to meet another man with an interest in the camera, Charles called on von Gloeden, returning afterward to the hotel rather later than Nixon had expected him with a small portfolio of photographs.

"Look at these!" Charles said with great excitement, untying the cover and removing two prints from within, as Nixon pulled his spectacles from his pocket. Charles placed into Nixon's hands a pair of exquisite photographs. One a view of Mt. Etna and the other a scene of the stunning local Greek theater. They were beautifully made, with a real feeling for light and shade, and Nixon nodded approvingly.

"These are quite lovely. Very picturesque," Nixon said.

"The photographer is a German baron!" said Charles. "He moved here years ago to recover his health. Lives with his sister over near the

Domenico. He's got a terrace full of birds and an old black dog named Nedda." Then Charles handed a second envelope to Nixon.

"There are also these..." Charles said as Nixon withdrew three smaller prints, each a beautifully composed male nude.

"Well, well," Nixon responded. "It seems the baron finds more to his liking in Taormina than the climate." Nixon shuffled the photographs in his hand. Nude youths posed alongside the trappings of classic antiquity, with pan pipes and amphora, garlands in their hair. "Very Homeric," Nixon said wryly, "but these are local boys, no?" Nixon placed a finger on the face of a particularly handsome youth stretched out in a columned courtyard. "I'm sure I have seen this one myself, in the town square."

"Gloeden says they are all boys from Taormina."

"Does he keep these boys around his studio?" Nixon asked.

"There is a houseboy there," Charles said, raising his eyebrows. "Gloeden calls him Il Moro!"

"The Moor," Nixon drew a long breath. "Gloeden does this photography here unmolested?" he asked in some disbelief.

"Apparently."

"Then he has indeed found his heaven on earth, but I should be cautious of some of these boys myself," Nixon said.

"What do you mean?"

Nixon held up one photograph showing three older boys, nearly men, leaning upon a crumbling wall in what appeared to be the Greek theater. He blocked with his hand the portion of the picture that showed their naked bodies, leaving only their faces in view. "Now Charles, if you came across this trio in a dark street in Naples, wouldn't you think it wise to walk the other way? Why they look like Neopolitan pickpockets!" Nixon was smiling a mischievous grin.

Charles scrutinized their faces. "Fully clothed perhaps, but if I found them in a dark street as they are, I would probably run into their arms."

They laughed, but in the ensuing years, on other trips, both Charles and Nixon grew to know Gloeden well. Charles spent hours in his presence, talking over photography and even assisting him on one of his shoots. Nixon found in the German baron a charming, sensitive man, bearded and dreamy-eyed and entirely devoted to his models. An evening in his artistic and hedonistic studio was unforgettable. Hung with tiger skins and ancient weapons, bordered with cascades of perfumed flowers, and enhanced with the flitting presence of boy models in gossamer chitons, Nixon had no doubt he was no longer in Boston.

The spring of 1914 was the last time Nixon and Charles ever saw Gloeden. Taormina was becoming a fixture on the tourist trail, and a few Americans took up winter residence there, including an elderly woman from Boston who'd known Mary Black. It was early April and Nixon and Charles had come to the end of their yearly travels. A party was attended at the studio and farewells said.

The Boston men were obliged pay a call on the elderly friend of Nixon's mother. A great dinner was served, but Charles managed to wiggle out of the dull conversation afterward and hastened off to Gloeden's for a final good-bye. It was this evening, while smoking on the terrace, that Nixon first heard the beautiful voice of Francesco, and plotted to hire the Italian youth and bring him back to Boston.

When Nixon finally returned to the small villa he shared with Charles, an anxious lover was waiting up for him.

"Nixon! I expected you hours ago. I was beginning to worry," Charles said. "I can guess you were listening to exacting detail of the hostess' last illness."

"No, it didn't go as far as that," Nixon replied. "How were the Neopolitan pickpockets tonight?" The joke had always remained between them as a description of the models of Gloeden, although neither took it seriously.

"Wild, as usual. Your health was much toasted. You should have made your excuses and come along. All the pickpockets missed you."

"I don't think so," said Nixon with a sly smile. "My dull evening turned quite exciting. Wait until you see what I found."

Thus it was Francesco, newly hired, who greeted Nixon and Charles as they breakfasted on Kragsyde's porch the sunny morning in July 1914. It was Francesco, smiling and handsome, pouring their coffee, a clean white apron lashed around his slender waist. *"Buongiorno!* Good morning, sirs!" delivered in the sonorous baritone, high above the summer sea.

Charles loved motors. He loved to examine, compare, and drive them. He could often be found at the new garage Nixon built at Kragsyde, with his head deep in the workings of one of them, consulting with Charlie Smith, the chauffeur. Smith was with the Blacks when the only vehicle driven was a carriage, and he still was called on to transport them in either manner, being as adept with the horses as he was with the sputtering but speedy Buick. One of the gardeners also had a motor, a Ford Model T Runabout, which Nixon referred to as the run-amok, and both vehicles were often parked in the yard, with all but one of the males of the household taking an interest in them.

On this bright day in late July, Charles suggested he and Nixon drive out to the Tabby-Cat Tea House in Wenham. A tiny picturesque building set beside the church in the charming town, the Tabby-Cat enjoyed a reputation for summer teas, and its business was brisk. Located in the midst of lovely country driving roads, its pretty stenciled rooms and roadside sign featuring a cat and a teapot were a landmark.

With Nixon as a passenger, who'd never desired to learn to drive, Charles skillfully and joyfully powered the new automobile through the village of Manchester-by-the-Sea and to the west toward Wenham.

"It's easy to drive, Nixon, you should give it a try," Charles shouted into the wind's roar, as the little grey auto had a canvas roof but no side windows.

"I'll leave it to you," Nixon answered, watching Charles manipulate knobs on the steering wheel and pedals on the floor.

"No cranking, either. Just a turn of this knob and we're off."

Nixon could understand the lure of the motor, the liberation it provided in being able to travel quickly, at whim. He knew too the days of his horses were numbered, but as long as he could ride out on one of them he would. He liked better traveling with something you could talk to.

They had their tea and proceeded onward, having decided to put the top of the Buick down, now that the midday sun had receded a bit and drifted toward the late afternoon. Heading northward they continued on, intending to circle though Ipswich and round back down to Kragsyde. The day was fine, and with the top folded back, full of sky and drooping elms. The motor progressed with a smooth chattering sound, almost lulling, as they passed stone walls, tidy orchards, slow wagons, and a man in shirtsleeves walking with a fishing pole and small bucket tied to his belt.

Somewhere beyond Ipswich, in the salt marshland, an old farmhouse appeared, with a group of men loading furniture into a wagon in the driveway. Charles' antiquing instinct was kindled, and he slowed the motor down.

"This is an old house," he said. "Shall we ask if they have any furniture for sale?"

"Good idea," Nixon replied.

As Charles pulled the automobile close to the edge of the road the men stopped loading and approached. The eldest removed his cap, and with the same hand wiped moisture from his forehead and scratched his head.

"Buick?" he inquired.

Charles nodded.

"The new one with the electric start?"

"Yes," said Charles, and with a quick twitch of his head indicated the men come closer and have a look. They craned their necks into the interior of the motor and watched as Charles demonstrated the small knob near the steering wheel that turned the car on and off.

"That is slick," the man said, and the others murmured in agreement. "Is it reliable?"

"So far," Charles said, smiling. "Are you breaking up housekeeping? I am always looking for old furniture."

The three men were brothers, with the surname of Eaton. The farmhouse had belonged to their mother, who'd recently passed away. They'd already divided what they wanted, and the remainder was indeed to be put up for sale.

The Eaton men led Nixon and Charles through the silent rooms of the old house. It was poignant, Nixon thought, looking at a dead woman's things, imagining her life here, her possessions to be scattered and sent separate ways. Yet there was nothing he and Charles had an interest in. It was all too new. Things made after the war.

"Is there anything older?" Nixon asked. "Furniture your grandparents may have had?"

"We can look in the barn," the shortest of the brothers, a man named Warren, said. "It's rubbish mostly."

At the barn Warren slid aside the large door. A creature of some kind rustled in the vast hollow loft. Old farm tools lay under decades of dust. A worktable hung from the wall, covered with rusted buckets, tag-ends of rope, a broken pulley block. The shaft of light from the open door cast the ancient space in a sallow light.

Nixon saw them first, the curved pieces of an old bed-tester sticking upright from a barrel. He stepped a little closer. A bedpost was tucked next to the wall studding. It was beautiful, Sheraton style, reeded, with an urn finial and leaf carvings. It would fit wonderfully in the empty bedchamber at Woodlawn.

When the bed sections were lifted outside into the sunlight, and it was ascertained all the parts were sound and complete, the bartering began. Nixon intended to offer fifteen dollars, as the men had seen the auto and sized up their financial situation, but at the end of their dickering twenty dollars was agreed upon.

Nixon fished into his pockets and sheepishly came up with only ten dollars.

"When I send the wagon around for the bed next week, I can include the balance," he offered.

Charles was likewise hunting in his wallet and found the remaining ten dollars required. Stepping toward Warren Eaton he passed him the money. "I'll settle the bill now," Charles said, slapping Nixon lightly and comically on his arm, "and the man with eyes bigger than his stomach can owe me."

The entire group laughed and shook hands once more before Nixon and Charles climbed into the Buick. The Eaton brothers watched as Charles turned the little knob and the car puttered to a start.

"It is a wonder," Warren Eaton said, shaking his head and waving his doffed cap to the Buick as it drove away.

The afternoon was slipping into the early dimness of evening. Occasionally the Buick flashed by a tree, but the landscape they passed was the dark meadow of the marsh, where no roads but their own opened into the flatness of the grassy sea. Now and again an island of real soil appeared with tall trees clinging to it, but the eastern sky was darkening beyond the rows of haycocks, and great overloaded wagons of salt hay drawn by sturdy horses silhouetted the horizon like beasts from another epoch.

"You're a wonder," Charles suddenly said, slapping Nixon again on the arm in jest.

"How so?" Nixon asked.

"Boston's biggest taxpayer and nothing in your pocket," Charles said in his most teasing voice. "You're lucky I was there to bail you out!"

"I spent it at the teahouse," Nixon shrugged.

"All I can say, is when we get that bed cleaned and put together, you'd better stay on your own side," Charles joked, and then leaned over and kissed Nixon quickly on the cheek, "as it is now half mine!"

Nixon rolled his eyes in mock disgust. "Keep your eyes on the road," he said.

The Casualty List
1915-1920

During the impossibly long moment Boxer hung suspended in the air above the cliff; in that moment when Charlotte Schetter dropped her parasol and met the creature's radiant Janus-eyes, and life and death entwined in a single fire that would burn in her memory forever; in that moment when Francesco, watching from the parlor window and seeing the doomed dog's raised paws, was returned, crossing himself, to the somber peasant church in Sicily where he cowered with boyish eyes beneath a nailed and writhing Christ; in that moment when Charles, stepping back to see around Charlotte, and first blaming a fault in his eyesight for the vision of the twisting, airborne batch of fur before realizing this was a perishing and not a nightmare the morning would dissolve; in that moment when Tena Grant, lifting her gaze from the heavy rug she was beating and fixing it on a favored animal's death, moaned through the hand that crossed her mouth; in that moment Nixon's heart grew old.

There were shouts of alarm, the cliffside alive with scrambling stable boys and weeping housemaids clustered on the porch of Kragsyde. The whispered consensus was the poor dog simply misjudged. He'd been away from Kragsyde the entire winter, confined in city rooms, and in his joy to be in the larger outdoors, rushed headlong into destruction. In any event, Boxer had disappeared, swallowed by the sea, to the horror of the many onlookers.

Supper that evening was muted, reduced to clipped statements and mild observations. That the animal met such an awful end under their gaze was one thing; that this happened only weeks after the torpedoing and sinking of the *Lusitania* was another. There was not a person present whose imagination was not already haunted by the thought of that awful submersion, the thrashing, wallowing victims, desperate pleading, and then silent, frozen bodies floating in oil and debris in the grey-green murk of the sea.

Nixon brooded the most, harrowed by a nagging dread. Beautiful Boxer, washed up in some shallow or sunk beyond all discovery, his bones mangled by the rocks and his silken coat salt-matted and putrid, eel-chewed, or riddled with clouds of sea fleas. The proud *Lusitania* too, gored and scuttled, trapping hundreds of souls, including innocent children. Nixon imagined its elegant rooms filling with water, passengers frightened and clawing. The beloved *Lusitania*, so many times in recent years the vehicle of his escape to freedom, smashed and drowned. He could see the splendid domed dining room once filled with laughter, the lovely staterooms where he'd slept with Charles, the grey brocade walls now waterlogged, the bed with the intricate brass garlands where Charles had twined his fingers plunged into a darkness that would never end.

As Boxer died, Nixon's age returned to him from its long years of absence. His age reentered his heart and he looked down the long tunnel of his years from the present, which had been his future as a young man. A future that was silent of all it had in store for him. A future that began when he'd not yet known how death can tease for years or snatch in moments. His seventy-two years returned with a terrible lucidity, sounding a tocsin, making apparent the trenches and poison gas in Europe, and stirring a reminiscence from his youth that now became a premonition. This awful dread was an undertow, and ahead lay a vast ocean of extinction.

A week after Boxer was found and buried, Charlotte Schetter climbed the main stairway at Kragsyde and tapped on the door casing of the cozy sitting room located above the massive arch. The entire household had taken pains to be gentle with Nixon, and she told no one how close she'd come to being knocked off the cliff by Boxer herself, the galloping dog brushing against her and causing her to drop her parasol before he made his fatal leap.

She'd come to Kragsyde at the summons of Nixon, who commissioned her to execute a copy of a valuable Gilbert Stuart painting of George Washington he'd purchased a few years ago. The painting resided at Beacon Street and Kragsyde, but Nixon wanted a copy made for Woodlawn. He and Charles were toying with the idea of presenting the old Maine estate as a museum, open to the public, much in the same way Isabella Gardner envisioned her Fenway palazzo. Nixon made provisions in his will that Woodlawn be left to Charles in life tenancy, and trusted his lover to manage the property and its presentation to the public as he best saw fit. At Charles' death, the property would go to the City of Ellsworth. To this end, the pair continued to decorate Woodlawn in a way that spoke of its history, and, as it would be foolhardy to hang such a valuable painting in an unoccupied house, they relied on Charlotte's talents to provide the solution.

Charlotte found Nixon propped against Morris fabric cushions, reading in his inglenook while the morning light was strong. She was not fully sure of why she'd come to him. Thoughts of Boxer troubled her. She believed she might never forget the look in the dog's eye as it realized its fate. She wanted to comfort Nixon, but she knew, in sitting with him, she would be comforted too.

"Nixon," she said, softly stepping into the dramatic room where the ocean could be viewed from every window. "I cannot look at George Washington any longer." Indeed her easel and the original painting were both set up in Agnes' old room, where she'd shut herself in, doing little but sleeping and working.

Nixon closed his book and looked at Charlotte's small figure in the doorway. Her eyes were weary but resolute; her hair was pinned unevenly, and she did look a bit ravaged. "Then you must take a rest."

"I can't rest. If I stop entirely, I shall lose my momentum."

Nixon continued to observe her, unsure of what to say. Charlotte was the daughter of unconventional parents, a free-spirited mother and a German-born father with idealist traits. What Charlotte said was not always a precise reflection of what she meant, and Nixon knew to discover that, he would have to let her continue speaking.

"May I paint you?" she asked.

Nixon met Charlotte in her temporary studio the following day, Agnes' old room, a space he never entered without the taste of his sister's memory. As Charlotte moved two chairs to face one another and adjusted her easel, Nixon turned his eyes toward the north light flooding the bow window. He saw the blurred outline of two women, a mirage that disappeared once he blinked and looked again. The woman before him had a deep experience of life, faced unequal struggles, and, orphaned early, had not enjoyed the luxury of a full youth. Now the war had come, bringing with it the half-mad pillorying of anyone German.

Charlotte possessed a voluptuous energy but also something stable and sensible, and Nixon enjoyed it when she glanced up at him in complete silence, her observant blue eyes just on the soft side of confrontation, her brush scraping the canvas swiftly. Unconsciously, she bit her lip in exertion as she worked. It would be easy to mistake her perseverance for obstinacy.

"I must tell you a story," she said, lowering her voice to its soft and feral tone, which sounded like a forbidden secret whispered into his ear.

"There is a place in Germany known as Rastede," she began, wiping one of her brushes clean and tucking it into the thick hair above one ear, as was her custom. "Rastede means resting place and was called such because the town was built on a site chosen by a dove. The families who settled there followed a dove who appeared to them. They wandered many miles in pursuit and in the place where the dove finally rested they built their town, naming the place Rastede."

"I was just thirteen, and spending the summer with my parents on the Peterstrasse in the neighboring town of Oldenburg. Neither of my parents was seriously ill then; I had no inkling of what was to come, and the days were the finest of my childhood. I had cousins living nearby, and in the house next door to them an American family came to stay. There were two sons. The more handsome son was my own age and still in the sourness of boyhood, but the elder was kind and nearly as beautiful, and my eyes followed him whenever they could."

Nixon smiled. He now knew the characters of the story, if not the ending.

"It happened that my cousins and the American family with their sons, Harold and Charles, went on a picnic to Rastede. Here was the great palace of the grand duke, surrounded by a forest as large as twenty Boston Commons and twice as thick. In the late afternoon of that day, when the forest was entirely silent, Charles and I went alone to see if we could find a magic tree much talked about by the townspeople. The tree was supposed to predict marriage. The forest was very dark. I remember we came upon deer who were unafraid and lifted their heads with curiosity as we passed near them. Charles took my hand, which caused my heart to pound, and we followed the directions given to us. Eventually we came to a large tree in a clearing, evidently the marriage tree as it was hung with many suspended sticks. One was supposed to toss a stick into the tree, and if you could aim it so it came to rest in a huge crotch in the center, you would be married. The number of tries it took to achieve this feat was the number of years before your wedding would come."

"Of course," continued Charlotte after a small glance at Nixon, "on that day when I was thirteen years old, I hoped my husband would be Charles. He was very gallant, seeking a branch from a nearby tree and trimming it with his penknife so it would be my size to toss. But as often as I tried, and I tried two dozen times, the branch would never find its mark. Charles finally tried himself, and managed to fix it solidly in place after four or five tosses. I was determined, so I tried again, and after a dozen more failures, fell laughing to the ground in defeat. Charles kissed me then anyway, and I thought the tree was wrong."

Nixon opened his eyes, realizing he'd held them closed during the entire length of Charlotte's story. "The tree was wrong," he said, "as neither of you have married."

Charlotte, who had ceased making brushstrokes, was breathing rapidly, almost breathlessly, her eyes vivid with mirth and fondness. Nixon noticed there were small smears of paint on her face and in her hair. She smiled slightly, arched an eyebrow, and bit her lower lip again before saying, "You and Charles have been married for years." Her voice trailed away softly, its mischievous tone both enduring and then dissolving like something slipping through his fingers.

It was the last beautiful story he was ever to hear.

Charles knew for certain he was in trouble on the day of Robert Peabody's funeral. For months he'd sensed harbingers, the gnawing pain in his lower back, swollen feet he had difficulty sliding into his shoes. Now, on this late September day in 1917, he discovered his fate while engaged in the most prosaic act possible. In the washroom of the King's Chapel in Boston, after the services for his friend had ended, Charles' urine came a coppery red.

Strange is the hour for those whose destiny appears defined. The rush of recognition, which courses through one's body like a searing heat and dissipates along the skin in little shivers, the sharply focused senses that manifest with the unaccountable exhilaration of early fear. When Charles returned to join the other mourners gathered in the entrance, their hushed voices sounded strident, and the somber old chapel appeared suddenly in keen angles. Outside, while waiting with Nixon for their motor to take them to the cemetery, autumn's splintery sun shot through the streets, glancing obliquely and almost audibly against the grey and narrow walls. In lifting his dazzled eyes to the source of the light, Charles gazed up at the splendid Custom House tower on State Street, admiring its pyramid-shaped roof which on this day rose nearly five hundred feet over the funeral of the man who had imagined it. Designed by Peabody before he became ill with the cancer that killed him, it was the tallest building in Boston, a true skyscraper. *There will be taller buildings here someday*, Charles thought, a great hope kindled by the exuberance of his newfound fear.

Later, while standing in the path beside the Peabody cemetery plot, among the ancient and tilting gravestones and sumptuous plantings, Charles was wracked by nausea and retreated to the Buick as the world reeled and tilted around him.

"Are you all right, sir?" inquired Charlie Smith, but Charles waved him away with one hand and shook his head, not wanting to answer. The chauffeur continued to watch him, with some concern, using the reflection in the tilted windscreen, but Charles merely slid down in the seat and rested sideways against its tufted back. Beside him, through the rectangular window cut in the automobile's canvas roof, Charles could see the steep road in the cemetery called Laurel Avenue, where his own parents were buried. A soft wind brushed the yellowing leaves of the overhanging trees in steady waves, carrying each syllable of the distant minister's doleful eulogy. Charles observed with perfect clarity the familiar objects, the line of parked motors, the glass of the hearse filled with lilies, the black armbands and drifting veils. He did not feel panic, only that his illness was, somehow…inopportune. His excited fear had left him and a ponderous fear arrived. His spirit grew heavy at the thought of fighting an invisible menace lurking within him. His engineer's mind tried to calculate, to evaluate, to measure what might be happening. His mind was thick with invented remedies, solutions, alternative outcomes, all while his stomach twisted lavishly in his gut.

It was not until he'd returned to Kragysde, his stomach settled, his supper eaten, and the bedclothes drawn up over himself and Nixon, that the next fear came. This was the midnight fear, furtive but never mysterious, and known to every mortal heart. Charles' sleepless eyes raked the ceiling as he recognized it.

Is it possible, he thought, *is it possible I may die?*

It was a fine evening for sitting out, rare for early October, likely the last of such nights for this season at Kragsyde. Nixon paused by the window of the stair hall, noting Charles seated in one of the chairs they'd reposed in during the past weeks of summer. The sun had declined, but the sky still held its radiated brightness, the lovely pause of twilight already brimming with the lush edge of a rising moon.

Nixon was not overly concerned when Charles took ill at Bob Peabody's funeral. For several years now, Charles suffered bouts of kidney stones, and unlike the sort that caused him to lie in bed twisting in pain, the milder attacks came just as this one had and passed with little incident.

"Kidney gravel," Charles had answered when Nixon climbed into the Buick at the cemetery and inquired as to his condition, and Nixon accepted this explanation without question. Bob Peabody's death had been anticipated, but it was still a day of sadness, burying a well-loved friend. The crush of mourners at King's Chapel was immense, including even the mayor of Boston. It was enough activity that Nixon's own stomach felt queasy and tired.

Normally Charles flourished. Compared with Nixon's more sedate temperament, Charles moved in a barely checked delight. His vitality and energy were such that the entire household looked forward to him. He was always getting up some antic, perching the servants' children in trees to pose for his camera, teasing the housemaids with some cheerful buffoonery, coaxing smiles even from the taciturn cook, Mrs. Carlson. The children clustered the driveway at the first sound of his returning Buick, knowing they could always beg rides, and Tena Grant could be brought to a flaming red blush when presented with one of Charles' handmade bouquets. If Nixon provided the kindness, it was Charles who provided the color in their days.

Nixon was thus glad to see Charles resting, watching the moon rise, with his fine hair being gently lifted in the fingers of the breeze. The trees, which had already started dropping their leaves, were full of deep shadows. The summer was ending, and Nixon rarely saw Charles, who was always moving, sitting so still.

The moon was trading places with the sun in the pageant of the skies when Charles first settled himself on the broad porch facing the sea. Francesco had brought him a small glass of whiskey, and it burned the back of his throat in a pleasant way when he gulped it in one swallow as the moon crept upward. This past summer, he and Nixon often sat here, as they'd done for years, watching the evening birds turn to bats, and the bats to stars. What views there were from this vantage! Although he sat lethargically, his thoughts pursued one another rapidly, some to blind alleys and others to conclusions, with only one that stuck painfully.

In another two weeks they would break up the household and return to Beacon Street. Charles would visit Doctor Washburn and make his new symptom known to him. The doctor would purse his lips and say very little, advising some change in diet or prescribe some powder to be dutifully dissolved and drunk. The medicine men had not made the advances his engineering brothers had. Today there were machines that could fly in the air, but people still died after taking a chill.

During the past week of sleepless midnights, Charles began to accept he might have failing kidneys. He dreaded illness and was daunted by the specter lying before him, but he conceded it might be the end. Death, which first appeared like a stranger Charles could not bear to look at, came to seem if not quite like a friend, then at least like something familiar. When Charles finally dared to meet its eyes, he realized the moon-bright face of death was not monstrous but tender, and that he himself had little to fear. It was Nixon for whom Charles trembled. Nixon for whom death would have no mercy.

Charles never knew how he'd pleased fate enough to be rewarded with Nixon. Sometimes he wondered if he'd been born for him, despite coming into the world eighteen years after his lover, and so far away it would seem they could never possibly meet. Sometimes he thought their pairing was accidental, two pedestrians absorbed in their own lives who, after bumping into one another, decide to continue walking together. In any event his love for Nixon was unequivocal, and the one great blessing of his life.

There was everything in Nixon to love. Charles loved him physically, his hungry blue eyes, his vigorous bearded face that belied his soft voice and affections. He loved his smell, all leather and soap and tobacco, and sometimes wet wool, when he pressed his face into Nixon's jacket.

Charles loved Nixon's kindness. Silently and unseen, Nixon cared for things. His servants were treated with sympathy and his animals sustained almost to extravagance. Nixon was a benevolent man who never failed to notice and never forgot.

Even more, Charles loved Nixon's secret heart. The unseen parts he'd never shown, but where Charles knew many unspoken things burned, small fires Nixon had banked but never let grow into a rage or flicker out and be forgotten. For encysted in Nixon was a brash virtue, a sad honesty that appraised everything with the same eye. It was this lucidity that Charles knew sobered his lover and made him cautious. Nixon neither favored nor frowned upon any man easily.

Charles always remembered their first conversation, which had been about goodness. Nixon confessed straight away he did not believe in it, and that day Charles was taken aback. Now, faced with his own extinction, Charles saw things differently. *Goodness,* he now thought, *can only belong to those who do not believe in it.*

The screened door shut lightly and Nixon stepped out to join

Charles. The moon was risen fully, casting its haunting beam across the sea, daring anyone it encountered not to notice it. Nixon gestured with his hand to indicate its magnificence, and Charles nodded silently in agreement.

"It's hard to believe it's indifferent," Charles said, and Nixon answered him with a questioning look.

"The moon," Charles replied, by way of explanation.

Nixon was quiet for a moment, leaning on the railing of the porch. "Yes," he said. "It's why man loves nature so much. The day and the night love us equally."

It was the moment of his illness when Charles would feel the sharpest pain, and he closed his eyes as it seared him. No matter how tightly his heart was wrapped around the man he loved, his body was conspiring to abandon him. Charles knew then he was right. Death would show Nixon no mercy.

A year later, on the third day of October 1918, Nixon sat at his breakfast table at Kragsyde with his head in his hand. Charles was upstairs dying, and Nixon was exhausted. He'd spread last evening's newspaper out before him but could not read it, and his poached egg was growing cold on its slab of toast. Francesco had brought some tea, and he sipped absently at it, his hand almost too heavy to lift the cup.

In the early summer of this same year, when the severity of Charles' illness was made fully known to him, he realized Charles' was the only death he'd never imagined. Indeed, Nixon always saw Charles as youth itself. In all the years of loving him, the younger man rose each day in an air of freshness and energy. He was endearing, and impetuous, full of ideas and plans that enriched each day of Nixon's life. It was Charles who taught the tentative Nixon the delights of caprice, Charles who opened his eyes to history, Charles who brought him new things to see and try. Everything about Charles was so vital, it was inconceivable he should die.

Now as Nixon stared at the newspaper he knew he was only one of millions to feel this way. No parent of the hearty son who'd farmed their land, or lost himself in *Gulliver's Travels,* or won the swimming race in the village pond expected this same son would become a war-battered corpse. No young father, who was in June dandling the firstborn child of his pretty new wife, would know that by September the child would be an orphan after he and this wife had died, days apart, their lungs hemorrhaged by the awful miasma of the Spanish influenza.

Nixon glanced at the war maps of the Argonne Forest. Arrows and diagrams indicated advances and capitulations. For more than fifteen hundred days now the newspaper had printed such maps. He thought of the tree in Charlotte's forest. He wondered if it were still there or if it were blasted, or cut for firewood.

"Backbone of the Grip Epidemic Not Yet Broken" the headlines announced. "Days Mortality '49—North and West Ends Hardest Hit. Private Nurses Help!"

It was true. Over the entire city so many people were sickening and dying, in some places there were not enough healthy people to care for or bury them. Every person with medical skill was called to help. Dr. Washburn was tending patients all over the city, but he was good enough to take the train every other day to Manchester to check on Charles. Nixon could have paid a fine wage for a nurse but decided to tend his lover himself. Nurses were urgently needed elsewhere, Nixon reasoned; but he was seventy-six years old, fifteen pounds lighter than he'd been in August, and nearly worn out. He turned the page of the paper, removed his glasses, and rubbed his tired eyes with his hand.

There was a commotion overhead in Charles' room, and Nixon rose quickly from the table to attend to it. Charles slept for hours now but was bad in the mornings, when he woke sometimes with nausea or painful cramps. He urinated infrequently, complained of headache, and developed a terrible rash on the inside of his elbows that itched torturously.

When Nixon came into the room he saw Charles had attempted to cross it unassisted, and snarling up his bedclothes, had overturned a basin of vomit he'd produced prior to his attempted rising. Francesco was squeamish about vomit but expert at soothing Charles, so while the Italian did this, Nixon sent Tena Grant to the cellar with the soiled linen and mopped up the floor himself.

Returning to his breakfast table, Nixon had gone cold. What remained of Charles' life was fleeing, and Nixon had no means to intercept it. He rested his head in his hand again, weary with every sort of fatigue but especially that of futility. Then he again saw the newspaper.

In his absence, Mellie Fraser had cleared the table. She'd removed all the dishes but left his newspaper open. In the center of the paper, where he'd probably jostled his teacup rising to tend to Charles, there was a dried circle of spilled tea that had ringed the bottom of the cup. He put on his glasses and let his eyes slide across the page. It was crowded from edge to edge with rows of tiny type. Only a few small headlines relieved the monotony of the letters, the grotesque categories in a declarative copperplate: "Killed in Action, Wounded Severely, Died from Wounds, Missing." This was the casualty list. There was one like it printed every day. Hundreds of individual lives lost or shattered, mounting in a week's time to thousands. Inside the ring where his teacup had sat, twelve young men from New York were pronounced dead.

Nixon laid his head on the table and wept. He wept a pity for these lost and unburied men, who had set out on ships to foreign shores where they expected their youth to protect their bodies; he wept a vengeance for Frank Crowninshield, who had walked again and again into a similar hell-furnace only to be burned when he was finally safe; he wept a repose for his father, who dug his own grave for his jealous brothers; he wept a thievery for Seth Tisdale, who had escaped with his crimes unpaid for; he wept a penance for his mother because he'd not taken the time to delve her mystery; he wept a manhood for his cousin Henry because he would have fathered sons as beautiful as he had been; he wept a voice for Agnes because hers had been cut out; he wept a wedding for Marianne and Richard; he wept a bravery for Caroline Crowninshield and Franny, because they had bent and bent and bent, and never broken; he wept a blessing for the priest John Bapst, who was his first lesson in being beaten and betrayed; he wept a devotion for Lucy and Boxer and the nameless little dog, and all the animals who had kept his company; he wept a vanishing for Charles, in whose dimming eyes Nixon would chase the final pinprick of light until it receded to the place beyond all knowing; and he wept a gratitude for all life had given him, as evidenced by what it had taken away.

When he finished weeping, and lifted his face from the newspaper his tears had wet, he walked away with the dead soldiers' names on him, smudged in ink against his cheek. In the rest of his long life, Nixon never wept again.

Charles died a week later, in the same bedroom where years ago they had come together, after the gift of a few final days of lucidity. Nixon sat with him and read to him, and although they both understood their time was short, they saw no reason to alter the normal routine of their tenderness, a persistent devotion that in a different world would have evoked accolades as to the ideal example of marriage.

Curled leaves skittered along the pavement behind the hearse carrying Charles' body to the cemetery, and Nixon's Buick followed behind. Harold Pitman sat in the front of the motor with the driver, Charlie Smith, and Christiana placed herself beside Nixon in the back. She was a tall and slow-bodied woman, pale and elegant. Nixon was relieved to lean himself against her in the car. His hands had resumed their old trembling these past few days and he hid them in his coat as they sat side by side. Nixon was both grateful and wounded by memory when she removed her glove and slid her hand into his pocket to hold his, stilling its quaking with the surprisingly strong pressure of her long thin fingers. She curled her head into his shoulder, and he pressed his aching head into the soft, perfumed nest of her hair.

The sky was the color of ashes, and although the cold air jolted Nixon into a state of wakefulness, his sight still seemed veiled, as though they were traveling through fog rather than through the glutinous air of a gloom as thick as smoke. The gaudy white-paneled hearse jumbled ahead of them, and through the little window that allowed a view of Charles' casket, Nixon watched the chrysanthemums lying atop it shudder. In their slow passage through the silent streets, there were shop windows with the shutters fastened tight, doorways hung with fluttering ribbons of black crepe. Everything was closed or vacant. Two women stepped down from a curb with their faces covered and Nixon saw one of them was weeping. They passed a van with a white sheet tied to its side with a red cross painted on it. White-masked policemen wearily waved them through the empty intersections, blunt and hollow-eyed.

Their small procession was simply one more in a steady stream of death. Each person nursed a common shadow, dread of the disease that swept through the bleak streets. Life itself was in abeyance. Loss was all that was left. Every tenth doorway was marked with a red lettered sign that said "Influenza." At the cemetery, Nixon watched Harold turn away from the minister's face when he spoke to him. Fear was the other contagion, severing as surely as death, leaving behind it a bleak and empty world.

This autumn day, Nixon followed his lover to his grave. It was not supposed to have been this way. In every story Nixon imagined about their lives together, he was to have died first. Now Charles was gone, and Nixon wondered if the thin air of his absence would always weigh so much.

There is nothing as disbelieved as death, Nixon thought while walking the path above the cliff at Kragsyde, two weeks after Charles died. Even though we daily avoid death, sidestep it with precautions of every sort, we don't admit its possibility, we never look into its face. Nixon had months to view Charles' death, time to shape it to form his grief, but he did not, and thus it remained a task he had to do. Walking outside helped. He enjoyed the ocean view that enfolded him and he took comfort in standing near the spot where he'd first seen Charles, surveying this piece of land that had become the longest witness of their days together. He thought of Frank Crowninshield often in these days too, calling forth from the memory of his heart the other man he'd watched die so slowly, whom he had so dearly loved. Nixon looked over the edge of the tall cliffside, pleased about the cave he knew lay below him to remind him of that first day of love.

There was no possibility of a public funeral for Charles. The influenza epidemic necessitated the closure of every church. Instead, a minister came and Charles was mourned only by the closest members of the family. In retrospect, this was a blessing. Surrounded by a small pool of familiar people and genuine grief, Nixon felt calmer.

Nixon found he took particular solace from an unusual source, and continued in the days that followed to puzzle on it. In the summer of Charles' illness, Francesco acquired a sweetheart, a pretty and very young girl named Maria. Nixon knew Francesco had recently passed the age of thirty, and did not believe Maria was any more than eighteen, but Nixon was not about to renounce a man for admiring a young lover. The girl was happy and lively with thick black hair, and she came to see Francesco on his days off, sometimes driving her brother's auto by herself, an act that rather astonished Nixon. She was a favorite with the housemaids as well. More than once, Nixon had seen Maria reading Tena Grant's palm, or sitting with Charlie Smith's children on the servant's porch, telling their fortunes with playing cards.

"She has the second sight," Mellie Fraser reported to Nixon one day, and he wondered exactly what she meant.

Maria joined Francesco at Charles' small funeral at Kragsyde. In nearly every aspect of her appearance she resembled a schoolgirl. She wore a dark, two-piece suit with a single button, a brimmed hat with a short veil, and a small gold cross suspended on a tiny chain. Her smile for Francesco, and indeed everyone else, was full of girlish affection.

During the twenty minutes when the minister was speaking, Nixon's eyes fell upon her at the same moment she was looking at him, and he found he could not remove them from her, save for moments of modesty, for the rest of the eulogy.

Maria sat impassively, with gloved hands folded in her lap and her tiny ankles crossed in small patent leather shoes with grey suede tops and a tall row of buttons. Behind her veil, set in the honey-colored skin of Italy, were the most unearthly eyes Nixon had ever seen. There was weariness in them, and pity, a deep tranquillity and valor. They stared directly into his, with a shuddering smoke-black beauty, revealing only a glimmer that mimicked the sought-for light at the end of a long tunnel. His mind staggered awkwardly before them; he looked away and then irresistibly returned. There was wonder in her eyes, a beautiful and awful timelessness that imparted the feeling he was being watched by Charles himself, or any of the other dead to whom he'd bidden farewell. It was inconceivable. She was an innocent, a simple girl with a giggling laugh, the daughter of a large working-class Italian family from East Boston, but her eyes held the calm and wisdom of ten thousand years.

"Mio Dio!" Francesco sharply set down the vase he'd been holding as he shouted these words, and elbowed his way around Tena Grant, with whom he'd been working at the sink. Tena turned and watched the Italian dash through the doorway, his big-knuckled hand gone white for a single clutching moment at the casing, and listened as he clambered down the winding set of stairs, uncharacteristically slamming the outside door. They were cutting flowers for arrangements, and she stood aghast with the scissors still open in her hands as she realized what Francesco had seen out the window and what had caused his alarm.

Mr. Black was standing on the sheer edge of the cliff, wavering, so close the toes of his shoes were hanging over it, in the same spot where Boxer had fallen. Her stomach went sick, and she turned her face away from what she was not prepared to see again, almost retching into the flowers in the basin but not before she glimpsed Francesco running down the path, his arms flailing, his apron a white flag flapping around him.

He heard the running feet and felt Francesco's hand grasping at the fabric of his jacket at the same moment. Nixon looked down at his own feet, just at the edge of the cliff, and realized completely the misunderstanding that had just transpired. A sense of some old and primal love threaded through him. He'd not been touched in this way since childhood, the dim recollection of a similar panicked fumbling long ago, his mother's hand at the small of his back preventing a thoughtless dash into the street before a moving carriage, or the careless stumbling off another precarious edge. The pleasure of being valued filled him, and the warming of embarrassment came next, as he turned, still gripped by the wary arm that held him, and faced Francesco.

By this time, Francesco realized his own possible error in judgment, but he was not willing to rely on it, and held Nixon tightly. Out of breath and trembling, Francesco chose his words carefully to salvage both their vanities. "You were so close to the edge, *Signore*. It is not safe."

"I'm afraid I was daydreaming, Francesco," Nixon said apologetically, and stepped back a comfortable distance from the edge as the Italian let him loose. "I am so sorry I frightened you."

Francesco was bent slightly, and resting his hands on his knees as he shook his head smiling while trying to regain his breath. He pointed with a nod of his head to the cliff's edge. "That soil may not be substantial."

Nixon laughed too. He'd been impressed how quickly Francesco had mastered the English language, and the valet's little quirks of translation amused him. Francesco had a naturally regal manner, and even in a situation as ridiculous as this, managed to maintain a suavity of speech. Nixon looked at the spot of uneven ground Francesco had called to his attention. "I think you are probably right," Nixon said. "It was careless of me to walk here. Thank you for coming to get me."

Francesco extended his arm for Nixon to lean on, but as the two men returned in the direction of Kragsyde, Nixon stopped.

"I was daydreaming of Maria," Nixon said.

The Italian, who was completely unprepared for this confession, regarded Nixon with an incredulous face. "*Signore?*"

"Francesco, does Maria have second sight?" Nixon suddenly asked.

The younger man's mouth curled in immediate disgust, and he gestured with his hand near his face, as if to ward the question away. "No," he answered, shaking his head, averting his eyes and tugging a bit on Nixon's arm to resume their ascent up the path.

Nixon held firm and would not follow him. "Miss Fraser says she does," he countered.

Francesco waved his hand again, this time in a swirling motion at the side of his head. "Women are superstitious. They think crazy things."

Nixon did not want to waste his chance to ask the question that for the last two weeks had grown with urgency inside him. He'd heard tales of a woman named Margery Crandon who operated a genteel séance parlor on Lime Street on Beacon Hill. Women from the highest ranks of Boston society left Mrs. Crandon's rooms with tales of spirit messages, but Nixon was inclined to imagine charlatans jiggling tea tables and trained actors mumbling behind curtains. Now that he'd looked into Maria's eyes, he was not so sure. Since he'd already inadvertently disturbed Francesco, he decided to take a chance. "What has Maria said to you about Charles?" Nixon asked.

Francesco released Nixon's elbow and faced him. The full light of midday blazed upon them. Drying leaves from the wind-bitten plants growing along the cliffside rustled in the unsteady breeze. Francesco's expression shifted from irritation to patience to uncertainty. He wiped his hands down the front of his apron and clasped them together almost as though he were readying to pray. "She said Mr. Charles is listening to music in heaven," Francesco admitted.

"Music?" Nixon questioned doubtfully.

"Maria thinks there must be a Music Hall in heaven."

"So heaven is like the Music Hall and Charles is there?" Nixon asked, deciding that second sight was perhaps indeed the business of superstitious women.

Francesco held out his hands and shrugged. "Women think crazy things, *Signore*. Maria told me she dreamed of Mr. Charles the night of his funeral. In her dream Mr. Charles told her heaven was like Mozart."

"Mozart?" Nixon clarified, his heart suddenly pounding. He thought of the narrow streets filled with clattering beer wagons, the lines of drying laundry, the scent of hops and yeast forever seeping through the loose windows, and the creaking stairway that led to the simple white iron bed in their hidden set of rooms.

Francesco nodded. "Mozart," he reiterated. "You see? It is all nonsense." The Italian's voice had lost its panic and returned to the warm cadence Nixon found so comforting and enchanting.

Mozart. The word hung between the two men like an apparition, but Nixon knew it was a ghost only he could see. Thus it could be trusted to be real. Maria had dreamt of Charles. A charlatan would whisper a consolation. It would take a spirit to whisper a secret.

"Yes, I see," Nixon answered, letting Francesco twine his arm again around his elbow and lead him toward the house. He could still feel a trace of the valet's frantic grasp at the small of his back. What strange angels he had around him! A Sicilian kitchen boy and the daughter of an East Boston butcher, he with the voice and she with the eyes of God.

Nixon did not expect anything special to be revealed in Charles' will, but in the overwhelming days of his illness, and in the grief that descended after, he'd forgotten Charles' humor. The will was a small batch of papers, folded thrice. Charles had handwritten the document on a day in early June on the porch at Kragsyde. Nixon remembered when Charles called two of the men up from the garden to witness it.

As the epidemic still raged in the city, it was decided to read the will at the home of Harold and Christiana on Chestnut Street, also on Beacon Hill. Only three men gathered in Harold's fine library, Nixon, Harold, and Charles' lawyer, the dull but capable Leonard Vine, whose slow, deliberate speech was emphasized by much nervous licking of his lips.

A warm band of sunlight streamed from the window of the small room, which held a low mantel displaying china, and a wall of bookcases bordered with fluted columns painted an ivory white. The walls were blue, and the room had the vague echo of disuse. An ashtray fashioned from an elephant's foot stood in a corner. Christiana and Harold had honeymooned on a steamer to Europe, but Harold still managed his hunting and camping trips.

"Shall we begin?" Mr. Vine asked, his tongue darting across his mouth like a lizard.

Nixon smiled inwardly when the sober Mr. Vine read out Charles' first bequest to him, "A half-interest in a four-poster bed." The sentence was as private and endearing as Charles meant it to be, and had a healing effect on Nixon as Charles lovingly intended, but there was another bequest that warmed Nixon even more. A small sum of money was set up in a trust, to be administered by Harold, to pay a monthly benefit to a "Harry Tulit of London." The money amounted to the wage one might pay a skilled workman. Nixon had never heard of Harry Tulit, but Harold remembered him.

"Why, he was a coachman's groom!" Harold reported incredulously. "Lived behind us when we were boys in London. He was about Charles' age. Sort of a grubby little beggar. He pushed me into the mud in the laundry yard one day. I wouldn't be surprised if he were no longer living."

"I believe he is," Leonard Vine said moistly, "as Mr. Pitman has provided a current address."

Nixon hid a real smile behind his hand, so neither the lawyer nor Harold would detect it. Charles was dead, and Nixon was still discovering reasons to love him. Apparently, Charles had his Frank Crowninshield too.

Nixon was to encounter Mr. Leonard Vine one more time, again in the company of Harold, on the day of the threatened police strike in Boston. Despite the jubilant end of the war in November, and the apparent end of the influenza epidemic the following winter, the year 1919 brought more violence and destruction. Parades turned into street riots, and strikes of every kind proliferated, disrupting services and feeding political frenzies that Nixon was beginning to feel he no longer understood. A great storage tank of molasses had burst, flooding parts of the North End and killing many people, the work of either an anarchist's bomb or greedy negligence, depending on whom one was to believe.

Now on this day, September 9, 1919, the police had promised they would strike at 5:45 PM, leaving the city vulnerable to every sort of mischief. There was a great commotion all day outside 57 Beacon Street, both in the Common and on the street, and just after noon Nixon walked out to have a look for himself. People of all sorts were streaming both toward and away from the State House, and he could detect the roar of a crowd nearby, probably in Scollay Square where the entertainment halls were located. Some sort of militia on foot and horseback was stationed in the front of the statehouse.

"Nixon!" he heard his name called in Harold's familiar voice moments before he saw him, walking across from the Common with Mr. Vine at his side. "Having a look?"

"Yes," said Nixon. "There seems to be quite a stir. Is there any word as to whether the strike has been avoided?"

"You remember Mr. Vine, of course," Harold said by way of introduction as Nixon and Leonard Vine acknowledged one another. "No word. As far as we can judge, the strike will take place."

Nixon nodded. "I see. I've got Maria, Francesco's girl, at the house. I think I'll ask her to spend the night. I don't like the idea of a woman alone on a streetcar now."

"Seems prudent to me," Vine said, sliding his tongue across his mouth.

"I doubt it will amount to much," Harold said. "They've got quite a force of temporary men. The mayor seems to have matters in hand."

Nixon looked over his shoulder to his townhouse steps. He wanted to get back and catch Maria before she took it in her head to leave. "All the same, I think it would be wise if we all tucked in behind locked doors. I don't like the look of things. I've seen a mob before."

As they parted company and Nixon had moved some distance away, Vine spoke up.

"Is he quite all right?"

Harold shook his head. "I don't know, Leonard. I think his head is all right but he's not the same since Charles died. He barely goes out, and seems content to stay at home with his servants. He's gotten rather morbid."

"What did he mean about seeing a mob before?"

"Pffft," Harold snorted. "That's just it. The only mob he's ever seen is the one around the bar in the first-class lounge on the *Mauretania.*"

The men laughed and continued on to Chestnut Street.

A Pause on the Threshold
1928

🌀 Chet Currier stuck his head up over the edge of the grave he was digging and cursed. "Dammit!" he cried in exasperation as he noted the distant metallic flash of the hood of a hearse driving through the grand marble archway of the entrance to the Green Mount Cemetery. He was supposed to have finished this grave two hours ago, but he started late, and old Eugene Hall wasn't expected with his setup until after noon. The funeral party wouldn't be here until three o'clock.

He stood on the wooden box he placed in the hole for a step and took a closer look. The vehicle had the grille of a Cadillac but looked to be a maroon color. It wasn't Eugene, and Chet didn't know of any red-colored hearses anywhere here in Montpelier or any part of Vermont, unless it was something new from Harris Ketchum's parlor over Waterbury way. Ketchum was always first to have something flashy.

Chet jammed his shovel into the earth, swept his brow with his forearm, and boosted himself out of the grave. The automobile coming through the gate was no hearse. It was a limousine, with a passenger and a driver and fenders covered with mud.

Spring had come to this part of Vermont as it usually did, from an uncertain start at the first of the month to full opulence just two weeks later. The good deep dirt in this graveyard was covered with soft new grass, and the trees were hung heavy with blossoms in hazy billows of pink and white. Chet had tended the Green Mount Cemetery for four

344

years now, since he turned twenty-four. He was a local man, rawboned, with straw-colored hair and a loose easy smile. He was not keen on the grave-digging part of the job but was proud of his care of the plantings, and with the arrival of this strange visitor he could not help but cast an eye of approval around the hillside graveyard. Decoration Day was coming, he'd been working hard, and the cemetery looked good.

As Chet began walking toward the grassy dip that served as a roadway, the great long Cadillac passed by him, circling carefully around his own stake-bodied truck which was pulled well out of the way, and presumably headed for the exit. Chet noticed the green Massachusetts license plate, splashed with dirt, and saw the discharged passenger walking slowly toward him.

The passenger was a man, well along in years, probably more than eighty. He still wore the old side-whiskers of fifty years before, the kind Chet had seen on his grandfather, and his body, which was probably once robust to the point of stockiness, was now losing its battle to preserve its flesh. "Halloo!" Chet sang out. "May I help you, sir?"

The old man had come up the roadway as far as Chet's truck, and he stopped and raised his head at hearing the greeting, looking toward the young man with a perplexity Chet had seen before in the faces of old men.

"Yes," the man said. "I believe you can." He wore a wing collar and suede-topped shoes, and leaned lightly on a stick of some polished wood, his old spotted hands gripping the gold ball adorning the top. "I am looking for the graves of the men from the Civil War."

"Oh. It's too bad your car left. The soldiers' lot is along the western side." Chet pointed to the distant opposite side of the cemetery. "In that lower corner, near the main road." Chet thought to offer the man a ride but looked at his truck doubtfully. It was muddy, and the bed was covered with squares of sod from the dug grave, arranged so he could replace them later. There was also his own passenger in the front seat.

As if to announce himself at the opportune moment, a low dog yawn rose from the front seat of the truck. A lengthy grey muzzle extended itself from the curved edge of the cab, and two brown eyes regarded the men.

345

The visitor smiled and approached the dog, touching his muzzle gently. "I see you've brought along your helper," the old man said.

"He's not much in the way of help. In fact, he's pretty foolish." The dog, who'd been seated regally with his forepaws crossed and his head alert, rose and shook himself vigorously within the cab of the truck. He was a huge thing with a swirling grey-haired coat and long legs. Somewhere in his blood a hunting hound of the Scotch or Irish variety dominated.

The old man continued to stroke the dog, pleased with him, running his hands along the dog's face and down his neck. Something in the way the man handled the dog suggested to Chet he knew a thing or two about them. "Your dog has aristocratic ancestors," the old man said.

Probably why he is foolish, is what Chet thought to say, but he stifled this answer. The man looked like he had aristocratic ancestors too. "Well he lives like a king, and eats like one too," Chet said instead. "I'm Chet Currier, caretaker. I won't shake your hand as mine are dirty. The king goes by the name of Smoky."

"I am Nixon Black," the old man said, placing another hand of affection on the big dog, "and I think Smoky is very fine. I thank you for your directions, and I shan't interrupt your work any longer." Mr. Black pointed with his stick toward the soldiers' lot. "The far corner, near the road?"

"Yes, you'll see them, all government stones. There aren't many, only eight interments. Men sent to the hospital here during the war. If you don't mind the dirt, I could drive you over."

"Not at all," Mr. Black said, shaking his head. "It's no trouble for me to walk. It's a lovely day and my stick is only for balance." As the elder man started on his way, Smoky did a strange thing. The big dog climbed over the door of the truck, his long legs easily reaching down to the step, and trotted to join Mr. Black, placing his nose in the old man's hand.

I'll be damned, Chet thought and then spoke out. "Smoky, come back, don't be a bother."

"I'd be pleased to have him with me," Mr. Black said, so Chet let him go.

Smoky was no puppy, and Chet watched as he and the odd Mr. Black from the muddy limousine crept across the roadways of the graveyard.

The dog was taller than the man's waist, and they walked side by side, two old pairs of withered flanks moving through the stones and spires of the dead.

They came here infrequently, men as old as the Civil War, asking to see the graves. They were all much the same as this Mr. Black, polite and almost chastened, with old memories flickering in their bleary eyes. They rarely spoke of themselves, and Chet often wondered who they were. Comrades from battles, he reckoned. The graves did not belong to soldiers from around Montpelier; one of those buried was even from as far away as Maine, and he never understood how these soldiers came to rest here. He supposed they had no families to retrieve them, or were poor or unknown. Chet was too young to participate in the Great War, which ended when he was just fifteen, and his thoughts of soldiering almost always ran to glory. It was only when confronted with these Civil War visitors bent with age as well as war that he suspected there might be something other, but they were not speaking, and he was not asking.

He finished digging out the grave for the afternoon's burial, looking often to the soldiers' lot where he saw the old man and Smoky around the graves, but in time he forgot them, and when Smoky jarred his memory by returning to the truck, he looked to the soldiers' lot again, just in time to watch a spotless limousine pull away.

Nixon had woken the day before that May morning of 1928 in the intractable throes of an impetuous notion. He suddenly wanted to see the place where his cousin Henry was buried, and his urge to make the journey was furious. No matter that Henry was buried in a cemetery he'd barely heard of, in a town he had never visited, in far northern Vermont. No matter the distance was probably more than one hundred and fifty miles; Nixon wanted to go now, he had to go now, and Charlie Smith would drive him.

Nixon burst into the garage where the chauffeur was up to his elbows in a basin of water, submerging an inner tube to locate a puncture.

"Charlie, can you drive me to Montpelier, Vermont?"

Charlie Smith turned to face Nixon in disbelief at what he'd heard. He chose to take the question as a joke. "Right now?" he said with a smile.

347

"As soon as you possibly can," Nixon replied, dispelling any notion of comedy.

"But, sir, I don't believe we can get there in one day."

"Then we can drive through the night!" Nixon said enthusiastically, and told him he wished to find the cemetery called Green Mount in that city.

In all the years he'd worked for the Black family Charlie Smith never heard Mr. Black speak without reason. Now he thought his employer had lost his head. Charlie began to make a list in his mind of the supplies such a trip would entail. He would need a spare tire, tubes, extra gasoline.

"Can we be ready to leave in an hour?" Nixon asked, in complete innocence.

Charlie was tempted to argue. He was certainly ready to dissuade, but something in his heart kept him silent. Mr. Black was eighty-five years old. Who knew how many years he had left? If he wanted this strange thing, then Charlie would try and do it.

They left Kragsyde two hours later. As news of the unaccountable journey spread through the household, the staff gathered by the front door to see them off. Mr. Black had given no thought to clothing, so Francesco packed a small valise with a change of clothes. Mrs. Carlson pushed a box containing enough food for a week into the trunk of the Cadillac.

During the day, the drive was pleasant. The sun was shining, most of the roads beyond Concord and toward Fitchburg were hard-surfaced and well-marked, but once they crossed the state line into New Hampshire the situation changed. Outside the town of Swanzey they came to a deserted crossroad, and making a guess based on the position of the sun, launched themselves into a series of bent and twisting country roads that seemed to do nothing but circle in upon themselves. Worse, they could not even find their way back to the place where they first became lost, and once they finally lurched into the village of Keene via some rutted and bone-rattling cow-path, they'd lost both time and, more significantly, daylight.

Charlie pushed hard in the remaining daylight on relatively good roads, now more confident of his direction since he could keep the

Connecticut River to his left, and they stopped near Bellows Falls just before dark and ate some of the food Mrs. Carlson prepared for them.

Mr. Black seemed eager to continue, so Charlie sighed and pointed the Cadillac toward Montpelier. In the dark of night, the byways of New Hampshire took on the look of a ghostly and dangerous world. The headlamps made futile progress in the blackness before them, and ditches and trees threatened at every turn. The wind picked up and it began to rain. Charlie was forced to ask for directions through the crack of the doorway of a suspicious farmer at Claremont. They were lost again somewhere near White River and turned away by a damaged bridge at Royalton, causing a double-back down a temporary road that consumed another two hours. Charlie swore at himself for not remembering the great flood that had ravaged this vicinity last November. Nixon slept from time to time as they traveled, but Charlie spent the unending hours tensed behind the wheel, peering into the menacing tunnel of the night through windshield wipers that could not keep pace with the rain.

When they finally arrived in the city of Montpelier early the next day, Charlie stopped at the Pavilion Hotel and asked directions to the Green Mount Cemetery. After stepping, bone-sore, from the mud-streaked limousine into a dry and distinct daylight, Nixon seemed to realize his folly. He had slept in an automobile all night in the same clothes and he'd put both his and Charlie's lives in some danger, yet he was compelled for his part to continue on. "This looks like a nice hotel, Charlie. Bring me to the cemetery and drop me off for two hours; meanwhile get yourself a meal and some rest. We will overnight here and head back to Boston tomorrow morning." Hearing this, Charlie wanted to fall on his knees in relief.

Nixon's heart was cheered when Smoky heaved his great shaggy body from the truck and joined him. He had no dogs of his own now. After Hub died in 1922, he'd never gotten another, afraid it would outlive him. His horses were gone too, replaced insufficiently by a Locomobile and the Cadillac that brought him here. He felt the familiar comfortable bump of an old dog's body as it pressed against his leg while they walked to Henry's grave. Nixon was sure the dog sensed his fear. He held Smoky's warm face in the palm of his left hand and thanked him for his company, grateful he would not have to walk alone to this last and awful place.

It was just a small stone, government-issued, with a shield and the name Henry Black carved upon it, but for Nixon its presence had grown large beyond all imagining in the years he'd thought of it. Henry was not killed at Petersburg. He died a week later, here in Montpelier in an army hospital from a fever that came after his leg was amputated. Why Uncle Alexander had not come to get his son's body and bring it home to Ellsworth, Nixon had never understood.

Smoky left Nixon's side and flopped down on the young grass between the graves, rolling and panting. The grass was very green. This corner of the cemetery was quiet, despite being near the main road. A broad river whose name Nixon did not know flowed briskly on the opposite side of this roadway. It was about the same size as the Union River in Ellsworth, where he and Henry once swam. Within the cemetery, a small hill rose behind the soldiers' lot. The cemetery was terraced and well-groomed with many blossoming trees, giving it a varied and pretty effect.

Nixon touched the top of Henry's grave. When they last saw one another they had both been boys. Nixon could not imagine Henry as a man. He could not see him in a uniform, with a beard, without a leg. It was a boy he knew. It was a boy Nixon saw here, buried, the bones of a tiny skeleton that tore and clutched at his heart.

The dog changed places again, this time coming close to Nixon and sitting beside his feet. Nixon wished he had a dog cake in his pocket, but he'd stopped carrying such treats long ago. A breeze wound its way around them, pushing along the river road and then thrust back by the presence of the small hill, curved robustly in this little cove of gravestones. It struck Nixon then that the winter wind would do the same, and in the long nights of February, Henry's grave would be covered in a deep drift of snow.

Nixon could envision no finer bed for Henry to rest in. Perhaps his urgent overnight dash to this strange place had been without caution, but it brought Nixon a peace that was wholly unexpected.

Charlie saw Mr. Black at the far end of the cemetery, standing with a big grey dog near a cluster of small gravestones. He steered the Cadillac, which he'd washed after his breakfast, down the narrow cemetery road to meet the older man. He watched as his employer reached down and touched the dog's head and then clapped his hands, sending the big dog away, trotting back in the direction of the entrance gate where the grave digger's truck was parked.

Drawing the car closer Charlie espied at once the reason for the trip. It seemed to be a soldier's grave with the name Henry Black carved upon it. Mr. Black had not spoken of the meaning of the visit in all their hours in the automobile together, but Charlie thought he grasped it at once and felt he ought to make some mention of it. As he opened the door of the car for Mr. Black, who was looking once more over his shoulder at the grave and the departing dog, Charlie said, "I think your brother is buried in a beautiful place, Mr. Black."

"Henry was my cousin, Charlie," Nixon answered. "I never had any brothers."

A tavern door, a yellow waistcoat, a toy soldier, a pot of glue, a train schedule. Nixon leafed slowly through the pages of his diary and read these entries he'd penned himself. Since the day, years ago, when Maria's dream of Charles was revealed to him, Nixon had taken care to note the highlights of his own dreams. That he might compose of these fragments some specific revelation seemed possible then, but now he knew they held no message for him.

Indeed, in reading the hopeful catalog of his nighttime reveries, he noticed there was not one human to be found among them. The faces and voices of those he loved most were faded, almost illusions. That the door of Haffenreffer's Brewery could return during a midnight dream, accurate to the sound of its creaking hinges, seemed impossible. That he could conjure, to the detail of touch, the pleating and covered buttons of Benjamin Pitman's waistcoat from the day with the Hawaiian queen at the Parker House seemed senseless.

He had no desire to revisit the days of his early boyhood, but in his sleeping hours he could smell the paint on his toy soldiers. Agnes' pot of scrapbook glue could likewise be summoned, but in daylight her beautiful voice could not be recalled. He could wake in the night with a throat thickened with tears from the dream of a train schedule with the name Albano on it, but he no longer knew the shape of Frank Crowninshield's smile.

Charles' absence from his dreams was the most awful, and Nixon could not account for it. When his lover died Nixon hoped his own old age would at least cut short his grief, but he'd lived on. It had been ten summers and snowfalls without Charles. Nixon had experienced many kinds of mourning, but none that was so constant or so full of sorrow. Fond memories of Charles were bitter too, simply a reminder of what was gone. Nixon never would have guessed that the worst thing to recall would be the success of their life together.

A red sail, a leaping fire, a horsecar, a bird's tiny feet. Nixon lived in a world of small things that had grown very large. Large things, in their turn, had become tiny. Nixon was a very wealthy man, but he'd stopped trying to accumulate wealth years ago. When his father died, he'd been shocked to discover the size of his estate. He could not imagine how he and his mother and sisters could ever spend it all, and he never again added deliberately to the size of his holdings. He cared for his estate, managed it with the diligence his father would have expected, but he did not coddle it, and his wealth grew anyway.

He was only a boy when he first began to understand the awful necessity of ascertaining others' motives. He'd not known then, how, as a wealthy man, this perception would become even more vital.

For a long time he'd known that the people around him looked to him with hopefulness, that he could no more approach people without his wealth than other men could approach people without their beauty, or their ugliness, or some whisper of their reputation.

Now he was old. He'd made his decisions, and he doubted that any-one in the future would ever guess the method of his choosing. The Boston Museum of Fine Arts would receive most of his money and nearly all of his collections because he, and Charles, and Agnes had loved it so. The animal charities would benefit because each creature he'd ever known had been perfect, the children's charities because of every boy who ever made a snow fort, the hospitals because of Marianne's illness. Charlie Smith would be able to retire because he drove all night unquestioning in order to satisfy the madness of an old man's caprice. Francesco should never have to work again because of the way the va-let's trembling hand had clasped Nixon's back. Charlotte Schetter would be able to paint as she wished for the rest of her life, simply because of the way she bit her lip.

It was only regarding the fate of Woodlawn that he had changed his mind. Many years earlier, when he still traveled with his horse and carriage, he'd been driving down Bridge Hill in Ellsworth and noted a woman crossing the street. She had a young girl with her, and on seeing Nixon she regarded him with disgust and turned her back to him, lean-ing over to whisper something to the child. This action, and the shape of her face, led Nixon to recognize her. She was one of Uncle Alexander's granddaughters. He felt anger at first, and then the old wariness of the town of his birth returned to him. *Hatred travels through generations, like eye color,* Nixon thought, and after sharing the incident with Charles, he removed the City of Ellsworth as the recipient of Woodlawn from his will.

Fortunately at the same time, a group of men from Boston were requesting donations of land with the idea of creating a public park in this region of coastal Maine. The idea began with Charles Eliot, the hus-band of a sister of Bob Peabody. Eliot, who'd been president of Harvard University, and his fellows modeled their new organization on the Mas-sachusetts Trustees of Public Reservations. Nixon and Charles agreed these men would be better overseers of the Woodlawn property. Nixon never forgot his boyhood observations of the wharves along the Union River. In the hands of the people of Ellsworth he feared Woodlawn would be like a scrap fought over by seagulls, torn from beak to beak until there was nothing left.

In truth the old homestead never really belonged to him. The men who loved it most were his grandfather and Charles. John Black told Nixon the histories, but it was Charles who most delighted in them, Charles who hoped to open the place as a museum, an idea that now seemed a folly. Nixon had visited his grandfather's house last summer and walked through the old place, penning a few identifying labels for the best of the paintings and furniture. He related some stories to the caretaker. Concealment is never difficult for the modest. It was all the history posterity was going to get.

A drawn curtain, a tin bath, a line of chained camels, a bowl of roses. It was the end of summer now, almost Charles' birthday. If he were still alive he would be sixty-eight years old. Nixon retrieved his diary on this day because the night before he'd dreamt of Agnes' bowl of roses. The old blue-and-white bowl sat as it had since the summer of 1886, on the hall table. Nixon had added petals from the rose garden every year since.

Nixon did not, as he'd earlier intended to, note the dream of the blue-and-white bowl in his diary. Instead he stood from his desk and walked out through the door onto the large porch overlooking the cove. Early evening had arrived, and the sky was darkening toward night and a coming thunderstorm. Nixon lit a cigar and stood for some time in the tired light. Soon they would have wood fires again and begin packing to return to Boston. Nixon watched as an automobile came along the cove road, its headlamps throwing two tiny beams before it. In the far distance he saw a sudden flash and heard a low roll of thunder. Sometimes he found he even wished for the uncertainty of youth again.

He placed the stub of his finished cigar in a small pot on a wicker table and paused on the threshold before entering the house. He stood very still and listened to the tall-case clock ticking. Stepping inside, he crossed before the looking glass and into the hallway where he sunk his hands into the petals in the old bowl. The flowers from forty summers, dry as shavings, fragile as the wings of dead butterflies. It seemed impossible the ones on the bottom had been placed there by his sister.

Outside he walked down the driveway past the greenhouse, clutching the bowl. The sky had turned to the color of an angry bruise, and the wind was turning the leaves of the trees over. One of the gardeners, a good-humored man named Al Robrish, stood inside the greenhouse twisting one of the long rods that operated the glass louvers on the roof to shut them.

"Line storm coming, sir!" the gardener said. "I'd get inside."

Nixon stopped and regarded the man but must have looked confused because Al Robrish added, "A storm on the equinox is apt to be a bad one."

"Yes," Nixon agreed, but continued to the rose garden, where plants stood dried and scrawny after the lushness of June. A few straggling blossoms held on, but the rain tonight would finish them. When Nixon emptied the bowl into the winds of the coming storm, the petals spun like torn bits of paper, whipping and swirling before him. He would throw the diary away tonight too. He had no need any longer to look back.

Later, from his parlor chair he listened to the violent storm assault Kragsyde. Jagged lightning ripped through the skies, and huge blasts of thunder rattled the foundations. Rain swept in heavy curtains across the porches. He sat by a fire that cowered each time a gust of wind tore across the chimney tops. The housemaids had gone together to the basement kitchen to play cards. They always did this during storms, afraid of their rooms at the top of the house. It was strange how old age brought both fear and fearlessness. Lightning did not frighten Nixon. It was not as though he'd never experienced anything sudden and awful. For Nixon there were greater fears. The fear of acceptance. The fear of the unchangeable. The fear, indeed, of losing his grief, because if he lost it what would be left? What message lay in dreams? What was the meaning of his long sojourn of grief? For these ten years he assumed he was trapped in a lengthy ending. Yet he was already forty years old when he first met Charles. Perhaps what he was really living was another lengthy start.

Nixon awoke wide-eyed into the vacant and particular silence of the middle of the night. For a moment he did not know exactly where he was. His body felt coated in a fierce heat. He listened for the sea but did not hear it, and instead detected the buried sounds of a nocturnal city. Yes, it was his Beacon Street room. It was autumn. Outside the trees would be bare, with only the oak leaves still hanging on. He peeled his coverlet off, seeking coolness in the still and familiar place.

His eyes roamed the colorless dark of the chamber, seeking sight along the ceiling molding, down the strips of leaked light around the closed window shutters. It was bright outdoors. There must be a full moon. This room was once his mother's, but he'd moved into it after her death so he could possess its view.

Nixon rose and drew his legs over the edge of the bedside, reached for his eyeglasses, and dug his toes into the wool of the rug that lay on the floor. It was a section of an old Kazak tracker, with overcast edges and a red diamond pattern in its center. Sometimes when he woke in the mornings and stared at the diamond without blinking, he could close his eyes and the red diamond would still be in his sight. It was too dark to view the rug now, but he knew what he would see: old and crooked feet upon it, pale-skinned and yellow-nailed, wormed with buried blue veins that writhed and twisted in magnificent knots up his legs. How many years since they were smooth? Clutching the bedpost, he stood upright and unbuttoned his collar. He believed his heart was pounding but then decided it was only the clock on the mantel ticking. He walked slowly toward the window on legs that were sere and un- steady. Nixon's nightshirt was a size too large for his aging body, sliding over one shoulder, billowing around him like a pearl-grey veil. He fum- bled open the latch on the interior shutter. From the upper corner of this middle window he could see the path in Boston Common where Charles had slid his hand into his jacket pocket.

Indeed there was a full moon. Its brilliance sharpened the streets and buildings, which cast long shadows and basked in the rare, pewter-col- ored light. A puddle in the street, created by a midday rain, reflected this illumination in unbelievable stillness. The moon side of the bare trees glittered as though cast in silver. *I have tried to notice,* Nixon thought of a sudden, *I hope I have never squandered.* His eyes then sought out the path and followed their accustomed route along it to the end of his sight, a point where the ground curved away, near an iron lamppost.

Nixon pressed his forehead against the windowpane, the outline of his face reflected in the glass. How cool it was, and how soothing! He breathed deeply and turned his gaze to the ball of light atop the distant lamppost. He felt pulled into the lure of it, slipping into its indifferent blank brightness. Furious with expectation. Shuddering on the raw edge of vanishing.

Stubbornly though, his face remained reflected in the window glass. His hair, once dark and wavy, now grey and limp, his dull and chalky eyes that were once the blue of a wet stone plucked from the bottom of a forest stream. He drew closer, and breathed on the glass a large circle of vapor that obliterated this face. "That's better," he said aloud.

The following afternoon, Maria climbed the stairway at 57 Beacon Street to summon Francesco. A boy from Underwood's was in the entryway requesting the clothing. The stairway always disquieted her. The eyes of too many portraits watched as she ascended it. She knew some of the paintings were of famous men. George Washington, of course, and a slightly larger one Francesco told her was Lord Cornwallis. It was the paintings of the women that gave her pause. The one who was seated holding roses, whom Maria dreamt lost her favorite son in a childhood sickness, or the tall woman in a blue gown, whose husband had beat her and loved her sister. *When Francesco and I are married we will not have such pictures on the walls of our home,* Maria thought. As she often did when in a crowd of strangers, she just looked away. Maria did not want to see their eyes or dream their stories.

Stepping into Mr. Black's bedroom, Maria found Francesco seated in a chair with his face buried in his hands. The room was strewn with Mr. Black's clothing, jackets and trousers scattered across the bed, stockings and neckties in a heap on the lowboy. An electric flatiron crackled in its stand on the ironing table. When Francesco raised his face to her, she saw it was wet with tears.

"I can't choose," he sobbed. "I can't decide."

In the end, it was Maria who chose the clothing Nixon was buried in.

The Vestige
1928-1930

Harold Pitman was daunted by the long line of keys laid out on the table before him. There were at least a hundred of them, tagged and arranged neatly in long rolls of pocketed felt, in four groupings, one for each floor of 57 Beacon Street. He dreaded the task ahead.

"I've sorted and labeled them," Francesco said, "so you shouldn't have any trouble, but as far as I know, everything within the house was always left unlocked." Francesco was dressed in street clothes, which was a strange sight to Harold's eyes, especially when the Italian opened the elegant front door that morning, allowing Harold inside. The entrance was soon to be Harold's own.

"I've left my own set here as well," Francesco said, pushing two keys on a single ring along the mahogany table. "They open the front and back doors. After today I won't need them again."

"No," Harold answered, observing Francesco's scrupulousness with a vague unease. "Sadly, not." Even in the street clothing, which made him indistinguishable from any of his North End kin, Francesco still comported himself like a king. There was also his voice, which sounded imperious to Harold's ears, and which seeded in his soul a small dislike for the younger man. Harold wanted this last meeting over as quickly as possible and decided to talk his way to the end of it.

"How is Maria? Are you both settled in your new home in... Arlington, is it?"

"She is well, thank you, and sends her best wishes to you and your wife. We are in Somerville now, until we can sail for Italy."

Ah, yes, Harold thought. *They always want to go back to Italy.* He did not understand, but it was no matter. Francesco could go wherever he liked. Nixon had made his former valet a well-to-do man.

"So you find marriage agreeable?"

Francesco answered with a completely straight face. "Yes, it is the same as being in service, but with a different boss."

Harold laughed at the joke, knowing Francesco had concocted it to answer this same question many times before. "I can agree with you there," Harold said, and then extended his hand. "I thank you, Francesco, and wish you and Maria every happiness."

"Good luck," Francesco said, a strange answer which caused Harold again to feel the man's impertinence, to imagine he'd seen the sliver of a smile around the Italian's lips. But the younger man stood solemnly and returned his handshake. Then Francesco looked around the room and up the staircase, this time with an unmistakable smile on his handsome face. "It is strange to leave," he said, as he lingered on the doorstep.

"I imagine it is," Harold answered, leaning against the casing and sighing, once he'd finally closed Francesco outside the door.

Harold had never been in the house alone, and the moment he latched the door behind Francesco, he felt the cold culpability of the interloper. He'd known for years he was to inherit this place. After Charles died, Nixon asked him if he would want it. Nixon was especially desirous that Christiana might live here, saying repeatedly how he could envision her within its walls. "The place needs a mistress again," Nixon would say. "It has been too long in an old man's hands."

As Harold walked the silent rooms, the old familiar furniture and objects crowded around him with what seemed like affection. The portraits on the stairway regarded him with curiosity. It was as though everything here was waiting to see what would become of it.

In another week the estate appraiser was scheduled to arrive. The man would need to go through and list everything in the house. At home in his own bed Harold was sleepless, worrying what such a search might reveal. Hastily, Harold arranged for a day in the house by himself before the appraiser was to enter. Francesco had to be telephoned, keys had to be readied. Harold did not know what he expected to find, but the thought of what lurked here frenzied him.

Alone with his conscience in Nixon's house, Harold now regarded the collection of keys with a different sort of trepidation. He knew they were, in fact, weapons. He knew he'd come here to commit a betrayal. He knew he was little more than an inquisitor, seeking to root out any object that bore testimony to Nixon and Charles' love.

Soon, Harold began to notice some things that were missing. Charles' photographs and equipment, for instance, and the glass plates he used to make his pictures. His brother had kept hundreds of them back in those crazy rooms he rented on Mozart Street so many years ago. The painting Charlotte Schetter made of Nixon was gone too, leaving behind a nail in the wall in the upstairs hallway where Harold was sure it had hung. Perhaps these things were at Kragsyde. He would have to go through everything there as well.

The thought of Kragsyde caused another surge of guilt. Nixon had left him that property too, again proclaiming his dreams of Christiana's presence there. But Christiana and Harold were accustomed to summering on the South Shore and Harold did not think he could ever be comfortable in the house where his brother died. There was no comparable bird hunting in Manchester. Nixon loved Kragsyde so much, he'd probably never noticed it was old and out of style. A young couple recently approached Harold about the Kragsyde property. Once he received the title, he told them, he was ready to sell.

Francesco was right: nothing was locked. In Charles' old room, the mattress was rolled and tied and a 1918 calendar stood on the dresser. A pair of his brother's gloves, which Harold recognized, lay on top of a lowboy. Table drawers revealed penknives, ash receivers, and a metal thermometer. Bureaus hid a pair of opera glasses, three puff jars, and a whisk broom. The photographic albums he did find, stacked in the library, contained a hundred pictures of the family, including some of himself, and another fifty pictures of horses and dogs. Writing tables disgorged stamp cases, blotting paper, and a volume written by Sir Walter Scott. Cabinets secreted matchboxes, a fan, a bonbon dish, a stack of sheet music, and a postcard picturing Pompeii. Endless trinket boxes were opened to reveal trinkets. When the drawer of the writing desk in Nixon's bedroom was yanked open, a single pen rolled in its emptiness.

There was nothing there, not even implication.

Frank Crowninshield removed his cuff links, tossed them into a brass tray above which an African mask grimaced on the wall, and undid his necktie and his collar. It had been a trying day. They were near deadline on the next issue of *Vanity Fair,* Nast was growling about expenses, Arnoux was late with the artwork for the cover, and a minor writer with a quibble about Frank's editing of his commas had to be diplomatically coaxed out of the office.

Frank parted the curtain on the large window of his apartment and looked out at the city of New York. It was a world of incessant life and din, and he loved every part of it. The nighttime traffic, bright with taxis that streamed below him; the brave soaring buildings, their tops pink at dawn and glittering like boxes of jewels at midnight; the screaming trains in their grand stations; the bump and jostle of the crowded streets; and the city's inhabitants, everyone who was bright and lively and important in the world.

Frank was named for a Boston uncle who'd died after the Civil War, and he'd come to New York bearing the good old New England name that implied a significant fortune, which the family no longer possessed. In the early days he trod the great avenues with an empty wallet and a predilection for art, music, the theater, and society. So he did what a poor young man of good background could. He fixed his jacket with a boutonniere, appeared at the doors his name would open for him, and lavished the hostess with an effusive flow of wit and taste, spiced with all the flattery she already expected.

Dinner invitations piled up, his reputation was cemented, and before many years Frank Crowninshield, the very image of old-school charm, was the editor of his own magazine, *Vanity Fair,* and the arbiter of all that was new and exciting in the city of New York. Friend and promoter of artists and writers of every stripe, celebrated toastmaster at the Knickerbocker and Dutch Treat Clubs, Frank had made quite a run. If there were some who scoffed that he was glib and superficial, he merely shrugged and smiled. It was his own secret that he did not believe half of what he said.

On this evening Frank arrived home tired. He was hungry, not having eaten anything since late afternoon, when he'd nibbled at an egg salad sandwich at Schrafft's, so he entered his small kitchen and assembled another sandwich for his supper. He then sorted through his mail, stacking the thick, square envelopes of invitations into one pile and the business correspondence and rubbish in another. His eye fell on the stern and unmistakable engraving of the return address of a law office, and he frowned. He set the sandwich on the plate in his lap and opened the ominous envelope with a quick slice of the heavy letter knife he kept on the table. He read the letter, took another bite of sandwich, and sat back heavily in the chair. The subject of the letter was a will. A man whom Frank did not know had left him twenty-five thousand dollars.

Weeks later, in the small hours of the night, Frank woke, turned on the light beside his bed, and sat on the edge of it. Some whisper of the past had come up to him, bearing the slightest image of the man from the will, George Nixon Black. Frank remembered a warm day in Stockbridge, the Massachusetts resort town where his parents had a summer home. Frank supposed it was at one of the garden parties his mother was fond of, but he'd no idea of the year, just that it was certainly before the Great War. Curiously what he most remembered about Mr. Black was his shoes. They were elegantly kept and English-made, probably Lobb's or Foster's he now knew. They were suspended on a pair of thin and crossed legs; Mr. Black had the delicate ankles of an old man, encased in fine stockings, tightly gartered. Mr. Black wore a pale linen suit, also English, and in Frank's picture of him, the elder man was turned away, speaking to whomever he'd been seated beside, but who had that been? Frank could not remember. From the waist up, the old man's features became murkier. Old-fashioned side-whiskers, perhaps a ring on his smallest finger, and, more vividly, eyes completely hidden behind a smoked pince-nez. George Nixon Black could only be recollected as one of the old ghosts of people his parents had known, but there was something else about him Frank vaguely remembered. Some talk, some scandal upon which Frank's mind could not put its finger.

Twenty-five thousand dollars. It was much more money than he earned, more money than he possessed, and more money than he'd ever dreamt of being given. Of course it enriched the rest of his life. The bequest anchored him during the awful years of the Depression and continued to help younger artists he believed promising. When Frank wanted to add to his own beloved collections of African art and the modernists others snickered at, like Picasso and the sculptor Despiau, he was able to afford far more than an editor's salary would have allowed. When in the early months of 1929 he became one of the first trustees of the new Museum of Modern Art, his net worth was not quite so precipitously lower than that of the other members.

Francis Welch Crowninshield, bon vivant, editor of *Vanity Fair,* and father of New York cafe society, never did know why he was the beneficiary of an old Boston philanthropist. He suspected an admiration for the magazine, or some old friendship with his parents, but Black was not a subscriber, and Frank's siblings were not named in the will. What Frank did not know was that he merely had the right name.

The baseboard groaned and screeched as Jotham Dodge ripped it from the wall. He was in charge of the second floor and he'd been round the rooms there all morning, removing the good woodwork from the walls and stacking it so other workers could load it into trucks. This house, the one they called Kragsyde, was about to be torn down, and he was one of the scrapping crew salvaging what could be sold and reused.

He set the bar into the wall above the molding and pounded it with his hammer, sending chunks of plaster flying, and worked his way down the length of each of the nice ten-inch-wide boards, prying them away from the wall with care so as not to split them. He then ran them across his knees and removed the nails with the hammer claw, flinging them into the bare brick firebox where they would be out of the way. The mantels had already been stripped and trucked off earlier in the week. It was not awfully hard work but for the crawling on hands and knees.

What Jotham thought as he tore the house apart was the waste of it. He'd been told the house was to be knocked down to its foundation so a new one could be built on the same site. Lord knows he'd heard a lifetime of stories about the crazy notions rich people who came from the city got into their heads, but this seemed untimely.

Since the crash last year, things had changed. There was talk that some of the swells who'd been hit hard might not open their houses this summer. If that were true, it would be bad on everyone. If some rich fool wanted to tear down one good house just to build another, so be it. At least someone had some money to spend. Jotham was glad of the job.

Jotham moved from room to room. Door casings in one pile, window casings in another, baseboards in a third. Wet patches of sweat formed beneath his armpits and across the back of his shirt. Despite the snow outside, the men had muscled a number of the windows open to keep themselves cool. He could hear the voices of other men bellowing, their tools clattering, footsteps thundering up and down the wide stairs, echoing in the empty rooms of the house.

Jothan howled in pain as he knelt on a nail, sitting back on his haunches and dropping his tools as he felt under his kneecap to remove it. As he rubbed his knee he looked at the tiny object he'd picked up. It was not a nail. He squinted and held it closer to his eyes. It was half of a collar stud, which probably came out of a crack in the floorboards somewhere. He held it in his forefingers and placed it in his mouth, biting down on it with his teeth. It gave a little. Solid gold. Probably the blue blood who dropped it never even bothered bending over to pick it up, just fished another out of a velvet box filled with forty more of them. Jotham flung it into the firebox with the rest of the trash. *Damned swells,* he thought, shaking his head in disgust, *nothing means anything to any of 'em.*

They were three days out to sea on the *Roma* when Maria fell ill from not sleeping. She had tossed and turned, refused most food, and remained in their cabin since they boarded. What Francesco knew was that her illness was not occasioned by the movement of the ship or the unfamiliar surroundings. Maria was afraid of their destination.

He'd seen the changes come over his wife the closer they came to the date of their sailing. Although Maria still spoke with enthusiasm about their upcoming move to Italy, he sensed her increasing wariness of it. She did not complain, and he did not ask her about it. He was unnerved himself by the things Maria sensed.

Francesco was disappointed too. He'd dreamt of this voyage for years, had always hoped he could make a success in America that would some- day lead him home. Now a success he'd never dared imagine was his. It was 1930. He'd been in America for sixteen years and was now a well- off man, in a first-class steamer cabin, with a beautiful wife, going back to Italy with his head held high. He and Maria would be able to live very well on what *Signor* Nixon had left him. Francesco's whole family could be cared for.

On this third night out, Francesco woke knowing Maria was beside him and still not sleeping. He turned on the small light on the wall beside the bed. Maria was lying on her back with her eyes open. He moved to her side of the bed and sat beside her, stroking her haunted, watchful face. *"Mia cara,* please tell what is troubling you."

"I am afraid, Francesco."

Francesco smiled softly and kissed his wife's forehead. "You don't need to be afraid, Maria, our new home will be wonderful. There will be sun forever and no more snow. My family will be in love with you."

"It's not that," she said.

"Then you must tell me, what is it?"

"I keep dreaming of soldiers," she said gravely, "and guns and bombs."

Francesco smiled again, and kissed her another time. *"Piccola* Maria, there is no more war," he said, placing his hands on her head and feeling his own heart freeze with fear. He knew better than to dismiss her vi- sions, but he knew not to show his concern. "You must sleep, my dear," Francesco said, touching the corner of Maria's eye gently. "Your eyes are getting dark circles."

"I am afraid to sleep," she answered, "and I'm cold." She turned to lie on her side, curling into herself, her hands pulled into tight fists beneath her chin.

Francesco reached for a blanket from the cabin closet, and Maria waved him away when he approached her with it. "The ship blankets are scratchy," she said.

Francesco sat on the bed and eyed the large trunk, which had been brought by the stewards to their cabin but remained untouched during the journey. He knew what traveled inside it. He'd packed it himself, keeping it with them in the stateroom rather than letting it be stored below with the other ship's cargo and returned full of moth holes. After crossing the room and turning on the desk lamp, he retrieved the key from his wallet and unlocked the lid. He raised the sheets of paper he'd placed on top and lifted out the great Russian sable coat that belonged to *Signor* Nixon. Francesco was willed all his employer's clothing and jewelry. Most of it he'd sold in Boston, but since the crash, no one wanted such an expensive fur coat. Francesco laid the beautiful coat across his lap and withdrew the paper he'd stuffed in its sleeves to keep its shape. It was the same coat *Signor* Nixon was wearing in the tiny oval painting on the dresser in Mrs. Black's empty bedroom. *Signor* Nixon must have owned it for many years. Francesco himself had brushed it a hundred times.

Francesco carried the coat across the room to his frightened wife. The scent of Beacon Street had emerged from the trunk, recalling the old stairways and kitchens, the paneled library, the closet in the bedroom chamber where the coat had hung. The fur smelled of *Signor* Nixon, and Francesco buried his face in the brown softness of it, into all that was familiar and now lost to him. Was there anything else in the world both as big and small as love? He was a thousand miles away from Boston, in the open sea on an uncertain journey, with his arms around a space where Nixon once existed. Francesco drew the heavy coat over Maria's shoulders, and she slept.

Afterword

Coup de foudre, the French say, which translates literally as a bolt of lightning—but means love at first sight. How better to describe the irresistible instant when a chance meeting alters a life? For who can ever expect the sudden place or glimpse or turn of the page that will change everything?

I first encountered Kragsyde in a book my father brought home one day from the school where he taught. I was barely a teenager and gave little more than a glance to the title or the text, but the photographs and drawings in this book gave me goose bumps.

These were the most beautiful houses I had ever seen. Not impossible fantasy castles or the monotonous ranch-style structures of my own time, but shingled, playful, shaggy houses, full of mysterious rooms placed at odd angles, rooms in which I could imagine myself. They had fanciful windows I longed to peer from, deep cool porches, wonderful turrets, and pennants flying from spires, promising endless summers. Even their names were romantic, names that might inspire novels or dreams: Grasshead, Sunset Hall, Wave Crest, Seabright.

I studied them all, but even my youthful eyes could discern the masterpiece, Kragsyde. This house was the pinnacle, with its fantastic arch large enough to drive through, its beautiful stones, its romantic perch above the sea. Completely beguiled, I clipped the photograph of Kragsyde from the book and pasted it in a scrapbook. The sepia photograph, held in my hands for the first time, both a daydream and a seed in my childhood mind.

Seven years later, I sat working in a sunny window in my college library. I was a sophomore and engaged to be married upon graduation to a man who was already on his path to becoming a master home builder. We often discussed the house we hoped to design and build. I was studying graphic arts and photography, but that day I was awaiting the delivery of several books I'd requested for an art history class project. When the stack slid off the library cart, I recognized the house on the cover of the top volume, *The Shingle Style and the Stick Style* by Vincent Scully. Like the *coup de foudre,* the magic of the attraction was again instantaneous, but in my case lightning had struck the same place twice.

My fiancé, James Beyor, and I decided to make a trip to Manchester-by-the-Sea to find Kragsyde. I'd shown the book to him, and we decided to visit the area where so many fine Shingle-style houses stood. We became more excited about our own plans as we drove, devising ways in which elements of the style could be incorporated in our own house.

Our search did not last long. Ten minutes after we'd entered the Manchester Historical Society's doors we learned from the docent, Frances Burnett, that Kragsyde had been torn down long ago. Sensing our disappointment, Ms. Burnett kindly offered to drive with us to the original site of the house. Rounding the edge of Lobster Cove and seeing the bare clifftop where I had always envisioned the great house standing was like witnessing an extinction. "The building plans can still be found in the Boston Public Library," Ms. Burnett told us, in a voice of consolation.

There is no colloquial French phrase to describe what happened next. In a small diner in Manchester, James and I ate lunch and commiserated. It was an easy first step to our mutual complaints that the world of nineteenth-century beauty was slipping away, replaced by cheap and poorly crafted objects. Yet it was frighteningly easier to come to our next wild thought. Why didn't we rebuild Kragsyde? We could do it. We knew how. It was a leap, a whim, an oath, an ambition, a naïveté, and a motif of the marriage that would follow.

The following day in the Boston Public Library we ran into our first difficulty. We didn't give much consideration to our jeans, our longish hair, or our obvious poverty when we entered the Rare Book division where the plans for Kragsyde were housed, but I suppose others did. It never occurred to either of us that interest would not be enough to open the archive vaults. We had no academic credentials, so the door remained closed. "You might want to call the man who donated the plans to us," the librarian suggested. So in the basement of the library that very afternoon, I did.

Wheaton Holden, a professor of architectural history at Northeastern University, was the man I called. He was an expert on the architects of Kragsyde, Peabody and Stearns. As an educator he was no doubt accustomed to youthful exuberance, and he possessed the wisdom to foster it.

"We're going to rebuild Kragsyde!" I told him over the phone.

"I think that's just great," he replied.

In a matter of weeks he had sent us copies of the plans and met with us to share the relevant photographs and drawings he'd amassed in his years of research. If Kragsyde was a seed in my childhood mind, it was Wheaton Holden who watered it.

Once I graduated in 1982 we'd saved as much money as we could, built a small model of the house, and bought an affordable seaside property that would suit the plans in a too-small town in Maine. The delight of daydreaming was about to be replaced by the hard discipline of work. For work it certainly was, performed by us, mostly on nights and weekends after returning home from our day jobs. Still, we embraced it with diligence and no small dose of delight, reveling in practicing a true craft, using old techniques and traditional materials. As finances waxed and waned, the progress was sometimes slow, but each month brought advances and a hard-won satisfaction in seeing the sepia photograph become tangible and as beautiful in our own century as in the century it was designed. We could now gaze out from the fanciful windows, and walk under the famous and fabulous arch, and we had built it ourselves.

Meanwhile, I was absorbed in another task of nostalgia. I started a business with James van Pernis, a college classmate, producing greeting cards and stationery printed on antique presses. Today Saturn Press is recognized as one of the earliest pioneers in the resurgence of letterpress craft printing, but in 1986 we were just foolish outliers who refused to let our graphic arts skills dissolve into a glowing screen.

I worked by day with tools from a passing era—cast-iron presses, lead type, T-squares, and ruling pens—and returned home in the evening to another kind of work, using construction methods that would have been recognizable to the men who built the original Kragsyde. Nothing felt new, but everything felt right.

As the house-building task was coming to a close, I turned my attention to George Nixon Black. To my nineteen-year-old self he was no more than the original owner of Kragsyde, but as we rebuilt his house, I felt his ghost in every corner. It took a decade of research to realize that the life of this elusive man was as romantic and compelling as the house he occupied—and that his was a story worthy of being told.

When George Nixon Black Jr. died in October of 1928, he left behind fewer than a dozen pieces of correspondence. A few handwritten sheets, all involving business matters, seemed all there was of his voice. Then I remembered his will. As an elderly man with a large fortune who had outlived his nearest relatives, what would his last wishes be, and what would they say about him? Seated beneath the humming fluorescent lights in a room at Boston's Suffolk County courthouse, with the will in my hands, I heard not only a man's voice but an amazing story.

In a document from 1900 when Nixon was fifty-eight years old, and a string of biennial codicils added until months before his death, Nixon pointed me to everything I later found out about him.

Here were hints of the family feud that began in the days of grandfather John Black and Franny, revealed by the abnormally small bequests Nixon gave to his paternal uncles and their descendants as opposed to the generous sums left to similar relatives on his mother's side.

Here were the longtime friends fondly remembered, their importance identified by Nixon's own descriptions of them. Sometimes only their names appeared, sometimes they were called "friend" or "sincere friend." I duly noted the important enhancements. Valued servants were also included, as well as some—like Francesco Gombi and Charles Smith—who received larger bequests than almost anyone else.

Here were the charities dear to Nixon—the Boston hospitals, local charities dedicated to animals and children, and most importantly, the Museum of Fine Arts.

Here too were the mysteries—the bequest from the quietest of men to the flamboyant New York editor of *Vanity Fair* magazine, and the large sum left to a little-known female artist of German ancestry with a Greenwich Village address.

Love was also revealed. On page twelve of the original 1900 will, I met Charles Brooks Pitman, the Hawaiian-born engineer who shared Nixon's address and was left the biggest sum of all.

The number of ways a historical novelist can narrate a subject are endless, but with Nixon's will in hand, I saw no better method then to stick as closely as possible to his true historical path. The people he introduced me to were already compelling, and those I had yet to meet even more so. Researching these individuals and interviewing their descendants allowed me to form a clearer picture of their interwoven lives. Their letters, diaries, and photographs made Nixon even more visible, and it is these sources that have shaped the characters I have written. Combining this documented evidence with actual events of the times has resulted in a story of historical accuracy. All but the most insignificant characters were real people, and their real names have been used. Actual events are told with an eye to exactitude, even to small details. The sable fur coat, the burning nightshirt, the barrel of onions, and the four-poster bed really existed. Attributed feelings and dialogue are imagined, but *The House at Lobster Cove* is a fiction based on ten thousand facts.

For those readers who wish to immerse themselves further into the subject, there is much that can still be seen of George Nixon Black and his world. The Ellsworth, Maine, family estate of Woodlawn can be visited. Tours are given in the summer months, and there the careful observer will find the blue-and-white Fitzhugh bowl, the George Washington miniature, Charles and Nixon's four-poster bed, the Laura Hills miniature paintings of Nixon and his mother, and dozens of other objects and settings referenced in this novel.

The Ellsworth of the tortured priest, John Bapst, is also there. The home from which the unfortunate man was kidnapped and the home where he was taken to safety both still stand, and although privately owned can be pointed out by any willing local historian. The now-vanished wharf where he was tarred and feathered borders a public riverfront park. The magnificent house once owned by Seth Tisdale and remodeled from Charles Pitman's plans is still the city's library. Although Charles' interior plans for the building were significantly altered in a late-twentieth-century renovation, the exterior of the building remains as Nixon and Charles would have known it.

In Boston, at the Museum of Fine Arts, any one of Nixon's colonial-era paintings or furniture pieces may be on display. His is still an active trust that benefits the museum and its many programs.

Not to be missed is a sunny late-afternoon viewing of the *New Jerusalem* stained-glass window at Trinity Church. Inside this glorious structure, which should be on the itinerary of any Boston visit, the recently restored John La Farge masterpiece and others like it are on prominent display.

The exterior of Nixon's home at 57 Beacon Street remains unchanged and can be seen easily from the street or Boston Common. It houses several private apartments today.

Nearly every character from the pages of *The House at Lobster Cove* is buried at Mount Auburn Cemetery in Cambridge, Massachusetts. Those who are not include John and Mary Black, who are buried in the tomb behind the Maine Woodlawn estate; Frances Wood Black, who finally left Ellsworth at her death to be buried beside her first husband in Wiscasset, Maine; and Henry Black in the soldiers' lot at Green Mount Cemetery in Montpelier, Vermont. I believe any one of them would enjoy a visit.

Alas, Kragsyde is but a memory. Its former site at Lobster Cove has been home to three houses since it was demolished in 1929. The complete set of architectural renderings for the famous structure are archived still in the Boston Public Library, but the marvelous original house has indeed been reduced to "a curling sepia photograph that is yearned for."

It is, I think, the responsibility of a historical researcher to consider whether or not their subject wants to be found. The elusive nature of the life of George Nixon Black certainly begs the question, and again his will provides the answer.

Twelve days after the death of Charles Pitman, Nixon entered the offices of his lawyers to change his will. The body of his companion of thirty-four years was buried, and there was no legal reason for Nixon not to bury the nature of their relationship too. Yet in altering the bequests he had intended for Charles to receive, Nixon inserted a single unnecessary phrase, a phrase he must have had in mind upon his arrival, a phrase that might have been opaque in 1918 but resonates clearly in our day:

"...whereas in my said will I made provision for my lifelong friend Charles Brooks Pitman, who is now deceased, and whereas I desire to recognize the steadfast and faithful friendship which existed between us for many years....."

In his last will and testament, George Nixon Black told us everything he wanted us to know.

Curiously, in searching for Nixon I also found myself. In my years of research, two different bits of ephemera floated up from the past.

The first came from the Manchester Historical Society, from the pen of Frances Burnett, the first person we met on our long journey. Buried in the archives was a copy of a letter she'd written in reply to someone who had sent her a newspaper article about our rebuilding of Kragsyde: "I well remember this young couple who visited the Society back in 1979," she wrote. "I took them to the site of the old house and told them it had been torn down. They had an old rattletrap car and I remember wondering how they could ever contemplate building such a mansion, but they have done it, and more power to them." Reading this letter wrenched my heart.

The second is the drawing on the cover of this book. A quick sketch by architect Robert Swain Peabody, from 1885, it is housed in the files of the Boston Architectural College, where no one has identified it. An architectural historian even asked me if I thought it was an early preliminary sketch for Kragsyde. Because it is not the iconic facade of the house, showing the famous archway, experts may not recognize it, but to me it is immediately familiar.

We never went back to the Boston Library to see the plans. With the help of Wheaton Holden there was no need to do so. Yet even though I never laid eyes on those original elevations, I know every line of the house. How could I not, after building it, after laying the rafters of those familiar rooflines and mixing the mortar for the enormous chimneys? I know how the shingles travel the eaves, and where the snow builds up in those valleys. I know both its past and its present—the huge shadowed porch where Nixon played billiards, where I today hang a hammock, and the bow window of the room where Agnes spent just a single summer, and where I find a sunny place for a blue-and-white bowl of flowers.

Acknowledgments

I owe many people for their help in bringing this novel into being. Foremost, I have been lucky to have the assistance of several institutions. Libraries played their vital role, and I thank the Boston Public Library; the Boston Athenaeum; the Phillips Library; and the public libraries in the Maine cities of Bangor and Ellsworth, as well as Northport, New York. For their assistance with research I am indebted to the archives at the American Kennel Club, Brown University, the Boston Architectural College, the Hawaiian Historical Society, Historic New England, Mount Auburn Cemetery, Massachusetts Institute of Technology, Newburyport Historical Society, Harvard University, University of Stuttgart, and especially those at the Manchester Historical Society in Manchester-by-the-Sea, Massachusetts.

The staff at museums have been remarkable. Their familiarity with and advocacy for their collections were evident in my every visit, and I salute them all. The Peabody Essex Museum, the Museum of Fine Arts, the Bishop Museum, the Isabella Stewart Gardner Museum, and Woodlawn Museum all helped to bring my characters to life. Special thanks go to Danny Newton of the White Oak Civil War Museum for driving me to the site of Nixon's burning nightshirt and for making that era come alive. In this same vein, I want to thank the men and women of the 2010 Civil War battle reenactments in Resaca, Georgia, for the conversation exchanged around the campfire, the rifle-firing lesson, and their enthusiasm and knowledge. The days spent with them were the most fun I ever spent in research.

The descendants of the characters of my novel deserve special mention. Their willingness to share their stories, diaries, letters, and photographs has made all the difference in creating characters who resemble real people and not official statistics. For this I thank Elizabeth Boyd, Jack Blanchard, Stuart Rodgers, Axel Magnuson, Judy McCarron, Ted and Susan Pitman, Michael Power, John Tulit, and Gigi Wilmers. I met them all as a researcher, and I continue with them as friends.

All authors have their facilitators, and I thank the following people for their support, guidance, and good cheer. Bill Cross, Colleen Cameron, Sarah Cunningham, Kathleen Rogers, Helen Deese, Bill Clendaniel, Sandra Goroff, David Demeter, Rebekah Raye, Carrie Brown, Bret Morgan, and Howard Mansfield. Each one helped advance the novel to publication. Lindsay Wood reminded me of the kindness of strangers. Lynne Warren provided the tipping point. The book has two special friends in Steve Fletcher and Carl Croft, my early champions and readers. Heartfelt thanks to you both, as you have truly hung on every word.

I extend my appreciation to the staff at Applewood Books and my editors, Jennifer Delaney, Susan Barba and Jeanne Gibson, for taking such pains to produce it with beauty.

I must thank my family for ten years of listening to me talk about the novel; my husband James, for taking the leap of building Kragsyde when we were both young; and to James van Pernis for doing my work and his as I abandoned Saturn Press to travel for research.

Lastly, I cannot forget those who have not lived to see the novel to its finish: Wheaton Holden, who believed in my youthful enthusiasm and Pat Teal, my indefatigable literary agent, who believed in the enthusiasm, of my middle age. There is also the late and much-lamented Pica, a wise and patient French bulldog who sat at my feet as I penned every word.

A Note on the Type

The text of this book was set in the present-day version of Bembo, recut in 1929 by Stanley Morison from the original face designed by Francesco Griffo for Aldus Manutius, the renowned Venetian printer. First used in a Renaissance travel book written by Pietro Bembo, the face was named for this author, who later became a cardinal. Bembo is a face of remarkable clarity, both elegant and beautifully proportioned.

The chapter-heading style, created nearly 400 years later and named Gutenberg, is the work of the prolific Victorian-era type designer Hermann Ihlenburg. With over 80 typefaces in more than 300 different sizes to his credit, Ihlenburg, a German-American, cut more than 32,000 punches in his career, mostly while working for the MacKellar, Smiths & Jordan type foundry. His signature artistic flair and dramatic and eccentric letter shapes echo both the exuberant era in which he worked and the elaborate mustache he wore.

Ihlenburg's Gutenberg typeface from 1888 is a rare survivor in metal type. Two complete fonts are housed in the collections at Saturn Press and were handset especially for this book.